BAD BLOOD

GALLOWBURN SERIES BOOK TWO

HEATHER ATKINSON

Boldwood

First published in Great Britain in 2021 by Boldwood Books Ltd.

Copyright © Heather Atkinson, 2021

Cover Design: www.judgebymycovers.com

Cover Photography: Shutterstock

A CIP catalogue record for this book is available from the British Library.

Paperback ISBN 978-1-80048-272-2

Large Print ISBN 978-1-80048-273-9

Harback ISBN 978-1-80162-902-7

Ebook ISBN 978-1-80048-275-3

Kindle ISBN 978-1-80048-274-6

Audio CD ISBN 978-1-80048-267-8

MP3 CD ISBN 978-1-80048-268-5

Digital audio download ISBN 978-1-80048-271-5

Boldwood Books Ltd
23 Bowerdean Street
London SW6 3TN
www.boldwoodbooks.com

1

The church bell chimed nine o'clock, the spire standing out starkly against the night sky. As autumn had just settled in it was getting darker earlier, the chilly breeze blowing discarded carrier bags and crisp packets across the cracked flags, damp hanging in the air.

Jamie glanced around but the square was deserted. A quiet area on the Gallowburn scheme was rare but there was a particular reason why this part of the estate had been abandoned, a reason Jamie was about to address.

Footsteps around the corner caused him to turn and he saw a figure dressed all in black emerge from the shadows, hood obscuring their face.

From the side of the church appeared a second figure, similarly attired.

As both men advanced on Jamie from different directions he looked from one to the other.

'We warned you to no' come here, Jamie Gray,' called the stockier of the two. 'This is our turf. The Blood Brothers are no' welcome.'

'And I told you to piss off,' replied Jamie. 'The Gallowburn belongs to us. You didn't listen, so I'm here to make you leave.'

'And you came alone? Big mistake,' said the stocky man as a third figure approached Jamie from behind.

The three men converged on Jamie, who remained calm, continually looking from one to the other, sizing them up. One carried a screwdriver in his right hand, one wielded a hammer and the third a baseball bat.

'You'll need more than those to take me down,' said Jamie.

But none of them replied as they continued their advance.

These three men had caused chaos on the estate lately with assaults, muggings and even an attempted rape. The latter had fortunately been foiled when the would-be victim had run inside the church to escape her pursuers. Even by Gallowburn's standards the violence they'd displayed had been savage, and the residents had turned to Jamie's gang, the Blood Brothers, to rid them of this menace. Of course, no one on the Gallowburn went to the police – that was a code of honour everyone had instilled in them from birth and it was never broken.

After sizing them up, Jamie decided the least dangerous of the three was the mouthy one with the baseball bat.

He slid his hand into his jacket pocket, fingers closing around the bike chain.

Before he could pull the weapon, there was a shout from the direction of the church and the other three Blood Brothers charged out clutching their weapons. Logan dashed down the steps, brown curly hair bouncing about. In one hand he wielded a crowbar. The rotund but no less fearsome Gary wore knuckledusters on each hand, and bodybuilder Digger had a baseball bat with nails hammered through it. As he ran he raised the bat above his head. Unfortunately he wasn't looking where he was going and he slipped on the bottom step, his war cry turning into one of panic as he toppled to the ground, the bat falling from his hand. Gary released a bark of laughter and dodged around him while Logan didn't even notice, too caught up in the frenzy of the moment.

As the three men surrounding Jamie whipped round to watch the Blood Brothers charging towards them, Jamie tore the bike chain from his pocket, drew it back and smashed it into the face of the man he judged to be the toughest. Logan took down the second man while Gary rammed his knuckledusters into the face of the third.

As the men lay groaning on the ground, Digger managed to pick himself up and limped over to join them.

'Oy.' He frowned. 'You didn't leave any for me.'

'Because you were too busy rolling around on the ground like a wee lassie who'd tripped over her skipping rope,' retorted Gary.

'You cheeky prick. I'll whack you with this bastard,' Digger replied, drawing back the bat.

'No, you won't,' said Jamie in a cold, hard voice. 'We do not fight each other. Got it?'

Digger nodded and lowered the weapon. 'Aye, Jamie, sorry.'

Jamie knelt beside one of their victims, who was still groaning in pain on the ground.

'Gallowburn is ours,' Jamie told him. 'No one fucks with it unless they want a holiday in Intensive Care. Piss off back to where you came from. If we ever see you around here again, you're dead. And to help you remember, here's a permanent reminder.'

He nodded at Logan, who slammed the crowbar into the gobby man's left knee, making him scream. No one came rushing to his aid. The Blood Brothers had put the word about that tonight they would be dealing with this latest menace, so the residents had wisely avoided the area.

'Looks nasty.' Gary grimaced. 'You're lucky he went for your leg and no' your wee cock.'

'Fuck off out of it,' Jamie told the interlopers.

The injured man's friends dragged themselves to their feet, slung his arms around their necks and staggered away as fast as they could, continually looking back over their shoulders at the Blood Brothers. So concerned were they at being followed they failed to notice the bench in front of them, and the three of them went sprawling over it, the injured man screaming again as he landed on his damaged leg. Gary and Digger burst out laughing.

'Well, that was easier than I thought it would be,' said Logan, the disappointment clear in his tone.

'Because they're cowards,' called a commanding, powerful voice, one that was clearly used to public speaking.

Gary turned to face the owner of the voice with a huge smile.

'Reverend Brown.' He beamed. 'It's lovely to see you, as always.'

His friends couldn't help but smile too. Reverend Valerie Brown, at forty-seven, was twenty-five years older than Gary and a woman of the cloth, but that had done nothing to dampen his raging crush on her. She was striking-looking rather than beautiful, tall and slender with piercing blue eyes and sharp, angular features, long dark hair pulled back into a ponytail. When she'd taken over as reverend of Gallowburn community church Gary had actually started attending services so he could gaze at her starry-eyed, failing to hear a single word she said as he lost himself in fantasies of the good reverend and himself in her vestry. None of his friends shared his crush but they all respected Valerie. She was one of the toughest women they knew, which was a huge compliment because Gallowburn was full of strong women.

'It's done?' she asked them.

All four men nodded, Gary's eyes wide and adoring.

'Good,' she said. 'You've done the Lord's work tonight, boys.'

'Aye, that's pure gallus.' Gary grinned.

'Get yourselves home before anyone comes along.'

'Is there anything else you need us to do for you?' said Gary, unwilling to relinquish her company just yet.

'No, thank you, Gary, but I'll certainly let you know if something crops up.'

'Great.' He grinned.

When she went back into the church, closing the door behind her, his grin fell. 'Why doesn't she like me?'

'She does,' said Digger. 'Just not in the way you want her to like you.'

'But why not?'

'Because shagging someone young enough to be her son would probably get her kicked out of the church,' said Jamie.

'Nothing can stop our love,' Gary said, gazing longingly at the church door.

'Oh, shut it, you soppy git,' said Digger as they made their way across the deserted square.

'Just because you've no love in your life.'

'Neither do you, unless you count your ongoing romance with your right hand.'

'Do you want me to stick that bat right up your arse?'

'Please don't start arguing,' sighed Logan. 'It's late and I'm knackered.'

Digger glanced at his watch. 'It's only just after nine o'clock.'

'Unlike you I was at work all day, stuck in a shitty office with people I hate.'

'Don't go if you hate it so much.'

'We can't all be supported by Mummy and Daddy. Some of us need to earn our own money.'

'I bet you could afford to pack it in, especially now people are paying us to protect them from roasters like those tits we just battered.'

'The extra cash is nice but it's not enough to give up work.'

'You should tell your da to pull his finger out,' said Gary. 'Lazy git that he is.'

'I don't want to discuss my da now,' Logan muttered. 'Let's just get home.'

'So you can cook him a fry up?' Digger grinned.

'Shut it, Rocky.'

They all smiled at this nickname as it reminded them of Allegra, however, their smiles were tinged with sadness. She'd christened Digger with this nickname because she'd thought all his bulging muscles made him resemble a bag of rocks.

'Things aren't the same without her,' commented Logan.

'I hope they lock that murdering bastard of a father of hers up for life,' spat Gary. 'You okay about the court case, Jamie?'

'I'll have to be, won't I?' he retorted.

Allegra's father, Cameron Abernethy, was up in court the next day for his daughter's murder. Her body had never been found but under Scottish law one wasn't needed for a successful prosecution. Jamie was to give evidence about how afraid Allegra had been of her father and of how he'd controlled her. Cameron was also being done for attempting to have Jamie killed. Craig Lawson, head of their deadliest rivals, had been in on the plan, and he'd already been tried and convicted, sentenced to nine years in Barlinnie. Cameron, however, could afford the best lawyers and had managed to swing things so he would be tried for Allegra's murder and the attempted murder of Jamie in one trial. He had clearly figured if he was found guilty of both crimes, then his sentences would run concurrently, knocking some time off.

The weight of the trial was bearing down on Jamie and not for the reason everyone thought. He alone knew that Allegra was still alive and well. He hadn't found out until after her memorial service when she'd come to him in disguise and told him the whole story. If it hadn't been for the ring she'd given him he would have thought he'd imagined seeing her again, the hallucination a product of the terrible grief he'd been crushed by. His fingers brushed the ring that he always wore on a chain round his neck, hidden beneath his clothes. It was an engagement ring, a promise that one day they would be together again, when everyone had forgotten about the whole sorry saga. That didn't look as if it was going to happen any time soon because ever since Allegra's disappearance there was always something in the papers about it. The Abernethy family was one of the richest in the whole of Scotland, so it was big news.

'Want me to come with you, pal?' Logan asked Jamie.

'I appreciate that,' he replied. 'But my maw's coming with me and DI Ross will be there.' He sighed heavily. 'I'm fucking dreading it.'

'It'll be a piece of piss,' said Digger. 'Abernethy's already been tried in the court of public opinion and been found guilty. What?' he added when they all looked at him.

'That doesn't sound like something you'd say,' replied Gary.

'It's not. I overheard my maw say it.'

'That's because you're a wee mammy's boy.'

'Shut it before I stick my spiky stick right up your bellend.'

'Stop arguing,' Jamie and Logan snapped at them in unison.

* * *

Jamie gazed at his reflection in the mirror. It was his day in court, giving evidence against Cameron Abernethy. He'd done his best not to look like a council estate ned, with his clothes well ironed and hair neatly combed. He'd even given himself a side parting. His mum had bought him a smart dark blue shirt, black trousers and a pair of black brogues. Ross had warned him that Cameron's defence would launch a personal attack on him and portray him as a thug whose word couldn't be trusted. He'd also warned him it was vital he keep cool and give his evidence calmly.

Jamie pressed his hand to the ring hidden beneath his shirt. He wished he could wear it on his finger but he couldn't risk anyone finding out. Christ, he hoped he didn't let Allegra down. She'd vanished so her father would finally get what he deserved. Cameron Abernethy had got away with killing his wife, Allegra's mother. At the time Allegra had thought he'd killed Jamie too after he'd got one of his lackeys to run him over in the street. Determined to see justice finally done, she'd set her father up for her own murder after he'd tried to kill her, and she'd done such a good job it was very likely he would be sent down. But Jamie was afraid of letting something slip that would tell everyone she was still alive.

'I feel sick,' he mumbled to himself.

'Jamie, are you ready?' Jackie yelled up the stairs. 'The taxi's here.'

He sighed at his reflection. 'Coming,' he reluctantly replied.

Jackie's heart went out to her son when he slouched downstairs, hands shoved into his trouser pockets, looking miserable. He'd been through so much and she hated it that he was having to go through this too.

'Ready, sweetheart?' she asked him.

Jackie wore a smart black trouser suit with matching black shirt. She was a lot slimmer these days. The stress of the last few months had drastically reduced her appetite, and she'd dropped a lot of weight.

With the loss of Allegra had come the realisation that she was all her boys had. Their only other living relative was their father and God only knew where that prick was. Even though Jamie was an adult, she couldn't bear the thought of him and Charlie being left alone, so she'd resolved to take better care of herself. She'd improved her diet and quit smoking, which hadn't been very difficult as she'd only been a social smoker anyway. This had led to her taking more pride in her appearance and she'd dyed her grey roots blonde, started wearing a little make-up and bought some new, more fashionable clothes, which had been necessary after the weight she'd lost. Thanks to Jamie bringing in more money, they'd been able to afford it. She looked ten years younger and the weight loss and make-up only sharpened and highlighted her intense green eyes.

'No, I'm no' ready,' muttered Jamie.

She linked her arm though his. 'There's something at the door that might cheer you up.'

She opened the front door to reveal, not only Digger, Gary and Logan, but Ephraim, the psychotic ice-cream-van man, Deirdre and Eric from the pub, Gerry who owned the local Italian restaurant and every resident of their street.

They all cheered when he emerged, the sight so unexpected he recoiled slightly.

'Stick it to the bastard, Jamie,' yelled Ephraim.

They weren't just there for him, they were there for Allegra too, she'd made such an impact on them all. The residents of Gallowburn were considered to be scum by a lot of people, especially by the likes of Cameron Abernethy, but they were good people with kind hearts and they buoyed Jamie's flagging spirits, made him think he might just be able to pull this off after all. The guilt raised its head again. They'd all mourned Allegra, and still grieved her, all the while she was sunning herself God only knew where. He had hoped she'd find a way of secretly contacting him, but he hadn't heard from her since the memorial service and he was starting to worry.

He gave them all an embarrassed little wave. The taxi waited at the kerb for them and he hastily got in.

'That was nice, wasn't it?' said Jackie as she got in beside him.

'I felt bloody ridiculous,' he replied.

'Don't be such a grumpy sod. They only wanted to show their support.'

'Aye, I know. Sorry, Maw, but I'm shitting it.'

'Well, don't. You speak your truth and get that disgusting beast sent down for life. I only hope Cameron makes a nice new friend in prison who repeatedly shows his appreciation for his fat arse.'

Jamie couldn't help but smile. 'Me too.'

'Ross called to warn me that outside the court is hoaching with reporters.'

'Fucking marvellous.' Jamie sighed, staring out of the window.

She took his hand. 'Just get through today, sweetheart, and you can finally put it all behind you.'

'I don't think it will ever be behind me.'

'You have to get on with your life one day, Jamie. Allegra wouldn't mind if you started dating again, she wouldn't want you to be alone.' Jackie was worried about her son, who hadn't gone near a girl in almost a year.

Once again Jamie felt dreadful. He wasn't interested in other women because he refused to cheat on the woman he loved. So many times he'd considered telling his mother that she was still alive and that one day they would be together again, but he was so afraid of her getting into trouble if anyone discovered the deception that he'd decided to keep it to himself.

* * *

Jamie had got used to reporters swarming around him, shouting out questions and snapping his photo, so he strode through the crowd of them outside the High Court of Justiciary in Glasgow as though they weren't there. He walked into the massive stone building through its grand colonnade of Doric columns.

Jackie, however, found herself surrounded on all sides.

'Get out of my way, you idiots,' she told the reporters, but they refused to budge.

Just as she was rolling up her sleeves to get stuck in, one reporter was pulled aside by DI Ross.

'Come on,' he told her.

She barged through the gap he'd created and hurried up the steps and inside the cool building, slamming the door shut behind them. The walls were lined with dark wood panels, the marble floor making it feel even more as if they'd stepped back into the past.

'Those reporters are like one of the bloody plagues of Egypt,' exclaimed Jackie.

'They're a pain in the arse,' replied Ross. He looked to Jamie. 'How are you feeling?'

'Nervous,' he replied.

'Just stick to the truth and everything will be okay.'

Jamie wasn't sure what the truth was any more.

2

The Glasgow High Court had been erected in the Victorian era but it had been extended over the years and Cameron's trial was taking place in one of the newer courtrooms, which were much more airy and brighter than the older part of the building.

As they walked to the reception desk, Jamie became acutely aware of the tunnel that ran underneath the building that had led from the cells to Glasgow Green, where the gallows had been – something else his history-loving grandfather had taught him. He too felt like a condemned man on his way to his execution, even though he was only a witness. Just one wrong word and he could be arrested and Allegra hunted down like an animal.

He handed over his citation – the letter telling him to attend court – to the receptionist, who directed them to the witnesses' waiting room.

'We can't go in there with you,' Ross told Jamie when they reached the waiting room. 'I'll take your mother into the courtroom, so you know we'll be there when you're called to give evidence.'

'When will that be?'

'Hopefully soon but anything can happen in a trial.' He patted Jamie's shoulder. 'Just hang in there, Jamie, and it'll soon be over.'

'Have you got any advice for me?' Jamie asked Ross.

'Just tell the truth and don't call the judge Your Majesty. It's amazing how many people make that mistake. Call him Your Honour. And don't swear.'

'I'll do my best,' he said with a nervous inhale.

'Good luck, sweetheart,' said Jackie, kissing his cheek before allowing Ross to lead her away, constantly looking back over her shoulder at him.

Jamie wasn't too proud to admit to himself that he didn't want his mum to leave.

With a sigh he walked into the waiting room to find it was empty. Whether that was because he was the only witness in the building or because he had to be kept separate from the other witnesses, he had no idea.

Jamie tried to distract himself by playing with his phone, but he kept returning to the photos of Allegra, hoping they'd give him strength.

He sat there for two excruciating hours before a court officer came in to tell him he'd finally been called. After confiscating his phone and telling him he could have it back later, the official led Jamie down the corridor to Court Five.

He was led into the room, which wasn't as vast or imposing as he'd imagined. It looked more like a large conference room and the judge was sitting behind a raised wooden bench. Jamie had imagined a decrepit hawk-like man, but he looked to be in his early fifties with thick steel-grey hair and a kind face. He wore the traditional wig and a bizarre white robe adorned with red crosses.

Jamie's heart started to thump in his throat as he was led straight to the witness stand, all eyes on him. He spotted his mum and DI Ross sitting in the gallery, the former looking pale and worried.

The fifteen faces of the jury watched him too, assessing him already, deciding if he looked to be an honest man or a liar.

Cameron Abernethy spilled out of a chair at the defence's bench, piggy eyes locked on him. The hatred emanating from him was so palpable Jamie could almost smell it. Cameron's demeanour wasn't tense or worried, it was smug and self-assured, as though he already knew he was going to get away with what he'd done. Even though he hadn't killed Allegra, he'd come very close. It was only because she was so feisty that she'd survived. Determination filled Jamie. This wasn't wrong. Cameron Abernethy was a monster who had tried to kill him and who'd murdered Allegra's mother as well as his accountant and God only knew how many other people. He deserved to go to prison for the rest of his life.

As Jamie didn't follow any religion, he was asked to promise to tell the truth rather than give a religious oath. The advocate depute went first for the prosecution, asking him about his time with Allegra and what she'd told him about her father. He repeated what she'd said about being afraid of him, how he'd controlled her life and how she'd been convinced he was responsible for her mother's death. He took great pleasure in repeating the incident at his house where he'd had to pretend to be a waiter in a restaurant when Cameron had called her demanding to know where she was. He enjoyed the fury in the fat bastard's eyes as he told that story. Obviously he'd had no idea he'd been fooled. Naturally the advocate depute treated him very sympathetically before the defence took over.

Jamie disliked the tall, frosty twig of a woman on sight when she rose from the defence bench, the ridiculous white wig of her profession balanced on top of her narrow head. Cameron had already gone through two solicitors before settling on this dragon, and Jamie could understand why.

After giving him a chilling smile, the woman tore into him, using his role in the Blood Brothers to paint him as a vicious thug who was tarnishing the reputation of a wealthy and successful man, a man Jamie was supposedly jealous of.

'Jealous?' exclaimed Jamie, losing his grip on his temper. 'Of that mental case? You're as crazy as he is.'

'We've only your word any of these incidents actually happened,' she countered.

'Well, Allegra would tell you but she can't because he killed her,' he retorted, pointing at Cameron.

'The evidence presented by the prosecution that Miss Abernethy is even deceased is circumstantial at best.'

'She is dead, only he won't say where she is,' Jamie said, pointing at Cameron again. 'I know you've all already seen the footage taken when he tried to kill me at Gallowburn where he brags about saying no one will ever find her.'

'No one will find her because she's out there alive and well.'

'If she is, then where is she?' Jamie retorted, trying not to think about the fact that the barrister was right.

'Who knows. Allegra is a woman of means with access to plenty of resources.'

'Resources she's never touched, you idiot.'

'Mr Gray,' said the judge in a surprisingly sympathetic voice. 'I understand emotions are running very high, but please try not to call the defence names.'

'Sorry, Your... err... Honour,' he breathed, running his hands through his hair. He looked to his mum, who urged him to calm down with a movement of her hands. Jamie looked back at the judge and forced a smile. 'I didn't use the name I really wanted to call her.'

'I can imagine.' The judge smiled back, earning an outraged look from the twig.

'Mr Abernethy claims you stalked him when you were released from hospital,' continued the defence.

'I didn't stalk him. I stood on the pavement across from his house. I didn't do anything wrong. He even called the police on me and they said I wasn't breaking the law.'

'May I ask why you indulged in this rather bizarre behaviour?'

'Because I wanted him to tell me what he'd done with Allegra's body. He ran out of the house at me. When I asked if she was in Cathkin Braes, where her car was found, he said I'll never know, that he'd separated us forever and that I'd never see her again – dead or alive.'

'A conversation we've only your word even took place. There were no other witnesses.'

'So what? It's true.'

'I'd like to play a section of the video captured at Gallowburn, taken by friends of yours who just happened to pass by at the crucial moment.'

Everyone's attention was turned to the large television screen. It was the first time Jamie had seen himself in full berserker mode and it was shocking. He looked insane. The defence lawyer paused the footage just when he was looking his most demented, as though telling the jury – look, this is your witness. How can you believe a word that comes out of this madman's mouth?

'Would you care to explain what was going through your head at that moment, Mr Gray?' she asked him.

'I was angry.'

'About what?'

'The fact that he'd killed Allegra, that he'd made her suffer for years, that she was terrified one day he was going to rape her. That was why she was leaving the country and I was also pretty angry that he was trying to kill me.'

'I'd say, Mr Gray, that you look ready to commit murder yourself.'

The prosecution objected to this statement, declaring that the defence did not possess psychic powers and could not possibly state what he was thinking, which was upheld by the judge.

'You wrapped a chain around Mr Abernethy's neck and attempted to strangle him,' continued the defence. 'You also threatened to hack off his hand with a machete.'

'Aye, so?'

'You accuse Mr Abernethy of being a violent individual but that's exactly what you are, Mr Gray, as is clearly shown in this video.'

'Oh, I'm sorry,' he said sarcastically. 'What should I have done? Not fought back and let them hang me? I noticed you didn't pause the video when that thing over there pinned a forged suicide note to my jumper while his paid lackey attempted to hang me from a tree. You didn't play the bit where he says my mother would be forced into prostitution and he'd be the first in the queue.'

'You launched a vicious attack on Mr Abernethy that he barely survived,' continued the frosty twig. 'He could have suffered brain damage.'

'Did he?'

'Excuse me?'

'Did he suffer any brain damage?'

'I ask the questions, Mr Gray,' she said as though he were simple. 'Not you.'

'So that's a no, then. Never mind though. If he had suffered any brain damage he could always have become a defence solicitor,' he snapped at her.

The woman's pale cheeks burned bright red when there were

titters from the jury, all of them going silent when she glared at them.

'Are you going somewhere with these questions?' the judge asked her. 'Because if you are, I suggest you get there quickly.'

'I'm just trying to show the jury that Mr Gray is an unreliable witness.'

'I was only defending myself,' Jamie leapt in before the judge could respond. 'You purposefully pressed pause on a bit where I look mental.' He turned to the jury. 'How many times have you had a photo taken where you look a bit like a loon? It happens to us all. She just picked to pause it there on purpose. And I don't have a history of violence. I've never been lifted in my life for anything, unlike your client.'

'If you'd allow me to respond, Mr Gray,' said the judge.

'Sorry,' Jamie breathed, wrestling with his anger.

'Thank you.' He looked to the twig. 'The video has already been viewed by the court. I suggest you move the questioning along.'

'Yes, Your Honour,' she politely replied, although her eyes flashed with annoyance. That annoyance was turned on Jamie. 'Mr Gray, you're leader of a gang called the Blood Brothers, based on the Gallowburn estate?'

'Aye,' he replied. 'So?'

'And what is the role of your gang in the local community? Do you organise trips out for the elderly residents, for instance? Provide meals for low-income families?'

'Do you?' he said, folding his arms across his chest.

'I'm not the one on trial here.'

'Neither am I. But you should be, defending scumbags like him,' he said, nodding at Cameron.

'Mr Gray,' said the judge, for the first time his voice heavy with warning. 'You are in danger of being in contempt.'

He sighed and nodded. 'Aye, sorry, Your Majesty... I mean, Your

Honour. Dammit,' he muttered, dragging his hands down his face. Bloody Ross.

Glancing at the jury, he saw they all seemed to be sympathetic towards him, especially some of the older women. They had a look in their eyes that said they'd rather like to mother him. Perhaps making a tit of himself wasn't such a bad thing?

'We keep an eye on the scheme,' said Jamie.

'What do you mean by that exactly, Mr Gray?' said the defence.

'If anyone has any trouble we help them out.'

'What sort of trouble?'

'A lot of the single mothers get hassled by some of the lads on the estate. We tell them to back off.'

'Are any of these warnings accompanied by physical violence?'

'A warning is usually enough.'

'And what other good turns do you do on the estate?'

'Some of the local businesses ask us to keep an eye on their shops for shoplifters and that.'

'I see. That is most commendable, Mr Gray. And what do you do if you catch a shoplifter?'

'We've never caught one yet because when everyone knows we're keeping an eye on the place, they all stay away.'

'Impressive. You must have done something to build such a reputation. What was that?'

'Dunno really. People just sort of respect us.'

'For no reason?'

'Aye.'

She frowned when it became apparent he wasn't going to elaborate.

'What can you tell me about the numerous clashes the Blood Brothers have with the Lawson family?'

'Not much.'

'Please elaborate.'

He shrugged. 'They're a family that live on the south side of the scheme.'

'Is it true that frequent fights have erupted between you?'

'There's a bit of a friendly rivalry, aye.'

'A friendly rivalry which led to the infamous Battle of Gallowburn.'

'I don't know much about that. I was too busy trying not to get hanged by Cameron Abernethy and his hired thug.'

'Several people were hospitalised, including five members of the Lawson family.'

'Then you know more about it than I do.'

The woman pursed her lips. She'd thought this witness would be a dumb meathead she could easily trick into tripping himself up, but he was avoiding all her traps with his vague replies. Even worse, the jury actually seemed to like his rough and ready charm. She'd wondered how an intelligent, educated woman like Allegra Abernethy could ever fall for someone like him, but now it was becoming clear.

'Is there any point at all to these questions, Mrs McCormack?' The judge sighed.

'I'm trying to establish the witness's character, Your Honour,' she replied.

'Trying to destroy my character, more like,' said Jamie.

'Mr Gray,' said the judge. 'You're on your last warning.'

He held up his hands. 'Sorry, Your Honour,' he replied, relieved when he got it right. He had to control his mouth better before he ended up letting Allegra down.

'It's safe to say that the witness has very clearly demonstrated his character,' the judge said, not without amusement in his eyes. 'Now please continue with your questioning.'

'Yes, Your Honour,' she said before looking back at Jamie, regarding him with predatory eyes. 'Mr Gray, how would you describe your relationship with Allegra Abernethy?'

Jamie's eyes filled with fondness. 'It was just... wonderful. I'd never met anyone like her before.'

'So she was unique?'

'Aye, undoubtedly.'

'In what way was she unique?'

'She was so brave and strong, and her sense of humour was amazing. She had this way of making everyone she met feel good about themselves. Wherever she went people just took to her. There's so many people in this world who are always pulling other people down, making them feel bad, but she did the opposite. Everyone on the Gallowburn loved her.'

'She sounds very special.'

A lump formed in his chest and he looked down at his hands, blinking back tears. 'Aye. She is.' He caught himself, panic shooting through him as he realised he'd spoken about her in the present tense because he was letting his emotions get the better of him. From the corner of his eye, he saw Cameron sit bolt upright in his seat. Jamie swallowed hard, ensuring he had complete control of himself before continuing. 'I mean was.'

Jamie glanced at Cameron, who was regarding him with narrow, suspicious eyes.

'Where did you first meet?' said the twig, drawing Jamie's attention back to herself.

'She came into the shop where I worked.'

'And where is this shop?'

'Baillieston.'

'And how far is that from Gallowburn?'

'Just under two miles.'

'What sort of shop was it?'

'I suppose you could call it cheap and cheerful.'

'What does it sell?'

'Toilet seats, cleaning stuff, cheap toys and make-up.'

What was Allegra Abernethy, the daughter of a millionaire, doing in this cheap and cheerful shop?'

'She wanted vape refills.'

'Is that when your relationship began?'

'No. I met up with her on my lunch break.'

'So you'd arranged to meet?'

'No. She was waiting for me outside.'

'Why was she waiting for you?'

'Because she, you know, liked me.'

'I see,' the barrister slowly replied in a way that indicated she couldn't see why. 'And is that when your relationship started?'

'No. I bumped into her after I'd finished work.'

'So she was still hanging around outside your shop how many hours later?'

'About four hours.'

'She waited all that time for you just to come out of work?'

'I don't know. I assumed she went somewhere else and then came back.'

'And then what happened?'

He recalled Allegra driving into John Lawson, and then locking him in her car and threatening to drive him all the way to London if he didn't let her drive him home, but he decided not to mention it. 'She gave me a lift home.'

'Allegra waited over four hours just to drive you a couple of miles?'

'Like I said, I don't know if she waited all that time, she never said. I don't think she did, she wasn't demented.' Sweat was starting to form between his shoulder blades. He didn't like this line of questioning; he had the horrible feeling it was going to lead some-where bad, but he wasn't sure how. Plus it was taking all of his concentration to keep referring to Allegra in the past tense. If he slipped up again this ice queen would pounce on him.

'And then what?'

'She dropped me off and stayed at ours for tea and, before you ask, the next evening we went out on our first date.' He glanced at Cameron, whose eyes were black with wrath. He'd had no idea this had all happened. 'That was when she told me she was terrified of her father, that she thought he'd killed her mother and that one day he'd do the same to her.'

'She told you all that on a first date, when you'd only just met?'

'Aye, she did, but she trusted me.'

'That's a lot to confess to someone you've just met.'

'If you'd known her you wouldn't think it was strange. She was straight up, in-your-face honest and spoke her mind. It was one reason why she was so incredible.' He looked Cameron's way. 'Some people can't handle that kind of honesty.'

'Did she tell anyone else about her fear of her father?'

'Naw, just me.'

'So this in-your-face honest woman told only you?'

'Aye.'

'After she'd known you for a single day, rather than tell her brother or best friend or her godfather, for instance? People she'd known her entire life and loved and trusted? Instead she chose to tell a complete stranger.'

'She wouldn't have told her brother, they never got on. She called him Daddy's little monster.'

'But there were other people she could have turned to, people with power and influence who could have helped her if she'd been so terrified. So why you?'

'Because I was the only one she felt comfortable talking to about it. It was how we were together...'

'In fact, Mr Gray, we've only your word Allegra said any of these things.'

'I am not lying,' he retorted.

'I didn't say you were. Allegra had a history of self-harming, which has been well documented by the counsellors she saw. Did she tell you about that?'

'Aye, she did. She'd cut herself every time her da' freaked her out. She'd wake up in the middle of the night to find him lying on top of her. He's sick, disgusting and she was terrified.'

'So terrified that she didn't seek any help from anyone?'

'She said he'd use his power and influence to destroy anyone who tried to help her – that's why we decided to go abroad together. It was the only way to get away from him. Allegra said if her dad found out about us he would get our house taken off us, that my little brother would be put into care and me and my maw would never find work. That's what he does to people,' he added, glaring at Cameron. 'That's why Allegra was so afraid to tell anyone.'

'Or this is all an elaborate lie made up by yourself. Allegra was mentally unstable, she had been ever since the death of her mother and she couldn't cope any more, so she took her own life and you are making up these allegations against her father because you blame him and you want revenge.'

'That is not true,' Jamie yelled. His eyes filled with tears, which he knew could destroy his reputation on the Gallowburn but he couldn't help himself. This stone-cold bitch was trying to destroy the woman he loved. 'He killed her and he was mad at me for having a relationship with her because I wasn't good enough in his eyes, so he tried to kill me too.'

'Mr Abernethy says his daughter's mental health really started to deteriorate when she met you. He says she committed suicide and he blames you for that. He admits to the attack on you because he wanted revenge on the man he says took his only daughter from him.'

'The lying bastard,' yelled a voice, but it wasn't Jamie, it was his mother. She'd risen from her seat, face purple with fury. Ross attempted to encourage her back into her seat, but she slapped his hand away.

'Do you want to be escorted out by Security, madam?' the judge asked her.

Jackie looked at her son and took a deep breath. He needed her here. 'No, Your Honour.'

'Then I suggest you sit back down and don't speak again.'

Jaw gritted, she slammed herself back into her chair while Ross attempted to calm her.

'Mr Abernethy isn't denying the attack on you,' the defence told Jamie. 'But he says he was acting in defence of his daughter, who took her own life because of her toxic relationship with you.'

'Toxic,' Jamie yelled. 'There was nothing toxic about it. It was pure and good and the most beautiful experience of my entire life, something *he* couldn't possibly understand because all he felt for her was the need to control and dominate her.' Jamie's voice cracked and, despite his best efforts, a tear slid down his cheek. 'He killed her and took her up to Cathkin Braes. What he did to her was so terrifying her nails were found stuck in some wood. People who commit suicide don't do that to themselves. Now he's trying to hide from everyone the fact that he's a monster who wanted to have sex with his own daughter. He's still trying to destroy her. He'll never stop.'

Jamie uttered this last sentence in a flat, exhausted voice before burying his face in his hands. The defence counsel glanced at the jury and saw fifteen pairs of sad, sympathetic eyes watching the witness.

'No more questions.' She scowled.

'Is that it?' a drained Jamie asked the judge.

'Yes, it is,' he kindly replied. 'You can step down.'

'Thank God for that.'

Jamie climbed down and was escorted to the exit by the same man who had led him in.

'Cheers, pal,' he told the court officer when he handed him back his phone.

'Jamie,' said Jackie, charging out of the court and flinging her arms around him.

He clung onto her, so glad she was here.

'You did smashing, son,' she said.

'Are you kidding?' he said, releasing her. 'I got angry and I even started crying like a big fucking pansy.'

'Firstly, there's nothing wrong with showing your emotion for that beautiful lassie you loved, and secondly, I thought you kept your temper pretty well. If it had been me I would have stuck the heid on that cold bitch.'

'Your maw's right,' said Ross, exiting the courtroom too. 'You did very well, Jamie. You gave simple replies and didn't let her twist your words, which was what she was trying to do.'

'She said I was lying.'

'The fact that we haven't found Allegra is the only thing the defence has in their favour and they're trying to cast as much doubt on the murder charge as possible. If the jury think Allegra could have taken her own life, then they will acquit.'

'You don't think they will, do you? Not with all the evidence you have against him.'

'In my opinion, no. We have a very strong case, but you never can tell.'

'What's that supposed to mean?' Jamie exclaimed.

'It means we'll just have to wait and see, but I do have some good news for you – we've been given the green light to reopen the investigation into Rebecca Abernethy's death.'

'What? That's brilliant.'

'Yes, it is. I can't tell you how happy I am to get a second shot at this, but you need to keep it quiet, for now. It hasn't been officially announced and it might not be until after Cameron's trial.'

'This is great news. I know how much it would have meant to Allegra...' Jamie trailed off, looking miserable, missing her like crazy.

Jackie linked her arm through his and patted his back. 'Come on, let's go home.'

'I'll escort you out,' said Ross. 'It's still hoaching with press out there.'

3

Digger, Logan and Gary were waiting for Jamie outside his house, and the sight of them lifted his spirits slightly.

'Some journos were hanging around,' said Digger. 'But we saw them off.'

'Thanks, lads,' replied Jackie. 'I don't want to see any more of the sods for the rest of my life.'

'How did it go?' Logan asked them.

'Shite,' sighed Jamie.

'Let's not discuss it on the pavement,' said Jackie, unlocking her front door.

They all walked inside, Jackie closing the door behind them.

'That fat prick tried destroying Allegra all over again,' seethed Jamie, tearing off his tie and hurling it across the room. 'He was trying to make out that she topped herself, and that I was making it all up about him being an abusive bastard.'

'The utter twat,' exclaimed Digger.

'That lawyer of his was one horrible cow,' said Jackie. 'I was this close to lamping her right in her snooty face.'

'Did the jury believe all that rubbish?' said Logan.

'I don't think so,' mumbled Jamie. 'They looked pretty sympathetic, although they might have just felt sorry for me. I called the judge Your Majesty.'

Gary looked down at the floor to hide his smile.

'Do you fancy coming down the pub?' Digger asked him. 'Let off some steam.'

'No, thanks,' Jamie muttered. 'I just want to be on my own.'

They all watched him slink upstairs.

'Thanks for being here when we got back boys,' Jackie told them. 'It was really nice of you.'

'I just wish we could have helped cheer him up,' said Logan.

'He'll come out of it in his own time. You know it's best leaving him alone when he's in a mood.'

'Do you fancy coming to the pub, Mrs G?' said Gary.

'No, thanks. I just want to sit down with a brew.'

'Well, we'll leave you to it, then,' said Logan, ushering the other two out of the door, Jackie throwing him a grateful smile.

Jamie lay face down on his bed, feeling miserable. He'd hoped his evidence would help convict Cameron, but he might have just made things worse. There was still no end in sight and at this rate he'd never be reunited with Allegra.

He tortured himself with thoughts of her romping on exotic beaches with handsome tanned men, forgetting all about him as they cavorted together in the sand. Sometimes he was tempted to sleep with a woman just for some payback, until he remembered that Allegra's betrayal was only in his own mind. She was incredibly loyal; she wouldn't cheat on him. One thing was for sure – the next few years were going to be torture.

* * *

Jackie collected Charlie from her friend Tricia's house, returned home and set about tidying the living room. There wasn't much to tidy as she'd given it a good going-over that morning, but housework soothed her when she was anxious and right now there was a lot to be anxious about. She was so worried about Jamie. Today was supposed to be the end of months of stress, giving evidence the last nail he had to hammer into that beast's coffin, but the game Cameron's defence was obviously playing was going to drag it out even longer. They wouldn't be able to move on until Cameron was behind bars.

She tutted when there was a knock at the door and she rolled up her sleeves, ready to see off whatever turd of a journalist was here to harass her boy.

'Piss off, you fucking leeches,' she yelled, yanking open the door.

She trailed off, body turning numb with shock as she gaped at the visitor.

'What... what are you doing here?' she managed to breathe.

Her ex-husband's face cracked into a smile. 'Nice to see you too, Jackie. It's been a long time.' He looked her up and down. 'You still look tasty, hen.'

Jackie just stared at him. The drunken mess she remembered had gone, replaced by a handsome, well-dressed man. Jamie had inherited his father's obsidian eyes and black hair. Jason's brooding looks had always made her weak at the knees before the pressure of children, marriage and paying the bills had taken over. Jason had slowly let himself go, putting on weight, descending into addiction and violence. Now he'd dropped all the extra weight and he looked fit and strong. His black hair was peppered with grey, but it was still thick and for once neatly cut and combed. There was something hard and determined in his eyes that hadn't existed before. She could detect no sign of the pathetic weakness he used to wallow in.

Her rage surged back, snapping her out of her shock. 'Don't even think you can pay me a compliment and then worm your way back into this house. Piss off out of it.'

'I'm here to help. I saw on the news what Jamie's been going through and I want to be there for him.'

'Seriously? Where were you when Cameron Abernethy murdered his fiancée and smashed his heart in two? Where were you when a car drove into him and snapped one of his legs? Where were you when he was almost strung up from the Hanging Tree?'

'In prison.'

'Well, there's a surprise,' she retorted. 'What did you do?'

'Robbery. I was an idiot.'

'Aye, I remember.'

'I was released three months ago. I would have come round sooner but I needed to get back on my feet first. I've got a good job, as you can see from the suit.' He smiled, gesturing to his dark blue jacket and trousers, light blue shirt and dark blue tie.

'Where'd you get that lot from?' she asked him. 'A charity shop?'

'No, Jackie. It was handmade by a tailor in the west end of the city. I'm earning good money and I thought now would be a good time to come back and help Jamie. I'm finally a father he can respect.'

'Respect has to be earned, Jason, and you're still the drunken bastard who beat both me and him.'

'I'm not the man you remember. I've changed.'

'Oh, aye? I noticed you haven't apologised for everything you put us through.'

'Saying sorry won't atone for what I did. Let me prove myself. Is Jamie in?'

'No, he's not,' she yelled. 'Piss off out of it, you loser, and never come back. We haven't needed you for the last eight years and we don't need you now.'

'You never divorced me. That says a lot, Jackie.'

'Because I couldnae find you and I didn't have the cash to pay someone to track you down. But now you're back we can finally get it sorted. I want nothing of yours, Jason Gray.'

'I looked you up on the council tax register. You're still using the name Gray.'

'Because I want the same surname as my boys. Jamie's old enough to change his last name but Charlie isnae without your permission and no way were we gonnae have different names to him. So, are you gonnae do the right thing for us all and give me a divorce?'

'No. I still love you, hen.'

'Love.' She snorted. 'What do you know about that? Well, if you're no' gonnae give me what I want then you're still useless. Bugger off.' Jackie's temper spiked even higher when Jason just stood there, refusing to move. 'Go,' she screamed, shoving him in the chest. 'You're fucking poison and I don't want you anywhere near my weans.'

'Maw, what's wrong?' said Jamie, appearing beside her in the doorway.

Jamie wrapped his arms around his mother and pulled her away from Jason as she moved to lash out.

It took Jamie a moment to realise who was standing on the doorstep, his father looked so different.

'Da?' he said.

'Hello, son,' replied Jason. 'It's good to see you.'

'Why have you come back?'

'I heard about the trouble you've had and I want to support you.'

'You've never supported me once in your entire life. Why start now?'

'Because I've changed.'

'Bollocks,' spat Jackie, who was struggling in her son's arms. 'Cockroaches like you never change.'

'Jamie's old enough to make up his own mind about whether he wants me in his life or not,' replied Jason.

'You've not even mentioned Charlie yet, or have you forgotten about him?'

'Course not, but I'm not sure he even remembers me.'

'He doesn't because you pissed off when he was a wee wean. We don't need you, so get lost.'

'Maw, calm down,' said Jamie, fighting to keep hold of her. He knew if he let go she would launch herself at Jason.

All the neighbours were at their windows now, looking to see what circus was taking place outside the Gray house this time, their attention drawn by Jackie's yells.

'I can see I'm causing some upset,' said Jason. 'I'll go to The Bonnie Brae. It's still there, isn't it?'

Jamie nodded.

'I'll wait for you there, son. If you don't show up I'll know you're not interested in talking to me.'

'That's right, piss off,' yelled Jackie as Jason exited the garden and headed down the street. 'You're not wanted around here.'

'Come inside, Maw,' said Jamie, managing to get her back in the house and close the door.

Jackie locked the door for good measure. She wouldn't put it past Jason to just stroll in.

'Are you okay?' Jamie asked.

Jackie raked her hands through her blonde hair, face bright red from all the shouting. 'I can't believe his cheek. After all those years he just waltzes back into our lives. The creep's got an ulterior motive, I know it. He won't do anything that doesn't benefit him. All that about wanting to help was utter shite. He's hoping to cash in on everything we've gone through.'

'Maybe I should go and talk to him?'

'Oh, no, Jamie, don't. He'll only tell you a pack of lies and I couldn't stand it if your heart was broken all over again.'

'I don't care about him enough for him to break my heart, but something's going on and I want to know what.'

'You're better off not knowing, because where he's concerned it's never good.'

Jamie nodded. 'You're right, Maw.'

Jackie breathed a sigh of relief and kissed his cheek. 'You're doing the right thing.'

'I haven't forgotten how he treated us. That's enough to make me never want to see him again.'

'Good lad.' She smiled. 'Now, how about I make us a brew?'

* * *

The atmosphere inside The Bonnie Brae was sombre, for once. All of Gallowburn had rallied behind Jamie and were still feeling the effects of Allegra's murder. Everyone wanted justice for her and the fact that Cameron Abernethy still wasn't behind bars was a slap in the face.

It's so wrong that Abernethy was let out on remand,' said Digger. 'At least he's on house arrest, so he's only allowed to go to court,' said Logan. 'That's something I suppose.'

'Justice doesn't apply to the rich and powerful,' commented Logan into his lager. 'If you've got enough cash you can literally get away with murder. It's all a fucking piss-take.' He and his friends were perched on stools at the bar, half a dozen of the tables taken up by more locals.

'You're right,' said Gary. 'They've no problem with banging up the likes of us, but rich twats can do what they like. It makes me fucking furious.'

'I'm raging,' announced Deirdre, the stick-thin hatchet-faced landlady who was one of the most feared people in Gallowburn because of her ferocity when dealing with unruly customers. 'We should have a riot, that'll let all those elitist bastards know how we're feeling.'

'Hey, that's a great idea,' said Digger.

'I've never understood riots,' said Logan. 'Why smash up where you live? It makes no sense. Anyway, no one gives a shite about the Gallowburn so nothing would be done to fix it after. We'd be left living in a smouldering war zone.'

'Then we smash up the street where the fucking prick Abernethy lives,' spat Digger. 'When all his posh neighbours moan about their fancy cars being torched and their hedges being torn up, everyone will have to take notice.'

'You've got a point there,' said Gary. 'Like it.'

'Don't encourage him,' Logan told Gary. 'All that would happen is we'd be slung into prison, leaving no one watching Jamie's back. The Lawsons might want payback and Abernethy definitely does.'

'What about him?' said Digger when the door opened and a well-dressed stranger walked in. 'He looks like an assassin.'

'Well, he's certainly not the type who usually hangs around here.'

Gary frowned. 'Why does he look familiar?'

Deirdre's eyes widened with realisation. 'Oh, no, you don't,' she yelled, running around the bar to block the newcomer's entrance. 'You're not welcome in my pub, Jason Gray.'

'It's Jamie's da,' gasped Logan.

'That bastard,' growled Digger. 'He beat the shite out of Jamie and Jackie.' He leapt to his feet, flexing his enormous muscles.

'Deirdre's right,' he told Jason. 'You're no' wanted around here, so why don't you fuck off?'

Jason frowned at him. 'Digger? Blimey, you've got bigger. I bet you could beat the crap out of The Rock.'

Digger preened himself at this praise before shaking himself out of it. 'Don't think a few crap compliments will mean you're welcomed back with open arms. I haven't forgotten that you broke Jamie's arm when he was ten.'

Jason held up his hands. 'You're right, I was a terrible father and I probably don't deserve a second chance, but I'm here to support Jamie and from what I've heard he needs all the help he can get.'

'He's got plenty of support.' Gary glowered. 'Don't you worry about that. He doesn't need you.'

'I've got some business I want Jamie to come in on with me. In fact you all could help. It's pretty big, you can earn some good money. Why don't you let me explain over a pint? If by the time I've finished my drink you still don't like what I've got to say, then I'll leave.'

'You're not getting a drink in here,' shrieked Deirdre. She produced one of Ephraim's home-made coshes from behind her back. 'And if you're not out the door in five seconds flat you'll have baws the size of prize-winning pumpkins. Jackie's one of my best pals and I remember every single time you broke her nose or knocked out a tooth, so get out before you get some of the same.'

All three Blood Brothers got to their feet.

'You'd better leave, Jason,' said Logan. 'While your kneecaps are still intact.'

'All right, I'm going,' he replied. 'I don't want any trouble.'

'Then you shouldn't have come back.'

Everyone watched him leave in silence, erupting into excited chatter when he'd gone.

'By Christ, that was a shock,' said Deirdre, returning to her place behind the bar and slipping the cosh into a cupboard before pouring herself a gin. 'Do you think Jackie knows he's back?'

'I reckon so,' replied Logan. 'He probably went to the house first and they told him to piss off, which is why he came here.'

'I don't know why. As if any of us would support him. He must be desperate.'

'He looked different,' said Gary.

'Aye,' said Digger. 'Like he was coined up.'

'And he wasn't a drunken slurring mess,' said Deirdre.

'Maybe he *has* changed?'

'Take it from me, boys,' she told them. 'People like him never change. He'll still be the same pathetic, abusive bag of shite he always was, just in a better suit.'

'Do you think we should tell Jamie?' said Gary.

'Not tonight. That poor lad's had enough crap for one day. Tell him tomorrow. Let's just hope Jason takes the hint and leaves Gallowburn, although I get the feeling he's here to cause fresh mayhem.'

* * *

Logan, Digger and Gary took Deirdre's sage advice and were on Jamie's doorstep first thing the following morning to give him the news of Jason's reappearance before he heard it from one of the gossiping old biddies that haunted the scheme.

A bare-chested Jamie opened the door to them, rubbing one eye with the heel of his palm, dark hair all over the place.

'Why are you lot here so early on a Saturday?' He yawned.

'We've got something to tell you,' said a grave Logan. 'You might want to sit down. It is pretty shocking.'

'Is it to do with my da?'

'Aye,' Logan sighed.

'He stopped by yesterday not long after you left. My maw sent him packing. When did you see him?'

'He came into the pub,' said Logan. 'We all told him he wasn't welcome and Deirdre chucked him out.'

'Nice one. He wanted me to meet him there but I refused to go.' Jamie opened the door wider. 'Come on in.'

They piled into the house to find Jackie dusting the living room while Charlie ate his cereal in front of the television.

'Morning, boys.' Jackie smiled. 'Have you all come for your breakfast?'

'Yes, please.' Gary grinned.

'No, thanks, Mrs G,' said Logan. 'We've already eaten.'

'Speak for yourself.' Gary frowned. 'I only had some toast.'

They all regarded him sceptically.

'Fine,' he sighed. 'Bacon and eggs too.' He rolled his eyes when they continued to stare at him. 'Black pudding, beans, tattie scone. And sausages.'

'Then you've had enough,' said Digger, making him pout.

'The boys saw Jason at the pub yesterday,' Jamie told his mum.

Her friendly smile vanished at the mere mention of her ex. 'That scabby horse's arse,' she snarled.

Logan looked questioningly at Charlie, who continued to stare at the television, oblivious.

'Don't worry about him,' said Jackie. 'He cannae hear a thing when he's watching the telly.'

'We told Jason where to go,' said Digger. 'And Deirdre barred him.'

'I'm glad to hear it,' she muttered. 'Waste of bloody space, he is.'

'He said he wanted to talk,' said Logan. 'That he had something big that we could help him with.'

'The only big thing that loser ever had was his drink problem,' said Jackie. 'Let's hope we've seen the last of him.'

'I'm no' sure he'll give up that easily,' replied Logan.

'Why not? The useless lump gave up at everything else in his life.'

'He seemed different – harder, stronger. I reckon he will try again.'

'I really hope you're wrong.'

The room filled with an awkward silence while Charlie continued to eat his cereal, still oblivious.

'So what are you up to today, Jamie?' asked Digger, clapping his hands together loudly, making them all wince.

Jamie yawned again and dragged his hands through his hair. 'We need to talk to Mr Cavenie at the corner shop. He's been getting some hassle.'

'From who?' said Logan.

'Dunno. That's why we need to talk to him.'

'I hope you're gonnae put a shirt on first,' said Gary. 'I'm in danger of throwing up my breakfast.'

'Ha fucking ha,' Jamie retorted, wincing when his mum scowled at him for swearing in front of his little brother. 'Sorry, Maw.'

'You'd better get dressed, Jamie,' she said. 'You've things to do. Mr Cavenie's a nice man.'

Jamie nodded and headed upstairs.

When he'd gone, Gary asked Jackie, 'So no chance of a bacon butty, Mrs G?'

'I don't have any bacon,' she replied. 'But you can have some of Charlie's cereal – crunchy pop pop crinklies.'

Gary blinked at her. 'Is that a real cereal?'

'It is and Charlie loves it. You can have some if you want.'

Gary eyed with distaste the multicoloured lumps floating in milk that had turned an odd pink colour. 'No, thanks. I've already had my breakfast.'

Ten minutes later Jamie was showered and dressed and the four Blood Brothers left the house together.

'So,' Logan asked Jamie as they walked down the street. 'What do you think about your da coming back?'

'Not much,' he replied. 'He's a fucking loser. I don't want anything to do with him. He probably thinks I got a big payout from the papers and he's trying to cash in.' Jamie had refused to give any paid interviews to the media, despite the huge financial incentives they'd dangled before him. He hadn't wanted to profit from Allegra's so called death, even though he could use the money. No amount of cash could give him what he really wanted – Allegra back by his side.

'I don't think you've seen the last of him,' said Logan. 'He seemed pretty determined. He's different to how he used to be. He seems stronger.'

'He said he's been inside.'

'Prison does strange things to people,' said Digger. 'When my cousin came out of Barlinnie he was one hard, nasty bastard. He only went in for drunk driving. Before that he was quiet and soft. He went through some traumatic shit and he was never the same again.'

'Maybe something happened to your da inside, Jamie?' said Gary. 'He could have been used as a sex toy over and over until he snapped and fought back and kicked the shit out of the big gimp called Bubba.' Gary clammed up, wondering if he'd gone too far, but Jamie chuckled.

'We can only hope.' He smiled. 'It would serve the twat right if he was some nasty sod's personal dildo.'

Sadness filled Jamie as they reached the street where Mr Cavenie's corner shop was. On the other side of the street was the tacky Italian restaurant where he and Allegra had had their first date, during which she'd told him how terrified she was of her father.

'You okay, pal?' said Logan, patting his shoulder.

Jamie nodded. 'Aye. Let's go talk to Mr Cavenie.'

They walked inside the small but well-stocked shop and patiently waited while the balding, bespectacled man behind the counter finished serving an elderly customer.

'Be with you in a minute, lads,' he told them.

'No rush,' replied Digger, studying the porn mags on the top shelf.

'You dirty bastard,' Gary told his friend.

'It's art,' he replied.

'If it's art why don't you ask your maw if you can put one of those pictures in a frame and hang it over the fireplace?'

'Don't you mention my maw,' Digger told him, wagging a finger before his face.

'Don't start arguing,' Jamie told them. 'You'll make us look like amateurs.'

Gary didn't like to add that they were amateurs, so he kept quiet.

'Thanks for coming,' Mr Cavenie told them as he walked around the counter after his customer had left.

Mr Cavenie was short, barely five foot three, a fact that wasn't evident when he was standing behind the counter as he'd had it purposefully built on a platform to raise him above the level of his customers, and the four Blood Brothers stared down at him in surprise. Digger had to bite the inside of his cheek to stop himself from laughing.

'We heard you've had some trouble,' opened Jamie, shaking Mr Cavenie's small pudgy hand.

'Aye, I have. It's those wee bastards the Reid brothers and no' just them but their sister too, nicking from the shop, smearing dog shite across the door, sticking nasty things through the letterbox and smashing windows. Three days ago I was unloading some stock from the van when they snuck up to the open doors and made off with a load of chocolate bars when my back was turned. Now I have to pay someone to stand guard while I unload the van. They even hang around outside the shop intimidating my customers and I'm losing business. I don't know what I've done to upset them, but it's got to stop. I'm at the end of my tether with it all. It's been going on for two weeks now.'

'Don't you worry, Mr Cavenie,' Jamie told him. 'We'll make them stop.'

'I'd really appreciate that. Just let me know how much I owe you.'

'We will, when the job is done.'

'I want you to see the security footage my cameras recorded,' he said. 'I know those wee bastards will say I'm lying but I can prove I'm not.'

He indicated the small television behind the counter, which was split into four screens, linked to the cameras dotted around the premises. Three of the cameras showed the inside of the shop from different angles, and one covered the rear of the premises. He pressed play on the remote control to show the Reid brothers clear as day stealing from the van parked out back. It was evidence that could easily get the Reids arrested but no one on the Gallowburn grassed to the police, and Mr Cavenie knew that if he did no one would ever go near his shop again. The Blood Brothers were his only option.

The boys nodded and left, Digger with his art magazine, which Mr Cavenie told him was on the house.

'Urgh,' said Gary when they were outside on the pavement. 'That magazine's full of female body builders.'

'Sorry,' replied Digger. 'They don't do one about vicars.'

'Valerie would never sully herself like that. She's got class.' Gary frowned at the picture of a blonde woman with a terrifying fake tan and bulging muscles. 'Does that actually turn you on?'

'Aye, it does.' Digger grinned.

Gary stared for a little longer before shaking his head. 'You're weird, do you know that?'

'If you've both bloody finished,' snapped Logan. 'We need to discuss how we're gonnae tackle the Reids.'

'What's to discuss?' Digger shrugged. 'We'll kick the shite out of them like we normally do.'

They all turned to Jamie for his opinion. Ever since Allegra's death they'd all noticed that he'd been even quieter and more brooding than usual.

'We talk to them first,' Jamie told them. 'We went to school with Paulie Reid and he was all right. You never know, Mr Cavenie might have done something to deserve it.'

The Reid family lived two streets away from the shop. Their house was one of the few well-maintained properties in this section of the scheme, freshly painted with no slates missing from the roof, no litter in the garden and a fully functioning fence and gate.

'Not what I was expecting,' said Logan, staring up at the house.

With an impatient sigh, Jamie strode up to the door and banged on it. The door was pulled open by a scrawny man of their own age with a face like a ferret. Thick red curls sprung out from his head.

'Jamie?' said a surprised Paulie, who was the elder of the two Reid brothers. 'What can I do for you?'

'Can I have a word?'

'You can but you'll need to do it on the doorstep. My da works nights and he's asleep upstairs.'

'Fine. Mr Cavenie at the corner shop said you and Mark have been hassling him.'

'Hassling him?'

'Aye. Nicking stuff and vandalising the shop.'

'It's not true, Jamie.'

'Don't bullshit me,' Jamie suddenly snarled, shocking Paulie into silence. 'He's already shown us the security footage. You didn't know he had that, did you?'

The flicker of Paulie's eyes informed him that he didn't.

Jamie thrust his face into Paulie's, causing him to duck backwards like a tortoise retreating into its shell.

'If you or your brother and sister gi'e Mr Cavenie any more trouble we'll be back with bike chains and baseball bats. You get it?'

'Aye, Jamie, I d-dae,' stammered Paulie. Like everyone else in Gallowburn, he'd seen the footage of Jamie beating the shit out of Craig Lawson and Cameron Abernethy that had been leaked onto the Internet and he did not want to be on the receiving end of one of those pastings. Craig Lawson had always been considered the ultimate predator on the scheme, no one could touch him, and the fact that Jamie had hammered, not only him, but a beast like Cameron at the same time had cemented his reputation as a man to be feared.

Jamie grabbed him by the front of his jumper and yanked him towards him with such force Paulie was left standing on his tiptoes.

'Good,' spat Jamie. 'And you'd better never fucking forget it,' he added, before shoving him away, sending him crashing to his hallway floor.

As their leader strode down the garden path, the rest of the Blood Brothers gave Paulie a hard look before following.

'You all right, Jamie?' said Logan as he strode down the street in angry silence.

'Aye,' he replied, coming to a sudden halt, causing his friends to almost fall over him. 'Actually, no, I'm not.' He sighed. 'I cannae stop worrying about my da. Why is he back now, after all these years? I cannae even be sure he's telling the truth about being inside.'

'Well,' said Logan. 'You are friendly with a local detective inspector who might be able to help you with that.'

'I don't want to get Ross involved. Who knows what's going to kick off now Jason's back?'

'Are you saying you want to talk to Jason?'

'No... oh, I don't know,' Jamie said, throwing his hands into the air. 'Even if I do, my maw will kill me. I just don't think his return can lead anywhere good.'

'Maybe you're best forgetting he even showed his ugly mug?' said Gary.

Jamie nodded. 'I think you might be right. He's always been bad news.'

'So what else are we going to do today?' said Digger.

'I thought you'd want to get home and have a wank,' said Gary, gesturing to the magazine sticking out of his inner jacket pocket.

Digger balled one meaty hand into a fist. 'One day, Gary, you're gonnae get such a smack...'

'I'm going home,' announced Jamie impatiently.

'But you've only just come out,' said Gary.

'Nae offence but I just want to be alone. I've got a lot to think about. See you later,' Jamie told them before slouching down the street, hands shoved into his pockets, head bowed.

'I'm worried about him,' said Logan as they watched Jamie go.

'Me too,' said Gary. 'But what can we do? You know what he's like. He never wants to talk about what's bothering him.'

'I don't know, but he's right when he said Jason's return can't mean anything good. All we can do is keep an eye out and help him deal with the trouble when it happens. We need to be prepared, boys. I get the feeling we've got a lot of trouble headed our way.'

4

Jamie was two streets away from his home when a figure stepped out in front of him.

'Don't you ever give up?' He sighed.

'I used to,' replied Jason. 'In fact I gave up everything – my job, my marriage, my home, my sons.'

'Stop it, you'll have me in tears,' Jamie said sarcastically.

'I mean it, Jamie, I want to be a father to you again.'

'Why now, after all this time? You'd better not be trying to cash in on what happened to Allegra.'

'No, Jamie, that's no' why I'm here, I swear. I have a business opportunity for you and your friends. I want to give you a future.'

'I assume this opportunity of yours is illegal?'

'Well, yes.'

Jamie rolled his eyes and shook his head. 'Do you think I'd get involved with anything like that with the police and press constantly harassing me? I mean, how fucking stupid do you think I am?'

'I'm trying to do right by you Jamie, for the first time in my life.

You'll be earning real money. Your house looks like it could do with some modernising.'

'Our house is fine as it is and I don't want you anywhere near it. I remember the beatings you gave me and Maw.'

'I wish I could turn the clock back, son, and take it all back, but I can't. When I was in prison I had plenty of time to think about the regrets in my life and losing you three has been my single biggest regret. I've finally grown up and I want to come home.'

'Piss off and leave me alone. I'm no' interested.'

Jason stood aside to allow his son to pass. 'I've made a deal with the McVay family,' he said as Jamie walked by him. 'I thought that would stop you in your tracks.' Jason smiled.

Jamie whipped round to face him. 'The McVays?'

He nodded. 'With Toni herself. You've driven off all the dealers in Gallowburn, leaving it free and clear for her product to be distributed. This is one of the few areas that has remained out of her reach, but she's seen its potential and wants to bring the scheme under her control.'

Jamie shook his head. 'No fucking way. Do you think we drove out the dealers to make way for you and that bunch of psychos? We did it to make this scheme a better place for everyone to live.'

'You sound so naïve, Jamie. All you've done is create a battlefield for every dealer within a seventy-mile radius. Drugs is big business, and you won't keep Gallowburn free from it for long. Someone will come along bigger and harder than you who will take you out to take control. You need the biggest shark on your side. That's the only real way to keep away the other dealers.' Jason's expression softened. 'Your intentions were pure but you've painted a bullseye on the backs of yourself and your friends. Every lowlife in greater Glasgow will see you as an obstacle to them making a ton of money and those psychos won't hesitate to remove you.'

It occurred to Jamie that he might actually have a point. 'How the hell did you meet Toni McVay?'

'I shared a cell with one of her people. He was released before me and told me to look him up when I got out. It turned out he was her second cousin as well as a lieutenant in her organisation. He told Toni I was from Gallowburn and she thought my inside knowledge of the estate would be useful.'

'What do you know about this scheme? You haven't been here for years.'

'And it hasn't changed in years. This is a great opportunity. The amount of money Toni pays changes lives.'

'Aye and no' for the better. I won't end up in prison like you.'

'Do you speak for your friends too? Surely you should put my offer to them before dismissing it so quickly. We're no' talking a few quid, Jamie, we're talking thousands and thousands of pounds.'

'I'm no' interested and if you know what's good for you you'll piss off before I lose my temper.'

'Toni McVay isn't the type to back down. What she wants she always gets and you do not want to stand in her way.'

'Just stay away from me,' Jamie muttered before slinking off down the street.

* * *

Jamie decided not to tell his mum what his dad had said. Any mention of the McVay family would send her into a frenzy of worry. Instead he arranged a meeting at Logan's house that afternoon with the rest of the Blood Brothers and Dave, Logan's dad.

After he'd relayed what Jason had told him he sat down and awaited their verdict.

'Bloody hell,' breathed Dave, his sweaty body spilling out of the armchair. 'The McVays. They don't come more heavy duty than that family.'

'They work with the Maguires in Manchester,' said Gary. 'And they're top of the tree in the whole of the UK, stronger even than the London and Irish gangs.'

'I know,' said Jamie. 'Which is why I don't want to piss them off.'

'Then it looks like you have no choice,' said Dave, swigging from a can of lager. 'You have to accept his offer and start working for them.'

'No,' retorted Jamie. 'We've never been drug dealers and we're no' starting now. We're trying to improve this scheme. Bringing in McVay drugs will finish it off once and for all.'

'And if you don't do what they want Toni McVay will scoop out your eyeballs, which is her favourite hobby, and keep them in a glasses case as a trophy. Is that how you see your future, stumbling about blind?'

'Course not but we can't do this. No one will have any future in Gallowburn if we let this happen. It'll be the beginning of the end, thanks to us.'

A profound silence filled the room, which was broken by Logan.

'Are you even sure Jason has the McVays' backing? He does have a reputation as a lying bastard. What if he's throwing their name about to make you cave in?'

'That's a bloody good point,' said Digger. 'It could all be a load of bollocks.'

'You need proof,' said Dave. 'I know Jason Gray of old, we went to school together. He'd tell any amount of lies if it got him what he wanted.'

Jamie thought Dave was a fine one to talk about lying, but he kept that to himself. 'Right, I'll ask him for proof. That should buy us some time.'

'What if he takes you to meet Toni McVay?' said a wide-eyed Gary.

'He won't because it's all shite. He's no' working for her, I'll bet my left baw on it.'

'But what if he does?' Gary pressed.

'I've no idea. By the way, no one mentions this to my maw. She'll go aff her nut.'

'Never a pretty sight,' muttered Dave.

Jamie's phone burst into life and he tugged the handset out of his jeans pocket. He listened seriously before saying, 'We'll be right there,' and hanging up. He looked to his friends. 'That was Mr Cavenie. The Reids are smashing up his shop.'

'To the Batmobile,' cried Digger before running outside.

'I assume he means my car?' said Logan as they regarded each other with puzzled frowns.

They followed Digger outside. He was waiting impatiently by Logan's black Volvo estate, which was held together by rust and willpower, and they all hopped in.

A few minutes later they pulled up outside Mr Cavenie's shop to be greeted by the sound of yelling and things being smashed, a group of customers gathered outside anxiously wondering if they should intervene. They sighed with relief to see the Blood Brothers, the decision being taken out of their hands.

Jamie plunged inside to find the two Reid brothers smashing jars of pasta sauce with baseball bats while Mr Cavenie cowered behind his counter. He popped up when his saviours ran in.

'Now you're for it, ya wee shites,' the shopkeeper told the Reids.

Jamie punched Mark Reid in the face and snatched the bat from his hands, using it to smash his brother in the stomach, and the two brothers crumpled to the floor.

'What the fuck did I tell you?' yelled Jamie, jabbing Paulie in the cheek with the tip of the bat. 'We warned you and you didn't listen.'

Logan's eyes widened when he saw a wild ginger harridan clutching a knife sneaking up on his friend from behind. 'Jamie, look out,' he cried.

Rather than attempt to snatch the weapon from her, Logan picked up a bag of flour sitting on the shelf where he was standing and swung it at the tip of the knife, which pierced the bag.

Digger and Gary – who had been standing outside the blast zone – watched the others vanish into the flour cloud, which cleared as it slowly settled to the floor. They burst out laughing to see their friends and the three Reid siblings coated from head to toe in flour. It was in their hair, their clothes and streaked their faces. Fortunately Logan still held the bag, the short stumpy blade embedded inside it.

'I didn't know your shop was haunted, Mr Cavenie,' guffawed Gary, making Digger laugh harder.

The girl blinked in astonishment but swiftly recovered herself and attempted to lunge at Jamie again, fingers curled into claws.

Jamie, who'd had it ingrained in him by his mother not to hit women, grabbed her by the wrists to keep her at bay.

'Bloody hell she's strong,' Jamie exclaimed, attempting to keep hold of her as she twisted and writhed, a shocking string of expletives pouring from her lips.

Digger snatched up an aerosol and sprayed her in the face, making her scream. Jamie released her and her hands went to her eyes.

'It's only deodorant,' Digger told his friends when they all looked at him. 'It's no' like it's insect repellent. She'll be fine.'

'Thanks, pal,' Jamie told him. 'You too, Logan.'

'If she tries for a third time, I'll take her on,' said Gary. 'I don't want to be the odd one out.'

'Here,' said Jamie, handing the shrieking girl a bottle of water. 'Rinse your eyes.'

She snatched it from him and poured it all over her face.

'Better?' he said.

She scowled and nodded.

'You look like a grey Merida.' Gary laughed. Ow,' he added when she punched him in the face, snapping back his head. He dabbed at his nose. 'You made me bleed, you bitch.'

'You got hit by a wee lassie,' taunted Digger.

'Shut it, you tit.'

'Why did you do this?' Jamie asked her. 'You were warned off.'

She shrugged. 'We were paid to. Our need for money is stronger than our fear of you lot, which isn't much, by the way,' she replied with a curl of the lip. 'You think you're such big men around here but you're just stupid little boys.' Her gaze was defiant as she regarded them one by one, except for Jamie. Only when her gaze settled on him did she appear uncertain. Like everyone else in Gallowburn, she'd seen the leaked footage of him beating the crap out of Craig Lawson and Cameron Abernethy.

'Who paid you?' Jamie asked her.

'Dunno, never seen him before.'

'Describe him.'

Another shrug. 'He was just some random guy.'

He sighed with impatience. 'What colour was his hair?' When she shrugged again he fought the urge to slap her.

'I didn't actually see him. He spoke to Paulie.'

The two brothers, who had remained quietly on the floor where they'd fallen in the hope that the Blood Brothers would forget about them, looked up at them warily.

'Get the arseholes up,' Jamie told his friends.

As they dragged her brothers to their feet, the girl took the opportunity to dart out of the shop.

'Let her go,' said Jamie. 'She can't tell us anything anyway.' He turned to Mr Cavenie. 'We'll get these twats out of your way.'

'Thanks, lads. I really appreciate your help.'

The Reid brothers were unceremoniously dragged outside, the customers gathered on the pavement bursting into applause.

'Thank you,' said Digger with his most charming smile as he hauled Mark Reid along the pavement. 'It was nothing, really.'

'You wantin' to sign autographs too?' muttered Gary.

'I don't envy poor old Cavenie having to mop up all that pasta sauce and flour,' said Logan.

'Where are we taking them?' Gary asked Jamie.

'Just down here,' he said, helping Logan haul Paulie down a back alley.

The two brothers were dropped into a manky puddle of water, which was so cold they gasped.

Jamie pulled his bike chains out of his pocket and swung them in a wide arc, one in each hand, the chains creating an intimidating buzz as they cut through the air. 'Now you're gonnae tell us who paid you to smash up Mr Cavenie's shop, and if you don't you'll end up in Intensive Care.'

'It was your da,' exclaimed Paulie.

'I knew it,' he hissed.

'No' yours, his,' he said, nodding at Logan.

'Are you fucking serious?' he said.

'Aye. He said he and Mr Cavenie had a falling out over something.'

'What?'

'Nae idea. He didn't say and I didn't care.'

'How much did he pay you?'

'Fifty quid each.'

'For all three of you?'

'Aye.'

'Bollocks. My da doesn't have a hundred and fifty quid to gi'e to wallopers like you.'

'Describe Logan's da,' said Jamie, who was still convinced his own father was behind it.

'Fat, sweaty.'

'That's him,' sighed Logan. 'But this doesnae make sense. He knows Mr Cavenie's shop is under our protection.'

'We need to have a word with Dave,' Jamie told his friend. He looked back at Paulie. 'But first, you and your brother need teaching a fucking lesson,' he said, whipping up the bike chains again, making them both shriek.

* * *

After dealing with the Reids, the Blood Brothers returned to Logan's house to speak to Dave. They explained what Paulie had told them and awaited his reaction.

Dave gaped at them with his mouth hanging open, which wasn't pleasant as he was eating Scampi Fries.

'It wasn't me, I swear,' he said when he'd recovered from his shock. 'I mean, why would I? I've no' had a falling out with Cavenie. He's a wee prick but I wouldnae do that to him. I get my lager from him, so I don't want to piss him off. And where would I get a hundred and fifty quid from? If I had a problem with him I'd tell him myself, I wouldnae send a bunch of wee ginger wankers after him.'

The Blood Brothers looked to each other and nodded.

'All right,' said Jamie. 'We believe you.'

Dave exhaled with relief. 'Thanks, lads.' Despite being Logan's father, he knew that wouldn't protect him should Jamie decide he needed a kicking. Logan would always side with his friend over him.

'Let's go back and kick the shite out of the Reids some more for lying about my da,' spat Logan. Dave certainly wasn't going to win father of the year, but he was his flesh and blood and Paulie Reid's lies infuriated him.

'Calm down,' said Jamie, grabbing his arm when he lunged for the door. 'Think about it. Do the Reids actually know what your da looks like?'

'They must do, they described him perfectly – fat and sweaty.'

'I am not fat and sweaty,' exclaimed Dave.

They all ignored him.

'Either they were lying,' continued Jamie.

'Which they fucking were,' snarled Logan, his curly hair seeming to stand on end. He was the most easy-going of the four Blood Brothers but when his blood was up he was ferocious.

'Or someone is setting Dave up,' added Jamie.

'Why set me up?' said Dave, the picture of innocence. 'I've never done anything to anyone. What?' he added when they all regarded him sceptically.

'Have you wound anyone up at the pub lately?' Logan asked him.

'No, not at all. I just sit there nice and quietly at the end of the bar with my pint, minding my own business. Okay,' he sighed when they all continued to stare at him. 'I might have said Gordon McDade likes to shag the dead but that's about it. He was pished at the time so he thought it was funny.'

'I find it hard to believe that anyone, no matter how drunk they were, would find a comment like that funny.'

'He did.'

'And you've not annoyed anyone else?'

'Not that I know of, but people are so touchy these days. They get upset over the slightest thing.'

'I'm still not convinced this isn't something to do with Jason,' said Jamie. 'It's too much of a coincidence.'

'But what would he have to gain?' said Logan.

'Maybe he wanted to test us?' said Gary. 'See what we could do.'

'Wouldn't he get someone more intimidating than the Reids to do that?' said Digger. 'They're just a bunch of fannies. Their wee sister was tougher than Paulie and Mark.'

'He's been away for years,' said Jamie. 'They might be all he could find.'

'We could do with talking to Jason,' said Logan.

'Maybe that's what he wants?' said Gary. 'It's a plot to get you to talk to him.'

'Oh, that's a good point,' said Digger.

'Great,' said Jamie. 'Now I don't know what to do.'

'Hold on,' said Logan. 'Paulie said the man who paid them was fat and sweaty and that's no' Jason. Could this be linked to Cameron Abernethy instead?'

'If it was him, he would have hired someone much scarier than those wallopers.'

'Or this could be from Craig Lawson.'

'Again, he has loads of cousins who are a hell of a lot handier than the Reids.'

'You're right, which can only mean the Reids were lying.'

'Let's go back there and kick the shite out of them some more,' said an eager Digger.

'Calm yer jets, Rocky,' said Gary. 'Why don't you sit down and read your creepy scud book?'

'What's that about a scud book?' said Dave.

'Here you go,' said Digger, tugging the magazine out of his jacket and tossing it into his lap.

Dave snatched it up, grin falling as he flicked through the pages. 'They're men, you dirty bastard,' he cried, flinging it back at him.

'They're no' men, you daftie,' said Digger. 'They're female body-builders.'

'You sure?'

'I know a woman when I see one,' he snapped back.

Dave's look said he thought that was highly doubtful.

'So,' said Logan. 'What's the plan?'

'If this is something set up by Jason to get my attention,' said Jamie, 'I don't want to fall for it. We just carry on keeping an eye out and dealing with trouble as it happens.'

'Sounds good to me,' said Gary.

'Me too,' said Digger without looking up from his magazine.

'Logan?' said Jamie.

His friend took his time replying and Jamie didn't hurry him along. Unlike the others, Logan always considered his options before making a decision.

'I think it's the only thing we can do,' he eventually said. 'I don't think the Reids were lying, they were too scared. There's more going on here than we understand. Whether that's to do with your da, Cameron Abernethy or the Lawsons, I have no idea. For all we know it could be someone else entirely.'

'Please don't say that,' sighed Jamie. 'We've got enough enemies.'

'Maybe we should gi'e the Lawsons a scare?' said Gary. 'Just to make sure they stay in their fucking place. If there is someone else up to shenanigans we don't want that family kicking off too.'

'That's actually a pretty good idea, Gary.'

'I do have them occasionally.' He grinned.

'Shall we do it now?' said Logan.

'How no'?' replied Jamie. 'It's Saturday, so they'll all be on the scheme somewhere.'

'Shall we hit John Lawson?'

'Naw. That cabbage is no threat. We'll go for Nick Lawson. He's the toughest in the family and he's Craig's first cousin. It'll send a stronger message.'

'Good idea. Let's go.'

'What's going on?' said Digger, dragging his gaze off his magazine when his friends marched for the front door.

'We're gonnae kick the shite out of Nick Lawson,' Gary told him as though he were simple.

'Great.' He grinned. 'I'm in.'

5

The Blood Brothers found Nick Lawson in the Gallowburn snooker hall, which lay close to the stream that marked the very centre of the estate. For this reason, it was frequented by residents from both the north and south sides of the estate, which was why it had a reputation for trouble. It had changed hands several times, the insurance premiums rising with each new owner. However, ever since the Lawson family had been subdued by Craig's arrest, it had been much more peaceful.

The Blood Brothers walked inside, their feet sticking to the ugly brown carpet, which was dotted with countless unmentionable stains. Half a dozen snooker tables sat in a row down the centre of the room, their glory days long gone with their ripped felt and stained wood. Over each table hung a large orange light, the shades a graveyard for unfortunate flies that had been drawn into its hypnotic glow. The walls were lined with pinball machines and fruit machines. At the far end was the bar, the bored barman reading the newspaper. He didn't even bother to look up when they walked in.

The only customers were Nick Lawson and four of his friends, two of whom were also Lawsons.

'What the fuck do you lot want?' Nick demanded of the Blood Brothers, brandishing his cue like a baseball bat.

'There's some shit going down on the scheme,' began Jamie. 'And we think you lot are behind it.'

'There's always some shit going on in Gallowburn,' replied Nick. 'So what's new?' His lips curled into a vicious smile. 'It said on the telly you were bawling your eyes out in court over your poor wee girlfriend,' he added, making his friends laugh.

'I'd like to see how you'd act if your girlfriend was murdered, you fucking prick,' retorted Gary. 'Oh, aye, that's right – you havenae got a girlfriend. You haven't had one since your last bird dumped you because you could only get it up by looking at a picture of Vin Diesel.'

'You lying bastard,' yelled Nick, charging round the snooker table at him wielding his cue, going silent when Jamie snatched it from his hand and broke it over his knee.

'Have you got anything else to say?' Jamie scowled.

'Just take it easy, all right, Jamie?' said Nick, holding up his hands. He too had seen the footage of him going berserker and he didn't like the wild look in his eyes.

'Did you pay the Reids to smash up Mr Cavenie's shop, which is under our protection?'

'No,' replied Nick, genuinely puzzled. 'Why the hell would I?'

'You tell me,' Jamie said, drawing back one half of the snooker cue.

Digger grabbed one of Nick's friends by the throat and pinned him to the wall when he moved to intervene.

'It was nothing to do with me,' Nick told Jamie. 'Honestly.'

'I don't want to take the chance,' said Jamie before smashing the piece of cue into the side of Nick's face.

As Nick dropped to the floor, the rest of the Blood Brothers tore into Nick's friends and twenty seconds later all the Lawsons were groaning on the floor.

'If you hear who did it,' Jamie told Nick, 'then you'd better let me know pronto, because if something else happens around here I'll be back to see you. Then I'll come back again and again and I'll never stop.'

Nick spat a tooth out onto the floor. 'Message received,' he lisped, the left side of his face already swelling.

'Good. Have you been to see Craig lately in Barlinnie?' He smirked.

Nick just glared at him.

The Blood Brothers left the snooker hall, the barman breathing a sigh of relief that nothing had been broken during the ruckus except a snooker cue. That, he could live with.

* * *

'All right, Maw?' called Jamie as he walked into the house. 'It's just me.'

He closed the front door behind him and wandered through the living room into the kitchen to find his mother unpacking half a dozen shopping bags with Charlie's help.

'Hi, sweetheart.' Jackie smiled. 'Did you get everything sorted out at Mr Cavenie's?'

'Aye, we did, but something strange is going on.'

'In what way?'

'The Reids said someone paid them to mess up the shop and we cannae work out why.'

Jackie froze, clutching a tin of baked beans.

'You okay, Maw?' Jamie frowned.

'This is something to do with Jason,' she whispered. 'I know it.'

'I'm not sure. They told us whoever paid them was fat and sweaty.'

'Then it was Davey boy.' She scowled.

'He said it wasn't.'

'Well, he would say that. He's a natural-born liar, that one.'

'I think he was telling the truth. Plus, he doesn't have a hundred and fifty quid to pay anyone.'

'I wouldn't put it past him to have stashed some cash away.'

'I really don't think it's him and neither do the others. He looked clueless.'

'He always looks like that.'

'Can I put that tin away, Maw?' Charlie asked her, indicating the tin of baked beans she held.

'Here you go, sweetie.' She smiled, handing it to him.

Humming happily to himself, Charlie neatly placed the tin in a cupboard.

'I wish you were as tidy as your brother,' she told Jamie.

'I thought you'd already accepted that I never will be.' He smiled.

'I live in hope. Anyway, this recent trouble must be down to Jason.'

'There's only one way to find out and that's by asking him.'

Jackie's outraged look said it all. 'I want to talk to you in private.' She looked to Charlie. 'Can you carry on putting all this away while I talk to your brother?'

'Course, Maw,' Charlie replied with his sweet smile.

'That's my boy,' she replied, ruffling his hair, widening his grin.

Jackie and Jamie retreated into the living room so Charlie wouldn't overhear.

'I'm willing to bet my left boob that your da is behind all this,' opened Jackie.

Jamie's face creased. 'Urgh, Maw. Couldn't you bet something else?'

'Trouble follows him wherever he goes and he's trying to bring trouble down on you too, so he can trap you into whatever daft scheme he's got into his head.'

Jamie didn't dare mention the McVays, knowing full well it would send his mum demented. 'I have to know for sure if this is down to him or not because, if it isn't, it could be to do with Cameron Abernethy, and I have to be prepared.'

Jackie sighed, able to see the sense of her son's words but not wanting him anywhere near his toxic father. 'Well, all right, Jamie. You're a grown man and I can't stop you from seeing him, but for God's sake take Logan with you. He's got a sensible head on his shoulders. I'd come with you myself but I know if I do I'll end up hitting the bastard.'

'Okay, Maw, I will.'

'Take my advice, Jamie – don't trust a word that comes out of his mouth. The truth doesn't exist for Jason Gray.'

'Don't worry, Maw,' he said, patting her shoulder. 'I'm no' daft.'

'I know you're not, sweetheart. I just wish you didn't have to deal with his pish on top of everything else you're going through. The best thing Jason could have done for you is to stay away. He doesn't want to help you. The only person he's ever helped is himself and bugger everyone else. He's only here because he thinks he can get something out of you.'

Jamie sighed and nodded. 'Aye, you're probably right, Maw.'

'I'm sorry to say this about your own father, sweetheart, but you have to be prepared. Do not believe a word that comes out of his mouth.'

'I won't,' Jamie replied, forcing a smile.

The sadness in his eyes broke Jackie's heart.

* * *

Jamie arranged a meeting with his father by calling him on the phone number that Jason had written down for him and slipped through his front door. He asked Deirdre for permission to meet his dad in the back room of The Bonnie Brae, which was where people went to discuss anything they didn't want overheard. At first she refused to allow Jason Gray anywhere near her pub, but when Jamie told her that his mother had given her blessing, she relented.

He and Logan waited for Jason to show up in the small, intimate room at the rear of the pub, the low murmur of voices and the clink of glasses coming from the main room was audible. There were no windows so no one could see in. Unfortunately that also meant no fresh air could get in and the room smelled stale and a little damp. The table they sat at had a wonky leg, the whole thing tilting when someone leaned on it, and the wooden chairs were hard and unyielding.

'I hope your da hurries up before we end up with piles,' commented Logan, shifting uncomfortably in his seat.

'It's no' the chair,' replied Jamie. 'It's your skinny arse.'

'That's the pot calling the kettle. How do you feel about this meeting?'

'Nervous. I've nae idea what he's gonnae come out with. Don't be afraid to speak up if you think it's all bollocks or that he's trying to trick me.'

'I will. Don't worry, pal, I've got your back.'

'Cheers,' replied Jamie with a grateful smile.

They went silent when the door opened and Jason walked in, looking as smart and together as he had the other day.

'Thanks for setting up this meeting,' he said with a pleasant smile.

He extended his hand to Jamie, who gave him a cold look before pushing out the chair opposite him with his foot.

'Sit down,' said Jamie.

Jason removed his gloves, unbuttoned his coat and took the proffered seat.

'Drink?' Jamie asked him.

'No, thanks, son. I gave up the booze years ago.'

'I suppose you had no choice in prison,' retorted Logan.

'You'd be surprised what you can get inside, and anyway I thought this chat would be between me and my son?'

'Logan's my best pal,' replied Jamie. 'As well as the smartest person I know.' *Apart from Allegra,* he thought. 'His advice has saved me from getting into a ton of trouble in the past, so he stays.'

'You think I'm here to get you into trouble?' replied Jason.

'Aye, I dae.'

'I see Jackie's been bad-mouthing me.'

'This is nothing to do with her. I remember exactly what you were like – the violence, the beatings. You stole all our money to buy booze so we couldn't even eat.'

'Aye,' he sighed, casting his eyes shamefully to the floor. 'I'm really sorry about all that, Jamie, son.'

'Sorry doesn't cut it after what you did. It's not my maw's fault I don't trust you. Don't you dare blame her for anything.'

'You've every right to be angry, I was a terrible father but that's why I'm here now, so I can make it up to you.'

'By turning me into a drug dealer?'

'By giving you the chance to make some serious money. What other opportunities are you going to get on this scheme?'

'How do we know you're telling the truth about the McVays?'

'You think I'd make up something like that?'

'Aye, we dae.'

'You want proof,' Jason said, delving into his coat pockets. 'Here you go.'

With that he produced a few tiny clear plastic bags from his pocket and dumped them on the table. 'Coke, methamphetamine and heroin.'

'Jesus,' breathed Logan, staring at the packages in shock.

'You're looking at forty grand's worth there, and that's just a small sample of my stock. Just think of the money you could make, lads, you could finally get yourselves off the Gallowburn, buy your very own place to live. I know Jackie always dreamed of a cottage by the sea. Charlie could go to a good school and grow up somewhere safe.'

'The Gallowburn is safe now,' retorted Jamie. 'Thanks to us.'

'So I heard, but have you been able to cure all the poverty? Find everyone jobs? Pay off all their debt? Put food on the table of hungry families? You can only do so much,' he added when Jamie looked down at his hands. 'Everyone who lives in Gallowburn isn't your responsibility. It's up to them to sort out their own lives.'

'And you think giving them drugs will help them do that?'

'No, but it'll help you. Charity begins at home, son.'

Jamie stared at the packages on the table. He could make his fortune out of all this but he would have to destroy other people to do it. There were better ways to make money. Plus, the thought of what Allegra would say if she found out he was involved in drugs was enough to prevent him from accepting, not to mention his maw. She'd hit the roof. Neither did he want to get locked up for years, because that was what usually happened to drug dealers. If he ended up in prison he'd never see Allegra again, and she was his future.

'We're not interested,' said Jamie.' This isn't who we are.'

'Come on, son, don't be daft. This is the opportunity of a lifetime.'

'I'll make my own cash and I don't need your help to do it.'

Jason sighed, snatched up the plastic bags and shoved them back into his pockets. 'The McVays are not people you turn down.'

'How do we know they're even involved? You could just be throwing their name about to scare us into agreeing to this.'

'You'll have to trust me, Jamie.'

He shook his head. 'No way. If you really are working for the McVays then we want proof. I'm no' taking your word for anything.'

'And if I do arrange a meeting, what then?'

'We'll see,' was all Jamie was willing to reply.

'Are you seriously going to tell Toni McVay that you won't allow her product to be distributed in Gallowburn?'

'Aye.'

Jason smiled and shook his head. 'You've got some baws, son, I'll gi'e you that. I'll set it up.'

'Aye, right,' said Jamie, looking slightly amused.

'I'm serious. This isn't a joke. I really am working for the McVays.'

'Course you are. Anyway, we need to discuss something else.'

'I'm listening.'

'Did you pay the Reids to smash up Mr Cavenie's shop?'

Jason's smile said it all. 'Aye, I did. Sorry, but I had to see what you all could do and, I have to say, I was impressed.'

'The Reids said the man who paid them was fat and sweaty.'

'That's what I told them to say if they got caught. I was hoping you'd blame it on your da,' replied Jason, nodding at Logan.

'You bastard,' exclaimed Logan, leaping to his feet.

Jamie grabbed his arm. 'Sit down.'

Logan complied, not taking his angry glare off Jason.

'Let me explain,' said Jason. 'I've heard that Dave has given you a lot of bad advice and got you into trouble. I thought it would do him some good if he knew what that felt like.'

'Your plan didn't work though,' retorted Logan. 'We knew he didn't have a hundred and fifty quid to pay the Reids.'

'I bet you asked him about it though?'

Logan's response was a glower.

'Who else have you been asking about us?' said Jamie.

'A couple of the Lawsons were happy to talk and there was Gerry in the restaurant.' Jason's expression softened. 'He told me all about Allegra. He seemed quite smitten. She sounds like she was a very special woman.'

'She was,' mumbled Jamie, looking down at his hands. For some reason he was afraid Jason would see the truth in his eyes. This man was a far cry from the drunken mess he remembered. Now he'd beaten his addiction, it seemed his brains had returned.

'Has Cameron Abernethy been hassling you?' Jason asked him.

'Naw, although I keep expecting him to. If he was going to make a move I thought he would have made it before I could give evidence against him.'

'He might just be biding his time. You need to stay on your guard.'

'I always do and I've got good people watching my back.'

'So I see,' said Jason, his gaze moving to Logan before slipping back to his son. 'But Abernethy might not be as obvious as before.'

'Logan,' said Jamie. 'Would you mind giving me a minute alone with my da?'

'No problem,' his friend replied, getting to his feet. 'I'll wait at the bar.'

Father and son didn't speak as Logan left the room, staring at each other in silence with identical obsidian eyes.

When he'd gone, Jamie leaned forward in his seat, resting his arms on the table, annoyed when it tilted.

'Do you really gi'e a shite about me, Da, or are you just

pretending so I'll help you out with your new business?' said Jamie, pronouncing the last word sarcastically.

'Of course I care, Jamie. I understand why it's so hard for you to believe after the way I've treated you, but the man I used to be is dead. I buried him in prison. I got off the drink when I was inside and suddenly I could see clearly again. I remembered how badly I treated you and Jackie and I hated myself for it. I finally realised exactly what I'd thrown away and it hurt, Jamie, it really hurt. If I could I'd go back and change things, become the father you deserved and the husband Jackie deserved, but I can't.'

'Why were you in prison?'

'I robbed an off licence, badly. I was caught on a security camera.'

'How long did you get?'

'Five years.'

'Jesus. Barlinnie?'

'At first. I got transferred to Addiewell in West Lothian before being sent back to Barlinnie.'

'Why?'

'The prison service likes to shift troublemakers about and when I was getting myself off the drink I went a bit demented with the DTs, acted out a lot. When I'd weaned myself off it properly I straightened out, started working out in the gym, lost a lot of weight. I really was a fat bastard at one point,' he said with a self-deprecating smile. 'I even got a certificate in industrial cleaning and my forklift truck licence. I did so well I got released eighteen months early.'

'And then you became a drug dealer,' said Jamie flatly, folding his arms across his chest. 'I'm so proud,' he added in a sarcastic tone.

'I could have become a cleaner or a forklift driver, working long hours for a pittance, paid taxes, found some dingy bedsit, but I want more, Jamie. There's nothing wrong with wanting the good things in life.'

'No, there isn't, but there are better ways to get them.'

'I don't force anyone to take drugs. If people want to stuff white powder up their noses or inject the brown into their veins, that's their business. Why shouldn't I cash in on their weakness?'

'Because you're cashing in on other people's misery, and do you think we're going to go from chasing all the dealers off the scheme to becoming dealers ourselves? That is not how I saw my future.'

Jason's smile was filled with fondness. 'You have your mother's ideals. She did a good job raising you.'

'Aye, she did, and she taught me better than to become what you want me to be. I'm no' dealing drugs. You get it? And you haven't even mentioned Charlie once, or are you no' interested in him because you cannae get him to deal for you?'

'Of course I'm interested in Charlie, but he was so young when I left. He doesn't even know who I am.'

'And whose fault's that?' snarled Jamie.

'I know it's mine, I'm holding my hands up here and I intend to make it up to him too.'

'How? By making him mug old pensioners?'

'You and your friends have got potential and I want to help you fulfil that potential.'

'But no' with drugs.'

'You really don't want to tell Toni McVay no.'

'Aye, right. Toni McVay.'

'I'm not making it up. I really am working for her.'

'I'll believe it when I see it.'

'Fine, but you'd better have a bloody good excuse ready when you tell her no because she does not take rejection well.'

Jamie's response was a smile. His dad looked worried. Good. He'd been called out on his lie and now he was panicking.

'Let me know when you've set up the meeting,' said Jamie, getting to his feet.

'I will and you'd better be prepared. Meeting Toni McVay is quite an event.'

'I'll be ready.' Jamie smiled before sauntering out of the room and joining Logan at the bar.

'Pint, Jamie?' Deirdre asked him.

'Please,' he replied.

'I hope you left that tosser a bloodied heap on the floor in there.' She scowled.

'I didn't want to stain your lino.'

'That was sweet of you but fuck the lino,' she replied, plonking his pint down before him.

'So how did it go?' Logan asked Jamie when Deirdre went to serve another customer.

'He said he'd set up a meeting with Toni McVay.'

'I wonder how he's gonnae pull that one off. Pay one of the Reid brothers to wear a dress and a black curly wig?'

Jamie spluttered into his pint. 'Aye, probably. Hopefully he's got the message and will piss off now.'

They went silent when Jason emerged from the back room, stood at the bar and regarded Deirdre expectantly.

She narrowed her eyes at him. 'I let you in my back room because Jamie asked me to but that doesn't mean you're welcome back here, so bugger off.'

'Okay,' he said, holding up his hands. 'I'm going.'

'Where are you staying?' Jamie asked him.

'I've got a flat in Hillhead, not far from Kelvingrove Park.'

'That's a nice area, that,' commented Logan.

'It is. Very.' He leaned in to whisper in Jamie's ear. 'You could live somewhere like it too if you took me up on my offer.' He patted his shoulder. 'Just think about it.'

When Jamie didn't reply, Jason left.

'I'm going to ask Ephraim if he can make me a twat repellent,' muttered Deirdre, glaring at Jason's retreating back as he left.

'I'm sure he'd have a lot of ideas for that.' Logan grinned.

'He'll go demented when he finds out Jason's back. He has a huge crush on Jackie.'

'Aye, we noticed.'

'If he does go mental that's Jason's problem, not yours,' Deirdre told both men before turning to serve another customer.

'Does your maw know you met him today?' Logan asked Jamie.

'Aye and she'll hit the roof when she hears what he had to say.'

'You can't tell her.'

'I don't want to but I cannae lie to her, and she will ask.'

'If you tell her that your da wants you to become a drug dealer she will hunt him down and snip off his baws with rusty hedge trimmers.'

'It'll serve him right if she does, but I'm not going to lie for him.'

'No, you're right. You cannae let him interfere in your relationship.'

Logan looked round when two women their own age walked in. Both were extremely attractive, one in a short black skirt, the other in a pair of tiny blue denim shorts, even though it was autumn and cold outside. When the women realised one of the Blood Brothers was looking their way they gave him their most alluring smiles.

'Hey, Jamie,' said Logan, elbowing his friend in the ribs.

'What?' he muttered, sipping his pint.

'Look at that pair of crackers,' he replied, nodding at the two women.

Jamie regarded them uninterestedly. 'What about them?'

'They're gorgeous.'

'Suppose.' He shrugged.

'And they're looking at us.'

'So?'

'Let's go and talk to them.'

'Why?'

'Jesus, Jamie, do I need to spell it out to you?'

'You go and talk to them. I'm no' interested.'

'It's been nearly a year, Jamie,' Logan said gently.

Jamie's eyes narrowed. 'What about it?'

'Allegra wouldn't want you to be alone and miserable.'

'Listen, pal, I know you're only trying to help, but just leave it.'

Logan held up his hands. 'Okay, whatever you want but I hate seeing you so down.'

'I'm no' down, I'm just fucking dandy,' Jamie muttered before draining his glass and waving it around until Deirdre spotted him, took the glass from his hand and refilled it. 'You go over there if you're so interested,' he told his friend.

'All right, I will,' replied Logan, getting up and taking his pint with him.

Jamie watched him settle himself beside the woman in the tiny shorts, who was the prettiest of the two. When Jamie felt the loneliness wash over him again his fingers went to the chain around his neck. He was so glad Allegra had given him the ring because it provided him with a lot of comfort, as well as the strength to endure the separation knowing they would be together again one day.

After finishing his pint he got up to leave.

'Night, Logan,' he said to his friend on his way out. Logan had his tongue stuck down his lady's throat.

'Aye, night,' Logan replied, briefly coming up for air.

The woman in the black skirt regarded him hopefully as he walked by, but Jamie ignored her and kept on going before disappearing into the night.

6

Jamie was tormented by dreams of Allegra. He was chasing after her but she remained elusively out of reach. Then, when he was just about to catch up with her, she was snatched away by a giant hairy bear. Jamie jumped awake, her voice screaming his name echoing in his head. He ran a shaking hand down his sweat-soaked face.

'Jeezo, I'm losing my mind,' he whispered to himself.

Daylight streamed through the thin curtains, to his relief. He was glad it wasn't the middle of the night because after that dream he wouldn't have been able to get back to sleep.

He wandered downstairs in his boxer shorts and T-shirt to find his mum helping Charlie with his school tie.

'Is it that time already?' Jamie yawned.

'Aye, it is,' replied Jackie. 'You slept in again. It's a good job you work for yourself now otherwise you would have been sacked from the shop.'

'Thank Christ I don't have to go back there. What?' he added when she frowned.

'You look like crap.'

'Thanks, Maw.'

'How did it go with you-know-who last night? I wanted to wait up for you to come home but I was so knackered I had to go to bed.'

'Oh, fine.' He shrugged.

'Me and you need a wee chat after I've dropped Charlie off at school, so don't go disappearing, okay?'

'Aye, okay,' he sighed.

After they'd gone, Jamie wandered into the kitchen to make some breakfast, tutting when the doorbell rang. He plodded through the house and pulled open the front door, not caring that he was in his underclothes.

A delivery man in a baseball cap and a high-viz vest was standing on his doorstep.

'Jamie Gray?' said the man.

'Aye.'

He thrust a parcel at him before turning on his heel and marching back to his van, which was parked at the kerb.

Jamie closed the door, frowning down at the parcel in his hand, which was wrapped in brown paper. He wasn't sure if it was his imagination or not but it seemed slightly sinister. He was loath to open it. What if it had been sent by his father and contained drugs? Or someone's eyeballs that had been scooped out of their owner's head by Toni McVay herself? He chided himself for being such a prick. His da wasn't so stupid as to send drugs through a parcel courier and Toni McVay didn't even know he existed.

He tore off the paper to reveal a brown cardboard box bare of anything that would give him a clue as to its contents.

Jamie took the box into the kitchen and placed it on the table, holding his breath as he slowly lifted the lid to reveal...

A blue teddy bear.

'What the hell?' He frowned.

It wasn't even a cute teddy. In fact it was an ugly wee bastard with a wonky snout and it was cross-eyed. Its expression was somehow both goofy and malevolent at the same time. He was quite sure that if Charlie ever saw it he'd burst into tears.

His confusion only increased when a ringing sound emanated from inside it. Turning it over, he saw the back was sealed with Velcro. He ripped it open and pulled out a mobile phone. The screen informed him that the number had been withheld.

He swiped at the screen and put the phone to his ear with a frown. 'Hello?'

'Hello, Dangerous.'

His head swam and he had to cling onto the kitchen table with his free hand. 'Allegra,' he breathed.

'I hope you don't mind me sending you the phone, but I had to speak to you. I've been going crazy. I'm missing you so much.'

Relief flooded through him like heavy rain after a drought. She hadn't forgotten about him; she was missing him as much as he was missing her. 'It's driving me crazy too. It's shite without you.'

'I wish I could see you in person but it's too dangerous. This was the only thing I could think of.'

'Only you would think of sending me a phone in a squinty-eyed teddy.' He grinned.

'Is it squinty? It looked cute on the website.'

'It's one ugly wee sod. You've not seen it?'

'Not in person. It's made by a family-run company in Aberdeen. I sent them the phone and asked them to put it inside as a gift, then paid them to post it to you. I've been glued to the online tracking for two days. As soon as it came up *delivered* I called the phone.'

'You're so bloody smart.'

'I know,' she said with a smile in her voice. 'I didn't want to send it to you directly from here in case it was traced back to me.'

'Where are you?'

'Italy.'

'I wish I could come out to you.'

'I'm working on a way we can see each other but it won't be for a while yet. At least we can talk until that happens.'

Tears of joy filled his eyes but he blinked them away. 'I cannae fucking wait to see you again.'

'Your voice sounds funny. Are you crying, Dangerous?'

He cleared his throat. 'Naw, I've... got a cold.'

'You don't need to hide your emotions from me. I like a man who can express himself.'

'All right, I admit I'm a wee bit choked up.'

'Me too. It's so good to hear your voice. I wear your ring all the time. I never take it off.'

'I can't wear your ring on my finger but I always wear it around my neck and it'll stay there until the day I can wear it properly.'

'That's so sweet. I still intend to marry you, Dangerous.'

'Good, because you're no' getting rid of me, Princess.'

'I wouldn't have it any other way,' Allegra said, the smile in her voice making him grin. 'I've been following the news. I read in the papers yesterday that you have been in court.'

'Aye. It was shite. I called the judge Your Majesty.'

'I feel so bad leaving you to go through all that and having to continually lie.'

'It's no' your fault. When you came up with your plan you thought I was dead.'

'I wish my dad was dead, then all this would end and we could be together. Actually, that's not a bad idea...'

'You gonnae send him an assassin in a box?'

'That or a bomb. No one would suspect me because everyone thinks I'm dead.'

'I don't think that's a good idea. It'll make things worse and guess who would be the prime suspect?'

'He's got lots of enemies, but I see your point. Don't worry, I wasn't seriously considering it.'

'That's a relief. Anyway, with all the evidence against him the fat bastard's going down.'

'I can't wait.' She released a long exhale, indicative of months of tension and fear. 'If only I'd gone to the police instead of setting him up for my murder, we'd be together now and I wouldn't be hiding like a criminal.'

'Hey, it's all right,' Jamie said gently when she started to cry. 'You thought he'd killed me, you were trying to get revenge for me and your maw, and it's looking like you succeeded. Ross told me they're reopening the investigation into your mother's death.'

'Wow, that's amazing, but I'd rather my father just got sent down for attacking us and we were together.'

'And we will be. This is just a delay, that's all. Are you okay out there? Are you safe?'

'Oh, yes, I'm fine, don't worry about that. I'm staying in a very respectable part of Florence.'

'Florence,' he breathed, the name sounding impossibly exotic to him.

'I've set up my own business.'

'Doing what?'

'It's a beauty salon. Well, technically I didn't set it up, I bought it off the previous owners when they retired. It was a real old biddy place but I made it modern and fashionable and it's doing really well.'

'Wow, that's amazing. Can you speak Italian?'

'I studied it at finishing school. I was pretty rusty but after speaking it every day I'm pretty fluent now.'

'How are you running a business if you're supposed to be in hiding?'

'I found a wonderful forger who set me up with all the documentation I needed based on the identity on the false passport.'

'How the bloody hell did you manage to find an Italian forger?' he spluttered.

'You can find anything if you have the cash to pay.'

'So you're okay for money?'

'Absolutely. My business is doing really well, so I'm opening a second salon.'

'What?' he exclaimed. Only Allegra could build a successful career while in hiding. 'I wish you'd be careful. You're supposed to be lying low.'

'Actually I'm not. No one's looking for me. They all think Allegra Abernethy's dead, which technically she is, and, anyway, I've changed my appearance. My hair is now short and black and I always wear the green contact lenses. I'm unrecognisable.'

'I'd love to see a photo.'

'I'd love to send you one, Dangerous, but I have to be careful.'

'I won't let anyone see it.'

'I know you wouldn't but I'm trying to protect you as well as myself. I tell you what, I'll send you a photo but more up close.'

'What do you mean?'

'You'll see,' she said, voice full of mischief. 'How are Jackie and Charlie?'

'Oh, fine. Missing you, though, as is everyone in Gallowburn.'

'That's so sweet.'

'My da came back.'

'What? Your father?'

'Aye. He wants me to become a drug dealer.'

'What?' she exclaimed again.

Jamie explained the entire saga to her. Somehow Allegra knowing what was going on made him feel better about the situation.

'The devious bastard,' she snapped when he'd finished. 'He's trying to trick you into doing what he wants.'

'That's what I think.'

'I know Toni McVay.'

This revelation should have surprised him, but it didn't. 'How?'

'She came to a few charity events I organised and I know she did some business with my father. I've no idea what it was but I bet it wasn't legal.'

'What's she like?'

'Attractive and charming but also coldly psychotic.'

'My da's full of shite. He doesn't know her.'

'What if he does?'

'He doesn't.'

'I'd feel better if you came up with a back-up plan, just in case you find yourself face to face with the inimitable Ms McVay.'

'I'll think of something but, don't worry, Jason's always been full of shite.'

'I wish I was there with you. I could help. Maybe I can find a way to sneak back into the country?'

'I'd bloody love that but it's too dangerous. The case is still all over the media. It just takes one person to recognise you and it's all over. No way are you going to prison for that bastard.'

'It's funny how we both have total arseholes for fathers.'

'It is, but we'll deal with them.'

'Aye, we will,' she said, a smile in her voice. 'Listen, I've got to go.'

'No, not yet.'

'Sorry, Dangerous, but it's time for me to start work, but I'll call you every day, I promise. We need to arrange a set time.'

'The time you called today is good, when my maw's taking Charlie to school.'

'Okay, and the weekend?'

'The same time because I'm usually in bed.'

'Sounds cosy. I wish I was tucked up with you.'

'Me too,' he said sadly.

He did consider asking her if there'd been anyone else, but he dismissed the idea. The fact that she hadn't asked him the same question proved her trust in him, and he wanted to show her that he had as much faith in her as she had in him.

'All right, Dangerous, same time tomorrow, then. It's been amazing hearing your voice.'

'Yours too. I can't wait until we're back together.'

'Me neither. And don't let your father bully you into anything.'

'I won't, you've nae worries on that score.'

'Good. Well, I've got to go,' she said reluctantly. 'Love you, Dangerous.'

'Love you too, Princess.'

'I'll send you that photo as soon as I hang up.'

'Looking forward to seeing it.'

Jamie stared at the phone after hanging up. That call had both delighted and pained him.

The phone pinged and he opened up the text message she'd sent, grinning at the very intimate photo, and lust surged through his body.

He texted back.

Tease

She responded with a goofy smile emoji, one eye winking at him.

Jamie shoved the phone into his pocket – he would guard it with his life. It was his only link to her. He then put the packaging and the empty box into the bin in the backyard so his mum wouldn't see it.

He picked up the squinty-eyed teddy and smiled, shaking his head. It would be smart to dispose of it, especially because it was so hideous, but it was from Allegra, so he couldn't bring himself to do it; he had so little of her as it was. Instead he christened it Squinty and hid it in the bottom of his wardrobe, even though it looked as if it might come alive in the night and crawl onto his bed.

There was a knock at the door and he jogged back downstairs, expecting to see Logan on his doorstep, bursting to tell him all about his previous night's conquest. Instead it was his father.

'Are you ready, then?' he asked Jamie.

'Ready for what?'

'To meet Toni McVay.'

Jamie snorted. 'Aye, right.' He frowned at his father's deadpan expression. 'Are you serious?'

'Deadly,' Jason replied with a twinkle in his eyes. 'Well, don't just stand there, get your coat and shoes on. It's not a good idea to keep her waiting.'

'You really want to go through with this?'

'It's not me that's insisting on it, it's you.'

'Fine, I'll play along,' said Jamie. 'Gi'e me a sec.'

Jamie closed the front door, leaving his father outside while he pulled on his coat and shoes, not wanting him to come inside. 'Okay, ready,' he said, opening the door again and stepping out.

Jason waited while he locked the door and together they walked down the garden path to the brand-new silver BMW four-by-four parked at the kerb.

'This is yours?' exclaimed Jamie.

'I told you Toni pays well,' Jason replied, unlocking the doors with the key fob. The SUV beeped and the lights flashed. 'Get in, then.'

'Quality.' Jamie grinned, jumping into the passenger seat, running his fingers over the dashboard.

'Nice, eh?' Jason smiled.

'Aye, it is.'

'Do you have a car?'

'Naw, not yet. I'm saving up for one.'

'I'll buy you one.'

'You don't need to do that.'

'I know but I want to. Have you got your licence?'

'Yeah, I got it a couple of months ago. But if you buy me a car my maw will probably torch it.'

'No, she won't. I'll talk to her.'

'Good luck with that.' Jamie chuckled. 'Where are we going?'

'I can't tell you. Toni never reveals locations to anyone who doesn't work for her. That reminds me, I'll have to blindfold you when we're halfway there.'

Jamie's eyebrows shot up. 'Eh?'

'Sorry, son, but if you want to meet her you have to do it.'

'Better a blindfold than having my eyes scooped out, I suppose.'

'Aye, it is.' Jason smiled.

Jamie studied his father closely. He seemed almost excited about this outing. 'So we're really going to meet Toni McVay?'

Jason picked up on the scepticism in his tone. 'Aye, we are, although you obviously don't believe it.'

'I didn't say that.'

'You didn't need to. It's in your eyes, but I don't blame you for being sceptical. I've been a shite father.'

'I won't argue with that.'

'I wanted to ask about your maw. Has there been anyone else?'

'She's had plenty of dates but no one permanent. There was a bloke called Dennis she saw for about a year. He was all right actually, he treated us nice, but she dumped him because he was boring.'

'So she's still single?'

'Aye, but don't even think of trying to get in there. She said she'd rather go with Hannibal Lecter than be with you again.'

'I can't blame her, I suppose.'

'No, you can't.' Jamie glowered.

'Shame. I always loved Jackie, although she never believed it. I remember our first date. Christ, she was gorgeous. Those eyes of hers were amazing. They still are. I couldn't believe she wanted to be with me. We'd known each other for years, we went to school together, but I didn't fall in love with her until I was nineteen and I finally recognised what an incredible woman she was.' He glanced sideways at his son. 'Did you feel like that about Allegra?'

Jamie nodded, looking down at his hands.

'She looked a beautiful woman too.'

'The most beautiful I ever saw,' Jamie mumbled.

'And were you really engaged like the papers said? It's hard to know what's true and what's lies with that lot.'

'Aye, it's true.'

'Was she your first love?'

'Yeah,' he sighed. *And the last,* he thought.

'That's really tough, pal.'

'Can we change the subject?' It felt as if he could put her in danger just by talking about her.

'Sorry. It's shite they let that Abernethy bastard out of prison on remand'

'I don't want to talk about him either.'

'There is something we should discuss.'

'What?'

'I saw that video of you kicking the shite out of him.'

'What about it?'

'I was attacked in prison. I was an easy target because I was scared shitless at first and all the other prisoners knew it, but I got so sick of the bullying I snapped. I went fucking mental on the two men who attacked me and I half killed them. The scary thing is I can't even remember it. From what the other prisoners told me I did the same thing you did – all that grunting and snarling, like a wild animal.'

'Really? Had you ever done it before?'

'Just once, when I was a teenager, when my anger got out of control.'

'You always seemed to be angry when I was a wean and I don't remember you getting like that.'

'I wasn't angry, Jamie, I was disappointed. I had such big dreams for my life and when I realised none of them were coming true the disappointment crushed me. I thought I'd be living in a big house with the fancy car and plenty of cash, the usual dream. I took my frustration out on you and your mum, which was really wrong of me, but back then I blamed you both for holding me back. Now I realise it was my own fault. I expected everything I wanted to drop into my lap. The problem was, I wasn't good at anything, so I had no way to earn all the money I wanted. I couldn't keep a steady job, so I turned to the bottle and it changed me into someone I didn't like. The more I hated myself, the harder I drank and the more I took it out on you and your maw. So that's why you never saw me that way, because, despite all the violence and shouting, I was never really angry. I was just sad and disillusioned.'

'If you want me to feel sorry for you, you'll be waiting a long time.'

'I don't expect you to, Jamie. I'm just trying to explain how it was and that you got that talent of yours from me.'

'I wouldn't call it a talent. I saw that video. I looked like a freak.'

'Everyone in Gallowburn is scared of you now because of that. It put the Blood Brothers at the top of the tree. If that's not a talent I don't know what is.'

Jamie was taking everything his dad was telling him with a pinch of salt. He could just be using it as a way to get close to him.

'Sorry, son,' said Jason, pulling the car over to the side of the road.

'Why, what's wrong?'

'Nothing's wrong. It's just time to put your blindfold on.'

After parking the car, Jason groped in the back seat for the black scarf that had been thrown there. Just before Jason tied the scarf around his eyes, Jamie took note of exactly where they were. They were just past Glasgow Royal Infirmary and heading west, the same hospital he'd been taken to after Neil Burrows had driven a car into him and all his dreams of living abroad with Allegra had been shattered. Involuntarily he shivered.

Jamie sat in silence as he and his father continued on their way, counting the time in his head and attempting to judge which way they were going, but he soon became disorientated. At least no one could see him sitting there looking like an idiot with a scarf wrapped around his head because the windows were tinted.

They only drove for another few minutes before Jamie felt the car roll to a halt and he heard the handbrake being applied.

'Here we are,' said Jason. 'Keep the blindfold on until we're inside.'

'Aye, all right.'

Jason caught the grin in his voice. 'You still don't believe me, do you?'

'I didn't say that.'

'You didn't need to. Right, it's time to go in. Stay where you are and I'll give you a hand.'

Jamie managed to unfasten his seat belt and open the door, but he needed Jason to guide him out of the car and across the ground, which felt uneven underfoot. He grimaced when his foot was engulfed in cold water.

'Sorry,' said Jason. 'I tried to steer you round that puddle.'

Jamie strained to hear any noise but all he could make out was the faint rumble of traffic somewhere behind him. There was the scrape of a door opening and the ground he was walking on became even, the temperature warmer. As he was unable to hear the traffic any more, he surmised he was inside.

'I'm taking off the blindfold now,' said Jason.

The scarf was pulled from his eyes and Jamie blinked to clear his vision, squinting against the harsh fluorescent lights. He found himself looking directly into the frowning face of a man with dyed black hair swept back off his face. A scar ran from each side of his mouth, cutting into his cheeks. His suit was smart and he wore an expensive watch.

'So, this is your son?' the man growled at Jason.

'Aye, this is Jamie. You don't need to do that, Caesar, he's clean,' he added when the man started patting Jamie down.

Jamie had to purse his lips so he didn't laugh at the man's ridiculous name.

'I don't take any chances with the boss lady's safety,' replied Caesar. 'Everyone gets searched, I don't gi'e a shite who they are.'

Boss lady? thought Jamie. His dad really was going all out with this charade.

'I've heard how much he likes his bike chains.' Caesar finished his search. 'Okay, he's clean.'

'Just like I said,' retorted Jason.

Caesar gave him a hard look before aggressively nodding. 'This way.'

They followed him down a dimly lit passage until they came to the last door on the left, which Caesar shoved open.

'In you go, laddie,' he said, placing his hand in the middle of Jamie's back and propelling him inside.

'All right, take it easy,' said Jamie, glaring at him.

'So you've got a bit of spirit, then,' said Caesar with a sinister grin that twisted the scars deeper into his flesh.

'Aye, I fucking dae,' retorted Jamie, infuriated when Caesar chuckled.

'He reminds me of myself at that age.' Caesar grinned at Jason. 'Way too fucking lairy.' He looked back at Jamie. 'It's how I ended up with these,' he added, gesturing to his scars. 'I met someone who didn't like my lairiness. Just bear that in mind, wee man.'

'Wee man?' exclaimed Jamie. 'Who the fuck do you think you are?'

'I may like your spirit, pal,' said Caesar, eyes narrowing. 'But don't think that will stop me from cutting off your baws and giving them to the boss lady as a pair of earrings. She likes presents like that.'

'As nice a gift as that sounds,' said a husky voice from deeper in the gloomy room, 'I'm sure they'd look much better swinging between Gray Junior's legs.'

Jamie peered into the shadows, able to make out a silhouette that for some reason seemed to glitter in the darkness. Beyond that he could see nothing.

Caesar hit the lights with impeccable theatrical timing, making Jamie squint as the harsh fluorescents overhead blinked into life, revealing the figure in all their glory.

The woman had long black curly hair that poured down her shoulders, and her eyes were dark and smoky. Her clingy red dress stopped several inches above her knees, revealing long shapely legs, and her feet were encased in matching heels that looked painfully high. The neckline of the dress plunged downwards, exposing plenty of creamy and very ample cleavage. A long fur coat was draped across her shoulders. It was then Jamie realised she glittered with all the diamonds she wore – around her neck, wrists and fingers and hanging from her ears. He'd never seen so much bling in his entire life and every single one of them was obviously genuine. Not a cubic zirconia in sight.

'You're Toni McVay,' breathed Jamie when black, shark-like eyes were turned his way. 'You're really her.'

'What did you expect?' she replied, her smile grim and humourless. 'Oh, I see. You thought I was some myth, a part of the local folklore.' She sighed as though hard done by. 'It's amazing how many people really do think that, despite how often I appear in the newspapers.'

'I knew you were real. I just thought no way would my da know you,' said Jamie, gesturing to Jason with his thumb.

'Why wouldn't he?'

'Because it wouldn't be the first time he's lied to me.'

'Strained relations?'

'You could say that.'

'Oh, dear,' she replied, her smile saying she was rather pleased about that. 'That's a shame, especially as your father speaks so highly of your abilities.' She uttered the last word in a sultry, breathy tone that made Jamie blush. 'I've followed your exploits very closely in the media, Jamie, and already you've impressed me. Caesar here will tell you how difficult it is to impress me.'

She sauntered up to Jamie, curvaceous hips swaying from side to side. Even though he knew she was psychotic he couldn't help but admire that sinuous movement.

'How did it feel pounding Cameron Abernethy into the dirt?' she asked him.

His eyes turned as black as hers. 'Fucking great.'

'I'll bet,' she said, the corner of her mouth lifting into a smile. 'I've watched the footage and it's not often you see such primal savagery.'

The husky moan she released made Jamie take a step backwards. He glanced uncertainly at his dad, who looked amused.

'Thanks,' mumbled Jamie.

'I think you and your friends would be a real asset to my organisation,' she said.

Jamie's heart sank. This wasn't what he wanted. 'I really appreciate that, Ms McVay.'

'Please, call me Toni.'

'Toni, but I don't want to be a drug dealer.'

He took another step back, expecting some form of violence to erupt from her or Caesar but they were both smiling.

'Oh, you really are adorable,' said Toni.

Slowly she walked around him and he thought that was what being circled by a shark must feel like. He had to force himself not to flinch when she ran her fingers through his hair.

'What you obviously don't realise,' she continued, 'is that it doesn't matter what you want. All that matters is what I want.'

'Meaning I don't get a say in this?'

'Why should you when so many others haven't? You see, you and your friends have done such a good job of cleaning up the Gallowburn that it is now a prime location for me to distribute my product. I never bothered with it before because the talents of my organisation were better put dealing in the more affluent areas. I didn't want to waste my time and money cleaning out packs of rabid dogs, but you've done all that for me and very efficiently too. I'm a woman who likes an easy life, luxuriating in a gossamer blanket of money, luxury and fabulous sex. So, when something is handed to me on a platter I can't resist.'

Jamie didn't know if what he was about to say would lead to him having his eyeballs scooped out of his head, but he had to stay true to himself. Keeping the future he wanted with Allegra firmly fixed in his mind, he took a deep breath. 'I'm sorry, Toni. I respect you so much, but I can't hand the Gallowburn over to you. Thanks to me and my friends the residents finally have a quiet life, and it's safe to walk the scheme at night. I can't let it go back to how it used to be.'

'You cheeky wee shite,' exploded Caesar. 'Who the fuck do you think you are?'

'No, Caesar,' said Toni when he slid his hand inside his jacket, no doubt going for his gun.

Jamie breathed a sigh of relief when Caesar's hand relaxed at his side. He tensed again when he received the full force of Toni's cold, pitiless gaze.

'I think you misunderstand, Jamie,' she said. 'You seem to think I'm asking for permission. When I want something, I don't ask, I fucking take, and anyone who gets in my way ends up spending the rest of their life without any eyeballs, if I allow them to keep their life, that is.' Her hand delved into the pocket of her fur coat and produced a glasses case. 'I bought this one especially for your eyes, Jamie. Black to match that gorgeous colour.'

'I don't think my son understands what he's saying,' interjected Jason.

'You don't need to speak for him,' hissed Toni. 'He's a fucking grown-up.'

'If you try dealing on the Gallowburn,' Jamie told her, 'me and my pals will sabotage you.'

'Jesus, Jamie,' breathed his dad. 'Don't you realise who you're talking to?'

'Aye, I dae,' he replied, not taking his eyes off Toni. He didn't dare.

Toni looked at the glasses case in her hand and sighed. 'Shame, I didn't want to use this, but it looks like I've no choice. Hold him, Caesar.'

'No, wait,' exclaimed Jason when Caesar wrapped his arms around Jamie's chest and held him fast.

Caesar was shocked when he found himself thrown off and he staggered backwards a few steps.

'Right, that's it, you lairy little shite,' he roared, drawing the gun from inside his jacket and pointing it at Jamie.

'No, don't,' cried Jason.

'Wait, I've got a proposition,' yelled Jamie, holding out his hands before him as he stared down the barrel of the weapon.

'Stick your proposition up your arse,' retorted Caesar, removing the safety.

'Let him speak,' said Toni.

'But, boss lady...' began Caesar.

'I said let him speak,' said Toni, her gaze not leaving Jamie.

Caesar sighed and stuffed the gun back inside his jacket.

'Thank you,' breathed Jamie, lowering his hands.

'It's rare for anyone to deny me what I want,' she replied. 'The sheer enormity of your balls has earned you the right to be heard, although that doesn't necessarily mean I'll like what you say.'

Jamie took a deep, steadying breath, giving himself the precious few seconds he needed to get himself together and gather his thoughts, well aware he was speaking for his life. He glanced at his dad, whose eyes flashed with annoyance. Clearly this wasn't how he'd expected the conversation to go.

'Me and my pals cleaned up the Gallowburn,' Jamie began, glad when his voice didn't tremble, despite his nerves. 'So the police don't bother with it any more. Plus the residents have a code of silence. No one on the Gallowburn grasses. They'd rather die than dae that. We've created a safe place.'

'Safe place?' said Toni, eyes glittering with interest.

'You can hide anything you want on the Gallowburn – stolen goods, even people on the run, and the police would never know. Best of all, no one would tell them either.'

Toni's black eyes flicked to Jason. 'You have a very intelligent son.'

'I get it from my maw,' replied Jamie.

Toni threw back her head and released a husky laugh. 'Sounds like your son thinks you're a bit of a prick, Jason.'

Jason gritted his teeth together and looked down at the floor.

'Go on then, Jamie,' said Toni. 'What's the catch?'

'That the Gallowburn stays drug-free. It wouldnae be a safe place any more if that stuff was getting distributed around the estate and the crime rate started to rise again.'

'Well, that is quite the offer,' she said thoughtfully. 'What do you think, Caesar?'

'I think the prick's after a serious kicking,' the big man snarled, glaring at Jamie. 'But he could still be useful.'

'I agree,' she replied, looking back at Jamie. 'As a matter of fact I have a little dilemma that you and your friends could help me with. All right, Jamie, you've got a deal. The Gallowburn will remain drug-free and I will use it to hide my secrets.'

'Thank you,' he breathed.

'You don't know what secrets I have. You may come to think the drugs were the lesser of two evils. And just so we're clear, this isn't a partnership. You and the rest of the Blood Brothers work for me now.'

'We do?' he said, eyebrows shooting up. Toni reminded him a little of Allegra when they'd first met. She'd forced him to go shoplifting with her then locked him in her car and threatened to drive him to London if he didn't tell her where he lived. Although Allegra was a far cry from this psycho, they shared a quality that made him almost well disposed towards Toni.

'Yes, you do,' replied Toni with a wicked smile. 'I promise the rewards will be great.' She sauntered up to him, letting her fingers trail across his chest as she whispered in his ear. 'I'm a very hands-on employer.'

'Oh,' he mumbled, not knowing what else to say.

'You're a good-looking man, Jamie. Obviously you take after your father, who has more than proved himself, which is why Jason will be running the operation on the Gallowburn.'

'He will?' Jamie said, heart sinking even further.

'You and your friends lack experience. You need a more mature person to guide you.'

'Couldn't he do that?' said Jamie, nodding at Caesar. Although he was a lunatic who wanted to shoot him, he thought he would be a better option than Jason.

'Piss off,' retorted Caesar. 'I'm second-in-command in this outfit, no' a babysitter. And I'm no' spending my time on that shitey scheme.'

'This isn't up for debate,' hissed Toni. 'I don't care what shite has gone on between you and your da. Whatever happened, get over it fast, because you will be working together.'

'If you say so, Toni,' replied Jamie, holding up his hands.

'That's more fucking like it,' she spat back. The anger cleared from her eyes. 'Any problems, Jason, you go to Caesar with them. He will decide if they're important enough to bother me with.'

Jason nodded. He'd quickly learnt that the fewer words you said to Toni, the more likely your eyes were to remain in your head.

'Excellent,' she said. 'This came at the perfect time for me. Now I don't need to worry about my little problem any more. Congratulations, Jamie. You've only worked for my firm for one minute and already you're in my good books, which is where you want to stay, believe me. Although, there is one thing that you've kept from me.'

'Have I?'

'I happen to know that a certain ice-cream-van man is still dealing drugs on the Gallowburn. Are you really surprised?' she added when his eyes widened. 'Didn't you think that I did a lot of research on your scheme before deciding it was a prime location for my organisation? I know the name of every dealer in the country. Most of them are too petty for me to bother with, but there's something different about Ephraim. There must be otherwise you would have run him off the scheme with the others. Why haven't you?'

'Because if we tried he'd chop our heids off and I'm no' exaggerating.'

'I went to school with Ephraim,' said Jason. 'He was mad mental even back then. He stabbed a teacher with a compass and that was a teacher he liked.'

'You failed to mention him when you were getting all self-righteous with me. So, your friend Ephraim can continue with his petty activities. He pays off the police to look the other way anyway, so that will help keep them off the estate, and I think that one day he could come in useful.'

'Nae offence,' said Jamie, 'but not even you could control him. He's a proper lunatic.'

'I like lunatics. They're a lot more interesting than the sane. And from what I've heard he likes money and I pay very well. Right, Jamie, do you have a car?'

'Naw.'

'Then we'll get you one. Obviously it can't be anything flashy or questions will be asked. Jason, sort out a motor for him, make it a crappy old banger.'

'Yes, Toni,' said Jason, while Jamie sighed with disappointment.

'And give him a burner phone,' she added.

Another nod from Jason.

Jamie looked from him to Toni, feeling bewildered, wondering how all this had happened so quickly.

As he looked back at Toni, for the first time in their meeting the hardness fled from her eyes.

'I met Allegra a few times,' she said.

Jamie felt the tightness return to his chest. 'You did?'

'At charitable events she organised. She was so beautiful. There was a spark about her that marked her out as special.'

'Aye, there was,' he replied, swallowing down the lump in his throat and looking down at the floor.

Toni grabbed his chin and tilted his face up to hers. 'I always wondered if it was true love or if the media made up a load of romantic old shite to sell more papers, but now I see that, for once, they were telling the truth. Your feelings for her shine out of your eyes and I should know – I've studied eyes for many years.' Her own eyes turned even blacker. 'Usually when they're sat in a glasses case after being scooped out of someone's head. Did you know that they retain the last emotion their owner felt before I tore them out? Usually when I look at eyes I see only fear. It's nice to see something different.'

Jamie stared back at her not daring to breathe or move. This was the weirdest conversation of his entire life.

She released his chin. 'She didn't deserve what her fat twat of a father did to her. Play your cards right, Jamie, do me proud and I might be able to help you out with Cameron Abernethy.' She treated them all again to that wicked smile of hers. 'I bet you dream of the tortures you'd like to inflict on him?'

His eyes were bright with rage. 'All. The. Fucking. Time.'

'It burns you up from the inside out, doesn't it?' she said, lowering her voice to a whisper.

His nod was as savage as his gaze.

'I'm looking forward to seeing how you get on working for me, Jamie. You really have no idea of your own potential. With the right guidance you could be one of my best.'

Jason did a good job of hiding his jealousy. She'd never said that to him.

Toni waved her hand dismissively. 'You can both go.'

'That's it?' said Jamie.

'For now. I'll be in touch soon, once the arrangements are in place. Caesar, give him a phone.'

Caesar nodded, produced one from his pocket and tossed it to Jamie with such speed he only just managed to catch it. Clearly he hadn't forgiven him for throwing him off earlier.

'This way,' muttered Caesar, leading them back the way they'd come.

'Goodbye, Jamie,' called Toni. 'I look forward to seeing what you can do.'

Jamie didn't get the chance to reply as he was shoved towards the exit by Caesar.

'All right, take it easy,' he snapped. 'Is it your time of the month or something?'

'Jamie,' said Jason, warning in his tone.

Jamie was practically thrown through the door and hit the ground hard. Outside the sunlight dazzled him after the gloom of the warehouse. He dragged himself to his feet, glowering at Caesar.

'Listen, you wee sod,' spat Caesar, jabbing a finger at him. 'You might be the boss lady's new pet but that won't stop me from shoving a knife right up your hole if you keep pissing me off. I'm watching you, laddie. Just one foot wrong and you'll find yourself strapped to a chair having your eyeballs scooped out of your heid with a rusty spoon.'

With that he stomped back inside, slamming the door shut behind him.

'Tosser,' muttered Jamie, dusting himself off.

'You need to be careful around him,' Jason told his son. 'I know he's got a ridiculous name, but he wouldn't hesitate to slit your throat. You've got to understand that these are serious people.

They're not the petty thugs you're used to dealing with on the Gallowburn.'

'So you think I should let him push me around and threaten me?'

'No. I think you should stop saying things that make him push you around and threaten you.'

'What's wrong with you?' said Jamie when Jason sighed and dragged his hands through his hair. 'Oh, I get it, you're pissed off at me for ruining your drug dealing, aren't you?'

'We could have had it all, son. We would have ruled that estate.'

'We still will with Toni McVay behind us, we just won't be dealing drugs and ruining people's lives.'

'Have you any idea of the secrets a woman like that has? God only knows what she'll have us doing. You might end up wishing you were dealing.'

'You should be saying thanks,' Jamie retorted. 'If my maw found out you were trying to turn me into a drug dealer she would have chopped off your baws.'

'Right now, Jackie is the least of our problems. Let's get out of here.' Jason sighed.

They climbed into his BMW.

'Won't the police wonder where you got the cash to buy this motor?' Jamie asked him as he set off. 'Aren't you still on parole?'

'Toni's already sorted that out. Technically this car doesn't belong to me, it's a company car. According to my parole officer and the tax office, I work as a chauffeur ferrying wealthy clients from the airport to a hotel and a couple of casinos Toni owns. I have to do it a couple of times a week to keep up appearances, so everything looks legit.'

'That's pretty clever,' commented Jamie.

'Toni thinks of everything.'

'I wonder what car I'll get?'

'You'll have to wait and see but if I were you I wouldn't get my hopes up,' replied Jason, his voice tight, telling Jamie he was still annoyed with him.

'Don't I need the blindfold back on?'

'Naw, it doesn't matter now you're working for Toni.'

'Oh, good.'

Jason set off and they both remained silent for the journey, which gave Jamie time to ponder his strange interview with the Queen of Glasgow, as the media often referred to her. He knew his life would never be the same again. Once you were in bed with the McVays you never got out. His mum's dream of a nice clean life for him had been shattered in a single morning and she would raise holy hell about it. However, what was at the very forefront of his mind was Toni saying she'd help him out with Cameron. Did that mean she would have him killed? Jamie knew it wasn't beyond her, she'd done it to plenty of others. Or would she just pluck out his eyes and leave him stumbling around blind for the rest of his life? That was a satisfying thought. Would either of those things help Allegra? She wouldn't be in danger from her own father any more, but if anyone found out what she'd done she would go to prison. Whether Cameron lived or died, it didn't matter. Allegra could never come home.

Jason glanced sideways at his son. 'What's up with your face? You look like a proper nippy sweetie.'

'I was thinking about Allegra.'

'And what Toni said about her da?'

He nodded. 'Aye.'

'Play your cards right and she'll get rid of him for you.'

'After what he's done I'm not sure killing him is punishment enough.'

'If death isn't enough, what is?'

'Naw, I mean someone else doing it. I want to kill him myself.'

'You ever killed anyone, son?'

'I've come close a couple of times.'

'Then you should think twice about doing it. It changes you forever. Once you've taken that step there's no going back. And life suddenly seems cheap.'

Jamie frowned at him. 'Do you mean you've...?'

Jason nodded.

'Was it when you were in prison?'

'I don't want to get into it. One day I'll tell you the story.'

Jamie wasn't sure he wanted to hear it.

8

Jason dropped Jamie off at Logan's house, leaving him to relate his meeting with the Queen of Glasgow to the rest of the Blood Brothers.

'Oh good," breathed Jamie when Logan pulled open the front door. 'You're in. I thought you might be at work.'

'It's my day off. What happened to you?' frowned Logan. 'You look shellshocked.'

'That's because I am. I need to talk to you, Digger and Gary.'

'It sounds serious.'

'It is.'

'Gary's already here eating us out of house and home. I'll gi'e Digger a call.'

'Is your da in?'

'Naw, he's gone to the bookies.'

'Good. I don't want anyone else knowing.'

Jamie thought Logan would ask him what it was about but he didn't, probably sensing it was bad news.

Jamie joined Gary at the small dining table tucked into a corner of the overstuffed front room while Logan made his call.

'All right?' Gary mumbled at him through a mouthful of beans on toast. 'How's it going?'

'It's been a long day and it's no' even dinner time.' Jamie sighed.

'Why, what's happened?'

'I'll explain when Digger gets here.'

'That bad, eh?'

'Aye,' he nodded. 'That bad.' Jamie hated himself for dragging his friends into something they probably wouldn't want to get involved in. The course of their futures had been altered without them having a say in the matter.

Digger, sensing big things were afoot by the tone in Logan's voice, arrived in record time and ten minutes later the four of them were ensconced together around Logan's dining table, which was so small their elbows touched when they leaned on it.

'Move up you big bag of rocks,' muttered Gary, digging his elbow into Digger's ribs.

'It's your fault there's no room, you lard arse.'

'Shut it,' snapped Jamie, in no mood for their shite.

They both went silent.

'So, what's happened?' Logan reluctantly asked.

Jamie regarded them seriously, his dark eyes harder than ever. 'My da wasnae joking. He does work for Toni McVay and, before you ask, aye, I'm certain, because I've just had a meeting with her.'

They all stared at him in shocked silence.

'You've met Toni McVay?' gasped Gary.

Jamie nodded, looking troubled. 'Aye.'

'What's she like?' said Digger. 'Is she well fit like everyone says?'

'She's a looker and scary as fuck. There's no easy way to say this but we work for her now, all four of us.'

Logan, Digger and Gary looked at each other in surprise.

Digger was the first to react. 'That's fucking awesome.'

'It is?' said Jamie.

'Aye, course. You don't get any bigger than the McVays. No one will mess with us ever again.'

'This is bigger than the Lawsons. Have you any idea what this means?'

'It means we're under the thumb of a psychopath who will tear out our eyes if we piss her off,' said Logan, looking miserable.

'I'm so sorry,' said Jamie. 'I didn't want this to happen. I tried to fight it but she would have killed me.'

'It's no' your fault,' said Logan sombrely. 'We all know who's really to blame.'

'The good news is we won't have to deal drugs. That was her plan but I managed to convince her my way was better.'

Logan perked up a bit. 'You mean she bought it?'

'Bought what?' said Gary.

'I told her that we've cleaned up the scheme so well the police don't bother to come here, meaning it's a safe place for her to hide her secrets.'

'What secrets?'

'God knows, but it's in her interest to help keep the place clean. When word spreads that the Gallowburn belongs to her now, no one will dare deal here again.'

'Until Toni decides she'll start.'

'She won't. She seemed really pleased with our idea. She's got the rest of the city for that.'

'Her secrets might be worse than the drugs.'

'Maybe, but it's the best I could do.'

Logan patted his shoulder. 'At least we're no' drug dealers. You did good, pal.'

'Thanks but there's more – we're going to be working with Jason on this. Toni said we needed someone experienced to guide us, so we're stuck with the bastard. So, what does everyone think?'

'Well, I think it's great,' said Digger. 'Apart from the bit where we have to work with Jason. We're in the big time now and the Lawsons will be running scared.'

'But what will we have to do for her?' said Gary. 'That's still no' clear.'

'We'll protect whatever she decides to hide on the estate,' replied Jamie.

'Like what? Drugs?'

'Naw. I reckon it'll be more like people needing somewhere to lie low for a while, maybe stolen merchandise.'

'When the police get wind of that they'll be back with a vengeance.'

'Then we'll have to do a good job of hiding it. We need to scout out the best places on the scheme. There's plenty of derelict buildings around here. That's something we can be getting on with while we wait for her to contact us.'

'How will she contact us?' said Logan.

'With this,' he replied, placing the burner phone on the table.

'Wow,' breathed Digger as though it were the holy grail.

'It's only a phone,' interjected Logan.

'Aye, but she's touched it.'

'Actually, she didn't,' said Jamie. 'Her second-in-command gave it to me, some grumpy bastard with a scarred face.'

'I don't know why you're so excited,' Gary told Digger. 'She doesnae have arms like Arnold Schwarzenegger.'

'Shut it, you fud.'

'If I could have stopped this from happening, I would,' said Jamie. 'Because once you're in with the McVays they never let you out. I feel like we've been forced into this because none of us really believed that my da knew Toni.'

'What's done is done,' said Logan. 'We just have to deal with it.'

Silence followed this grim pronouncement.

'You never know,' said Gary. 'It could be our big chance for a better life. Toni might be a psycho but I heard she pays well.'

'So my da says,' replied Jamie. 'I'm bloody furious with the bastard. He even blindfolded me so I wouldn't see where I was being taken.'

'Bloody hell, that's a bit heavy duty,' exclaimed Digger frowning.

'It doesn't get any more heavy duty than the McVays,' continued Jamie. 'I hope you're no' all pissed off with me. This wasn't my choice for our future, but I thought it's better than being murdered because she does not like being told no.'

'There was nothing else you could do,' said Gary. 'And at least we'll be earning a decent wage.'

'Your da looks to be doing pretty well for himself out of it.' Digger told Jamie.

'Aye, isn't he just?' he replied bitterly. 'So, you're no' angry about the mess I've got you all into?'

'Naw,' said Gary. 'This could be the chance we've been waiting for.'

'I agree.' Digger grinned. He clapped his hands together so loudly they all winced. 'The birds will be all over us when they realise how minted we are.'

Jamie looked to Logan, who was the most intelligent of them all, the one who really thought things through, unlike Digger and Gary. 'What do you think?' he asked him.

'I don't know,' Logan slowly replied. 'Only time will tell how it will pan out, but I repeat – this is not your fault. It is what it is and nothing can change that. We've just got to deal with it. I'm just relieved you got out of that meeting in one piece.'

'Cheers, pal,' said Jamie tightly.

'Like you said,' continued Logan, 'she might decide not to bother with us. I'm sure she's got a lot on her plate.'

Jamie could tell Logan didn't believe that any more than he did.

* * *

Jamie returned home feeling a little down. He hated that his friends' futures had been taken out of their hands by a psychopath who would kill them all if it benefitted her. He'd already decided he wasn't going to tell his mum about his deal with Toni. Not only would she hit the roof, but she'd go after his dad with a power drill. It was better they keep it quiet for as long as possible.

'All right, sweetheart?' Jackie smiled when he walked through the front door, which led directly into the living room.

'Aye, no' bad, Maw.'

She frowned as he flopped onto the couch. 'Are you okay? You look done in.'

'It's been a long day,' he sighed.

'It's only dinnertime.'

'Is that all?' he said, genuinely surprised. He felt as if he'd lived years in a single morning. The meeting with Toni had irreparably altered him but as yet he wasn't exactly sure how.

Jackie's eyes narrowed suspiciously. 'Have you seen that deadbeat da of yours?'

'Aye, just to ask him if he paid the Reids to smash up Mr Cavenie's shop. He said yes.'

'The vicious wee sod,' she exclaimed. 'Just you wait till I get my hands on him.'

'No, Maw,' he said when she stormed for the door. 'Me and the lads are handling it.'

'The only way to handle Jason Gray is with something big and heavy in the back of the head.'

'Please don't rock the boat.'

'Rock it? I'll capsize it and drown the sod.'

'No, Maw,' he said with such authority she stopped in her tracks. It wasn't what he said, more the way he said it.

'You sure you're okay, son?' She frowned.

'Aye, but don't make things worse. I will handle it.'

'Okay, if that's what you want. You hungry?'

'A bit.'

'How does cheese on toast grab you?'

'Sounds great.' He smiled.

'Coming right up and, by the way, you're picking Charlie up from school today. Old Mrs McGee up the road isnae very well, so I'm going to do some cleaning for her.'

'No worries.'

She smiled and patted his face. 'You might be the big man around here, son, but you're still a good boy.'

He forced a smile, feeling terrible. What would she think of him if she knew he was working for the McVays?

* * *

Once she'd washed up after dinner, Jackie went round to Mrs McGee's, so Jamie decided to take the opportunity to call Allegra and get her take on recent events.

'Buon pomeriggio,' said her voice when the call was answered. 'Come posso aiutarla?'

'Eh?' replied Jamie.

Her response was another smooth stream of Italian.

'Hello?' he said when it went silent on the other end.

'Sorry,' Allegra eventually replied. 'I was with a client.'

'Oh, sorry. Do you want me to call back?'

'Not a chance, Dangerous,' she purred, making him smile. 'Maria's attending to her.'

'Who?'

'One of my staff. I'm very lucky to have her. She's such a hard worker and very good at her job.'

'How many people do you employ?'

'Seven.'

'You employ seven people?' he spluttered.

'Sì,' she replied.

'You're bloody amazing.'

'I know. I'm glad you called actually because giving old Mrs Bianchi a pedicure is not pleasant with all her bunions.'

'Urgh.'

'I told her this was an urgent call and I had to take it. It wasn't a lie. I couldn't wait to speak to you again.'

'Me neither.'

'How's it going with your dad?'

'Oh, well, I only had a meeting with Toni McVay.'

'What?' she exclaimed. 'Oh, my God, you've still got those gorgeous eyes of yours, haven't you?'

'Aye, they're still safely in my head.'

'Thank God.'

The concern in her voice made him smile. 'The bad news is I work for her now. She gave me no choice.'

'Oh, no, you're not dealing drugs, are you?' she replied, lowering her voice to a whisper.

'No, thank Christ.' He related the entire episode to her. When he'd finished, there was a pause.

'That was clever of you, Dangerous,' she said. 'You do know that woman has a lot of dark secrets?'

'Aye, I'm sure she does but I won't be a drug dealer. That's the important thing.'

'What did your dad think of it?'

'He seemed a bit pissed off but I couldnae gi'e a shite. It was his fault I was there in the first place. And he told me he did pay the Reids to attack the shop. He wanted to test me and the lads.'

'What do the rest of the Blood Brothers think about all this?'

'Digger and Gary reckon it might be a good thing, but Logan was more wary.'

'Who do you agree with?'

'Logan. There is the chance this could go very bad for us.'

'You must do everything she says, babe, even if you disagree. Telling her no might result in her scooping out your eyes, or worse. I know you have your principles but they're not worth your life. I heard that when someone really annoys her, she doesn't just take it out on them. She goes after their family too.'

'I've heard that myself.'

'Do as she says, and you'll be fine. Anyway, it's only temporary because you'll be coming out to me in a few years.'

'Years,' he said miserably.

'It'll fly by. The next thing you know we'll be back together.'

'I cannae wait that long. I need to see you.'

'I wish I could, Dangerous, but it's not the right time.'

He huffed with frustration.

'Hopefully the court case will be over soon and my dad will be locked up and then the fuss will start to die down. You never know, you might be able to come out here sooner than expected.'

This buoyed his spirits a little. 'God, I hope so. This is driving me demented.'

'Me too,' Allegra replied, voice tinged with sadness. 'I will regret running from Glasgow for the rest of my life. If only I hadn't blindly believed my father I'd still be with you.'

'I'm going to make the fat bastard pay. Toni mentioned your da. And you. She told me you met at a few charity events. She also said that if I play my cards right she might be able to help me out with Cameron.'

'What did she mean by help out?'

'Get rid of him.'

'That would be very handy.'

'How would you feel if that happened?'

'Delighted. Then it would all be over and once the fuss of his death had died down you could come out to me.'

'I want to be the one to kill him,' he growled.

'Your voice has never sounded more dangerous. It is so sexy but don't do it, babe. It'll change you and I love my Dangerous just the way he is.'

'I fucking dream about killing him. I would have already done it if my pals hadnae pulled me off him.'

'How would you have done it?'

'Strangled him with my bike chain.'

'That is so hot,' she breathed. 'But leave it to someone who's had plenty of practice. There is another way to deal with him.'

'What's that?'

'Remember what I said when you were trying to stop Craig Lawson?'

'Discover their fear,' he said, a smile curling his lips.

'It could help with my father. I never did find out what he was afraid of but there will be something. It could help with your dad too.'

'God, I love you, Princess.'

'I love you too, Dangerous.'

Jamie determined to discover his father's fear first. It would be easier than finding out Cameron's. He needed a way to control him and hopefully use him to keep Toni off his back. His first port of call for information was his mother.

He decided to ask her that evening when Charlie was in the bath and she was washing up.

'All right, Maw?' he said, slinking into the kitchen, hands in his jeans pockets.

'You've got great timing, Jamie.' She smiled. 'Could you pass me that pan off the hob?'

'Course,' he said, picking it up and handing it to her.

'Thanks, love,' she said, dunking the pan into the suds before attacking it with a Brillo pad.

'Can I ask you something?'

'You can ask me anything, you know that.'

'It's about my da.'

Her face twisted into a sneer as she drew the pan out of the water, dripping with suds, and slammed it down on the draining board.

'Why do you want to talk about that useless bawbag?'

'I want to know if he's afraid of anything.'

Jackie's eyes narrowed and her lips twisted into a vengeful smile. 'I remember Allegra saying you need to discover a person's fears if you want to bring them down. Is that what you're up to?'

'I'm no' sure yet, but I thought it might be useful to be prepared.'

'In that case I'll tell you. Apart from being terrified of doing an honest day's work, he hates heights. Any higher than a stepladder and he greets like a wee lassie. He can't stand slugs either. That's no' a phobia but he cannae stomach their slime. He calls them satan's bogies.'

Jamie sniggered.

'And he has a superstition about magpies. If he sees one he has to salute it and say a wee poem.'

Jamie wondered what Toni McVay would say if she knew she employed someone who saluted birds and recited poetry at them. 'Why does he do that?'

'Because he's a tit. Always has been.'

'What made you marry him?'

'Well, he was very charming, at first, and he was so handsome too, before he got too fond of the bevy and became fat and bloated. Then he started looking like the slugs he so hates. Granted, he looks better now he's dropped all the weight, but he's still a twat. There's no changing that. Anything else you want to know, son?'

'What's the best way to get the better of him?'

'Well, holding a knife to his throat worked for me, but I don't want you doing the same. You know my feelings about knives. I only did that because I was desperate to protect you and Charlie and because I didn't have an elephant gun.' She pulled off the yellow rubber gloves and tossed them onto the draining board. 'I suppose I can't stop you, no matter how much I want to, you're a grown man, but take my advice – he's bad news. Did he take you anywhere?'

'Just for a drive,' he nonchalantly replied. He hated lying to his mum, but he had no choice.

'If he asks you to go for a drive again, say no. Trouble follows him everywhere he goes and he'll end up dragging you into it.'

The chimes of the ice-cream van echoed from outside.

'Oh, great,' sighed Jackie. 'Ephraim's here.'

Ephraim was the biggest psychopath in Gallowburn, which was saying something. His ice-cream van was a front for the drugs and homemade weapons he flogged around the scheme. He was the only drug dealer the Blood Brothers hadn't run off the estate because if they'd tried he would have come after them with a machete and lopped off their heads – that was the standard way he dealt with people who annoyed him. Ephraim had also had an enormous crush on Jackie ever since they were at high school together and his adoration hadn't waned over the years, despite her never once showing any interest in him. When on his rounds, he

always parked his van right outside their house hoping for a
glimpse of his paramour.

'I want a wee word with him,' Jamie told his mum.

'Don't let him sell you a blade,' she replied.

'Course I won't, Maw,' he said as he headed out of the door.

Jamie stepped outside to see the pink ice-cream van with its big
smiley face painted on the front and eyelashes on the headlights. A
queue was already forming made up of dodgy bastards in baseball
caps and tracksuits, hoods up to obscure their faces. Only once
they'd been dealt with did those who actually wanted to buy an
innocent ice cream queue up.

Ephraim was at the serving hatch, frowning severely at his
nervous customers, who all did their best to avoid his gaze.

That sharp gaze snapped onto Jamie as soon as he opened the
front door and remained fixed on him as he walked down the
garden path towards the van.

'Step aside, you bunch of fannies,' Ephraim roared at his
customers. 'Let the lad pass.'

They all physically jumped and quickly obeyed.

'All right, Jamie?' said Ephraim, as polite as he could ever be
with his gruff voice. He had a lot more respect for the Blood Brothers, particularly Jamie, after the Battle of Gallowburn.

'Aye, no' bad,' Jamie replied, stepping up to the counter. 'How
about you?'

Ephraim ignored the question. 'I heard your da's back?'

'He is, unfortunately.'

When Ephraim's left eye twitched, everyone in the queue took
another step back, Jamie looking at them over his shoulder in
amusement.

'What does Jackie think of it?'

'No' much. She hates him.'

'So she's no' taking him back, then?'

'God, no.'

'Oh, right,' Ephraim said, taking a deep relaxing breath, muscles unfurling. The dangerous gleam returned to his eyes. 'If that walloper ever comes to me for an icey I'll lop off a piece of him and stick it in the freezer. He hurt Jackie. Nobody hurts Jackie.'

When his fingers started to twitch as well as his eye everyone retreated another step, all except Jamie.

'I need to ask you for something a bit different,' said Jamie, snapping Ephraim out of his violent thoughts.

'Oh aye, like what?'

'You got a piece of paper?'

'How?'

'I want to write down what I need. I don't want that lot to hear,' he said, jabbing his thumb over his shoulder at the queue.

Ephraim sighed, nodded and delved under the counter before straightening up clutching a notepad.

'I suppose you want a pen too,' he said, dumping a biro onto the counter along with the notepad.

'Cheers,' said Jamie, picking up the pen and scribbling something down. When he'd finished he turned the pad around for Ephraim, who picked it up and frowned at it.

'I've never been asked for that before.'

'Can you get it?'

'Aye, nae bother. Gi'e me a couple of days. You got the cash?'

Jamie nodded. 'You wantin' a deposit?'

'Naw, I know you're good for it.'

'Cheers, pal. I'll see you tomorrow, then.'

'Wait,' he said when Jamie started to walk away. 'Can you gi'e Jackie these?'

Jamie felt a bit of a tit as he walked back to the house clutching a huge bouquet of red roses. He could see the lads in the queue were itching to laugh and crack a joke, but they wouldn't dare take the piss out of Jamie Gray or Ephraim.

'Has Ephraim started selling flowers now?' said Jackie when her son walked through the front door. 'That's a lot better than the stuff he usually sells out of his van.'

'No, he hasn't. He asked me to gi'e them to you.'

'Oh, Christ,' she sighed. 'When's he going to get it through his thick skull that I'm no' interested?'

'Aww, he's in love.' Jamie grinned.

'They are lovely,' she said, inhaling their scent. 'It's been a long time since anyone bought me flowers.'

'What about that bunch you got off that bloke who took you out a couple of weeks ago?'

'That cheap bastard nicked them off a grave. The thick sod forgot to take out the card, which said, "Missing you my beautiful wife. Love Fred".'

'Classy. Want me to kick his head in?'

'It's nice of you to offer, sweetheart, but I kicked him in the baws. I'll bet it was a few days before he was able to stand up straight.'

'Nice one.' He grinned.

'So, what did you talk to Ephraim about?' Jackie said, trying to sound casual but failing.

'I was just seeing if he had any new weapons,' he replied, failing as badly as his mother at sounding casual.

'Did he?'

He shook his head.

'Oh, good,' she said with relief. 'Right, I'd better get these in some water.'

Jamie watched her bustle into the kitchen with the roses, which he knew had made her day, even if they had come from Ephraim. He made a mental note to buy his mum flowers more often. All this lying to her was really getting to him. Throughout all the nightmare with the Lawsons and Cameron Abernethy she'd known everything that had gone on pretty much from the start and she'd done nothing but support him, which was why it was so tempting to confide in her now. But if she knew what his dad had got him into, she was more than capable of starting world war three over it. Neither did he want her getting caught up with the McVays. But what if she found out from someone else? Gary and Digger had a hard time keeping their mouths shut. Finding out from someone else would make it ten times worse.

9

Cameron stared thoughtfully out of the window into his enormous back garden as he sipped his coffee. For the last few days he'd been unable to shake the feeling that he'd been had. First Allegra had tricked him by dating that fucking scrag-end Jamie Gray for months. Then he'd thought he'd killed her, only for her to bash him over the head with a wheel wrench. Now he suspected she wasn't actually dead.

It had been a strategy of his defence to try and use the fact that her body hadn't been found to cast doubt in the minds of the jury that she was indeed dead. He hadn't believed it himself, because he'd assumed she'd staggered off injured and bleeding and fallen down and died somewhere. Granted, Cathkin Braes was enormous, but surely her body should have been found by now? Plus, he hadn't thrown her shoe into the marsh at Cathkin Braes, which was where the police had found it while searching for her body. Neither had he done anything to her in the bird hide at the marsh, where her false nails had been found embedded in the wooden floor.

At first he'd thought some predator had come across her when she was injured and finished her off. However, it had been Jamie's reaction in the courtroom that had made him really think that she could still be alive. It hadn't been so much the fact that he'd spoken about her in the present tense, but more the little git's reaction to it – panic. He'd seen it light up his eyes and he'd quickly corrected himself. It seemed only he had noticed this reaction. He'd mentioned it to his solicitor, but she'd dismissed it as a simple slip of the tongue. Even his own defence thought he was guilty. He'd been considering how conveniently the evidence had stacked up against him and he was starting to suspect he'd been well and truly set up by Allegra, which meant the little cow was still alive. If she was, he doubted she was still in the country. The case had made the national news and she was such a striking-looking girl that someone would have spotted her by now.

He had to hand it to her if she had escaped the country; she was clever, and he admired her ruthless streak. How he wished her brother Fenston had her smarts. His son had been a disappointment; he was more of a sneaky wee turd than the powerful, pitiless force Cameron had hoped he would be. Fenston was so useless he'd failed in his attempts to have his father ousted from his own company when he'd been locked up in prison. Cameron hadn't been angry with his son for trying. For the first time in his life he felt his son had actually done something he would have done himself. Finally he'd thought he was becoming a chip off the old block, but when Cameron had been released, Fenston's bottle had deserted him, and he'd given up his attempt at a takeover. Once again his son was the fawning little toad Cameron loathed.

Of his two children Allegra had been the risk-taker, the one with the most guts and the brains to match. It was just a shame she'd been born a girl. If she'd been the one trying to oust him from the company, he knew he would now be sitting in some damp bedsit, flat broke and defeated. Had she been a son he would have brought her in on the business, he'd have left her a lot of money in his will and she would have been his true heir. Instead she'd been born with nothing between her legs and he was lumbered with the toad.

Cameron knew a lot of his friends and acquaintances considered his attitude to women outdated, but in his mind there was no place for women in business. He did permit them to toil in more menial positions in his company, but that was it. One ridiculous, horse-faced bitch had tried to sue him for failing to promote any women into the upper echelons of his company, but he'd crushed her pathetic attempt to take a single penny from him. Now it was striking him that if he had brought Allegra in on the business he could have shaped her into the person he'd wanted her to be. She wouldn't have gone anywhere near Jamie fucking Gray and he wouldn't be in this mess now, a prisoner in his own home looking at some serious jail time. And his nose would be its normal shape. Cameron scowled as he slid his fingers up and down the knotty bridge, a permanent reminder that he'd lost to a twenty-one-year-old scrag-end from a manky scheme.

Cameron was now convinced Allegra was out there somewhere, alive and well. The question was, had her fucking boyfriend known all along? Judging by his behaviour in the aftermath of her disappearance, he was inclined to say no. Jamie Gray's desperation to find Allegra's body had been eating him alive; Cameron had seen it in his eyes when they'd clashed. But several months had passed. If he hadn't known back then he definitely knew now. But the main problem was getting the little bastard to talk. If anyone put a finger on Jamie, Cameron would be the prime suspect and he couldn't risk a single bad mark against him with the trial going on. But if Jamie did know Allegra was still alive, then it was probable he knew where she was too. Bringing his daughter home was the only way to clear his name...

'Come in,' he called when there was a knock at the door. 'What do you want?' He scowled when Fenston walked in.

'There's a Mr Mullen to see you,' he replied, looking vaguely puzzled.

'And why haven't you brought him through?'

'I wanted to check that you want to see him.'

'Of course I want to see him. I invited him here.'

'Yes, sorry. I'll send him in.'

'Good, and we don't want to be disturbed. I don't care if there's a comet hurtling towards the earth, you do not interrupt us. Do you understand, boy?'

'Completely,' Fenston replied, throwing his father one of his suspicious stares before leaving.

'Prick,' muttered Cameron, draining his coffee and slamming the cup down on the windowsill.

The door opened again and in walked a tall, broad-shouldered man with penetrating grey eyes and a sombre expression. He was handsome and confident with thick dark hair very neatly combed into a side parting. He walked with a distinguished military bearing.

'Mr Abernethy,' said Mullen, extending a hand out to him. 'It's good to meet you.'

Cameron noted that his hand was large and strong, every nail cut to precisely the same length. Clearly Mullen was a very meticulous man. 'You too, Mr Mullen,' he replied, shaking his hand. 'Please, take a seat.'

'Thank you,' replied Mullen, taking the proffered armchair and unbuttoning the jacket of his very expensive and tasteful dark blue suit.

'Drink?' said Cameron.

'No, thank you. I'd prefer to get down to business.'

Cameron nodded approvingly and took the armchair opposite his guest.

'You mentioned this was something to do with your daughter?' opened Mullen.

'I did. I take it you've heard all about the court case?'

Mullen nodded.

'Good. Then I don't need to go into all the bloody details. The truth is, I didn't kill Allegra. I believe she's still alive and I need you to find her.'

Cameron paused to examine the effect his words had on the other man, but Mullen just stared at him impassively, waiting for him to continue.

'I'm assuming she's gone abroad,' went on Cameron. 'The only way to make this stupid court case go away is to produce her alive and well.'

Mullen nodded once as he considered his words. 'In order to find her, I need to know everything that happened the day she disappeared, and I need the plain unvarnished truth. Not the version your lawyers put forward.'

'Why?' barked Cameron.

'Because to find someone who's run away you need to understand their motivation. Past experience affects future decisions. In this case, I need to know if she's run away out of fear, revenge or for a completely different reason. I assure you I won't judge. What went on between you and your daughter really doesn't matter to me. You're paying me to do a job and I intend to do it to the best of my ability, but I need as much information as I can get.'

'Fine,' sighed Cameron, getting up and pouring himself a whisky.

He slumped back into the armchair and took a swig of his finest single malt. 'We got into an argument about the scrag-end.'

'Scrag-end?'

'Jamie fucking Gray from that shitty estate.'

'Gallowburn.'

Cameron nodded. 'They got engaged and I wasn't happy about it.'

Mullen didn't bother to ask why. The reason was obvious.

'The row became heated,' said Cameron. 'Allegra went crazy and started attacking me. She said no one was going to stop her from marrying Jamie, especially not me. I was pretty pissed off, I can tell you, after everything I'd done for her. She kept a knife in her bedside cabinet that she used to cut herself. One thing you should know, Mr Mullen, is that my daughter is extremely unbalanced. She self-harmed for years. I managed to get the knife off her but in the fight I accidentally stabbed her in the shoulder.' He studied Mullen carefully to see if the man was buying his story, but his expression was so impassive it was impossible to tell. 'I thought I'd killed her and I panicked, so I put her in the car. I was going to take her to hospital but she woke up and went crazy again. When I stopped the car to tend to her, she hit me over the head with a wheel wrench and knocked me out. Although I didn't see her, I know she ran off.'

He reached the end of his story and Mullen was staring at him with unreadable grey eyes. Cameron wasn't accustomed to feeling unnerved, but that assessing stare made him uncomfortable.

'Aren't you going to say something?' he asked Mullen.

'Sorry, Mr Abernethy. I was just going over in my head the various reports I've read about the case. You put Allegra in the boot of the car.'

'Says who?' he practically snarled.

His anger failed to affect Mullen. 'The police. They found her blood and hair in the boot but nothing in the back seat or front passenger seat.'

Cameron shot to his feet, huge body trembling with outrage.

'You're a fucking copper, aren't you? Did Ross put you up to this? I bet he did, the sneaky prick.'

'No, Mr Abernethy, he didn't. I'm not a police officer but I do have a lot of contacts in various police departments who give me access to confidential information. I wouldn't be able to do my job without them.'

'And they gave you access to the files on Allegra?'

Mullen nodded.

Cameron studied him carefully for any signs of deception. He could always tell when someone was lying, except his daughter. She was the only person who had ever fooled him.

'All right, you win,' Cameron sighed. 'I thought I'd killed her and I stuck her in the boot and drove her up to Cathkin Braes to get rid of her, but the rest of it is true. When I opened the boot she hit me and knocked me out. After that I've no idea what happened to her.'

'Thank you for being candid, Mr Abernethy. Now I can see the path more clearly. Allegra ran because she was afraid of you.'

'And because she wants to see me punished. She's got it into her head that I killed her slag of a mother.'

'Did you?'

'No. She died in a car accident.'

When Mullen gave him another assessing stare, Cameron refused to give in and admit anything.

'Okay, Mr Abernethy,' said Mullen when it became clear that tactic wasn't going to work a second time. 'Is there anywhere or anyone special to her she might have run to? Anywhere she felt safe?'

Cameron knew his daughter so little, all he could do was shrug. 'Not that I know of, but she does like the high life so, wherever she is, it'll be expensive, probably by the sea.'

'Does she have access to any funds?'

'Probably. The girl's sneaky and resourceful.'

'Is there anyone that could be helping her?'

'I've been thinking about that and there's only three people I can think of – Tarquin Austin, her godfather, but he buggered off to Thailand to open an elephant sanctuary. Can you believe it? He sold all his businesses to shovel elephant crap. Then there's Veronica Jones, Allegra's best friend. She comes from a wealthy family. Not as wealthy as mine but she does have access to a lot of money. Then there's the fucking scrag-end,' he hissed, hands curling into fists.

'I'm guessing Jamie Gray doesn't have any money?'

'The little twat doesn't have a pot to piss in, but he does know a lot of dodgy bastards who can get hold of things like false passports and IDs. He wasn't the first scheme rat Allegra messed about with. There were others from other estates.'

'Would you be able to give me their names and addresses?'

'Yes. I dug up all the dirt on them, the ones I knew about anyway.'

'Was Jamie the only one she got engaged to?'

Cameron's nod was savage. 'I don't know why though. She could have had anyone she wanted. A bloody viscount was interested in her. She could have married into royalty but, oh, no, not Allegra. She preferred some little prick who lives on a manky council estate. I'm sure she only did it to piss me off.'

'Is it possible she felt any real emotion for him?'

'No, it's not,' Cameron yelled. 'And what the fuck does it matter? I'm paying you to find her, not give her fucking counselling.'

Mullen's expression was deadpan. 'It matters because, if she is alive and genuinely in love with him, she may try to contact him. However, if she only got engaged to him to spite you then she wouldn't risk exposing herself like that.'

'Oh, I see,' said Cameron, feeling a little foolish for giving into his rage so quickly. 'In that case, yes, I do think she had real feelings for him. Christ knows why, he's a skinny, broke, wee prick with absolutely nothing going for him.'

'It could be advantageous to watch him and delve deeper into his life.'

The corner of Cameron's mouth lifted into a humourless smile. 'And if you find anything that could damage his reputation in the eyes of the jury and show the world he's a lying scumbag, then that could be very useful too.'

Mulled nodded.

'Excellent,' said Cameron, smiling as he fantasised about tearing the little git's reputation to shreds. All those newspaper reports making him out to be some tragic Romeo figure made him want to vomit. There was even a Jamie Gray fan club, for Christ's sake, made up of daft bints who posted images of him on social media and whined about how gorgeous and tragic he was. The only tragic thing was that the stupid bitches had nothing better to do with their time. He'd expose Jamie Gray for what he really was and shove it down the throats of all those idiots. Allegra was out there alive somewhere and if anyone knew that it was Jamie. He couldn't wait to see the prick in the dock.

'What else do you need?' he asked Mullen.

'Everything you can tell me about Allegra, and I need to see her room too. I understand the police have taken anything of interest but her likes and dislikes will give me a clue as to where she is and what she's doing. I understand her bank accounts haven't been touched, so she'll be supporting herself somehow.'

'Well, there's more to that than has been said in the papers or that the police know.'

Mullen raised a questioning eyebrow.

'Some money was stolen from me – a hundred and fifty grand, to be precise. I think she has it.'

'That amount of cash would go a long way. It's more than enough to buy a new identity.'

'I'm well aware of that. It must be the only way she's been able to stay hidden.'

'It wouldn't be too difficult for her as no one's been looking for her.'

'I bet she's changed her appearance too. She's good with hair and make-up. She did once mention that she'd love to open her own salon, but I put a stop to that. No daughter of mine works for a living.'

'Interesting,' said Mullen, the corners of his mouth turning down as he went deep into thought.

'So, where will you start?'

'With Jamie Gray. I think you're right and if anyone knows where she is, it's him, and he probably got her a false passport. But I will speak to these other exes of hers on the other schemes.'

'You can't tell Jamie you're looking for Allegra.'

'I don't intend to. I can be very discreet.'

'Discretion won't persuade a bunch of scheme rats to tell you about false passports.'

'I have methods of persuasion, some more intense than others.'

'That sounds more like it. Torture the information out of the little bastards,' Cameron said, before draining his glass and slamming it down on the small table by the arm of the chair.

'I require 50 per cent of my fee up front, plus expenses as I go along. You have my account details. The remaining 50 per cent will be paid when I conclude my investigation, whether that ends with me bringing Allegra home or finding out that she really is deceased. You must accept my findings. My job is to discover the truth, whether you like that truth or not.'

'As long as you can back up your findings with plenty of evidence, we won't have a problem.'

'I will. I always do.'

Cameron studied Mullen hard before picking up his phone and stabbing at the screen with one large sausage-like finger. 'The first 50 per cent has been transferred.'

'Thank you,' said Mullen, getting to his feet. 'I'll be in touch soon.'

'And you'll keep me informed every step of the way?'

'Naturally. I'll need those names and addresses emailing to me.'

'I'll do it now.'

'Thank you for your time, Mr Abernethy. I'll see myself out.'

Cameron just nodded, watching him leave, glad he'd gone. There weren't many people he felt were his equal, but Mullen was in that illustrious few. If anyone could find his daft bitch of a daughter, Mullen could. Now Cameron could sit back and imagine how he would make her suffer for the rest of her life for the hell she'd put him through. He would insist the police didn't press charges against her. It would take all of his influence and a lot of cash to convince them not to, because she'd wasted a huge amount of their time and resources, but he would manage it. He thought his best bet would be to get a psychiatric evaluation done on her saying she wasn't right in the head and wasn't competent to stand trial. That should stop any talk of her being prosecuted. He could always threaten to sue the police for wrongful arrest and imprisonment if they tried to press the issue.

He would play the forgiving father who was just relieved his daughter was home safe, tell the world it wasn't her fault, that she wasn't in her right mind. Then he would have her locked up in a private institute where his money would dictate all the clinical decisions. After a few months of being stuck in a loony bin receiving unnecessary treatment she would be much quieter and compliant, and he would bring her home where she would forget all about the scrag-end. Once all the fuss had died down and everyone had forgotten about Jamie Gray, he would have him killed, properly this time. Cameron wouldn't risk using a method where Jamie might survive. Finally, the little prick would be gone and Allegra would never leave him again.

* * *

'Why have you dragged us to this manky alley?' Logan asked Digger, shivering against the biting wind and shoving his hands deeper into his coat pockets.

Out of the four Blood Brothers, only Digger appeared unaffected by the cold in his light jacket with just a T-shirt underneath. Idly Logan wondered if all the steroids Digger took were responsible. It seemed this alley was favoured by all the local dogs because they had to keep dodging little brown logs lying on the cobbles.

'I've found the perfect place to hide secrets,' announced Digger.

'It won't be secret much longer if you shout about it like that.' Jamie scowled.

'Oh, sorry, but I really have,' he said, coming to a halt in front of a small, squat brick building with a thick metal door and mesh covering the windows.

Digger produced a key from his pocket and unlocked the door, which screeched as he shoved it open.

'This workshop belongs to my granddad,' he explained. 'His best pal left it to him in his will, but as he's in a care home now with dementia he won't be using it. The beautiful thing about it is that my granddad never had it transferred into his name, so no one will link it to my family.'

They stepped into a fifty-foot-square bare room with a concrete floor, and a light bulb dangling from the ceiling. A door in the west wall led into a tiny toilet with a sink. Inside it was no warmer than it was outside. When Digger hit the light, Jamie closed the door.

'Jimmy, that's my granddad's friend, loved metalwork,' explained Digger. 'He had some pretty expensive equipment in here, so the building's watertight. That's why he had that door fitted and the mesh. No one ever managed to break in in all the years he had it. And, best of all, no one comes down this alley anyway.'

'I'm no' surprised,' said Gary. 'Unless they're a dog needing a shite.'

'So,' said Digger like a little boy awaiting praise. 'What do you think?'

'I think it's bloody perfect,' said Jamie. 'Nice one, pal.'

'Cheers.' Digger grinned.

'And you're sure your family won't come sniffing round?'

'Sure. They've forgotten all about this place and my granddad won't be using it.'

'Then I can let Toni know we've found somewhere.'

'Aren't we going to need more security than a steel door and some mesh?' said Logan.

'I'm already on that,' replied Jamie. 'We'll have it this afternoon.'

'This is moving fast,' sighed Logan.

'Tell me about it pal,' said Jamie grimly.

10

Despite them having everything ready for Toni, it was another couple of days before her secret was delivered by Jason and Caesar, along with three more men. All four Blood Brothers turned out for the occasion and Jamie made the introductions.

'Is Toni no' here?' said Digger, trying to sound casual but failing.

'No,' snapped Caesar. 'She wouldnae sully herself by coming down this dog's toilet of an alley.'

Jamie shook his head at Digger, who had opened his mouth to backchat Caesar.

Digger, who spotted the suspicious bulge under Caesar's left arm, nodded and closed his mouth again.

'What's in it?' said Gary as Jason and the three men heaved a large heavy box that measured about seven feet by five feet off the back of a white Transit van and carried it inside.

'None of your bloody business,' said Caesar, who was making no attempt to assist his sweating colleagues. 'And if you know what's good for you, you won't peek either. What's the old saying? Curiosity killed the fat wee prick.'

'I am not fat,' Gary retorted. 'It's glandular.'

'I bet it's chips.'

'Shut up, Gary,' Jamie told his friend.

Gary nodded and went silent, glaring at Caesar.

Jason noted the influence his son had over his friends, and he was bloody proud of him. Jamie was clearly a natural-born leader.

Finally the four men manoeuvred the heavy box into the centre of the room and dumped it on the floor before doubling over and panting. Caesar studied the room and nodded approvingly.

'You've done good, lads,' he said. 'It won't be easy for anyone to break in here. The boss lady will be pleased.'

'How long will the box be staying?' Jamie asked him.

'Until the boss lady says otherwise.' He regarded them all one by one. 'And no one touches it, you get it? If I think you've been taking a look I'll chop off all your sticky fingers and shove them up each other's arses. Do you understand, fannies?'

They all nodded sombrely.

'Good.' Caesar looked to his men. 'Let's go. It stinks of shite around here.'

'I'll see you later, son,' Jason told Jamie. 'I'll bring your new motor over.'

'New motor?' said Gary eagerly as the five men hopped into the Transit van.

'Don't get excited,' replied Jamie. 'Toni's already said it'll be an old banger, so no one will ask questions. It won't be anything flash like my da's.'

'Oh, well. An old banger's better than no car, I suppose.'

All four of them looked at the box.

'It looks like a coffin,' said Gary. 'What?' he added when they all frowned at him. 'I'm only saying what you're all thinking.'

'Sadly you're right,' said Logan.

'Surely they wouldn't hide a deid body here?' said Digger.

'It's no' a body,' said Jamie. 'Toni McVay's got away with murder for years because she's good at hiding bodies. She doesn't dump them on people she doesn't know if she can trust yet.'

'Unless she's trying to set us up?' said Gary.

'Why would she do that? And that would be a stupid thing to do to me when I'm so much in the public eye with the trial. Let's lock up and get out of here,' he added, wanting to get away from the grim object.

They left the workshop, Digger locking the door. 'I'd feel better if you held onto this,' he said, holding the key out to Jamie. 'I'll end up losing it.'

'Nae bother,' said Jamie, taking it from him and slipping it into his jeans pocket. 'Is there a spare in case this one gets lost?'

'Aye, safely stashed in my undies drawer at home.'

'Urgh,' said Gary.

'They're clean undies,' Digger snapped at him.

'Well, I could use a drink,' said Logan, sounding weary.

'Great idea.' Gary grinned. 'Let's celebrate.'

'Celebrate what?' said Jamie.

'The first day of our new lives.'

'We haven't been paid yet,' said Digger.

'But we will be, and we'll be paid bloody well too. What's up with you all, you miserable gits?'

'I don't like the look of that box,' said Logan.

'Me neither,' said Digger.

'Let's not worry about that now,' said Jamie. 'Let's get out of here and have a bevy, we've earned it.'

Their moods all lifted when they stepped into the welcoming warmth and life of the pub after the cold dankness of the workshop and its macabre delivery. Deirdre greeted them with a smile.

'All right, boys?' she said. 'Four pints?'

They all nodded.

'Take a seat. Eric will bring them over,' she said, gesturing to her husband, who was chatting to a customer sitting at the bar.

'Oh, I will, will I?' he retorted.

'Why not? You've done sod all else all day, you lazy bastard.'

As they launched into a domestic, the Blood Brothers hastily took a seat at a table on the other side of the room.

Sensing someone watching him, Jamie looked round to see a furious red face surrounded by a cascade of red curls. He nudged Logan and nodded in Sasha Reid's direction. He in turn nudged Digger, who nudged Gary so hard he was almost knocked off his chair.

'Careful, you big dumb rock,' Gary told him.

Digger nodded in Sasha's direction and all four Blood Brothers stared back at her.

'She's a bit fit when she's not covered in flour,' commented Gary.

'What would Valerie say if she knew you were here lusting after another woman?' Digger asked him.

'Shut it, Rocky.'

They watched as Sasha shot to her feet and stomped across the room towards them, the eyes of all the Blood Brothers – except Jamie – locked on her long and shapely but very pale legs.

'I hope you're happy with yourselves,' she yelled at them.

'Always.' Digger grinned.

'My brother's in hospital with a broken leg.'

'Why, what happened?' said Logan. 'Did he have an accident?'

'Accident, my arse. It was you lot.'

'Us?' said Gary with mock shock. 'We don't do things like that.'

'Oh, yes, you do. What do you want?' she snapped at Eric when he appeared at the side of the table clutching a tray of drinks.

'What does it look like?' he retorted, nodding at the tray in his hands. 'And if you don't simmer down you'll be barred.'

'They broke my brother's leg,' she said, gesturing to the Blood Brothers with a violent stab of the hand.

'He probably deserved it. He's a trouble-making wee jobby and if someone finally put him in his place, then good on them.'

'Don't you fucking dare,' Deirdre screeched at her when she drew back her hand to slap the tray out of Eric's grip. 'You do and I'll mop it up with your head. That hair of yours looks pretty absorbent. Now sit down like a good wee lassie or piss off out of it.'

The room was silent as Deirdre's furious scream died away.

'This isn't over,' Sasha spat at the Blood Brothers before flouncing back to her seat, allowing Eric to finally put the pints down on the table and return to the bar.

'She's mental, is that one,' commented Gary.

'You're right,' said Jamie. 'We need to keep an eye on her. You and Digger can do that. I get the feeling you'll enjoy it.'

'Too right.' Digger grinned. 'Especially if we get to keep an eye on her when she's in the shower. Only joking,' he hastily added when Jamie scowled at him.

The door opened and the Blood Brothers sighed when John Lawson strolled in with two of his cousins.

'Oh, jeezo,' sighed Digger. 'Not that dick.'

John's gaze connected with Jamie's as he walked across the room. He hadn't caused them any trouble since his older brother had been sent to Barlinnie, but Jamie was sure it was only a matter of time.

They watched as he walked up to Sasha, who leapt to her feet with a grin, wrapped her arms around his neck and kissed him.

'Urgh,' said Gary. 'She's got really bad taste.'

They all winced as the kiss grew more passionate.

'Gi'es me the baulk,' said Digger.

Sasha smirked at the Blood Brothers, as though she'd taken some big revenge by dating their enemy, not that John Lawson was much of an enemy. He certainly didn't have his older brother's smarts, although he was roaming free while Craig was locked up, so maybe he had more brains than everyone thought.

'They can only have just started dating,' said Logan. 'He only split up with Kylie Watson a couple of days ago.'

'It looks like our enemies are joining forces,' replied a thoughtful Jamie.

* * *

The three men pried at the mesh covering the windows of the workshop, but it stubbornly refused to come away.

'It's bolted to the wall,' one of the men dressed all in black muttered to his friend. 'Go for the bolts, not the fucking mesh.'

'Oh, aye, right,' he replied, sweating under his balaclava.

'You're making too much noise,' hissed the first man when he started hammering at them.

'It's the only way to get them out.'

'No, it's not. Try prising them out, not hitting them, you fucking dick.'

'Don't call me a dick,' retorted the first man, waving the hammer menacingly.

'Be quiet, the pair of you,' spat the third man in a deep, authoritative voice. 'Do you want to wake up the entire scheme? Now try to get that mesh off...'

They all cried out and staggered backwards blindly when the lights that were mounted to the front of the building burst into life. A few seconds later the lights went out again, leaving them stumbling about unable to see.

'What's happening?' cried the first man.

'I've nae—' began the second man before he was knocked unconscious by a baseball bat to the back of the head.

His friends were also helpless to defend themselves because their vision still hadn't cleared. Four masked figures laid into them with coshes, baseball bats and bike chains. When the intruders were subdued, Jamie pulled the balaclava off his head, face shiny with sweat.

'Bloody hell, these things are hot.'

'Hey.' Digger frowned, rolling up his own mask. 'My maw used her best wool to knit us these.'

'I think we could use something more breathable,' panted Logan, peeling his balaclava off his red, sweaty face.

'I like mine,' said Gary through the mask. 'It's all warm and toasty.'

'Let's save the discussion till later,' said Jamie. 'We cannae scare the shite out of anyone talking about knitting.' He pointed to the man he'd hit in the face with the bike chain, who was attempting to push himself up onto all fours with a pained groan. 'Let's see who it is.'

Digger planted his enormous foot in the middle of the man's back and pushed him back to the ground while Gary pulled off his balaclava.

'Polyester.' He grinned at his friends, holding up the mask before tossing it aside. 'He's still sweaty but I think that's because he's been battered with a bike chain.'

Jamie crouched before the man, who glared at them, the left side of his face swollen and bruised.

'I don't recognise him, do you?' Jamie asked his friends.

They all shook their heads.

Jamie pulled the masks off the other two men, who were still out for the count.

'I don't know any of them.' Logan frowned. 'I felt sure they'd be Lawsons.'

'But how would the Lawsons know about this place?'

'I don't know. No one should.'

Jamie straightened up when a fourth man emerged from around the corner, clapping.

'Caesar?' He frowned, squinting into the darkness.

'Aye, it's me,' replied his gruff voice. 'Well done, boys.'

'These are your men?'

'They are. They're here to test your security.'

'And did we pass your test?'

'With flying colours. The boss lady will be pleased. You had hidden cameras installed, didn't you?'

Jamie nodded. Earlier that morning, Ephraim had come through with the security equipment he'd asked him to get.

'And that was a good trick with the lights. Very smart.'

'Thanks,' said Jamie.

Digger realised he was still standing on one of Toni McVay's men and hastily released him. 'Sorry, pal.'

'Ya wee bastard,' the man spat, dragging himself to his feet and brushing himself off.

'I don't think you can call him wee.' Caesar chuckled. 'He's bigger than you. He's like a fucking ox.' He looked back at the Blood Brothers. 'My lads weren't expecting you to beat the shite out of them.' He delved into his coat pockets with both hands and produced four bulging rolls of notes, tossing one to each of the Blood Brothers. 'A gift from the boss lady to show her appreciation.'

'Cheers,' breathed a wide-eyed Gary, gaping at the money in his hand. He'd never seen so much before.

'Wake them up, will you, Cal?' Caesar told his angry friend, gesturing to the two men who were still unconscious on the ground. 'We need to move the box out of there.'

'Already?' said Jamie.

'Aye. Want to see what's inside?'

'No, thanks. We're good.'

'That's the smart answer but, sorry, the boss lady insists. Open up the workshop.'

Jamie reluctantly unlocked the metal door and shoved it open while Cal roused his friends, who got to their feet grumbling about having a headache. They all stepped inside the workshop, Jamie switching on the fluorescent lights, making them blink.

Caesar took a key out of his pocket and stood before the box, a sinister grin on his face. 'You ready, boys?'

They all nodded seriously, Gary swallowing hard.

Caesar unlocked the box, but the lid was so heavy it took both him and Cal to open it.

'Take a swatch, lads,' said Caesar, the way his scars twisted as he smiled making them all shudder.

Reluctantly they peered inside and frowned.

'It looks like a packet of crisps,' said Gary.

'Aye,' replied Caesar.

'Is it a clever disguise for some hidden jewels?'

'Pick it up and see.'

Gary looked to Jamie, who nodded.

Slowly Gary reached out a hand and gingerly took a corner of the packet between thumb and forefinger, his friends anxiously looking on as he lifted it out of the box.

'Open it, then,' snapped Caesar, making Gary jump.

He pulled open the packet and peered inside.

'What is it?' said Digger, eyes wide.

'Salt and vinegar.'

'Eh?

'It really has crisps inside.'

There was a moment of silence as the Blood Brothers all looked at each other before Caesar burst out laughing, his injured friends weakly joining in.

'You should see your faces.' He guffawed. 'You were expecting priceless jewels or drugs when it was crisps all along. Don't worry, lads, they're crinkle cut, the good stuff.'

'Why the hell would you put a packet of crisps in a lead box and dump it here?' demanded a very put-out Digger.

'You hear that?' Caesar asked his friends. 'The fucking donkey doesn't get it.'

Jamie jammed his elbow in Digger's ribs when he opened his mouth to yell at Caesar, silencing him.

'It was a test,' explained Logan. 'They wouldn't leave anything valuable with us until they knew we could be trusted to look after it.'

'Aye, you're right,' said Caesar, wiping away tears of mirth. 'In a few days you'll get the real package. We'll let you know when.' He rolled his eyes when they stared at him stonily. 'Don't look like nippy sweeties, you should be celebrating. You did good tonight and you got paid more cash than you've ever seen in your lives.'

There was a crunch from Gary's direction. 'The crisps are good too,' he mumbled, crumbs falling from his lips.

'Glad to hear it.' Caesar looked to his men and with a jerk of the head told them it was time to leave.

'Wait,' said Jamie. 'What about the box?'

'It can stay here until we bring the first delivery. We're no' humping that out of here in the dark.'

'It would be a terrible breach of health and safety,' said Logan a little sarcastically, earning himself a fierce Caesar scowl.

None of them spoke until the McVay heavies had got back in their van and driven off.

'Well, that was... weird,' said Jamie.

'We were shitting it about what was in that box,' said Digger. 'And all the time it was a packet of bloody crisps. The McVays really have a sick sense of humour.'

'Let's lock up and get out of here,' said Jamie. 'We don't want anyone finding this place.'

Once the workshop was secured, they meandered back through the estate, all lost in their own worlds, lacking their usual high spirits, the only sound the crunch of Gary eating the crisps.

* * *

'Piss off, will you? Just bloody piss off out of it. You're not wanted round here.'

The yelling woke Jamie, who lifted his head from the pillow and squinted at the clock. It was only seven in the morning. It took him a moment to realise it was his mum shouting.

He leapt out of bed and tore downstairs in just his boxer shorts, jumping the last few steps and racing towards the front door, which was standing open, Jackie yelling at the figure standing on the doorstep.

'Maw, what's going on?' he demanded.

'This prick won't bugger off,' she told him, pointing at Jason. She frowned at her son. 'Jamie Gray, I didn't raise you to stand naked on the doorstep.'

'I'm no' naked, Maw, I've got my undies on.'

'That's something at least. Go and get dressed. I'll deal with this,' she said, turning her attention back to Jason, her green eyes shooting fire.

'Why are you here, Da?' Jamie asked him.

'I just want to talk to you, that's all,' he replied.

'I'll meet you in Raymond's Rolls around the corner from Di Giorgio's.'

'Aye, I've seen it.' Jason looked back at his ex-wife. 'It was nice seeing you, Jackie.'

'Well, it wasn't nice seeing you,' she huffed, slamming the door shut in his face. She scowled at her son. 'Why do you want to meet that useless lump?'

'We have things to discuss,' Jamie replied.

Her green eyes narrowed. 'He's dragged you into something, hasn't he? I knew he would. He heard all about the Blood Brothers on the news and he thought he could use you. That's all he's here for. He hasn't even bothered to ask about Charlie. Thank God he spent last night at his friend's.'

'Has Charlie asked about Jason?'

'A couple of vague questions but he doesn't know him like you do. Oh, please don't go to see him, Jamie. He'll only drag you into something dodgy.'

'I can handle it, Maw,' Jamie said, hugging her. 'I promise everything will be fine.'

'Whatever he says, don't believe it. All he knows is lies. I know you want to get ahead in this world but whatever stupid scheme he's got in mind isn't the way to go. You're a good boy and you're smart. You can make it without him.'

'I'll meet with him and tell him not to come here again.'

'You mean that?'

'Aye, I dae, and I'll ask him why he's not bothered to see Charlie.'

'Don't do that because then he might want to see him out of spite and I don't want your brother exposed to his poison too. Charlie's so innocent.'

'You're probably right. I'll go and get dressed, then I'll sort out the walloper.'

Jackie anxiously watched him dash back upstairs, wishing she could stop him from seeing his waster of a father. She would have to find a way.

* * *

'So, she let you out, then?' Jason smiled when Jamie sat opposite him at a table in Raymond's Rolls.

'Course,' he replied. 'I'm a grown man.'

'I've not ordered yet because I didn't know what you'd want.'

Jamie turned to the big, hairy, middle-aged man serving behind the counter. 'I'll have a cup of tea and a roll and sausage, please, Ray.'

'Nae bother, Jamie,' replied the gorilla. 'What about your da?'

'How did you know he's my da?' replied Jamie. Raymond had moved onto the scheme five years ago, so he hadn't known Jason Gray.

'Because it's all over the scheme that he's back and you look just like him.'

'Suppose.'

'I'll have coffee and a roll and sausage too, please,' said Jason.

'Coming right up,' replied Ray before getting to work.

'I've got your new car,' Jason told his son. 'It's parked on the next street. I didn't want to bring it to your house because I thought Jackie would go aff her nut. Thank Christ I didn't because after seeing how she was I think she would have taken a sledgehammer to it. In fact she still might. How are you going to explain the car to her?'

'Simple. I'll tell her the truth.'

'I don't think that's wise.'

'I've lied to her enough and I'm no' doing it again.'

'All right, if you think that's the right thing to do, but she will go ballistic. Then again, I suppose you can handle her better than I can.'

'No one can handle my maw,' said Jamie with a hint of pride. 'She's like fire and she's capable of burning anyone, including you.'

'Aye, I know. You don't need to tell me. Anyway, the tax is already paid on the car, it's got a full year's MOT and it's insured under my name. I put you on as a named driver, so you're good to go.'

'Brilliant, cheers, Da.'

'Don't thank me, thank our friend.'

They went silent when Ray plonked their rolls down on the table. He wore a white short-sleeved T-shirt, revealing very meaty forearms coated in thick black hair. Jason grimaced when he noticed one of those hairs on the table by his left hand. He was just relieved it wasn't on his food. As Ray went back to the counter to fetch their drinks, Jason swept the offending hair onto the floor with a serviette.

Their mugs were unceremoniously dumped on the table too.

'Enjoy,' muttered Ray before ambling back behind the counter.

Jamie picked up the ketchup bottle and squirted some onto his roll.

'The car will give you so much more freedom,' Jason told his son.

'Am I allowed to use it whenever I want or is it just for business?'

'You can use it whenever you want. Toni is a very generous employer. One day soon she'll upgrade you to something better.'

'What has she given me?'

'A silver 2008 Vauxhall Vectra. Don't pull a face,' said Jason, eyes dancing with amusement. 'You've got a free car.'

'Suppose,' Jamie mumbled. He took a bite of his roll and chewed thoughtfully before saying, 'After you left us, did you have any more weans?'

'You're wondering if you have brothers and sisters?'

Jamie nodded.

'No, I didn't. You and Charlie are my only kids. I was so useless with you two I didn't think it fair to inflict myself on anyone else.'

Jamie thought that was the most mature thing he'd ever heard his father say. 'Were there any, you know, women?'

'A couple. Nothing you'd call serious. Have you had any serious relationships, other than Allegra?'

'Naw,' Jamie muttered into his roll.

'Don't be shy talking about her.'

'I'm not. It's just... difficult.'

'I can only imagine. You know, Jamie, I still have friends in Barlinnie and I've asked them to keep an eye on Craig Lawson for me.'

'Why?'

'Let's just say we clashed a few times when I was inside.'

'You did? Why didn't you say anything before?'

'I thought I'd given you enough surprises.'

'Well, I appreciate you keeping an eye on him, but he can't do anything to me from inside a prison.'

'I wouldn't put it past him, and men like that always want revenge.'

'At least Cameron won't be using him to do anything, not after Craig gave evidence against him.'

'Don't assume anything, it's dangerous. You've got to expect trouble to come from any direction.'

'That's a cheerful thought,' Jamie said wryly.

'But true. Now you're working for Toni you need to be prepared for anything.' Jason broke into a smile. 'I heard you gave Caesar's men a good hiding.'

'We did.' Jamie grinned. 'They seemed... surprised.'

'Aye, they were. They thought breaking in would be a piece of piss, but not only did they not get in, but they had the shite kicked out of them too.'

'It was fun.'

'I can imagine.'

Father and son smiled at each other from over their rolls.

'I've got a friend with a boat,' said Jason.

'What sort of friend?' said Jamie, eyes narrowing suspiciously. 'Do you mean Toni?'

'No,' Jason chuckled. 'This friend's legit. It's a beautiful cabin cruiser moored at Inverkip Marina. He said I could borrow it, so how do you fancy a wee hurl out in it? We could go down the west coast.'

'Really?' replied Jamie, trying not to show his excitement.

'Yes.' Jason smiled. 'Have you ever been on a boat before?'

'No, but I've always wanted to.'

'Then now's your chance. Are you free on Friday?'

'Aye.'

'I'll pick you up at nine o'clock. The marina's only a fifty-minute drive, so it won't take us long to get there.'

'Great.' Jamie grinned. 'I'll look forward to that.'

'We'll relax, catch up. It'll be fun.'

Jamie couldn't help but beam. His dad actually wanted to spend quality time with him. It seemed he was interested in him and not just here for what he could get out of him after all.

11

Isaac Lawson, cousin to the Lawson family in Gallowburn and Allegra's ex-boyfriend, exited the front of the house on the Easterhouse scheme where he occupied the top floor flat. He shoved his hands into his tracksuit top, pulled his Burberry baseball cap down lower and set off up the street, keeping his head down against the cold wind, accompanied by the scrape of a discarded polystyrene carton from the chip shop.

As he walked, he became conscious of someone following him. Glancing back over his shoulder, he saw a tall, dark figure just a few paces behind him.

Isaac's hand gripped the small knife hidden in his jacket tighter. He turned the corner and looked back again, relieved when the figure carried on down the street without so much as glancing his way.

When he looked back round he cried out and stumbled back a couple of paces. Before him was a large man who stood so tall and straight he looked like a soldier on parade.

'Stay back,' cried Isaac, yanking the knife out of his pocket and pointing it at the man, but his mouth fell open when the weapon was knocked from his hand and landed in the gutter. He lunged for it but the man grabbed him by the scruff of the neck and pushed him up against the wall.

'Just relax,' said Mullen. 'I only want some information. If you tell me nicely and give me no bother, I won't have to hurt you.'

'Piss off, you walloper,' cried Isaac, eyes bulging when the hand around his neck started to squeeze.

'Not wise, Isaac, but, then again, I didn't expect you to be. I just want you to tell me if you ever gave any false documents to Allegra Abernethy.'

Mullen released Isaac's neck so he could talk. Isaac coughed and spluttered, massaging his aching neck. 'Documents?' he gasped. 'What do you mean?'

'ID cards, passport, that sort of thing,' Mullen impatiently replied, looking up and down the darkened street to make sure they weren't being observed.

'Naw. Why should I? And what does it matter? She's deid.'

'You're sure you never gave her anything?'

'Aye, I'm sure.' A lecherous grin spread across his face. 'I gave her plenty of something else though. She couldnae get enough of me.'

'Don't lie, you're embarrassing yourself. Did anyone on the scheme get her anything like that?'

'How the hell should I know? Is that it, only I've got somewhere to be?' snapped Isaac, attempting to be tough and failing.

Mullen nodded. 'We're done here. Thank you for your time.'

Isaac watched him walk away. Only when he was certain he was out of earshot did he dare mutter the word, 'Prick.'

* * *

Mullen returned to his car – a small, understated black five-year-old Hyundai i10 – and started the engine, leaving Easterhouse behind. Tomorrow he would try the next name on his list. He was anxious to work down the list of idiots Cameron had given him so he could get to Jamie Gray, who he thought most likely to know about Allegra's true fate. There were only two names left on the list. The next name – Danny Barker – was in Barlinnie for attempted murder. Mullen hadn't wanted to visit him personally because it would mean leaving a trail behind him, but he had a friend inside who had easily got the information he'd needed from Danny. The lad had thought he was a tough guy for attempting to kill a fifteen-year-old kid, until he'd ended up in a category A prison and discovered he was nothing more than a silly, cowardly little boy, and had been repeatedly taught the error of his ways with several beatings. Sadly, Noah Anderson, who had moved to Possilpark, would have to wait until tomorrow night as through his contacts Mullen had discovered he spent most of his nights going about the streets dealing drugs. Mullen needed to reach him earlier in the evening, before he could leave on another of his night-time forays. Inwardly Mullen sighed. All these silly kids thinking they were gangsters. He would enjoy teaching them all a lesson, especially Jamie Gray.

* * *

Jamie's temperature soared and his face flushed bright red as he indulged in an increasingly erotic conversation with Allegra over the phone. Abstaining from sex was hard enough and this conversation wasn't helping, even though he was really enjoying it. Allegra had called him for their morning chat while his mum was taking Charlie to school.

'We must be able to meet up somehow,' he exclaimed, his entire body aching for her.

'I'm working on it,' she replied, sounding equally frustrated. 'I'm tempted to come out there.'

'Or I could come to you?'

'Too risky. There's a lot of attention on you right now and questions will be asked if you suddenly leave the country.'

'I really want to see you, but I don't want you to get arrested.'

'Me neither, Dangerous, but there might be a way, even if we can only be together for a few hours.'

'There's a lot I can do to you in a few hours,' he groaned.

'Oh, yes. I'm imagining them all right now.'

'Me too.'

'God, I need to cool down. I've got to get back to work in ten minutes. So, how are things with your dad and the McVays? Is there an update?'

'Plenty actually.' He told her everything that had happened, Allegra laughing as he described beating up Caesar's men.

'Serves them right.' She giggled. 'God, I wish I was there, it sounds so exciting. I love Italy but it is pretty quiet.'

'I can't imagine it ever being quiet around you.'

'It won't be when we're together, Dangerous, I promise you that.'

'I can't wait, Princess. Actually, I need your advice.'

'Oh, good, because that's the only way I can help you right now.'

'Should I tell my maw everything?'

'It's a difficult one. I know how much you must hate lying to her, but the truth will kill her.'

'I know and she'll probably go after my da with a frying pan. She got herself a new one after she did hers in battering Craig Lawson around the head. It's bigger and heavier than the last one. She'll go mental. This isn't the future she wanted for me.'

'Is it the future you want for yourself?'

'I dunno. It's the chance to make some serious money but I don't want to end up in prison or dead. Plus Toni McVay is so unpredictable. She might decide one day that I'm no use to her after all and kill me and scoop out my eyeballs.'

'I don't think so. Yes, she's a psycho, but first and foremost she's a businesswoman. As long as you're useful to her, you'll be safe. People only leave her firm with her permission or if she has them killed.'

'It wouldn't be so bad if it had been my choice to work with her, but it was forced on me, and now I'm trapped.'

'Jackie's a smart woman. She'll work it out eventually. It's probably better coming from you than someone else.'

'Aye, you're right,' he said, Allegra's words confirming what he felt deep down. 'I have to tell her. I'm not looking forward to it though.'

'She's your mother and she loves the bones of you. She won't take it out on you.'

'She'll take it out on my da. What worries me is that she doesn't realise how much Jason's changed. He's no' the spineless waster he used to be.'

'You don't think he'd hurt her, do you?'

The concern in her voice made him smile. 'No, not physically. He knows I'd kill him if he laid a finger on her, but he might hurt her in another way.'

'You must make it very clear to him what you'll do if he does hurt her.'

'I already have but I'll tell him again, just so he's clear.'

On the other end of the line, a soft, feminine voice called Allegra's name.

Allegra sighed. 'Sorry, Dangerous, I've got to go. Sofia's having trouble with some acrylic nails. God, I hope she's not put them on upside down again. Same time tomorrow?'

'Definitely. My favourite time of the day.' He smiled. 'And I'm gonnae tell my maw as soon as she gets home.'

'Good for you. It's the right thing to do.'

'Aye, I know. Speak to you tomorrow, then.'

'Aye, you will,' she said in a strong Glaswegian accent, making him grin. 'Love you, Dangerous.'

'Love you, Princess,' he said before hanging up.

He wandered downstairs, willing away the lust that still had hold of his body. God, he hoped she found a way to visit soon; he wasn't sure he could take the frustration for much longer.

Jamie made himself a cup of tea, poured out a bowl of cereal and carried them into the front room to eat in front of the telly, his mind on Allegra as he chewed thoughtfully.

When his mother didn't come home he started to worry. Half an hour ticked by and he wondered if he should call her, but it wasn't unusual for her to go on somewhere else after dropping Charlie off at school. She could have gone to the shops or on to one of her friends' houses, but with everything going on he didn't like it.

He took out his phone and stared at the screen before sighing and dumping it on the couch. Calling his mum and demanding to know where she was would not go down well with her. She was a grown woman who was more than capable of looking after herself. He would talk to her when she came home.

* * *

Jackie knew something was wrong. She felt it deep in her bones. Her oldest son was in trouble; he was being secretive and it was something to do with that bastard of an ex-husband of hers. She'd never get it out of Jason, so she was going to speak to someone she thought might be able to give her the answers she so desperately wanted. She knocked on the front door of the house Logan shared with his dad. The red door was shiny and new. Dave had been forced to replace it after the Lawsons nearly knocked it off its hinges while searching for John Lawson's lost phone, stolen by Logan.

'All right, Mrs G?' Logan yawned when he answered the door wearing jogging bottoms and a white T-shirt. He raked his fingers through his dark curls, sending them springing about his head.

'Sorry for waking you, love,' she replied.

'You didn't. I was already up. I just didn't get much sleep last night.'

'Any particular reason why?' Jackie said suspiciously.

'Naw. It was just one of those nights.' In truth he'd lain awake for half the night worrying about what the future held for him and his friends. Would they be successful in their new endeavour or would they end up dead in a ditch with holes in their heads?

'Can I come in?' Jackie asked him. 'I need to talk to you.'

Logan was immediately on his guard. Jackie had realised something was going on and she wanted to see if he knew anything about it. He had no choice but to let her in. Jackie Gray was not the sort of person you turned down. 'Yeah, course,' he said, opening the door wider.

'Thanks.' She smiled, stepping inside. She came to a halt in the living room. 'Oh. You're here.'

Dave McVitie's large sweaty body occupied the armchair in front of the telly. 'Course I'm here,' he told her. 'I live here.'

'Do you ever go out?'

'Yeah, actually,' he retorted.

'To the bookies or the pub, I bet. Not to go to work. All that responsibility is dumped on poor Logan's shoulders.'

Dave's pudgy face creased unpleasantly. 'If you came here just to have a pop at me you can bloody well leave.' He swallowed hard when her eyes narrowed, glad she wasn't holding a frying pan. He'd seen first-hand what she could do with one of those.

'Do you want a cup of tea, Jackie?' said Logan.

'No, thanks.' She smiled. She always had a ready smile for Logan, who was like another son to her. 'I just wanted to ask you a question. What's going on?'

Dave and Logan glanced at each other before looking back at her.

'What do you mean?' said Logan innocently.

'Jamie's being secretive and I'm sure he's hiding something from me. I know it's to do with that scumbag father of his. Now you two are going to tell me what's going on and I want the truth.'

'What makes you think I know?' said Dave. 'The lads don't tell me anything.'

'Because you knew all about that catastrophe with the Lawsons before I did. In fact, you caused it.'

'Not this time. If anything is going on, then it's nothing to do with me.' Dave looked to his son. 'Is anything going on, Logan?'

'No, nothing at all,' he casually replied while Jackie's green gaze bored into him.

'You're lying,' she said. 'Didn't you learn your lesson after last time, Logan McVitie?'

'It's really not my place to talk about it.'

'So, something is going on, then?'

'Well, maybe, but you need to discuss it with Jamie.'

She looked to Dave. 'Aren't you going to say anything?'

'What do you want me to say?'

'Make him tell me what's going on.'

'I can't make him do anything. As you're always telling me, he's a grown man now.'

His tone was filled with so much smugness she wished she had brought her frying pan. She would have loved to smash it into his smirking face. Jackie turned her attention back to Logan. 'Is that all you've got to say on the matter?'

'It is. I'm sorry, Jackie, but it needs to come from Jamie.'

'Then it is something to do with Jason?'

Logan nodded.

'I knew it,' she spat. 'I'll kill him.'

With that she stormed out, slamming the front door shut behind her.

'I hope Jason Gray can run fast.' Dave chuckled.

Lava flowed through Jackie's veins as she made her way home. Jason had got her son and his friends into something so heavy they felt they couldn't tell her and the thought of what that could be terrified her. She'd recognised he was a very different man from the one she'd married. If she held a knife to his throat now he'd take it off her and laugh in her face. She wanted to hunt the bastard down and kill him for what he was doing to her boy, she could see the weight of whatever Jamie had been dragged into was pulling him down. But first she had to find out exactly what was going on and if Jamie refused to tell her she would find a way to make him.

* * *

'Come back, you bastard, I'll break your fucking legs,' yelled Noah Anderson, who was flailing impotently on the floor of his manky flat in Possilpark, battered and bruised.

Mullen smiled. He admired the boy's spirit but that same spirit had meant he'd had to resort to more persuasive techniques to get the information he wanted. It wasn't something he enjoyed or took pleasure in but needs must in his line of work. Noah hadn't been sensible like the others, and just told him what he wanted to know. After some coaxing, Noah had revealed that he'd got hold of a false passport for Allegra in the name of Helen Wilkinson. He hadn't made it for her personally, it had come from someone who lived in Springburn, who Mullen was now going to visit. The name on the passport was all well and good but the passport number would be even better. Then he could get his friend to run a trace. It would be interesting to see if the passport had been used or not.

Mullen drove to the address Noah had given and parked down the street to watch the building, which was a new-build red-brick terraced house with a surprisingly neat garden. It looked well maintained, but, then again, someone who dealt in such a nefarious business wouldn't want to draw attention to themselves by getting complaints from the neighbours. So many would-be criminals made that mistake. They were unable to control their baser impulses, leading to nothing but trouble from the locals and police. Leading a quiet life and being polite to others was the best cover, only most of them were too stupid to understand that.

Mullen noted the child's bike propped up against the wall of the house. It said a lot for the occupant that it hadn't been stolen. It seemed Matt Dawson would be a tougher prospect than the other neds he'd spoken to.

Climbing out of the car, Mullen walked up the garden path and knocked on the door, which was opened by the man Noah had described – tall, toned arms, neatly combed dark hair, wearing a smart dark-blue shirt and blue jeans. The man looked intelligent and together. From inside the house came the sound of a child laughing, accompanied by a cartoon playing on the television.

'Hello?' said Matt politely.

'Mr Dawson?'

'Aye,' he replied, suspicion gathering in his hazel eyes.

'I want some information about a passport you provided someone.'

'I don't know what you mean.'

When Matt attempted to close the door, Mullen put his foot in it. 'I'm not here for trouble,' he said. 'And I'll pay you well for your time.'

'I don't deal in passports.' Matt's eyes widened when Mullen opened his coat to reveal a gun tucked into the waistband of his trousers. He made no move to draw it, but the threat was clear.

'I've no wish to hurt anyone, Mr Dawson, as I said, I only require some information, but I *will* do whatever is necessary to get it. I believe your child is in the house. It would be best to give me what I want so I can be on my way.'

Dawson sighed. 'All right.'

'Very sensible.'

'What do you need to know?'

'Last year you provided a passport in the name of Helen Wilkinson. I need the passport number. Do you keep any records?'

'Yes.'

'I would be very grateful if you could check them for me.'

'I don't need to check them. I store the records in my head,' he replied before reciting a number.

'You're certain that's the one?' said Mullen, impressed by the man's memory.

'Yes. I like to keep track but I don't want to leave a paper trail.'

'You're a very wise man. It would be best for you if you stayed that way,' Mullen replied, sliding his free hand into his coat pocket. 'Relax,' he added when Matt's eyes widened. 'It's just a token of my gratitude. Buy the wean something nice.'

'Thanks,' said Matt, taking the roll of notes Mullen held out to him.

'I would be very appreciative if you never mentioned this conversation to anyone.'

'It's already forgotten.'

'Good. I anticipate you'll do very well in life, Mr Dawson. Thank you for your time.'

Mullen headed back down the garden path, smiling when he heard the front door slam shut behind him followed by the click of the lock. That was usually the effect his presence had on people.

* * *

Cameron roamed the grounds of his home. They were huge, affording complete privacy, which was a relief when he had the press constantly harassing him. Despite the extensive size of his home, it was starting to feel small, especially the gardens after walking round them for what felt to be the one thousandth time. Before all this had started he'd rarely had time to enjoy his garden and at first he'd taken pleasure in exploring all its nooks and crannies – the ornamental koi pond, Japanese garden and huge summerhouse. Now he was sick of the lot of it. He had the mad urge to bulldoze everything and start again just to give himself something different to look at. If this house arrest didn't end soon he was quite sure he'd go mad. He was hoping Mullen could help him end this nightmare, when the man himself called.

'I hope you've got good news for me,' said Cameron into his mobile phone. 'I'm considering tearing up my garden just for something to do.'

'Actually, Mr Abernethy, I do,' he replied. 'One of those men on the list you gave me got hold of a false passport for Allegra in the name of Helen Wilkinson.'

'What?' Cameron rasped, coming to a sudden halt beside the koi pond. 'Has it been used?'

'Yes. It was last used to enter Italy.'

'But Italy's a big country, she could be anywhere, or she might have gone elsewhere in Europe.'

'This is an excellent lead. If she is in Italy then she will need some form of identification to stay in a hotel or hire a car, for instance. It's a starting point to trace her. I'm sending one of my best people out there.'

'No. I want you to go.'

'Mr Abernethy, I can assure you that Natalie is the very best.

She is fluent in Italian, has Italian family and contacts out there. Plus a fellow female is more likely to put Allegra off her guard.'

'So, you think she is alive, then?' he said excitedly.

'It's very possible. I can't be 100 per cent certain that it is her using that false passport. It could have been stolen from her.'

'Fuck,' muttered Cameron.

'Has Allegra been to Italy?'

'Yes, a few times. She knows the language too – she studied it at finishing school.'

'Which parts of the country did she visit? She would probably go somewhere familiar to her, especially if she's feeling scared and alone.'

'Err, she went to Milan and Rome and there was somewhere else, what was it? Oh, yes, Florence. I remember the last one because she kept banging on about the architecture.'

'So you think that's the likeliest place to start out of all the three?'

'Probably, but Allegra is so unpredictable it's hard to know what she'll do. That's the most important thing you need to remember about her.'

'Noted.'

'What will you be doing while Natalie goes to Italy?'

'I'll be watching Jamie Gray.'

12

Jamie jumped up off the couch when the front door slammed shut, and his heart sank when his mother stormed into the front room with a face like thunder. Her furious gaze softened when she saw him.

'All right, sweetheart?' she said.

'Aye, I'm no' bad. There's err...something I need to talk to you about.'

Jackie hoped this meant her son was finally going to confide in her. 'It's to do with your da, isn't it?'

He nodded and looked down at his feet.

'Let's sit down and have a wee blether about it.'

As they sat beside each other on the couch, Jackie took in a few deep breaths to try and keep calm. If she started demanding answers he'd only clam up. His dark eyes were stormy and she could see his toes wiggling in his socks. She could read her boy like a book and he was in trouble.

'Me and the lads,' he began. 'We're in deep.'

'I knew it. Are you in deep because of Jason?'

'Aye.'

'Oh, God. It's drugs, isn't it?'

'No, Maw, it's not, I swear to God.'

'What, then? Weapons? Stolen cars?'

He shook his head. 'Secrets.'

'Blackmail?' she gasped.

'No. He took me to meet someone. They wanted us to deal drugs on the scheme but I said no, we've cleaned this place up, apart from Ephraim. They didn't like that, they got angry so I said because the police didn't bother with the scheme any more it would be a good place to hide secrets.'

'What do you mean by secrets?'

'That's the problem. I'm not sure yet because they haven't given us any secrets to hide, apart from a packet of crisps.'

'A packet of crisps?'

'That was just a test to make sure we were up to the job, which we are. God, I'm explaining this really badly.' He sighed, dragging his hands down his face.

'Start at the beginning,' she said gently.

'I didn't believe Jason knew these people, I thought he was bull-shitting, so he set up a meeting with them to prove he was telling the truth.'

'Them? How many of them were there?'

'Just two. They liked my idea of hiding secrets on the Gallowburn.'

'Who are these mysterious 'they'?'

Jamie took a deep breath. 'The McVays.'

All the blood drained from Jackie's face. 'What?' she cried. 'As in Toni McVay?'

'Aye. I met Toni and her right-hand man, Caesar.'

Jamie had prepared himself for shouting but Jackie remained still and silent, face ashen. 'Are you okay, Maw?' he said when she'd been silent for a full minute.

'The McVays,' she rasped. 'You mean that family of drug dealers and murderers?'

He sighed. 'Aye.'

'Your own father took you to meet a woman who enjoys ripping people's eyeballs out of their heads?'

Jamie just nodded. There was a storm gathering around his mother; he could see the fury glittering in her bright green eyes. The odd thing, though, was her silence. When she was in a temper she shouted and screamed and threw insults about and it worried him that she wasn't doing that now.

'Maw,' he said, putting a gentle hand on her arm. 'You're scaring me...'

She leapt to her feet, face flushing bright red. 'I'll fucking kill him,' she yelled. 'The pathetic, worm-dicked loser is fucking dead.'

'Maw,' exclaimed Jamie, leaping up to follow her when she rushed into the kitchen and began rooting through the drawers. 'What are you doing?'

'Finding something to batter his brains out with,' she snarled, snatching her frying pan out of the cupboard. Her smile was wicked. 'Perfect.'

'Please, Maw,' he said, rushing after her as she stormed towards the front door. 'You cannae do this.'

'Yes, I can.'

He put himself in front of the door. 'Listen to me. He works for Toni McVay. If you go after Jason, she'll go after you.'

'I don't care about that mad cow,' she retorted.

'You should. I've met her and she's insane. Please, Maw, me and Charlie need you.'

This heartfelt plea broke through the red mist and Jackie went still, holding the frying pan limply by her side. Jamie took the opportunity to snatch it from her.

'I knew that man's return would mean something bad for you,' she said, hanging her head. 'He didn't come back to get to know you or to finally be a proper father. He came back to recruit you.' She raised her head, the gesture taking a lot of effort as the sadness swept through her. 'I had such a bad feeling that he'd get you into something heavy, but I didn't think it would be this bad.' She sank onto the couch and sighed. 'The McVays of all people. You had a chance at a good life, Jamie, you're a bright lad with a good heart, but he's taken that from you now and the only person who can free you from it is Toni herself.'

'It might not be so bad, Maw. I've already been paid a few grand just for protecting a packet of crisps. Caesar was so impressed with the way we passed their test that he gave us five grand each. The real secret will be delivered in a few days.'

'Delivered where? Not here, I hope?'

'No. We have somewhere safe, somewhere no one knows about.'

'Where?'

'I can't tell you for your own good.'

Jackie was going to argue, then thought better of it. She didn't want to know.

'I shouldn't have told you all this,' he said. 'But I hate lying to you. That's been the worst part of it all.'

She pulled him into a hug. 'Ever since I fell pregnant with you I wished I'd found you a better father. Never have I felt that more than right now.' She released him and took his face between her hands. 'But if I had, you wouldn't be my Jamie and I wouldn't change you for the world. Now you work for the McVays we're going to be stuck with him.'

'I've already told him not to come round here again and he agreed not to.'

'Even if he does stick to his word, which will be a first, he'll still be hanging around the Gallowburn, he'll still be in your life. You don't know what he's like, Jamie. He's poison. Actually, not even that word is strong enough to describe him.' She paused to think, before continuing. 'He's like one of those fish in the Amazon that swims into your cock and lodges itself there with spikes.'

'Urgh.' Jamie grimaced.

'That's what he is. He got himself jammed in and he'll never leave.'

'I preferred it when you called him poison.' Jamie winced. 'But you see now why you can't go after him? He's a very dangerous man, not just because he works for the McVays, but because of what he's capable of.'

'I get that. He has changed, but in other ways, he's still the same.'

'Me and the lads can handle this and we're already in Toni's good books. This could work out well for us and the money will make life easier.'

'I don't want it,' Jackie said when Jamie placed a roll of notes in her hand.

'Please take it, for me. We need a new cooker and Charlie's school uniform's getting too small for him.'

'I don't like taking this dirty money.'

'Me neither but you deserve nice things and to have an easier life. Get yourself some new clothes, go to the hairdresser...'

'What's wrong with my hair?' She frowned, patting it.

'Nothing, but I know you've been wanting to get it done. Well, now you can. Please, Maw,' he continued when she still looked uncertain. 'For me.'

'Well, okay,' she sighed. 'I'm glad you told me the truth.'

'But you can't tell anyone else.'

'I won't. I'm no' daft.'

'I know.' He smiled.

'You've been carrying all this on your shoulders, as well as Allegra's death and the trial.'

Pain lanced through Jamie. That was something else he was lying to her about.

She patted his face. 'I'm so proud of your strength.'

'I don't get that from my da. I get it from you,' he said, making her smile. 'You should know,' he added. 'Jason bought me a car. Well, technically the McVays did but he brought it round.'

The excitement in his eyes at finally having some transport was such that she couldn't find it in herself to criticise. 'Really?' she said, attempting to muster some enthusiasm. 'What sort of car?'

'A Vauxhall Vectra. It's thirteen years old but they had to give me something that would match our income. They'll give me something newer soon.'

Jackie forced a smile. 'That's great, sweetheart.'

'You really think so?'

She could see how much he wanted and needed her approval and for her to tell him that it would all work out. With everything he had going on, the last thing he needed was for her to get on his case. 'Yes, I do,' she said, hugging him, her heart brimming over with love for him. She was so terrified for his future.

'I'll bring it round to show you.' He grinned when she released him.

With a sad smile, she watched him leap up, stuff his feet into his trainers and pull on his jacket. His enthusiasm meant that he missed the tears shining in her eyes.

Jamie rushed out of the house, ran onto the next street with a grin on his face, the weight of lying to his mother lifted. He couldn't believe she'd taken it so well. He jumped into the car, started the engine and drove it around the block, parking in the space outside their house.

Jackie came out to admire the car, making all the right noises to appease her son while inwardly she was raging. Jason had got her son involved with gangsters, and not just any gangsters but the

McVays, the most feared family in Scotland with close ties to other organised crime families, not just in the UK but around the world. She remembered reading once in the papers they had links to Columbian drug cartels. Her son was in deep and if he wasn't careful he would drown.

*　*　*

Mullen watched Jamie Gray and his mother Jackie from his car that was parked further down the street. Both were looking at a tatty old Vauxhall. Judging by Jackie's face she wasn't very pleased about it, although she was trying to show some enthusiasm and failing. Jamie, however, was so busy enthusing over his crappy car that he didn't notice. Mullen attempted to work out why the fact that her son now had transport didn't make the woman happy. Did the thought of him driving on busy roads make her nervous? Did she think it was a death trap? He forced himself not to jump to conclusions. For all he knew she always looked like that. He thought her rather an attractive woman. Judging by the photos he'd seen of her, she'd lost some weight recently and she had pretty eyes. She was one of those women who had a natural air of dignity about her. Here was a strong woman who should not be underestimated. Jackie Gray was a woman to be respected.

When his phone began to vibrate in his pocket, he took it out and put it to his ear, his gaze not leaving the Grays.

'Mullen,' he said. 'Oh, hello, Mike.' A slow smile spread across his lips. 'Excellent news, thank you.'

He hung up and pondered whether he should call Mr Abernethy with this latest development or visit him in person, and decided it was too important to tell him over the phone.

Mullen watched Jamie get back in the car and drive off while Jackie returned to the house. He let Jamie get a head start before following but Jamie only drove for a couple of minutes before pulling up outside the house of his friend Logan McVitie. They would have to keep, so he drove straight to the Abernethy home, calling Cameron on the way to warn him of his arrival. He'd already got the impression that Cameron was not one for unexpected visitors.

Mullen was greeted at the front door by the slimy son who clumsily attempted to question him about what he was doing for his father. Mullen politely rebuffed all his attempts. Realising he wasn't going to get anywhere, a sulky Fenston showed him into the large lounge. In Mullen's opinion, Cameron was a desperate man. When he'd first contacted him to ask him to find his daughter, Mullen had thought he was a guilty man attempting to find a scrap of evidence to cast doubt on his guilt in the eyes of the jury. Mullen hadn't seriously thought he'd actually find proof Allegra was alive, not until he'd got the details of that false passport.

'What have you found out?' demanded Cameron the second Mullen had closed the lounge door behind him.

Mullen thought it interesting that Cameron wasn't even attempting to be a good host any more. He had no time for niceties. Nor was he trying to hide his emotions.

'The passport allegedly given to Allegra was used a few months ago to get back into the country,' replied Mullen.

Cameron's face turned ashen before immediately morphing into a violent shade of beetroot. Mullen thought that couldn't possibly be good for his heart; the man didn't look very healthy as it was.

'You mean she came back here, to Glasgow?' rasped Cameron.

'Yes. I'm now certain Allegra is the one using the passport as the day she flew into Glasgow was the day of the memorial her friends arranged. She flew in from Italy that morning and flew back that evening. If it had been any other day it would still have been possible someone else was using the passport but that's far too big a coincidence to ignore.'

'Because it's not a coincidence. It was her.' The beetroot colour blossomed into purple. 'The bitch,' Cameron yelled. 'The vicious, conniving, scheming little bitch. We need to get proof it was her. Can you get any security footage from the airport?'

'I'm afraid not. Airports only keep footage for thirty days. Anyway, it would probably be useless even if they had because no doubt Allegra changed her appearance to return to the country.'

'Fuck,' yelled Cameron. 'I bet she came back to see the scheme rat. That bastard knows where she is.'

'Natalie will be flying to Rome in a couple of hours. If Allegra is in Italy she will find her and I've already started watching Jamie Gray.'

'What's the little twat up to?'

'He has a new car. By new, I mean a thirteen-year-old Vauxhall Vectra.'

Cameron snorted. 'I wouldn't use a shit heap like that as a plant pot. What idiot gave that prick a driving licence?'

'I'll be watching him very closely. If he is in contact with Allegra, I will find out.'

'He is, I can feel it. Christ, I can't wait to see the pair of them in the dock.'

'I'm going to approach the mother, Jackie Gray.'

'Jackie?' Cameron frowned. 'That cow won't tell you anything and she won't be easy for you to manipulate. She battered Craig Lawson's head in with a frying pan.'

'I'll be subtle.'

'You're going to romance her, aren't you?' said Cameron, amused by the idea. 'Good luck with that. She looks the type who enjoys squashing men's genitals with her boot heel. If she didn't have two kids I'd have said she was a lezzer.'

'She's my best way into the Gray home.'

'Rather you than me. I bet it's a shithole inside. It probably stinks too.'

Mullen didn't respond to these puerile comments. 'I'll also be continuing covert surveillance on Jamie Gray. I might find something that will damage him in the eyes of the jury, throwing his evidence into doubt.'

'That would be fun,' said Cameron with a grim smile. 'Is there anything I can do to help? I can't go anywhere but I do have resources and contacts.'

'I appreciate the offer, Mr Abernethy, but no, thank you. That's what you're paying me for.'

Cameron sighed with frustration but didn't argue. Mullen wasn't the type to budge.

He turned to the window to look out at the garden he'd been getting so sick of. The urge to destroy it had gone. He was saving up that energy for his bitch of a daughter and her scheme-rat lover.

* * *

Jamie smiled as his dad pulled the BMW into a parking spot at the marina at Inverkip, on the west coast. Jason was actually taking him out on a boat trip. It was the first time they'd ever been on an outing together. Jamie had been tempted to suggest bringing Charlie along, until he'd remembered what his mum had said. He'd expected Jason to suggest it himself, but he hadn't, leaving Jamie once again to wonder if he cared at all about his younger son. It had rankled, but Jamie was so excited about the trip that he hadn't wanted to spoil it by getting into an argument.

They wended their way down the pontoon, which split off in different directions as they wandered through the maze of boats. The view was astonishing, the water clear and blue. Across the water was the mainland curving around the Firth of Clyde, which fed into the Atlantic Ocean, the town of Dunoon and the mountains of the Cowal peninsula visible.

Jamie went rigid when he felt the pontoon swaying beneath his feet.

'You all right, son?' Jason grinned.

'It's moving.'

'That's because it's on water,' Jason replied, grin widening. 'Don't worry, we're nearly at the boat. Want me to hold your hand?'

'No.' Jamie sniffed. 'I'm fine.' He nodded at the three-storey town houses that lined one side of the marina. 'I wouldn't mind one of them.'

'I know, nice, eh? Play your cards right and one day you'll be able to buy one and I mean buy outright. You won't be a slave to a mortgage.'

'Yeah, that'd be great,' he mumbled, knowing his future didn't lie in Scotland. It was in Italy, with Allegra.

'Here we are,' said Jason, coming to a halt before a large white motorboat.

'Awesome.' Jamie grinned. 'It looks like something James Bond would drive.'

'Fortunately we're not going to be chased by villains with machine guns. We're just going out for a nice wee cruise.'

They climbed onto the boat and Jamie felt a bit better now he was off that constantly moving dock. He looked up at the grey sky. 'Do you think it's going to rain?'

'It doesn't matter if it does. We can go in the cabin.'

They motored out of the marina and headed south, the ferry to the island of Bute crossing their path up ahead. Houses and blocks of flats lined the sea front on the coastline to their left as they passed the village of Skelmorlie. Above the flats was a cliff on which more properties sat and Jamie regarded them enviously. Right then he swore to himself that one day he would get his mum a nice place like that. Now he was working for the McVays he had a chance of achieving that dream.

'The old sugar barons built those houses,' Jason told him, indicating one of the older red sandstone buildings. 'There were more but they were knocked down to make way for the flats. They built them so they'd have somewhere nice to stay in the summer and so they could be close by to catch the steamer across the water to Bute from Wemyss Bay. They actually pushed back the tide to build their summer homes because the sea used to reach the bottom of the cliff.'

Jamie smiled as his dad reminded him of his granddad, who had always enjoyed giving him a history lesson.

'Imagine having enough money to push back the sea,' breathed Jason.

Jamie glanced at his dad, not liking the gleam in his eyes. In that moment he recognised how much Jason craved money and power. It meant he would stop at nothing to get what he wanted.

They left Skelmorlie behind, the houses and blocks of flats morphing into fields.

'We're going a bit far out, aren't we?' said Jamie as the coastline got smaller. 'Are we going to Bute?'

'No, we're no' and don't worry, we're perfectly safe.'

Jamie spotted a small fishing boat not much bigger than their own boat this far out too, reassuring him a little. 'We're getting a bit close to that other boat,' he commented.

'Stop worrying, Jamie, I know what I'm doing,' said Jason, who appeared to be steering the boat directly at the fishing boat, which was being stalked by a flock of seagulls.

'Da,' Jamie said, warning in his voice, gripping onto the edge of the boat and bracing himself for impact when it appeared they were going to collide. To his surprise, the fishing boat pulled up alongside them.

'All right, Jason,' called the tubby, bearded fisherman who looked like a cliché in his woollen jumper, sou'wester and yellow waterproofs.

'How's it going, Colin?' Jason replied, switching off the engine.

'Not so bad. It looks all clear.'

'Nice one. Let's do this quickly.'

'Do what?' Jamie frowned.

Both men ignored him.

Jamie leaned over the rail to peer into the fishing boat before recoiling from the fishy smell.

'What the hell are you doing?' he demanded when Colin opened up a hatch in the deck and started to toss Jason wrapped brick-sized packages. His dad had opened up the metal storage box on deck and was catching them and neatly stacking them inside.

Once again both men failed to respond. Jamie jumped when an enormous seagull landed on the rail beside him and squawked loudly, as though it too wanted answers.

'Those are drugs, aren't they?' exclaimed Jamie.

'Never mind all that,' said Jason as he worked. 'Help me put them away.'

'Piss off. I'm no' touching them.'

'Weans,' chuckled Colin. 'I'm glad I never had any.'

'How many more?' Jason asked him as he continued to catch and stack.

'Another five.'

Jason had put away another four bricks when Colin said, 'Oh, shit, it's the coastguard.'

'Crap,' exclaimed Jason, turning to look at the orange boat. 'They're still a distance away. Give me the last two.'

Colin chucked them to him and Jason stacked them inside the storage box, slammed the lid shut and padlocked it.

He straightened up and looked to Jamie. 'You said you can swim, didn't you?'

'Aye, why?'

Jamie released a cry of surprise as his dad shoved him in the chest, knocking him backwards into the water. The breath was squeezed from his body as the dark, icy water closed over his head. Kicking his legs, he broke the surface and gasped for breath.

'Jamie, the ladders,' yelled a voice.

He looked up to see Jason pointing to the ladders at the side of the boat. Jamie swam over to them, grabbed them and hauled himself up onto the first step. The weight of his waterlogged clothes made the task extremely difficult and the cold was sucking all the strength from his limbs.

Jason grasped his hands and pulled him up the last few steps. Jamie collapsed onto the deck where he lay shivering and shaking, trying to catch his breath as the orange rib pulled up alongside them.

'What's going on here?' demanded the suspicious coastguard.

'My son,' said Jason, wrapping a blanket around Jamie. 'He fell overboard. This man saw it happen and kindly came over to see if he could help.'

The coastguard looked to Colin, who nodded.

'Is that what happened?' the coastguard asked Jamie.

Jamie looked up at his dad, whose eyes were heavy with warning. 'Y...yeah,' he stammered, shaking violently with cold. 'It's my... first time... boat... lost my balance.'

Sympathy filled the coastguard's eyes. 'Do you need any medical treatment?'

'No, thanks. I'll be fine,' he said, teeth chattering.

'If you're sure?'

'I... am.'

The coastguard's eyes danced across the deck of both boats but saw nothing suspicious. 'All right, you,' he told Colin. 'On your way.'

Colin nodded and gave him a smile and a salute before starting the engine and steering the boat around theirs before heading south.

'You'd better get back to shore and get that lad warmed up before he gets hypothermia,' the coastguard told Jason.

'I will, thank you. We'll head straight back to Inverkip.'

'Good.'

'Come on,' said Jason, helping Jamie to his feet. 'Let's get you inside.'

They entered the cabin, Jason closing the door behind them to keep out the cold air, breathing a sigh of relief when he saw the orange rib speed away. 'Thank God,' he sighed. 'Get those wet clothes off,' he told Jamie. 'I've got some dry ones you can wear.'

He turned up the heater and Jamie started to peel off his sodden clothes. It was only when he unfastened his jeans that realisation struck.

'My phone,' exclaimed Jamie, pulling out, not his usual phone or even the burner Toni had given him, but the one Allegra had sent him. 'Oh, Christ,' he exclaimed when he saw it was water-logged. 'It's switched itself off and it won't come back on.'

'Take the SIM card out,' Jason told him. 'If you can dry that out your data might be saved.'

Jamie frantically tore the back off, which wasn't easy as his fingers were almost numb, and he took out the SIM card. 'It's soaked,' he cried.

'Not to worry, I'll buy you a new one.'

'But this one can't be replaced.'

'Why not? It's just a phone.'

'You don't understand,' snarled Jamie as despair clawed at him. His one link to Allegra had been ruined.

'Why? What's so special about that phone?'

'Nothing,' he muttered.

Jason frowned at him, eyes flicking suspiciously from his son to the phone, before he opened a cupboard and produced a pack of tissues. 'Wrap the SIM card in one of these to dry it off. They're made to be pretty tough, so hopefully it should still work.'

Jamie snatched the packet off him, pulled out a tissue and carefully wrapped the SIM card in it with hands shaking with cold, before placing it on the small table.

'Get the rest of those wet things off before you catch your death,' said Jason.

Jamie peeled the rest of his clothes off, even his socks and underwear, and pulled on the thick wool jumper and blue jeans his dad held out to him, As the jeans were way too wide Jason gave him a belt, which he had to fasten at the last notch just to get them to stay up. Once Jamie was dressed, Jason wrapped another blanket around his shoulders.

'I'm sorry about that, son,' he said. 'But I had no choice.'

'You could have thrown yourself in.' Jamie glowered at him, the ruined phone still clutched in his hand. One of the very few things he had of Allegra and his own dad had ruined it.

'Y...you could have warned me,' he said, still shivering uncontrollably.

'If I had, your reaction wouldn't have seemed natural. You had to appear surprised for it to work. Do you want a coffee?' his dad asked, switching on the kettle in the small galley kitchen.

As Jamie warmed up with the help of the coffee and the heater, he slowly filled with hurt. His dad hadn't wanted to spend time with him. He'd just wanted an excuse if he was caught with that other boat. What had promised to be a good day that would leave him with some happy memories had been destroyed and Jamie was left feeling like a stupid little boy with a father who clearly didn't give a shit about him. Well, Jason had shown his true colours and what his priorities were. He'd chosen drugs over his own son and for that Jamie would never forgive him.

13

Jamie remained in sullen silence for the short journey back to the marina. Jason continued to point out various landmarks, oblivious to the fact that his son wasn't responding, or maybe he simply didn't care.

It was with a sense of relief that Jamie jumped off the boat back onto the pontoon.

'What about...?' began Jamie, nodding at the storage box where the drugs were hidden.

'Someone will be along shortly to take the boat up to Glasgow. Our job is done.'

'It's not my fucking job,' snapped Jamie. 'You tricked me into it.'

'I was trying to show you the ropes, Jamie...'

'This is fuck all to do with me,' he hissed. Despite his fury, he still had the presence of mind to keep his voice down. Although no one appeared to be within earshot you never knew who was around.

'I'm not discussing this here,' said Jason. 'Let's get back to Gallowburn. You need a hot shower and a warm meal. Here's your clothes,' he added, holding out a carrier bag containing the sodden bundle.

Jamie snatched it from him and stormed down the dock, his trainers making an annoying squeaking sound. As they exited through the gate back into the car park, Jamie whipped round and drove his fist into his father's face. A stunned Jason was knocked off his feet and as he lay groaning on the ground Jamie patted him down and took his car keys.

'Maw was right,' said Jamie, looking down at him coldly. 'You are a fucking loser.'

Jamie ran over to the BMW, unlocked it, jumped in and tossed the damp carrier bag onto the plush leather of the passenger seat.

Jason hauled himself to his feet and chased after the car as Jamie tore off.

Jamie smiled grimly as he watched his father's reflection getting smaller in the rear-view mirror before vanishing altogether.

Before heading back to Glasgow, Jamie stopped at a phone shop in Greenock to see if the phone could be saved. He was told it couldn't but to his relief the SIM card was still working, so he bought a cheap pay as you go. If his dad had ruined his only connection to Allegra he would have hunted him down with a shotgun.

It was only when he pulled onto the Gallowburn that Jamie realised he wasn't even insured to drive his dad's car. He parked it in the small car park outside Di Giorgio's and switched off the engine. He gazed at the restaurant, recalling his first date with Allegra, his hand going to the ring around his neck.

'I wish you were here,' he murmured to himself. She'd know exactly how to handle his father, although he was pretty sure she'd be proud of him for nicking his car and leaving him stranded.

Before getting out, he decided to have a rummage in the glovebox. Jason was keeping a lot from him and he wanted to find out what that was.

His blood turned to ice, as cold as if he were back in the water, when he found a handgun hidden beneath the manual for the in-car entertainment system.

'Jesus,' he breathed before slamming the glovebox shut. For good measure he pulled the sleeve of the jumper over his hand to wipe his prints off the glovebox, steering wheel, handbrake, gearbox and door. He got out, closed and locked the car before wiping the handles of both the driver and passenger doors, before dropping the keys down a drain and walking the rest of the way home.

Although it was only a few minutes' walk, halfway there he started to shake with cold again. His coat was in the carrier bag and was still soaking wet and his feet felt like blocks of ice. The blue sky he'd so enjoyed on the boat trip had gone, the Glasgow sky grey and threatening.

'Oh, that's just fucking marvellous,' he exclaimed when large, cold drops of rain started to fall.

The brief pleasure of taking Jason's car faded with each step until he felt truly miserable, as well as furious and humiliated about being used. The squelch his trainers made only blackened his mood even more, as did the rain that was growing heavier, soaking the dry clothes he'd changed into.

He stormed into the house, shivering and dripping water all over the floor, angrily kicking off his trainers.

'Hi, love.' Jackie smiled, putting aside the book she was reading. 'How was your trip?'

'I don't want to talk about it,' Jamie muttered, dumping the carrier bag – which was now leaking water – in the kitchen and striding for the stairs. 'I'm going for a shower.'

Jackie's heart sank. Obviously the trip Jamie had had such high hopes for hadn't gone as planned.

She got up to investigate the bag he'd left in the kitchen, puzzled when she pulled out a bundle of wet clothes. She recognised them as the clothes he'd gone out in that morning. Next she examined his trainers, which were similarly wet. Had he fallen overboard?

After putting the clothes in the washing machine and placing the trainers on the radiator to dry, Jackie anxiously waited for Jamie to emerge from the shower.

When he finally reappeared wearing his thickest jumper and jogging bottoms, hair damp, she said, 'What happened? And don't say nothing because I've seen your wet clothes and shoes.'

He sighed and sank onto the couch, curling up into a ball, looking so unhappy her heart broke.

'I don't want to talk about it,' he muttered.

'You went into the water, didn't you?'

He nodded sullenly.

'Are you hurt?'

'No, but I cannae get warm,' he replied, wrapping his arms around his chest.

'I'll make you a cup of tea,' she said, getting to her feet. 'Do you want something hot to eat?'

'Aye, please.'

When he stared down at his hands, pulling a loose thread on the cuff of his left sleeve, she knew no more information would be forthcoming, so she went into the kitchen to prepare his food. He was an adult so she couldn't force him to talk, but clearly something bad had happened on that boat.

As she put the lasagne in the oven, tutting when it took a few goes to get the bloody thing to light, a horrifying thought occurred to her. She slammed the oven door shut and rushed back into the living room.

'Did you do something to Jason?' she said.

'You what?' He frowned.

'You didn't drown him, did you? I don't care about him. I just don't want anything bad to happen to you because of him.'

Despite how miserable he felt, Jamie laughed. 'No, I didnae drown the prick. He's fine, but I did nick his car and leave him stranded at the marina. Then I dumped his car outside Di Giorgio's.'

'Good, but why did you do that? You were so looking forward to that trip.'

His smile dropped. 'It wasn't like I thought it would be.'

'Is he the reason you ended up in the water? Did the bastard push you in?'

'Please, Maw, I really don't want to talk about it or even think about it ever again.'

'He had an ulterior motive for that boat trip, didn't he? Jason Gray does nothing unless he can gain from it, but why push you into the water? What would that get him?'

Jamie refused to reply, picked up the remote control and switched on the television, avoiding her searching gaze.

'I wish you'd confide in me Jamie,' she said. 'After what you told me about the McVays, surely you can tell me about this?'

'Leave it, Maw,' he muttered, keeping his gaze on the television.

'Why won't you tell me?'

He looked at her. 'Because I feel like a fucking idiot for thinking my own father would want a real relationship with me,' he yelled.

The pain in his dark eyes brought a lump to her throat. 'I'm sorry it turned out that way,' she said gently. 'I'd hoped I was wrong.'

'Well, you weren't. He's a fucking waste of space, end of story,' Jamie said, grinding the heels of his palms against his eyes.

Jackie was about to comfort him when the sound of footsteps on the stairs alerted them both to Charlie's presence. Jamie looked up and forced a smile.

'All right, wee man?' he asked his little brother.

'Maw said you went on a boat,' said Charlie, eyes sparkling with excitement. 'What was it like?'

'Fun but cold,' replied Jamie with as much enthusiasm as he could muster, which wasn't very much.

'I want to go on a boat.'

'I'll take you one day.'

'When?'

'When the weather gets warmer.'

'I can't wait.' Charlie grinned.

Jamie envied his little brother. Their father was a stranger to him, so he'd never once been let down by him. Jamie would love to be free of that pain.

'Can I watch my cartoons?' said Charlie.

'Here you go,' said Jamie, handing him the remote control.

With Charlie in the room, Jackie was forced to drop the subject of the boat trip. After serving Jamie his lasagne and a cup of tea, she said she was popping to her friend Tricia's and asked Jamie if he could watch Charlie.

'Aye, fine, Maw,' he replied, tucking into his food.

'Thanks, love.' She smiled, kissing the top of his head. On her way out she ruffled Charlie's hair, making him grin. She paused at the door to look back at them sitting together on the couch watching television. Her beautiful boys.

Instead of heading to Tricia's, though, she went in the opposite direction and walked the few streets to Raymond's Rolls. She took a table by the window with a cup of tea and a doughnut to watch Jason's BMW, which was still where Jamie had abandoned it.

Four cups of tea and two doughnuts later, Jason finally turned up. Jackie dumped the money on the table and rushed out, racing across the street as he got in the car. She yanked open the passenger door and jumped in beside him.

'Jackie,' he exclaimed, eyes lighting up. 'It's great to see you.'

'Well, it's not great to see you,' she retorted. 'I want to know what you did to my boy. He came home freezing cold and upset and he refused to talk about it.'

'I see,' Jason said slowly.

'Well, I don't, and I want fucking enlightening right now.'

'All right, calm down, hen.'

'I am not your hen,' she said, jabbing her finger in his face. 'Whatever you did to Jamie hurt him badly. He's back at the house in bits.'

'It was just a misunderstanding, that's all, and he's a grown man. He doesn't need you to fight his battles for him any more. He's perfectly capable of fighting them himself,' he said, gesturing to the left side of his face, which was swollen and bruised.

'He did that to you?'

'Yes. Our boy has one hell of a right hook. He nearly knocked me out, which isn't easy to do.'

'Because you've got a thick head,' she retorted. 'Now you're going to tell me exactly what happened on that boat. I know my Jamie and he doesn't get depressed for no reason.'

'Look,' Jason sighed. 'I didn't want to embarrass the lad any more than he already has been, but I steered the boat a little erratically back into the marina. I caught the edge of the dock and he fell in. You know how self-conscious lads that age are. They get easily embarrassed. He got angry and blamed me.'

Jackie's eyes narrowed. 'My boy does not hit people and nick their cars because he gets a bit embarrassed.'

'Well, maybe *our* boy has a side you don't know about,' Jason said, leaning into her. 'He hit me and left me stranded. I had to get the bus back to my flat so I could get my spare car keys, then I had to get another bus here. He's caused me no end of trouble today but I'm being understanding because I know he's going through a lot, what with the court case and losing Allegra.'

'Yes, he is going through a lot and all he wanted was a fun day out doing something he's never done before with his da and you couldn't even give him that. I don't believe all that crap about an accident. You pushed him into the water for some twisted reason of your own.'

'How can you be so sure? Don't you think his fiancée being murdered on top of almost being killed himself is bound to change him? No one can come through something like that unscathed.' He leaned in even closer, so their lips almost touched. 'There's a darkness inside our son,' he whispered. 'And it was put there by the Abernethys.'

'Not the Abernethys,' she retorted. 'Just Cameron. Allegra gave him nothing but joy and love, something you wouldn't understand.'

'And I'm working on changing that. I didn't mean for him to fall in the water, Jackie. I just wanted a nice day out with Jamie.'

'Well, it seems you've ruined any chance you had of forming a relationship with him, if that is really what you want, because he hates you more than ever now. Well done, Jason, another success. From now on you stay away from both *my* kids. If you go near either of them ever again, I will make you regret it. I'm also seeing a solicitor about a divorce. I want shot of you for good.'

When she moved to open the door, Jason grabbed her arm.

'Get off me,' she yelled.

He grabbed Jackie's face in both hands and kissed her, but she shoved him in the chest and slapped him hard across the face.

'I still want you, Jackie,' he breathed, dark eyes piercing. 'I never stopped loving you.'

Her lip curled. 'Never stopped? I don't think you ever started. You're incapable of loving anyone but yourself.'

'I know all you've ever wanted is a family.'

'I have a family.'

'Not a proper one.'

'I don't need a man to complete my family. We're doing very well as we are.'

'Don't tell me you don't get lonely, Jackie. Jamie said you've had dates but no one's ever really stuck around.'

'Because I don't need anyone except my boys.'

'Every woman has needs,' he said, reaching out to touch her face. 'You're still a looker and I love your fight.'

'I had no choice but to fight when I married a waster,' she said, slapping his hand away. 'You're not here to win your family back, you're here to drain us dry. I know you've got Jamie in deep with gangsters.'

His gaze hardened. 'He told you?'

'Aye, he did. Don't look so surprised. Children tell their parents things when they share a close relationship.'

'He shouldn't have told you that,' he said, eyes flashing.

'Well, he did, but don't worry, I'll keep my mouth shut.'

'Don't you see this is a good thing for him? He's in danger from Cameron Abernethy and the Lawsons. Craig wants revenge for being put back in prison.'

'Craig and Cameron can be beaten but how do we beat the McVays?' Her eyes filled with tears. 'You've put a noose around Jamie's neck as surely as Cameron and Craig did when they tried to hang him from the hanging tree, only he can't take this one off. I hated you before, Jason Gray, but now my feelings go beyond hatred. If I had a gun in my hand I'd shoot you in the head right here, right now.'

'I know you don't mean that, Jackie. You loved me once.'

'You're right, I did, many years ago before you turned into a violent, drunken bully. Then my love turned into loathing and disgust. Despite your flash car and expensive suit, you're still the pathetic little man you were back then.'

He grabbed her by the face with one hand and squeezed, making her wince. 'You never did know when to shut that gob of yours, did you, Jackie?' he snarled.

'There's the real Jason,' she said, eyes mocking. 'No matter how hard you try you'll never be anything more than a weak bully.' She could see he was contemplating further violence. 'Go on, Jason,' she goaded. 'Beat me up. Then Jamie and his friends will come after you with everything they have. They might be young but they'd tear you apart. Unlike you, I've seen up close what they can do. I wonder what your new employer would say about the disruption to business?'

He pushed her away with an irritated sigh. 'Get out, Jackie, while you still can.'

'I'm going. I don't want to stay near you one second longer than I have to. But keep away from Jamie. I won't warn you again.'

His upper lip curled. 'What can you possibly do to me?'

'Try me and find out. You're not the only one who's changed,' she said before pushing open the door and getting out, slamming it shut as hard as she could.

As she stormed away she massaged her face, which ached from where he'd grabbed her. Jason had shown his true colours. He wasn't interested in his family and he was still the same violent scumbag he'd always been.

And he was going down.

* * *

Mullen watched Jackie Gray stalk away from the car with interest. He'd witnessed the altercation between her and her husband. Although he had no idea what it had been about, he felt sure Jamie had been the topic of conversation. Mullen had watched Jamie and his father return to the marina and Jamie punch his dad and take his car. He'd then followed Jamie to the phone shop and then back to Gallowburn. The lad had been so consumed by whatever had happened on the water that he hadn't noticed he was being tailed. Mullen enjoyed covert surveillance, looking into other people's lives. Experience had taught him never to assume anything, so he didn't know why Jamie had suddenly turned on his father. It was obvious to Mullen that Jason Gray was bad news; he'd met plenty like him in his time. How he wished he'd been able to follow them out onto the water, but he would have stood out too much and blown his cover.

He watched Jackie storm around the corner and vanish from view. She'd held her own against a violent man. It seemed he'd been correct in his judgement that she was a woman to respect. He was going to enjoy getting close to her. The question was, how should he go about it?

* * *

Jackie told Jamie nothing about her confrontation with his father because she didn't think it would help. Thankfully Jason stayed away from them for the rest of the day, while Jamie remained sullen and morose.

At seven o'clock that evening, Jamie got a call from Logan telling him he and the rest of the Blood Brothers were in the pub. Thinking he could do with drowning his sorrows, Jamie told him he was on his way and he set off on the short walk to The Bonnie Brae.

He'd only just turned the corner onto the next street from his home when he heard running footsteps behind him. Jamie spun round, pulling his bike chains from his coat pockets, drawing back the right one as he turned, sending it into a wide arc – a move he'd got down to a fine art – and whipped it across the face of the hooded figure sneaking up behind him carrying a baseball bat. The figure's head snapped sideways, blood erupting from his mouth and spraying across the wall of the house they were standing beside.

Jamie lashed out with the chain in his left hand, hitting a second attacker across the chest, who shrieked and fell backwards.

Strong arms wrapped around Jamie's chest, pinning his arms to his sides and he was held as a fourth man, face likewise obscured by a hood, appeared in front him. As the man drew back his fist to punch him, Jamie kicked him in the stomach and as the man doubled up Jamie kicked him in the face and he fell. Jamie threw back his head, catching the man holding him on the bridge of the nose. There was a satisfying crunch and Jamie was released. He turned and struck the man in the face with the bike chain.

The first man he'd knocked down had got back to his feet and pulled a knife, which glinted in the streetlights. He lashed out, catching Jamie on the left upper arm; he grimaced as the blade nicked his skin. He slammed both chains into his assailant's hand, forcing him to drop the weapon.

Jamie glanced over his shoulder and groaned when he saw two more men charging up to him.

* * *

Mullen smiled from the warmth and comfort of his car as he watched Jamie Gray pulverise his attackers all by himself. The lad was a terror. Mullen had considered setting up an attack such as this using his own people so he could charge in and save the day, but now someone else was doing it for him and Jamie appeared to have little need of saving. However, when two more men pelted down the street towards Jamie, both of them carrying knives, he decided now was the time to intervene. Cameron Abernethy would not be happy if his best lead to Allegra was stabbed to death in the street.

'Oy,' yelled Mullen, jumping out of his car.

While one of the pair started to attack Jamie, who neatly dodged all the knife thrusts, his friend turned to Mullen and waved his knife aggressively.

'Fuck off, old man,' he yelled at him.

Mulled raised an eyebrow. 'Old man? I'm only forty-four.'

'That's fucking ancient,' he spat. 'Now do one before you get hurt.'

'I'll show you ancient,' replied a cool Mullen.

He grabbed the boy's arm and twisted, enjoying his screech of pain before punching him in the face. The boy's eyes rolled up to the heavens before he toppled backwards.

Mullen looked to Jamie, who was clearly tired after fighting the other four and he was favouring his left leg.

Mullen swept Jamie's assailant's legs out from under him and kicked him in the face, knocking him out.

'Cheers, pal,' panted Jamie.

'No problem,' Mullen replied. 'Are you all right?'

'I just got nicked,' he said, clamping a hand to his injured arm.

'I can take you to hospital,' he said, gesturing to his car parked across the street.

'No need, my maw can patch me up. She's done it often enough.'

'Where do you live?'

'Just around the corner. I can get there on my own, thanks.'

'I'll drive you.'

'No need, I'm fine.'

'You don't look fine,' said Mullen as Jamie's left leg went out from under him and he fell against the wall. 'And what if there are more of them waiting for you?'

Jamie chewed his lip, not wanting a stranger to know where he lived, but if anyone else jumped him he wouldn't be able to fight them off. 'All right, thanks, pal.'

'You're welcome.'

'I need to see who they are first,' said Jamie, stuffing his bike chains back into his pockets and pulling back the hoods of one of his assailants. 'Fucking Lawsons,' he spat.

'Friends of yours?'

'God, no.'

'You okay?' he asked as Jamie winced.

'I broke my leg last year,' he said, slowly straightening up. 'It aches sometimes and it started hurting when I kicked that dobber. I would have used my right leg instead but I cannae put all my weight on my left leg.'

'Let's get you to the car so you can sit down,' said Mullen, striding across the road, Jamie slowly hobbling after him.

He held the passenger door open for Jamie while he struggled in. The lad was clearly in pain from his injured arm and leg, but he didn't utter a single sound to show it, earning Mullen's respect. He had to admire how tough Jamie Gray was.

Once he was in, Mullen closed the door, walked around the car and got into the driver's seat, leaving the Lawsons groaning on the pavement.

'Where did you learn to fight like that?' Jamie asked him as he started the engine.

'I served for eleven years in the Royal Marines.'

'Impressive.'

'So were you,' replied Mullen,. 'You took down four of them alone. I didn't think I needed to intervene, until I saw the other two.'

'If my leg hadn't started playing up, I could have taken them on too.'

'You've got some talent, but it didn't look like you've had formal training. You learnt to fight on the street, didn't you?'

'Aye. You've no' much choice if you live around here.'

'I can imagine. Which way am I going?'

'Turn left at the end of the street and my house is halfway down.'

Mullen put the car into gear and set off. 'My name's Scott Kendrick,' he said, using one of his well-established aliases. 'What's yours?'

'Jamie Gray. So, what were you doing on the Gallowburn? I've never seen you around here before.'

'I'm on business. I'm a pharmaceutical rep and I paid a visit to the local health centre.'

'It's a bit late in the day for that,' said Jamie suspiciously. 'It shut over an hour ago.'

'I stopped for something to eat at the fast-food place near it then I got lost. It's a bit of a maze around here.'

'Aye, it is,' replied Jamie, relaxing as his suspicions were allayed.

'I pulled over to put my home address into the satnav. It seems you have someone watching over you, Jamie. I could have chosen any street to stop on, but I chose that one.'

'Maybe you're right,' Jamie replied, gritting his teeth together, sweat beading on his forehead as the ache in his leg and the pain in his arm intensified. 'It's that house there,' he said, gesturing out of the window.

Mullen indicated and pulled the car up outside the house next door as Jamie's own car was parked directly outside the Gray home.

'I'll help you out,' said Mullen, shoving open his door and getting out. He assisted Jamie out of the car and up the path to the front door. The lad seemed to be in even more pain and it was difficult for him to walk, one hand clamped to his injured arm to stop the bleeding.

Jamie pushed open the front door, unaware of Mullen's sly smile.

14

'Oh, my God,' cried a voice. 'What happened?'

Jackie rushed up to her son and Mullen found himself up close with the Gray matriarch.

'It was the Lawsons,' breathed Jamie. 'They cornered me on the next street. Don't worry, we beat the crap out of them.'

'For God's sake, haven't they learned their lesson yet?'

'Where's Charlie? I don't want him seeing me like this.'

'In the bath.' Jackie frowned at Mullen. 'Who are you?'

Mullen stared into a pair of dazzling green eyes. She looked younger up close and he thought how attractive she was. That air of strength and dignity he'd spotted in her was almost palpable. 'My name's Scott Kendrick,' he replied.

'He helped me with the Lawsons, Maw,' said Jamie. 'And he brought me home.'

'In that case, I'm very grateful to you, Mr Kendrick,' said Jackie. She looked back at her son. 'Oh, God, Jamie, you're bleeding. Let's get you into the kitchen.'

Mullen helped Jamie limp through the house. Contrary to what Cameron Abernethy had assumed, the Gray home was clean and

tidy and the scent of cinnamon hung in the air. The only downside
he could see was that it was small.

He assisted Jamie to sink into a chair at the dining table.

'What happened to your arm?' Jackie asked her son as she
helped him off with his coat.

'It was a blade,' he muttered, knowing the effect that news
would have on her.

Mullen watched all the colour drain from Jackie Gray's face and
for a moment he thought she might faint. 'Are you okay?' he
asked her.

She shook herself out of it. 'Fine. Do you need to go to hospital,
Jamie?'

'Naw. You can patch me up. I don't want word getting out, it'll
only bring the bloody press back to our door.'

She helped him off with his coat and then his jumper, Jamie
wincing as he slowly pulled his arm out of the sleeve.

Jackie rolled up the sleeve of the white T-shirt he wore under
the jumper. 'Christ, Jamie,' she breathed when she saw the gash in
his arm. 'This is beyond me. It needs stiches and I'm no' a doctor.'

'If you would allow me,' said Mullen. 'I've had medical training.'

Jackie glanced questioningly at Jamie, who nodded. 'All right,
then,' she said, taking a step back.

'The wound is only superficial,' said Mullen, examining Jamie's
arm. 'Fortunately your thick coat and jumper took most of the
damage and the bleeding's already stopped. Do you have an adhesive dressing?' he asked Jackie.

'I've got an all-singing, all-dancing first-aid kit,' she told him.
'My boys are always getting into scrapes, especially Jamie, so we
need it in this house.'

She retrieved it from a cupboard, dumped it on the table and
opened it up.

'That's just what I need,' said Mullen, plucking a wrapped

dressing from the box. He pulled on the latex gloves that were part of the kit, before getting to work. 'I'll clean the wound first,' he said, opening up a sterile wipe and gently wiping away the blood.

'It doesn't look anywhere near as bad now the blood's been cleaned off,' said Jackie with a shaky breath of relief.

Mullen glanced her way. He recognised the anxiety in her eyes. She wasn't just upset because her son had been injured; she wasn't the type to go to pieces in a crisis. It was the fact that a knife had been mentioned. During the research he'd done on her he'd discovered that she'd witnessed her brother being stabbed to death in the street. That would have an effect on anyone.

Jamie winced as Mullen cleaned his wound and smeared antiseptic cream on it, but he refused to utter a single sound of pain. Mullen had to hand it to the boy, he was bloody tough.

'This adhesive dressing will join the separated skin,' said Mullen as he wrapped it around Jamie's arm. 'Taking it off will smart a bit because it's tough stuff and doesn't come off easily, so make sure the wound has fully healed before removing it.'

'I will,' replied Jamie. 'Thanks, pal.'

'You're welcome. Now you need to rest that arm.'

'Go and rest on the couch,' Jackie told her son. 'Do you want a brew?'

'I'd rather have a bevy.'

'Not a good idea,' said Mullen.

'Fine, I'll have a tea,' Jamie sighed. 'I'd better let the lads know I won't be going to the pub tonight,' he said, slowly rising from the chair and limping into the living room.

'Put your leg up on the couch,' Jackie told him.

'I will, Maw,' he called back.

'Would you like a brew too?' Jackie asked Mullen.

'I don't want to impose,' he replied, pleased with how the evening was progressing.

'It's the very least I can do after what you did for Jamie.'

'In that case, I'll have a cup of tea, please. Milk, no sugar.'

'I've got some snowballs too, if you're interested?'

'My favourite.' He smiled. It was true, the small round coconut-covered cakes were his favourite, but he didn't indulge often because he liked to watch his weight. In his job fitness was essential.

'So,' said Jackie as she filled the kettle at the sink. 'Can I call you Scott?'

'Please do.'

'Thanks for helping my boy, Scott. He's been through a lot lately – you may have seen him in the papers – and this fresh nonsense is the last thing he needs.'

'Ah, that's why he's familiar. The Abernethy case.'

She slammed the kettle onto its base and switched it on. 'Don't go mentioning that to him, it only upsets him.'

'I wouldn't dream of it.'

'Thank you. I wish the bloody press would be so understanding.'

'Have they been giving you a hard time?'

'It's been a nightmare, from the moment Jamie was hit by that car driven by one of Cameron Abernethy's cronies. It eased off a bit after Abernethy was put in prison. Then the idiots let him out and it started up again. Now Jamie's given evidence it's quietened down but I know the sodding cockroaches will come back when the verdict is given.' She surprised herself by how quickly and easily she'd opened up to this stranger. 'But you don't want to hear about all that.'

'It sounds like you needed to get it off your chest.'

'Perhaps. So, tell me about yourself, Scott.'

'There's not much to tell, really. I'm a pharmaceutical rep. Single, no children. Ex-Royal Marine.'

'Royal Marine?' she said, eyes sparkling. Jackie had always liked a uniform. 'That's very interesting. How did you go from that to a rep?'

'I sustained an injury that meant I was unable to continue serving.'

'What injury? Oh, I'm sorry, I shouldn't have asked that. I can be a nosy cow sometimes.'

'It's all right. It was a bullet that did it. Unfortunately it ended my career.'

Although she was incredibly curious, Jackie didn't push him for details, sensing it was an uncomfortable topic for him. 'That must have been very difficult for you.'

'It was, but one thing they teach you in the military is how to adapt. That training helped me get on with my life.'

'That's good to hear.' She smiled.

After Jason's return, Jackie had been put off men for life, but she liked this one. He was strong and upright, and it helped that he was very handsome.

'What on earth is that?' said Mullen when there was the crash of the front door followed by a cacophony of voices.

'That'll be Jamie's friends,' replied Jackie, loading up the tea tray with the teapot, cups and a plate of snowballs.

'You mean the Blood Brothers? I read about them in the newspaper.'

'That's them. The media made them out to be ferocious, and they can be when they want, but they're all good boys at heart.'

Mullen couldn't believe how well tonight was going. It couldn't have gone better if he'd planned it himself. Everyone he wanted to meet all together in the one house.

'What the bloody hell happened?' demanded Digger. Before Jamie could reply, he continued, 'Fucking Lawsons. I'll rip their heids off and kick them down the street.' This statement was accompanied by a lot of muscle flexing.

'They jumped me around the corner,' replied Jamie. 'But me and Scott fought them off.'

'Scott?'

They looked round when Mullen stepped into the room.

'Who the bloody hell are you?' demanded Digger.

'Don't be so rude,' Jackie told him, carrying in the tea tray and placing it on the coffee table. 'He helped Jamie.'

'Aye, sorry, pal,' said Digger, extending his hand to Mullen. 'Cheers for that.'

'It was no problem,' replied Mullen, shaking his proffered hand. 'And please, call me Scott.'

'I'll bet it was no problem. The Lawsons are a bunch of wee lassies.'

'Are you okay, Jamie?' Logan asked him.

'Aye, I'm all right,' he replied. 'I got slashed on the arm and I hurt my leg kicking one of them, but other than that I'm fine.'

'Slashed? You mean they were carrying knives?'

'A couple of them were.'

'Jesus,' breathed Logan, wrapping his arm around Jackie. She smiled and patted his hand.

'Oh, quality.' Gary grinned. 'Snowballs.'

Jackie slapped his hand away when he reached for one. 'Scott gets first pick after what he did tonight,' she said, picking up the plate and holding it out to him.

'Thank you.' Mullen smiled, selecting one, and Jackie handed him a saucer.

Next it was Jamie's turn and only when he'd chosen his snowball was Gary permitted to pick one. He pouted at his. Jamie and Scott had taken the biggest two.

'Why would the Lawsons do this now?' said Digger.

Jamie wondered if he'd pissed off his dad so much Jason had set him up. After he'd pushed him off the boat, he wouldn't put it past him. Then he thought Toni McVay wouldn't be impressed if her newest employee got stabbed, so he ruled it out. 'Let's discuss it later,' he said, glancing Scott's way.

'Oh, aye, right,' Digger replied. 'You missed a show in the pub. Kevin Walker said his pint was flat and Deirdre went for his goolies with those tongs she uses to pick up ice cubes. His squeal was so loud it nearly shattered the glasses.'

Jamie chuckled. 'I wish I'd seen that. Kevin's a walloper.'

'Deirdre?' said Mullen.

'The landlady at The Bonnie Brae,' explained Jackie. 'She's pretty fiery.'

'She sounds it.'

As Mullen ate his snowball, he studied the other three Blood Brothers. Gary seemed to be the joker of the pack, with a startling fondness for snowballs. Digger clearly loved to work out and, judging by his overly aggressive demeanour, flushed skin, enormous muscles and prominent jaw, he was a regular user of anabolic steroids. Then there was Logan, the quiet, contemplative one. Mullen got the impression he was the most level-headed and he seemed intelligent and thoughtful. He could have been the leader of the group, but he lacked the edge and natural magnetism Jamie had. Jamie Gray was a born leader, he didn't even need to try. All very different personalities but together they made a formidable team. Even Gary, the tubby joker, carried an air of menace that said he could go from amiable to ferocious in a second. Small wonder they now owned this scheme. They would certainly be a tougher prospect than the lads on the other schemes that he'd encountered during the course of his investigation, who in comparison had been silly kids trying to act like grown-ups. He could imagine the Blood Brothers would be serious contenders in a few short years.

He spotted the framed photo of Jamie and Allegra together hanging on the wall. They looked happy, arms wrapped around each other as they smiled at the camera. While his friends talked, Jamie looked up at the photo before looking back down at his hands, swallowing hard. Mullen wondered if that look meant Allegra really was dead and Jamie was still mourning her or that she was alive somewhere and he was missing her. Whichever it was, there was no doubt their relationship was a love match. The pain in Jamie's dark eyes was bright and intense.

'Scott,' said Jackie. 'Would you like the last snowball before Gary snaffles it?'

'That's very kind but no, thank you,' he replied. 'I like to watch my weight.'

'You certainly do a good job,' she said with a flirtatious smile that made all the Blood Brothers grin, except Jamie, who cringed.

'Hello, wee man,' said Gary when Charlie wandered into the room in his pyjamas, hair damp.

'Hi, Gary.' The boy smiled, delighted to see his brother's friends. 'Are you having a party?'

'Naw, we just came to see Jamie. His leg's a bit sore.'

'Oh, no,' said Charlie, rushing to his brother's side. 'You won't have to go into hospital again, will you?'

'Course not,' Jamie said with a reassuring smile. 'It just aches in the cold weather. Nae bother.'

'That's good,' Charlie said with relief. 'I don't want you to go into hospital ever again.'

'Me neither, wee man,' Jamie said, hugging him.

Mullen was a little shocked by the closeness that very obviously existed in this family, as well as between the Blood Brothers. They clearly loved and cared about each other, which was the last thing he'd been expecting. He'd thought they'd be a pack of hyenas, constantly turning on each other.

'Can I have a snowball too, Maw?' said Charlie, perching on the edge of the couch beside his brother.

'No, sweetheart,' replied Jackie. 'The sugar won't do you any good before bed.'

'Aww.' He pouted.

'But you can have some toast.'

'Yay, I love toast,' he exclaimed with such enthusiasm they all smiled, even Mullen.

Jackie headed back into the kitchen to make him his snack.

When it became apparent the Blood Brothers weren't going to discuss anything sensitive in front of him, Mullen decided his job was done for the day, he'd got the measure of them all. Now it was time to take advantage of the fact that he'd got his foot in the door.

He glanced at his watch. 'I'm sorry, I really must be going. I have to be up early for work.'

'Well, thank you so much for everything you did for Jamie,' said Jackie. 'You can't know how much we appreciate it.'

'Any time.' He smiled.

'I'll see you to the door.'

She ignored the grins of her son and his friends, Charlie obliviously tucking into his toast.

'Thank you for your hospitality,' said Mullen, turning to face Jackie on the doorstep. 'I hope I don't seem forward but I wondered if you'd like to have dinner with me tomorrow night?'

Jackie attempted to hide her delight but her eyes sparkled with it. 'I'd love to.'

'Great.' He smiled. 'There's a wonderful restaurant I know in the city. Shall I pick you up at seven?'

'Perfect. I'll see you then.'

'I'll leave you my phone number, in case anything crops up,' he said, handing her his card.

'Do you want mine in case you can't make it?'

'I can safely say that won't happen.' He winked at her.

Jackie was smiling like a teenager as she looked down at the card in her hand. It said Scott Kendrick, Pharmaceutical Sales Representative, the top emblazoned with the name of his company. This was accompanied by a phone number and email address.

She closed the door and frowned. 'What are you lot looking at?'

'You got a date, Mrs G?' Digger grinned.

'Aye.' She sniffed. 'So?'

All their grins increased, even Jamie's.

'He seems a good one,' said Logan.

'Yes, he does,' she replied, trying to stifle a smile and failing. 'What of it?'

Jamie's eyes danced. 'You're blushing, Maw.'

'I'm not, it's just... hot in here.'

'Aye, that's what it is.' He smiled.

'Right, we'd better get you to bed, sweetheart,' Jackie told Charlie.

'But I'm not tired,' the boy whined.

'Well, I am, so come on, upstairs.'

'Okay, Maw,' he said, getting to his feet. 'I don't want you to be tired.'

Jackie beamed and ruffled his hair.

Once they'd gone upstairs, the Blood Brothers were free to discuss the attack on Jamie.

'I reckon it's payback for what we did to Nick Lawson and his pals at the snooker hall,' said Logan.

'That makes sense.' Jamie nodded.

'Going after you with knives is a bit drastic though,' said Gary. 'I'd expect that from Craig Lawson but no' them. Or maybe he put them up to it?'

'Why now?'

'Revenge.'

'I dunno. It feels a bit obvious for Craig. Or Sasha Reid could have got them to do it as payback for breaking her brother's leg. After all, she is shagging John Lawson.'

'That sounds more like it,' said Digger.

'How have you got on with watching her?'

'She spends most of her time at John's house, the pub or the swimming pool,' replied Gary. 'She pure loves swimming and you should see her in her costume, man, her legs are incredible.'

'So it's back to us not walking the streets alone until we find out what's going on,' said Logan.

'If everyone knew we worked for the McVays they wouldn't dare go near us,' said Digger.

'We have to keep that quiet,' Jamie told them. 'So keep your gob shut about it or Toni will take your eyes and baws.'

'Two of my favourite body parts.' Digger sighed.

'If you keep using steroids you won't have any baws left,' said Gary. 'They'll be the size of toaty wee grapes.'

'There's nothing wrong with my baws,' exclaimed Digger, tugging at his belt. 'And I'll prove it.'

'Do not get your baws out in my maw's living room,' Jamie told him.

'Sorry, Jamie,' he said, fastening his belt, to all their relief.

'Whatever the reason for the attack on you tonight,' Logan told Jamie, 'we have to hit back.'

Jamie nodded. 'Aye, I know. Like we havenae enough going on without this shite. We need to target John Lawson this time. He's in charge since Craig was locked up and we need to make an example of him to make the rest of the family back off. With everything going on with the McVays we don't want to be dealing with the Lawsons too.'

'All that can wait. Rest that leg. Hopefully it'll be better by the morning.'

'Aye, it should be.'

'Mrs Harris, the auld biddy who runs the hairdresser's, is getting hassle from a pal of hers and her husband. She wants us to have a word. We can sort that in the morning and then we'll come round when we're done to discuss what's to be done about the Lawsons.'

'All right. See you all tomorrow and thanks for coming.'

When they'd gone, Jamie's eyes darted to the picture on the wall of himself and Allegra. He took the new phone he'd purchased out of the pocket of his jogging bottoms and sent her a text message asking how she was. When he heard footsteps coming down the stairs, he hastily shoved it back into his pocket.

'Did I hear someone down here yelling about getting their baws out?' said Jackie as she walked into the room.

'Aye, it was Digger.'

'Oh,' she replied in a way that indicated that explained everything. 'Did he?'

'No, we stopped him.'

'Thank God for that. You know, every day when I pick Charlie up from school I ask him what sort of day he's had and every time he just says *fine*. Then, when I'm reading him his bedtime story, he decides to tell me all about it. You used to do the same. I swear it was only so you could stay up later.'

'In my case it was.' He grinned. 'I cannae say the same for Charlie. He probably doesn't want you to leave him on his own.'

'Probably, the poor wee mite,' she said, sinking into the armchair. 'How are you feeling? Do you need any painkillers?'

'I'll have a couple of paracetamol before I go to bed.'

'What a crappy day you've had, son,' Jackie said sadly.

'It's no' been the best but at least you got a date.'

'With an ex-marine too,' she said, unable to hide her smile. 'There's something sexy about that.'

'Please, Maw.' He winced. 'I don't want to hear about that.'

'Best of all,' she said darkly, 'he could kick Jason's heid in.'

'I hope that's no' why you agreed to go out with him?'

'Course not. I like him and he's very handsome. Makes a nice change from the ugly window-lickers I usually get landed with.'

Jamie laughed. No matter how low he felt, his mum could always make him laugh, unlike his dad, who just broke his heart.

15

Jamie's leg felt brand new the next morning. His arm twinged a bit but at least he could move it normally. As he knew his friends were coming round, he texted Allegra to ask if they could have their daily conversation a bit earlier. It was a weekend, so his mother wouldn't be out of the house taking Charlie to school, but she was cooking in the kitchen with the radio on, and Charlie would be sound asleep for another good hour, so it was safe to talk.

A minute after he'd sent the message, his phone rang.

'Hello, Dangerous,' she purred in his ear.

'All right, Princess.' He smiled. 'Christ, it's good to hear your voice.'

She picked up that something was wrong immediately. 'Oh, God, what's happened now?'

The events of the previous day poured out of him. It was a relief to finally tell someone what his dad had done to him. His pain must have been loud and clear in his voice because when she spoke, her own voice shook with emotion.

'Right,' she said. 'I'm coming out there. I'm not having you going through this alone.'

'As much as I would love that, I can handle it. Don't worry about me, I just needed to unload. I didn't tell my maw what Jason did because she would literally kill him.'

'It's what he deserves,' Allegra snarled. 'I feel like doing it myself, and when are those Lawsons going to learn that they could never beat you because they're too stupid and cowardly?'

'They got their heids kicked in and my maw has got a date with the man who helped me batter them.'

'I hope he's decent. There's not many men out there deserving of Jackie Gray.'

Jamie's heart swelled with love for her. 'Aye, he seems to be. He's an ex-marine and a hard bastard but he's also polite and that.'

'I hope he treats her well. She deserves a good man.'

'She's having dinner with him tonight, so we'll see. I'm sure she'll handle him if he turns out to be an arsehole.'

'I've no doubt, but it's you I'm worried about. You're going through so much.'

'I can handle it.'

'I know how strong you are, but everyone has their breaking point. I've been working on a way to come back for a visit. I have to see you, Jamie.'

'You've no idea how much I want to see you too, but please be careful.'

They chatted for a little longer, until he heard the noise enter the house that usually accompanied the arrival of his friends. He said goodbye to Allegra, before pulling on his jumper and jeans and making his way downstairs, glad when his leg didn't give him any gyp.

He entered the living room to find Jackie taking his friends' orders for breakfast, which they'd all apparently had to miss because they'd gone out to give Mrs Harris's friend and her husband a stern warning. Apparently all the fuss had been because

Mrs Harris had given her friend a bad haircut and she'd wanted revenge. The Blood Brothers' warning had been enough for her to decide to forgo that revenge.

'You should have seen her hair, man.' Gary laughed. 'She looked like a fucking monk. I cannae blame her for being pissed off.'

'Mrs Harris paid up,' said Logan, producing a few notes from his pocket and dumping them in Jamie's lap. 'That's your share.'

'But I wasn't even there.'

'It's only fair. You cut Digger in when he was ill with raging diarrhoea.'

'It was a stomach bug, no' raging diarrhoea,' retorted Digger.

'That's no' what your maw said.' Logan looked back at Jamie. 'And you cut me in on a job when I was working at the call centre.'

'We're all agreed on this,' said Gary. 'So just take the money.'

'Well, okay, then,' said Jamie, pocketing the cash. 'Cheers.'

'Nae bother,' said Logan. 'And thanks to Digger and Gary's spying, we know that John Lawson stayed over at Sasha's house last night.'

'How?' said Jamie. 'Her da' would have gone aff his nut.'

'Her parents have gone away for the weekend. We can follow John from there. We shouldn't tackle John at the Reids' house as their parents are all right and it would be disrespectful.'

'Aye, they're a nice couple,' said Gary. 'It's a shame they raised three fuds.'

Charlie got up too at the sound of his brother's friends and they all enjoyed breakfast together at the table, Logan slapping Gary's hand away when he tried to take his toast off his plate.

'Oy, that's mine,' he barked.

'Aww, come on, man,' whined Gary. 'I'm still hungry.'

'You're always bloody hungry. You've probably got worms.'

'Worms?' Charlie frowned. 'You mean like a pet?'

'No, wee man,' said Digger with relish. 'You can get worms in your stomach that eat all the food you swallow, meaning you're always hungry.'

Charlie turned white and he stared at Digger in shocked silence before he let up a wail. 'Maw, I don't want worms in my stomach.'

She leapt to her feet and rushed to comfort a sobbing Charlie. 'You've no' got worms, sweetheart, I promise.'

'But what if the worms crawl in through my belly button?'

'They cannae get in through your belly button. Nothing can.'

'Sorry,' mumbled Digger, hanging his head when Jackie glared at him.

'You fanny,' Gary told his friend. 'You know how sensitive he is.'

'Why don't you have a drink of water?' Jamie told his little brother. 'Worms hate water, it makes them dissolve.'

Charlie stopped sobbing and looked at his brother. 'Really?'

'Aye. I'll get you a glass.'

Jamie got to his feet, filled a glass of water from the tap and handed it to him. Charlie took it from him and glugged it down.

'There you go,' said Jamie, retaking his seat. 'If there were any worms then they're all gone now.'

'Thanks, Jamie.' Charlie smiled happily, putting down the glass. 'You should have a glass of water too, Gary, to dissolve your worms.'

Logan couldn't stop the laugh that burst from his chest and he started to choke on the piece of toast he was chewing. Jamie slapped him on the back to dislodge the blockage.

'Cheers, pal,' Logan told him, eyes watering.

Satisfied her younger son was once again his usual sunny self, Jackie retook her seat. 'I don't know,' she sighed. 'Nothing's ever peaceful with you lot around, is it?'

When they'd finished eating, Digger helped Jackie clear the table and wash up, as a penance for upsetting Charlie earlier before she announced she was going into the city to do some shopping.

'I'll drop Charlie off at Tricia's on the way,' she said. 'He's got a playdate with Kieran.'

'Why are you going into the toon today to do your shopping?' Jamie asked her. 'You usually do that on a Wednesday.'

'I just fancied a change, that's all.'

Jamie smiled. 'You're gonnae get an outfit for your date tonight, aren't you?'

'Maybe,' Jackie said, trying to repress a smile and failing.

Jamie took the notes Logan had given him out of his pocket and held them out to her. 'Why don't you get yourself something really special?'

'You don't need to give me that, sweetheart, you've already given me some money.'

'I know you, Maw, you never spend anything on yourself because you always feel guilty, even though you shouldn't. Get something designer and some new shoes and you can have your hair done too. Salons are open on Sunday'

'Why do you keep saying I should get my hair done?' She frowned, running her fingers through it.

'I'm just saying you should treat yourself.'

'You should, Mrs G,' said Logan. 'You deserve it.'

'You're right, I do.' She smiled. 'But I'm no' taking your money, son. You gave me more than enough to get what I need and to get a new cooker.' She pulled on her jacket and shoes and slung her handbag over her shoulder. 'I don't know what time I'll be back, so you might have to make yourself lunch. Don't worry about Charlie, he'll have his at Tricia's. Charlie,' she yelled up the stairs. 'Hurry up or you'll be late.'

'Coming,' he called back, racing down the stairs after getting dressed.

'See you later, boys,' said Jackie.

'Bye,' they called in unison.

'I've been thinking about Scott,' began Logan.

'Aww, are you wantin' a date with him too?' Gary sniggered.

Logan ignored him. 'Don't you think it was a bit weird that he was in the right place at the right time last night to save your arse? I mean, I'm glad he was, but out of all the streets in Gallowburn he was on that one.'

'What are you saying?' said Jamie. 'That it was a set-up?'

'No, I'm not saying that at all. It was probably just a coincidence. Ignore me.'

'He's going on a date with my maw, so if you think he's dodgy...'

'Actually, I don't. He seemed all right. It's all this stuff with the McVays, it's making me paranoid.'

Jamie nodded. 'I know what you mean.' He'd been pondering what to tell his friends about the previous day and had decided he wouldn't tell them about Jason shoving him off the boat, it was too humiliating. But there was something else he felt he should share with them. 'My da carries a gun.'

They all stared at him in shocked silence.

'You mean a real one?' breathed Digger.

'Aye, course I dae. It was in the glovebox of his car. He doesn't know I saw it.'

'What was it like?' said Gary with awe.

'It was a black handgun.'

'What sort?'

'Nae idea.'

'Isn't it a bit stupid to drive around with one of those in your car?' said Logan. 'What if he's pulled over by the police?'

'I thought it was a bit daft too,' said Jamie. 'Which means he's scared enough to carry protection like that.'

'You mean someone could be after him?'

'Maybe.'

'I suppose that makes sense. Why else take a risk like that?'

'So who's he scared of?' said Gary. 'The McVays?'

'I don't think so,' said Jamie. 'Whenever he talks about them he seems proud. I reckon someone else has it in for him and I cannae blame them for that – he's a proper walloper.'

'This gets worse and worse.' Logan sighed. 'Maybe you shouldn't go about with him any more, Jamie, for your own safety?'

'That'll be difficult after Toni said he's our contact. We have to go through him for everything.'

'Oh, yeah,' Logan muttered.

'Maybe no one's after him and he just likes carrying a gun?' offered Gary. 'It probably makes him feel like the big man.'

'Now that does sound like Jason,' said Logan. 'We must be careful not to jump to conclusions.'

Jamie produced his phone when it pinged. 'It's a message from Jason. He wants to meet me at Raymond's Rolls.'

'Are you going?'

'I suppose I should. It might be something to do with Toni.'

'Want us to come with you?'

'That would be good, thanks.'

'Great,' said Gary. 'I pure love Ray's haggis rolls.'

Digger pulled a face.

* * *

Jamie had no idea what sort of reception he was going to get from his father after he'd punched him and nicked his car. Jason was already at the café, sitting at the same table he and Jamie had occupied on their last visit. While Jamie took the chair opposite him, his friends took a table by the window, far enough away to give them their privacy but close enough should there be any trouble. Gary enthusiastically ordered a haggis roll and a vanilla slice while the others ordered coffee, still full from the breakfast Jackie had made them.

'Hello, son,' opened Jason. 'Thanks for coming.'

'You managed to get back your car, then?' said Jamie icily

'I had a spare set of keys.'

'I wish I'd dropped those down the grate too.'

'So that's what happened to my other set.' Jason couldn't help but smile when Jamie nodded. 'I've got to hand it to you, son, you did me over good and proper. I suppose I deserved it.'

'Aye, ya did, ya bastard,' Jamie hissed.

'I understand why you're upset.'

'No, you don't. You don't have a bloody clue. You never have.'

'I did what I had to do to save both our hides. You would have been nicked too.'

'I wouldn't have been in that situation in the first place if it hadn't been for you.'

'Look, my job is to prepare you for working for Toni. Knowing how to get out of dangerous situations like that is all part of it.'

'Oh, no,' said Jamie, lowering his voice to a whisper. 'That is not a life I want. I made that very clear.'

'Don't be naïve, Jamie,' whispered back Jason. 'Toni only said you wouldn't be dealing drugs to reel you in. One day she will expect you to graduate, and saying no will cost you your life. I've seen what she does to people who refuse her and I don't want the same for you.'

'If you didn't want me involved you shouldn't have dragged me and my pals into it in the first place,' spat Jamie through gritted teeth.

'Everything I do is for your own benefit. I can't mollycoddle you. The only way you're going to learn is to throw you in at the deep end.' Jason held up his hands. 'Sorry, bad choice of words.'

'I get that, but I thought you wanted to spend the day with me,' retorted Jamie, the hurt clear in his eyes. He was being careful to keep his voice low. The last thing he wanted was anyone over-hearing.

'I did.'

'No, you didn't. You just wanted someone to shove into the water if you got spotted. You took me out on that boat knowing that was what you might have to do to me, you total bastard.'

'All right, I admit I did know it was a possibility, but I thought it was a remote one. I chose the safest location possible so it wouldn't have to happen.'

Jamie shook his head, jaw gritted. 'I fucking knew it.'

'But I did want to spend time with you too, to try and repair our relationship.'

'Well, you fucked that up, *Jason*, because it's more broken than ever.'

'I've messed up big time but it's no' too late.'

Jamie's eyes bored into his father. 'Who are you scared of?'

'Eh?'

'I know you're worried someone's coming for you. Who is it?'

'What makes you think I'm scared of anyone?' he said curiously. 'Oh, I see, you peeked in my glovebox, didn't you?'

'You need protection like that, but from who?'

'No one in particular. It's just there in case I need it. When you work for the McVays you don't need to be afraid of anyone.'

'Except the McVays themselves.' Jamie glowered. 'And you're taking a hell of risk driving around with that in your car. It could land you five years in prison.'

'What can I say? I enjoy taking risks. You do too, Jamie, I've seen it in your eyes. You love the adrenaline rush and once you're addicted you can never break free.'

Jamie ignored the fact that his father was right. 'You've fucked up my life, dragged me into something I never wanted to be involved in, and did it never occur to you that if the police find out what I'm involved in it will destroy my integrity with any jury and spoil the case against Cameron Abernethy? He could get away with what he did.'

'That won't happen.'

'He's a rich, connected bastard and tossers like that have the habit of getting away with murder because our society is so fucked up. If that does happen I will come for you.'

'You're tough, Jamie, but you're inexperienced. You need me to guide you.'

'I need fuck all from you. The only time I'll speak to you is to do with business and I'll never call you Da again.' Jamie got to his feet, planted his hands on the table and loomed over Jason. 'And I recommend you stay away from the Gallowburn. Bad things happen to people who wander around the scheme when they're no' welcome.'

With that, Jamie sauntered to the door, feeling better for getting all that off his chest. Jason didn't speak as he watched him leave.

'Let's go,' Logan told the others.

'But I haven't eaten my vanilla slice yet,' said Gary.

'Bring it with you,' Logan replied impatiently.

The rest of the Blood Brothers left the café, glowering at Jason as they went; Jason merely looked amused.

'Jamie,' said Logan, hurrying to catch up with his friend. 'Are you okay?'

'Aye, fine,' Jamie replied. He took his phone out of his pocket when it started to ring, glad of the interruption. 'Hello?' He paused to listen before replying. 'We'll be there in ten minutes,' he added before hanging up.

'Who was that?'

'The reverend.'

Gary's eyes lit up. 'Valerie, my angel?'

'You are such a fanny.' Digger chuckled.

'She said she's got something important to discuss with us,' said Jamie.

'Finally she's realised her true feelings for me,' said Gary. 'And now she wants to tell the world.'

'Aye, you keep dreaming,' said Digger.

16

The Gallowburn church was the original one, built in the fifties when the scheme had been created. It had survived two arson attacks and a copious amount of vandalism and stood in proud defiance, the tallest landmark on the scheme with its towering spire.

The Blood Brothers found Valerie at the rear of the church, staring in thoughtful contemplation at a large image of Christ on the cross.

'Thanks for coming, boys,' she said without turning to face them, keeping her gaze on the image.

'How did you know it was us?' said Jamie.

'Just a feeling,' she replied. 'And Gary's aftershave is very memorable.'

'Thanks for noticing,' he said shyly, blushing.

Valerie finally turned to face them. 'Let's talk in the vestry,' she said, indicating a door off to one side.

'Relax,' Logan whispered in Gary's ear when he turned positively scarlet with excitement. 'She means all of us.'

Gary walked into the vestry last, the scene of so many of his fantasies, feeling unworthy of being brought into this inner sanctum.

Valerie sat behind her desk, Jamie and Logan taking the two chairs opposite her, leaving Digger and Gary to stand.

'Word has come to me about something very serious occurring on the estate,' began Valerie.

She looked so grave that Jamie started to worry she knew about their connection to the McVays. He glanced at his friends; it was clear they thought the same thing.

'It involves John Lawson and Sasha Reid,' she added.

All four Blood Brothers relaxed.

'Apparently,' continued Valerie, 'they've got themselves involved in a very dark business, namely breaking into the homes of the older residents on the scheme, tying them up and robbing them.'

'What?' exclaimed Jamie. 'How long has this been going on?'

'Two weeks.'

'Why have we never heard about it?'

'Because they terrified their victims so much they were too afraid to speak out. I know of three victims, who are all parishioners of mine. There might be more I don't know about. They break in at night, when the victim is asleep, usually by smashing a pane of glass in the door or by forcing the door open. They restrain the victim before they even know what's happening and then ransack the house. They're very blatant about it, they don't bother to hide their identities, and threaten them with all sorts of horrible physical harm if they tell the police or you. I only found out because one of my parishioners couldn't cope any longer and confided in me. The poor woman was shaking like a leaf just telling me about it. I had to slip some of my best Scotch into her cup of tea to calm her down.'

'You drink Scotch?' said Gary in an adoring tone.

She nodded once, sharply. 'After this I noticed two more of my parishioners were acting the same as Lizzy – scared, jumpy – so I spoke to them too and they gave the same story. All three victims are very old, frail and female.'

'Did John and Sasha hit them at all?' said Logan.

'They didn't need to because they terrified them so much, but they trussed them up like turkeys, leaving rope burns on their wrists and ankles. Before they leave, they loosen the ropes so their victims can free themselves. It's a miracle none of them had a heart attack. If John and Sasha aren't stopped they will end up killing someone, even if they don't mean to.'

'Do these women all live in the same part of the scheme?' said Jamie.

'Yes. This part, to be precise. All three live a two-minute walk from the church.'

'The nasty, manky bastards,' spat Digger. 'Oh, sorry,' he added when he realised he'd cursed on hallowed ground.

'That's all right,' she replied. 'I understand how you feel.'

'We need to stop this,' said Jamie, his friends nodding in agreement.

'I'm afraid I can't afford to pay you much...'

'No need,' said Gary. 'This is on the house. We wouldnae dream of charging.'

He trailed off when Jamie turned in his seat to glare at him.

'Only if Jamie agrees,' he hastily added.

Jamie turned back to face Valerie. 'As Gary said, we wouldnae take a penny. Someone's hurting old yins on the scheme, so we're gonnae stop it.'

'Thanks so much, boys,' she said. 'That's very good of you and the spiritual rewards you'll reap for this good work will far outweigh the material ones.'

Digger pulled a face.

'We'll sort it,' said Jamie.

Valerie nodded. 'May I talk to you in private, Jamie?'

'Err, aye,' he replied, puzzled.

'We'll wait for you outside,' said Logan.

He had to usher out Gary, who had gone rigid with jealousy.

'Before you begin,' said Jamie when his friends had left, 'you should know that I'm no' religious.'

'That's not why I want to talk to you,' replied an amused Valerie. 'I just wanted to check that this task I've given you won't be too much for you.'

'Like John Lawson could ever be too much for me,' he said belligerently.

'I don't mean like that. You have so much weighing down on your young shoulders – losing your fiancée, almost being killed, the court case and now I've heard that your estranged father has returned. I thought carefully about coming to you with this because I didn't want to pile any more pressure onto you, but there was no one else to turn to. I dismissed going to the police because, not only would my congregation stop coming to the church, but it would probably be set on fire again. You have become the ones the people on this estate go to when they have a problem and sometimes they forget just how young you are.'

'I'm twenty-two,' he retorted.

'Which is still very young. This arrangement of yours does put food on your table, but I want to caution you against taking on too much at your age. It breaks my heart that so many young people take drastic action because they simply can't cope.'

'Don't worry, I'd never hurt myself. I wouldnae dae that to my family and pals.'

'I'm very glad to hear it. It's wonderful that you have such supportive people around you. Don't ever be afraid to say if things get too much, okay, Jamie? There's no shame in it. If you want to talk to someone, then I'm always here.'

Jamie nodded, uncomfortable about discussing his feelings with someone he didn't know very well. 'Thanks,' he mumbled.

'Well, that's all I wanted to say. Let me know when you've sorted it out.'

With that she picked up a book sitting on her desk, opened it and started to read.

'Right,' he said, getting to his feet. 'I'll be off, then.'

Valerie looked up from her book. 'Thank you for coming, Jamie. You're doing the Lord's work.'

'Aye, that's... great,' he said uncertainly.

He left the church to find his friends gathered on the pavement outside the door, Gary uncharacteristically agitated, pacing up and down and running his hands through his hair.

'What the fuck was that about?' demanded Gary the moment Jamie set foot outside the door. 'What did she want? What did you talk about? Did you touch her?'

Jamie frowned. 'Why the hell would I touch her?'

'Because she's a beautiful angel.'

'To you maybe. To me she's just a middle-aged woman.'

'Don't you dare talk about her like that,' thundered Gary, thrusting his face into Jamie's. 'Or I'll knock you the fuck out.'

Jamie was so astonished he didn't know what to say and Logan and Digger were gaping at the pair of them. Gary had never threatened Jamie before, he wouldn't dare.

'What's wrong with you, you walloper?' Jamie demanded of him. 'It looks like your angel has sent you bloody doolally.'

'You're no' good enough for her,' spat Gary, face contorted with rage. 'No one is.' He shoved Jamie in the chest. 'Come on, square go, right now.'

'If you don't get out of my face,' Jamie hissed at him, 'I'll knock you to the fucking ground.'

The threat in Jamie's tone broke through the red mist that had claimed Gary, who finally came to his senses.

'Jeezo, I'm sorry,' Gary exclaimed. 'I don't know what came over me.'

'Said the nun to the bishop.' Digger grinned.

'You went fucking demented, you fanny,' said Jamie.

'I couldnae help it. I was jealous because I wanted to be alone with her in her vestry.'

'We were only talking. It's no' like we were shagging up against the wall.'

'Aye, I know. Ignore me, I'm a tit.'

Jamie felt sorry for him. He knew what it was like to be in love and Gary had it bad. 'It's okay, pal, forget about it. Want to figure out how to stop John Lawson and Sasha Reid?'

He smiled and nodded. 'Too right I do.'

* * *

Jackie felt out of place as Scott escorted her into the five-star restaurant in the west end of the city. She was glad Jamie had convinced her to treat herself because she'd bought a designer skirt and blouse for her date and anything less would have been unsuitable for this venue. The elaborate pillared entryway had been intimidating enough, but Scott had made it worse by telling her this place had a Michelin star. She couldn't remember the name of the restaurant, as it was French, and she felt nervous as the maître d' escorted them to an intimate table by the window, looking out onto the busy street. The glasses on the table sparkled and the cutlery gleamed.

They took their seats, their drinks order was taken and they were handed menus before being left alone. Jackie glanced around the room, taking in the diamond jewellery, expensive watches and elegant clothes of the other customers and felt like a fish out of water. Not one of them looked as if they lived on a scheme like the Gallowburn. But tonight neither did she, thanks to the clothes and the expensive haircut she'd had done at a trendy salon.

'This is my favourite restaurant.' Scott smiled. 'The food is incredible. Their truffle croque monsieur is out of this world.'

'I don't know what that is.' Jackie blushed.

She stared at the menu, which was gibberish to her as it was all in French. For a moment she felt stupid and embarrassed, until she recalled that she was a strong, proud woman and she shouldn't be ashamed for not knowing about posh food or how to speak a foreign language. She was willing to bet all the stuck-up tarts around her wouldn't last a day in her shoes.

'I can't speak French,' she said. 'I don't understand the menu.'

His smile was gentle and kind. 'Not to worry, neither do half the people that come in here, they just pretend they do. I once saw a man order escargot, not realising it meant snails. Rather than admit he'd made a mistake, he shoved every single snail down his throat before rushing to the toilet.'

Jackie laughed her loud, dirty laugh, which made Scott smile.

'How about I order for you?' he said.

'Well, okay. What should I have?'

'That depends on what food you like.'

'I have simple tastes. I love a big warm stew or casserole, especially this time of year when it's cold outside, with lots of thick, crusty bread, and soups too. I love making my own soup. Ooh, I recognise one,' she said, pointing at the menu. 'Crème brûlée. I love that but I don't often get the chance to eat it.'

'Okay, so how about the Soupe au Pistou, which is a seasonal vegetable soup, followed by the Poulet Basquaise, a famous French stew with chicken, ham and peppers? To finish, a crème brûlée.'

'Sounds smashing.' Jackie smiled, stomach rumbling in anticipation.

She was grateful when the waiter – who actually wore white gloves – brought them a bottle of white wine. Although she knew it must be expensive, she glugged down half the glass the waiter poured out for her. It might have been posh but to her it didn't taste any different from the cheap plonk she and her friends bought from the local off-licence for their girls' nights in. Still, it did the trick and steadied her nerves a little.

'Are you all right?' Scott asked her when the waiter had gone. 'You seem nervous and I don't think you're the type of woman who gets nervous often.'

'You're right, I'm not normally but I've never been to a place like this before.'

'It's only a restaurant,' he said gently.

'No, it's a very *posh* restaurant. I'm used to Di Giorgio's on the scheme with its scampi in a basket, uncomfortable chairs and seventies décor. I'm not used to hardwood floors, silver service and waiters in gloves.'

'Think of it as a new experience.'

'I feel like I don't fit in.'

'No, you don't, because you're better than the lot of them put together. You're a special woman, Jackie. Don't let anyone tell you any different.'

'How do you know I'm special? You've only known me five minutes.'

'Because I'm a very good judge of character. And I think you're beautiful.'

'I'm not beautiful,' Jackie said, blushing again. It had been a long time since she'd received a genuine compliment from a man. She was used to men asking her if she fancied a shag or telling her they thought she was all right only when they were blind drunk.

'Yes, you are, Jackie, and your eyes are like emeralds. The way they catch the light is enchanting.'

Mullen wasn't trying to flatter her and he certainly wasn't lying. It was just what he thought and he had no qualms about saying it.

Jackie wondered if he was the first genuinely honest man she'd ever met, but a part of her urged her to reserve judgement on that for the moment. 'Thanks,' she said. 'And you're very handsome.'

'Thank you.' He smiled.

'I like your suit. I'm used to men who think they're still in their twenties wearing tracksuits and baseball caps, unable to face the fact that they're adults. It's pathetic.'

'The women I meet are either shallow or brainless, so it's refreshing to finally meet a woman who's neither.'

Jackie was starting to feel like a teenager again. Did this man actually like her for herself and not for what he could get out of her or a quick shag? She'd seen the prices on the menu; this place was not cheap, so he was willing to spend a bit on her. Even if nothing came of this date, it was nice to be spoilt.

He asked her about her life, and she found herself opening up to him about meeting Jason and having her babies. When the first course was brought to their table, she realised she'd been monopolising the conversation for twenty minutes. She inhaled the delicious aromas emanating from the soup and her stomach rumbled a little too loudly in anticipation.

'Sorry.' She cringed.

'Don't worry about it,' he replied. 'Mine's been doing that ever since we walked in. It always does when I come here.'

'This smells amazing.' Jackie smiled, eagerly picking up her spoon. 'Anyway, that's enough about me. Tell me about yourself. I hardly know anything, and don't say there's nothing to tell because I won't believe it. You've obviously led an interesting life.'

'Well, I suppose I have. Where shall I start?'

'At the beginning – where you were born and raised.'

'Well, I'm the youngest of six.'

'Six?' she said, eyes widening. 'That must have been a busy house.'

'It was. I have three brothers and two sisters. We lived in a three-bedroomed house in Possilpark. My mum was a housewife and my dad worked in a factory. He didn't earn much.'

'Tough times?'

'In a way but we were lucky. Our parents loved each other and they loved us. It was a fight to put food on the table and pay the bills, but my childhood was still a happy one.'

'That's nice.'

'In a way, you remind me of my mother.'

'What?' she said, smile falling.

'I don't mean like that. I mean the way you are with your boys, struggling to raise them alone.'

'But your da...'

'Died when I was nine of a brain aneurysm. No one had any idea, he just keeled over one day without warning. He was dead before he hit the floor,' he said quietly.

'Oh, I'm sorry, Scott.'

'Thanks,' he replied with a tight smile. 'Everything landed on my mother's shoulders. Despite her grief, she rolled up her sleeves, got herself two jobs, showed my older brother and sister how to cook so they could look after us younger ones and got on with it. Life was still a struggle, but we were happy. Well, as much as we could be without our father. Sorry,' he added sheepishly, a little surprised at himself for opening up so easily. 'I suppose that's a little more than you wanted me to share.'

'Not at all, I'm glad you did. So many men find it difficult opening up, so your attitude is very refreshing.'

'Glad to hear it. What about your childhood?'

'Mine was similar really. Poor but happy. I had one brother but he died,' she said, looking down at her soup to hide her pain.

'I'm sorry to hear that.'

'He was a wonderful brother, kind and protective. Jamie reminds me of him a lot – he's the same with Charlie as my brother was with me.' Jackie's eyes took on a faraway look. 'When I was with him, I knew everything would be okay.'

'That's nice.' He smiled.

Jackie cleared her throat to get rid of the lump forming and took a glug of wine. It was incredible to her how comfortable she felt in his presence; she'd even managed to forget that they were in a snooty restaurant. 'The soup's lovely.'

He gazed across the table at her. 'It's not the only thing that's lovely.'

Mullen smiled inwardly at the way Jackie beamed back at him. This was going very well indeed.

* * *

Jamie frowned when he heard a noise just outside his front door. His mum was still out on her date and Charlie was asleep upstairs. He wondered if it was his imagination, so he muted the television. When he heard a thud against the door, he leapt up, ran into the kitchen, retrieved his bike chains from their hiding place and raced back to the door. He pressed his ear against it to listen, frowning when he heard furtive whispers, followed by silence.

Jamie yanked open the door, leaping aside when two figures stumbled inside.

'Maw,' exclaimed Jamie. 'What are you doing?' When he realised Scott's arms were locked around his mother's waist and hers around his neck, he added. 'Oh, sorry.'

'It's a good job you were holding me, Scott,' said Jackie. 'Or I would have gone flat on my arse.'

'Why are you making out on the doorstep at your age?' said Jamie.

'At my age? You're no' too big to be put over my knee,' she retorted, making him grin.

'Sorry, Maw. Want me to go to the pictures?'

'That won't be necessary.' She sniffed. 'Me and Scott were just saying goodnight. He's got to be up early in the morning and the taxi's waiting for him.'

'I'll call you tomorrow, Jackie,' said Scott, giving her hand a gentle squeeze. 'Jamie.' He nodded.

Jamie smiled and nodded back.

'Goodnight,' purred Jackie, watching as he walked down the garden path and got into the taxi. Only when it had set off did she close the door.

'I take it your date went well?' Jamie asked her.

'It was lovely. That man knows how to treat a lady. He took me to a Michelin-starred restaurant. I've never ate food like it. Then we went to a cocktail bar for drinks and we even danced. I haven't danced in years. Honestly, I feel ten years younger and all for being treated nicely by a good man. He's a great kisser too. That was a very nice bonus.'

'I didnae need to know that last bit, Maw.'

She didn't even hear him because she was so caught up in her happy memories. 'He said I was beautiful.'

'You are beautiful.'

'You're so sweet.' She smiled, patting his face.

'So you're seeing him again?'

'Aye. He's working tomorrow but he's going to call to arrange another date soon.'

'That's great, I'm glad, Maw.'

'How would you feel if I got into a serious relationship? I know it's been a long time and we've got so used to it being just the three of us, but I really do like this man.'

'Me and Charlie would be fine with it. You deserve someone who treats you right and you can't be alone forever.'

'Thanks for understanding, sweetheart.'

'I know how hard feeling lonely can be.'

'Oh, Jamie, I'm sorry. Here's me banging on about my date when you're still mourning Allegra.'

'It's fine, don't worry about it. I'm happy for you. If it hadn't been for you, I wouldn't have got through everything that happened with Allegra. I want you to be happy and you don't need to worry about me.'

'You're my baby, Jamie, I'll always worry about you. It goes with the territory of being a mother. And anyway, I am getting ahead of myself. I only had one date with Scott. I might discover something horrible about him, like he chews his toenails or he likes watching *Britain's Got Talent*.'

Jamie couldn't help but laugh.

17

The shadows darted across the road and ran down the back street, their forms blending in with the night.

'This way,' one whispered to the other, indicating a gate leading into a tiny backyard. They pressed their weight against it, but nothing happened. 'It's locked.'

'No problem,' whispered the second figure. 'Boost me up.'

The first figure formed a cradle with their hands and the second figure used it as a step to reach the top of the wall beside the gate. They grabbed onto it and scrambled over, landing silently on the other side. They studied the gate with the assistance of a small torch, located the bolt and unlocked it, allowing the first figure entry, who then quietly closed the gate behind them.

Together they crept up to the back door and crouched down together to study it. After some furtive whispering, one of them produced a crowbar from inside their jacket and smashed the window that took up the top section of the door. They reached inside with a gloved hand and fumbled for the lock. They turned it and it clicked open. The pair of them snuck inside and closed the door behind them.

They paused in the tiny galley kitchen to listen, making sure they hadn't been overheard before heading deeper into the house. As with all the houses on the Gallowburn, the living room was poky, most of the floor space taken up by the two couches. The décor was faded and dated.

The intruders padded to the bottom of the stairs and once again paused to listen before slowly making their way up the steps, pausing every time there was a creak, but no one stirred. The house remained silent.

At the top of the stairs they hesitated to take stock once again, looking left to right, wondering which way to go.

Following the gentle snores, they turned right, towards one of the two bedrooms. Quietly they pushed open the door. The room was dark but the moon was full, its silver light pouring through the thin curtains, highlighting the shape asleep on the bed. The taller figure nodded at the smaller one, who produced a roll of tape from their pocket and tore off a piece, ready to slap onto their victim's mouth before they had time to scream.

The figures prowled closer to the unsuspecting form on the bed, preparing to spring...

But they both recoiled in shock when the figure sat up and roared at them, not in the expected high, frail voice but in a deep, booming one.

'Jesus Christ,' yelled John Lawson before turning and attempting to sprint for the door.

He'd only made it a couple of steps when he smacked into a large immovable object and was sent crashing to the floor, landing on his back.

'What the fuck's going on?' yelled Sasha.

Light flooded the room, making them blink. John found himself staring up at Digger, who was grinning from ear to ear.

'That was pure funny, ya fanny.' Digger laughed.

Sasha was startled to see the lump in the bed wasn't an old lady. In fact, it was Gary tucked under the covers, looking very pleased with himself. He even wore an old lady's nightcap on his head, looking like the big bad wolf's worst nightmare. The bedroom door was slammed shut and locked, Jamie and Logan standing before it.

'Oh, shit,' she sighed.

'What are you lot doing here?' demanded John, slowly sitting upright, rubbing his aching lower back.

'We heard you two were doing over old yins,' said Jamie.

'No, we're not,' John yelled automatically.

'How did you know?' an eerily calm Sasha asked Jamie.

'A wee bird told us. That's all you need to know, so we put it about that Mary, who owns this house, had a collection of expensive old coins. We knew you'd hear about it in the pub and come straight here, you cowardly bastards.'

'It's no' what it seems, Jamie,' said John, feeling nervous when he saw that wild look in Jamie's eyes.

'What is it, then, John?' he spat. 'Because to me it looks like a pair of jobbies have been attacking the most vulnerable people on the scheme. Not even Craig would have done that.'

'Aye, he would. He'd do anything for some easy cash, but it wasn't my idea.'

'Shut it, you idiot,' hissed Sasha.

'It was her brother's,' he added, pointing at Sasha.

'You are such a fucking coward,' she said in a low, cold voice. 'I don't know why I'm with you.'

'Because you love me,' he retorted.

An undignified snort was her reply.

'Oh, dear,' said Gary. 'Lovers' tiff?'

Sasha just glared at him.

'So, what happens now?' rasped John, his tone indicating he already knew the answer.

'We're gonnae kick seven shades of shite out of you,' said Jamie. 'And we're gonnae enjoy it.'

John just sighed and hung his head. Sasha, however, had more fight. She made a run for the door, puzzled when none of the Blood Brothers attempted to stop her. She pulled the door open to be confronted by Jackie, who was quivering with fury.

'Where do you think you're going, madam?' she demanded.

'Get out of the way, you old cow.'

'Old? I'll give you old.'

Jackie punched Sasha full in the face and she staggered backwards, a hand to her bleeding nose, swaying on her feet before she tripped over John and landed on the floor beside him.

'We don't hit women,' Jamie told Sasha. 'Luckily my maw's no problem with it.'

'Too right I don't,' said Jackie. 'Especially nasty wee bitches like her who can only attack the helpless.'

Sasha sat up with a groan, dabbing at her delicate nose. 'You made me bleed, you old hag.'

'Why so much of the old?' retorted Jackie. 'Is that the only insult you know? You'll be my age one day, or maybe not if you carry on the way you are.'

Sasha just glared back at her, resembling a particularly malevolent pixie.

'What are we going to do with them?' Jackie asked her son.

'Well,' said Jamie. 'First we're gonnae gi'e John a good hiding. You can do what you want to Sasha. And then we're gonnae talk to her brothers.'

'You'll leave them alone,' screamed Sasha, making them all wince.

'Make a rammy like that again,' Jackie told her, 'and I'll staple your lips shut.'

Sasha scowled but remained silent.

'Clever girl.' Jackie smiled.

'If you don't want us to pay them a visit,' Jamie told Sasha, 'then you'll tell us why they came up with the idea to rob all these old women.'

'It's simple,' said Sasha. 'Because they're easy targets. We need some cash and they've got it. There's no big plot behind it, if that's what you're worried about. Not everything's about you around here.'

'Good to know. Lads, gi'e him a good kicking,' Jamie said, gesturing to John.

Jackie joined her son in the corner of the room, well out of the way as the other three Blood Brothers laid into John with their fists and feet. John's yelps of pain grew weaker. Sasha had got up out of harm's way and sat on the bed, impassively watching her boyfriend being beaten to a pulp.

'That is one cold wee cow,' said Jackie.

'Aye, she is,' replied Jamie.

'There's something wrong in that pretty heid of hers. Definite faulty wiring in there.'

'Probably.'

'They won't go overboard on John, will they?' said Jackie.

'They won't. They know what they're doing.'

Gary, Digger and Logan did indeed stop attacking John before any serious damage could be done to him. His face was bruised and swollen, blood trickling from his nose and split lips, but nothing had been broken.

'While you're down there,' said Jamie, standing over him and glaring down at him, arms folded across his chest, 'did you tell any of your family to attack me around the corner from my house the night before last?'

'Naw,' he wheezed. 'That wasnae me. Nick arranged it to get you back for twatting him at the snooker hall.'

'All this violence,' sighed Jackie. 'Constantly back and forth, retaliating against each other. It makes me so sad.'

'Right,' said Jamie. 'It's time to get you out of Mary's house.'

Digger and Gary dragged John to his feet and marched him to the door and downstairs.

'Your turn now,' Jackie told Sasha.

The girl got to her feet, nose in the air. 'I can manage on my own,' she sniffed before strutting out of the room.

Jackie stuck close behind her as they made their way downstairs and into the living room.

'Dump him outside on the back street,' said Jamie, pointing at John.

'Come on, ya big jessie,' said Digger, dragging him along by one arm.

Gary moved to assist, saw his friend had control of the situation and left him to it, John groaning with pain when Digger dragged him into the door jamb leading into the kitchen.

'And you,' Jamie told Sasha, 'will stay away from all the old yins' houses in the scheme and don't think you can scare them into silence because we will find out. You'll stay away from us too. If you cause any more trouble, then my maw will batter your melon in with her frying pan.'

'And I'll enjoy myself too,' said Jackie with a predatory smile.

'This is the only warning you're going to get,' added Jamie.

'What big tough men you are,' snorted Sasha. 'Getting your maw to sort your problems out.'

'Only because they don't hurt women,' said Jackie. 'That's the mark of a true man. When you grow up you might learn that, although I feel sorry for any man who tries to hurt you. You're the type to stick poison in their tea or slit their throat while they're sleeping. I can see that crazy in your eyes.'

Sasha stared back at her, eyes narrow and sly. 'Or maybe I'd do both, just for good measure.'

'It wouldnae surprise me. Go on, get lost.'

With a hard look, first at Jackie, then at Jamie, Sasha slunk out.

'You want to watch that wee madam, son,' said Jackie. 'I'd say she's more dangerous than the Lawsons and her brothers put together. The bad is deep in her bones. It's a special type of bad, beyond the usual ned shite on this scheme. She's a female Craig Lawson.'

'Urgh,' said Gary. 'It's a bit creepy that John's seeing her.'

'After tonight that relationship will probably be over,' said Logan. 'His cowardice seemed to disgust her.'

'Let's hope so,' said Jamie. 'If their relationship ends then she won't be able to use the Lawson family to get her own back on us for hurting her brothers.'

'She should be mad at her brothers for being wee fannies,' said Digger.

'Well, hopefully the old folk on this scheme should be safe now,' said Jackie. 'You did some good work tonight, boys.'

'You did a lot of it, Mrs G,' said Gary. 'It was awesome how you dealt with her.'

'That's what people get for calling me old.'

'You're no' old. She's just a dick.'

'True, but mark my words – you've no' seen the last of her.'

The five of them headed home together, the other three Blood Brothers branching off into their various houses until it was just Jackie and Jamie left. Jamie walked with his bike chains clenched tightly in his hands, alert for trouble. He wouldn't put it past the Lawsons to have another go at him, but they got home safely.

Jackie sent Charlie's babysitter on her way with ten pounds in her pocket and headed upstairs to check on her younger son. As she came back down, one of Jamie's phones rang. He was dismayed to realise it was the burner phone Toni had given him.

'What's wrong?' Jackie asked him.

'This is the phone the McVays gave me,' he replied, staring at it in his hand.

'You'd better answer it, I suppose.'

'Aye, suppose,' he said, putting the phone to his ear. 'Hello?'

Jackie anxiously watched her son, whose shoulders slumped with resignation. 'Aye, we'll be there.'

'Well?' she said when he'd hung up.

'The first secret is being delivered tomorrow morning.'

'What is it?'

'They didn't say. It's a secret.'

'Oh, God, I dread to think what it is.'

'At least it won't be drugs.'

'But what if it's guns or stolen goods?'

'Knowing Toni, it could be anything. I'm off to bed, Maw. Night,' he said before slinking upstairs.

Jackie watched him go, his shoulders hunched. It wasn't right someone so young had so much pressure. He should be out enjoying himself, going to nightclubs and dating women. She'd worked so hard to give him the best life she possibly could, but it had all been in vain. Jason had come in and destroyed all her good work and there was nothing she could do to make it all better for her son. She felt such a failure.

* * *

'Jeezo, I'm even more nervous than last time,' said Gary, who was practically hopping from foot to foot.

The Blood Brothers were all gathered together outside the

workshop, as per the McVays' instructions. It was eight o'clock in the morning.

'Try and keep a lid on it,' Jamie told him. 'They'll pick up that you're nervous and it'll make them edgy, which won't be good for anyone.'

'You're right,' Gary replied, taking a few deep, calming breaths. 'I need to chill a bit. I know, I'll think of me and Valerie together in her vestry.'

'It won't help if they pick up on the fact that you're feeling horny too,' commented Logan.

'They're here,' said Jamie as another white Transit van backed up down the alleyway.

It was a different van from the one they'd brought during the failed attempt to break into the workshop as it had a different licence plate. Either that or the plates had been changed.

Jamie experienced a moment of tension when Jason got out of the driver's seat, expression so neutral Jamie couldn't tell what he was thinking. They hadn't seen or spoken to each other since Jamie had told him he wanted nothing more to do with him. As Jason moved to open the rear doors of the van, he gave his son a nod, which he didn't return.

'Oh, God, he's back,' muttered Digger when Caesar got out of the front of the van too.

'All right, wee men?' Caesar cheerfully asked the Blood Brothers.

Logan arched an eyebrow. 'Wee men?'

'Relax, I'm only messing with you. When your baws drop hopefully you'll get a sense of humour.'

Jamie cast Gary and Digger warning glances over his shoulder, telling them not to respond. He could trust Logan to be sensible enough to keep his mouth shut.

'You ready for your first big secret?' Caesar asked them.

All four nodded seriously.

'Good. Open the doors, then, Jason.'

He obeyed and the Blood Brothers peered curiously into the back of the van from a distance, wondering what was going to leap out at them. The last thing they were expecting was a tubby middle-aged man clutching a blue carrier bag that clinked with bottles. His clothes were loud and flamboyant and on top of his head was balanced a ridiculous orangey-blond wig.

'Where the fuck am I?' slurred the short, rotund figure. 'Who are those wee scrotes?' he added, pointing at the Blood Brothers.

'Who are you calling a scrote?' demanded Digger.

The man straightened up to his full five feet six inches. 'I am—'

'Shut your hole,' Caesar told him.

The mystery man's eyes flashed with annoyance, but he went silent.

'Wee men,' said Caesar, 'meet your new secret. Secret, here are your wee men.'

Digger grunted and shook his head but managed to keep his anger in.

'They don't look very wee to me.' The mystery man frowned. 'That one's positively obese,' he added, pointing to Gary.

'Obese?' he exclaimed.

'And that one,' he continued, pointing to Digger. 'Well, I'm not sure what that is. Some sort of weird hybrid between a donkey and a bull elephant.'

'Who's this fucking fanny?' demanded Digger.

Caesar chuckled. 'Charming, isn't he? That's nothing, believe me. The good news is he only insults people when he's drunk. The bad news is that he's drunk all the time. You're not to ask his name. You don't need to know who he is and why he's here. If you want something to call him, you can call him... Donald.'

'Why Donald?' The mystery man frowned again.

'Because you wear a wig.'

'I do not,' he retorted, staggering slightly.

'It blew off when you got into the van, which was a bit of a giveaway.'

'Oh, aye, I forgot about that. So why does that mean I should be called Donald?'

'Because of Donald Trump.'

'Is that some sort of rhyming slang?'

'No, it's because you wear the same wig,' exclaimed an exasperated Caesar.

'Does Donald Trump wear a wig?'

'I don't know but that's your fucking name and you'll like it.'

Even Logan, the most sensible and quiet of them all, was fighting as hard as his friends to keep a straight face.

Caesar rolled his eyes. 'Jesus Christ.' He looked to the Blood Brothers. 'Good luck, boys. Your job is to protect him, but I'll understand if you give him the occasional slap.'

'So we've to keep him in the workshop?' Jamie frowned.

'Aye.'

'Workshop?' said Donald. 'Sounds delightful. I adored woodwork as a boy. I can spend my time whittling. Why is that funny?' he asked when Gary sniggered.

'Whittling. Is that code for something?'

'Yes. It's code for you're an idiot.' He looked to Caesar. 'Must I be inflicted with these children? Can't you find me any grown-ups?'

'You've pissed off all the grown-ups, so you're stuck with the weans now,' replied Caesar.

Donald tutted. 'Well, are you going to help me down or am I to stand here like a mobile exhibit?'

'Help the prick down, Jason.'

Jason took Donald's arm and assisted him to jump out of the back of the van, keeping him upright when he almost fell.

'I'm too old for this.' Donald sighed, straightening his wig, which had slipped. 'I should be sunning myself on a tropical beach somewhere, not being driven in the back of a van to the armpit of Glasgow.'

'Hey,' said Jamie. 'You can insult us but no' the Gallowburn. This is a good place with good people.'

'Then why is it littered with dog jobbies?' the man replied, looking at the ground in disgust. 'I nearly landed in one.'

Jamie ignored the comment. 'Caesar, can I have a word with you?'

'Naw. You want a word with someone, speak to your da.'

He looked uncertainly at his father, who stared back at him.

'Whatever's gone on between the two of you,' said Caesar, 'get over it fast, before you lose your eyes.'

'We can talk over here, son,' said Jason, heading into a corner of the alley.

Jamie looked back over his shoulder at Logan, who nodded encouragingly.

'So, what's wrong?' Jason asked him in a friendly tone.

'The workshop isn't set up to take a person. There's no bed, heating or cooking facilities. There's a cludgy and sink but it needs some cleaning. We can't keep him in there.'

'Don't worry, we've got all that stuff in the van.'

'I cannae see Caesar cleaning a toilet.'

'He won't. To make up for pushing you into the Firth of Clyde, I'll clean the toilet myself.'

'You'd really do that?' said an astonished Jamie.

'Aye. I'm no' too proud.'

'I'm warning you, it's bad.'

'I'll cope, and it can't possibly be worse than the ones I had to clean in prison.'

'Cheers, I appreciate it.'

'No problem. Gi'e us a hand unloading the stuff off the back of the van.'

'All right,' said Jamie, feeling slightly more well disposed to his father.

The rest of the Blood Brothers also helped while Caesar and Donald stood to one side, watching as they carried the furniture and supplies into the workshop. There was even a roll of thick carpet to put down on the cold concrete floor.

'Who do you think this arsehole is?' Digger whispered to Gary as they worked.

'Nae idea,' he whispered back. 'But it's no' surprising he's in trouble with the gob on him.'

Twenty minutes later the cold, bare room had been transformed into a cosy den for Donald with a lamp, armchair, camp bed, camping stove, matches, television, microwave, portable fridge, a stack of books and a supply of food, water and alcohol. True to his word, Jason pulled on a pair of rubber gloves and set about cleaning the toilet, which hadn't been used in years. Jamie watched him closely and he didn't grumble or even pull a face.

'Will this do you?' Caesar asked Donald.

Donald produced a bottle of gin from the carrier bag, unscrewed the lid and took a big swig. 'Well, I suppose it's an improvement on what it was. It'll look even better when I'm completely pissed.'

'A thank you would be nice.' Digger frowned.

'You want me to thank you for keeping me in this cell like I'm an animal in a zoo?'

'Animals have better manners,' said Logan, narrowing his eyes at him.

Donald looked him up and down. 'You seem an intelligent boy. You can help me unpack.'

With that he held the carrier bag out to Logan, who took it from him and pulled out a bottle of vodka and another bottle of gin.

'Is this it?' he asked Donald.

'That is everything I need in the world. As long as I have them I can cope with anything.'

'How long is he going to be here?' Jamie asked Caesar.

'Three or four days,' Caesar replied. 'Don't worry, we don't expect you to become his permanent carers. Then we can get him out of the country.'

Jamie was itching to ask who this man was and why the McVays were protecting him, but he knew better.

'He's got enough food for today and tomorrow, but you will need to bring him more supplies the day after,' added Caesar. 'And I want you to check on him at least twice a day.'

Jamie nodded in understanding.

'You sure you can handle this?'

'Nae bother.'

'Donald can be a handful, so make sure he doesn't run out of alcohol – it keeps him nice and quiet. If he runs out he goes into a rage and we don't want him banging on the door and attracting attention.'

'Understood. We'll work it in shifts so there's always someone to look after him.'

'Good lad. Maybe you're no' such a wanker after all?'

'That's the nicest thing you've ever said to me.'

Caesar didn't smile but his eyes twinkled with something that could almost be described as good humour. He produced a roll of notes from his pocket and held it out to Jamie. 'To cover your expenses.'

'Cheers,' he replied, taking it from him and slipping it into his pocket.

'Look after Donald and you'll get double the pay you got after beating the shite out of my men.'

This statement lessened some of the worry Jamie had about this latest job. 'Great.'

'Right, has your da finished scrubbing the cludgy?'

Without waiting for an answer, Caesar wandered into the tiny bathroom to check on Jason's progress. Jamie joined his friends in watching Donald wander aimlessly about the small room, studying each item of furniture that had been placed inside it.

'I wonder who the hell he is,' whispered Gary.

'It's probably best we don't know,' whispered back Logan.

'You don't think he's another test, do you?' said Digger. 'Like the packet of crisps was?'

'Naw,' said Jamie, watching Donald pick up the small camping stove, frown at it as though attempting to puzzle out what it was before replacing it on the floor. 'This is the real deal.'

When it was time for Caesar and Jason to leave, the latter hesitated by Jamie. 'Can I have a word, son?'

Jamie nodded and joined him outside the workshop.

'I know you're still pissed off at me,' began Jason, 'but can we meet for a coffee?'

'Why? You wantin' to discuss anything in particular?'

'No. I just want to spend time with you, genuinely. No ulterior motives, promise.'

Jamie was reluctant to open himself up to more hurt. 'No.'

'Come on, son.'

'You had your chance and you blew it. You're no' making a fool of me again. I'll be civil to you for the sake of business but that's all.'

'Jason, let's go,' called Caesar.

'Coming,' he replied before looking back at his son. 'Please, Jamie.'

'You'd better go. Caesar's getting impatient.'

'Jason,' barked Caesar, proving his point.

'All right, I'm coming,' he called over his shoulder, looking hopefully once more at Jamie, who folded his arms across his chest, gaze stony. With that Jason slunk back to the van.

Jamie watched Jason and Caesar get back in the van and drive off.

'What did he want?' Logan asked Jamie.

'To meet up. I told him to piss off.'

Logan patted his shoulder. 'Good call.'

'Jamie,' said Gary, exiting the workshop. 'You'd better come quick. Donald's going off on one because there's no foot spa.'

'Foot spa?' replied Jamie.

'He says he's got bunions and he needs one.'

'Jesus,' he sighed, rolling his eyes.

18

Mullen watched from his car as the white Transit van rolled by. He was careful to sink low into his seat to avoid being seen. He'd followed the Blood Brothers to this back street but had been unable to park down it because he would have been spotted. Instead he'd been forced to wait on the road that ran across the top of the alley, attempting to see what was going on and failing. He hadn't even managed to see who the occupants of the van were as it had come up on him from behind.

The van was there a good half-hour before it exited the alley.

'Jesus,' he breathed when he spotted the occupants.

One he recognised as Jason Gray, Jamie's father, but that wasn't a surprise. It was the second man in the van who was the shock. Caesar, second-in-command of the McVay family and Toni McVay's long-time lover.

Things had just got a hell of a lot more complicated.

His phone beeped and he smiled at the message that popped up. Jackie had been reeled in hook, line and sinker, which had been a surprise as he'd thought she'd be a tougher prospect. Part of him felt guilty, which wasn't an emotion he was accustomed to feeling. Jackie Gray was a good, decent woman, not the vicious, base creature he'd assumed she'd be. She was also very attractive and good company. She'd had such a hard life and she was potless, but she hadn't let it get her down. Jackie Gray was a fighter.

His phone beeped again as he received another message and he smiled as he replied. The next step in his plan was to get more access to the Gray home, namely to search Jamie's room. If there was anything to find, he would find it there.

He also pondered what to do now he knew the Blood Brothers were somehow involved with the McVays. He wouldn't tell Cameron in case he told every media outlet in the country, or the police, and the McVays would not appreciate that. Toni would demand the eyes of whoever was responsible and she wouldn't stop at Cameron, she would want to know his source too.

Mullen needed to find out exactly how the Blood Brothers were linked to the McVays and take it from there. He'd encountered Toni before and had narrowly avoided losing his eyes when a case of his had brought him to her attention. She wouldn't be so forgiving a second time.

Mullen hunkered down even further into his seat as the Blood Brothers strolled out of the alley. He was in a silver Toyota, so Jamie wouldn't recognise the car. They didn't notice him and passed by, talking so quietly he couldn't hear what they were saying.

When they'd turned the corner at the top of the road and vanished from view, Mullen got out of the car and jogged to the mouth of the alley, grimacing when he stood in a dog turd.

It was a dead end, just an ugly, squat building with a thick metal door. The windows were covered in mesh and something had been put over them from the inside to black them out, so he could neither see nor hear anything.

Mullen considered secreting a camera somewhere but he didn't have one on him and he didn't know if there were already cameras here, which was why he was keeping his distance from the building. The last thing he wanted to do was get caught on film and blow his cover.

Sighing with frustration, he returned to his car, scraping the dog mess off his shoe on the kerb before getting in, smiling when he received another text from Jackie.

* * *

Jackie was distracted from her worries about what else the McVay family were getting her son involved in by text messages from Scott. It had started off as a friendly chat and now they'd progressed to saying they'd missed each other and that they'd both really enjoyed their first kiss and couldn't wait for more. It made Jackie feel young. Scott texted her again.

I could come round now.

I'd like that but I've got to take Charlie to school soon.

Even though she couldn't wait to see him again she refused to rush into anything. She had to bear in mind her children's feelings and introduce Scott gradually into their home.

In that case, tomorrow can't come soon enough.

Her attention was drawn from the conversation when Jamie returned. She sent Scott a final message saying she'd see him later and cast her phone aside.

'Well?' was all she said.

'It's no drugs or weapons, Maw. You can relax.'

'I don't think I'll relax ever again. So, what was the delivery?'

'I cannae say but we've got it under control. It could have been worse.'

'That's something, I suppose.' She forced a smile. 'Brew?'

'Aye, please, Maw. I'm freezing.'

* * *

After his mum had left to take Charlie to school, Jamie slumped onto the couch, exhausted. He'd worry all day about Donald. The man looked to be in his mid-fifties but he had all the maturity of a ten-year-old. Digger had said he'd check on him that afternoon on his way to the gym. Fingers crossed Donald would behave himself and wouldn't burn the place down.

As he hadn't got much sleep the night before, worrying about the McVay delivery, Jamie decided to try and grab a couple of hours, so he took his brew to bed and curled up beneath the duvet, knowing he probably wouldn't get back to sleep as thoughts of Allegra, Cameron, the trial, the McVays, his father and Donald would spin through his head. The only time he felt peace was when he spoke to Allegra.

Taking out his phone, he flicked through the photos of them together. They were due to talk again tomorrow and he couldn't wait.

To his surprise, after he'd finished his cup of tea his eyelids grew heavy. Feeling cosy and warm, he soon drifted off to sleep, exhaustion winning out over his troubles.

* * *

It hadn't been difficult for Natalie to track down Helen Wilkinson on her arrival in Italy. She'd done an online search on that name, checking business as well as personal records, and up had popped a beauty salon in Florence. Unfortunately there was no picture of Helen on the salon's website, so she made the three-hour drive from Rome to Florence.

The city in central Italy was beautiful, full of renaissance architecture, the dome of Florence cathedral dominating the skyline. Natalie wasn't that familiar with Florence, her family and contacts in the country being centred around Rome, but it was just as lovely. She climbed out of the car, closed the door and locked it before tilting her face to the sky, enjoying the warmth of the sun soaking into her skin, a relief after the constant rain Glasgow had had lately. Even though the salon was on a busy street, the sweet scent of the colourful flowers bursting from the huge hanging baskets dangling from the walls of the shops filled her nostrils. It was an immaculately clean city, not a scrap of litter anywhere, the people elegant and beautiful.

She'd booked an appointment for a manicure at the salon, using her fluent Italian. As she walked through the door, excitement gripped her. She was close, she could feel it. She hadn't wanted things to progress so quickly. In truth, she had hoped this case would drag on so she could spend a few weeks in Italy, visiting family and friends and hooking up with Alessandro, her old flame. There was always the chance that the Helen Wilkinson who owned this salon wasn't Allegra Abernethy and part of her hoped that was the case, but the stone-cold professional in her was keen to catch her quarry.

Once inside she was greeted by a young, perky woman who introduced herself as Maria. She looked to be around Allegra's age, but she was far too short.

Maria seated her at a table and set about removing Natalie's old, chipped nail varnish. As Maria worked, Natalie took the opportunity to study her surroundings. The salon was large, offering a range of different treatments. It was very tastefully decorated in muted pink, fawn and cream. The effect wasn't garish or girly but rather classy and sophisticated. From what she'd researched of Allegra, she knew she was a woman with style and taste and this place looked as if it had received her magic touch, but that didn't mean Helen was Allegra. Natalie had hoped there would be photos on the walls of each staff member but there were none.

'I wondered if Helen Wilkinson was here?' Natalie asked Maria in Italian. 'I heard that she's a wonderful hairstylist. I was hoping to get my hair done by her.'

'No. She's gone away for a few days.'

'Oh, that's a shame. Do you know when she'll be back?'

'Probably not until the middle of next week, maybe even longer. She likes to travel.'

Natalie wondered if Maria was lying as she kept her head down as she talked, but that could just mean her attention was focused on her work. 'So you don't know when she'll be back, then?'

'No idea.'

'I see,' Natalie said, eyes continually darting about the room, studying each member of staff. It was a busy place and there seemed to be six of them working, including Maria. All were female but they were either too short or the wrong body type to be Allegra, and she was certain none of them were Allegra in disguise.

'Do you live in Florence?' Maria asked her.

'No,' replied Natalie. 'I'm staying with friends. I came from Rome. I realised my nails badly needed doing and this salon was recommended to me.'

'Oh, how nice.' Maria beamed. 'We have only been open eight months but already we are so popular.'

'That's great.' Natalie smiled. 'Do you enjoy working here?'

'Yes, very much. I love my job.'

'That's good. Sadly these days too few people enjoy what they do.'

'Do you enjoy your work?' Maria asked her as she applied the first layer of varnish to the nail on Natalie's left index finger.

'Yes, I'm one of the lucky ones too. I'm an architect.'

'Very interesting.' Maria smiled. 'I don't think I've ever painted an architect's nails before.'

Natalie asked Maria a few more questions about the salon but none of her answers indicated whether Helen Wilkinson was Allegra Abernethy.

'There, all done,' said Maria, putting the lid back on the bottle of nail varnish.

Natalie admired her handiwork. She had to admit she'd done a wonderful job. Each one of her nails had been smoothed and rounded and all were exactly the same length. She'd painted them a deep, luscious plum colour.

Maria indicated the small white nail-polish-drying machine on the table. 'If you rest your hands under there, it will dry your nails for you. We don't want them to get smudged.'

Natalie placed both hands under the machine.

'Scusi,' said Maria, getting up and heading down a short passage at the back of the salon and taking the stairs up to the first floor.

She knocked on the door at the end and a voice told her to come in.

'Sorry for interrupting,' she told the woman sitting at the desk in the salon's office. 'But there's a client downstairs who's a little strange.'

Allegra turned to face her with a smile. 'Oh, no, old Mrs Ricci hasn't come in for the full Brazilian wax again, has she? She screamed the place down last time. I don't know what she wanted that done for – she's eighty-three, for God's sake.' Allegra's Italian was as fluent as Natalie's.

'No, it's not her. It is a woman who's never been here before. She seemed very interested in you. She said she heard you're the best hairstylist and wanted her hair done by you...'

'And I don't cut hair.'

'Exactly. I just got this strange feeling from her, so I told her you'd gone away for a few days and that I didn't know when you'd be back.'

'Oh, Maria, you are such a treasure,' said Allegra with a fond smile.

'There was something else. When she speaks in Italian she sounds Scottish. I know this because I have been there on holiday. As you told me you came here from the UK to get away from someone who was stalking you, I thought I should warn you.'

Allegra felt herself go cold.

Maria curiously watched as her employer paled beneath her tanned skin. 'Are you all right, Helen?'

She forced a smile. 'Yes, thank you. I'm just a bit tired. You know, I might take a short holiday after all. I think I could use the break.'

'You have been working very hard.'

'Do you think you could manage to run things in my absence?'

'Yes, it won't be a problem. Francesca can always help me.'

'I really appreciate that, thank you. I'll make sure you're paid extra for your trouble. Is the customer still here or has she left?'

'She's still here, waiting for her nails to dry.'

'What's her name?'

'She booked under the name Claudia Gallo.'

Allegra nodded and Maria, taking this as her cue to leave, headed back downstairs to see to her client.

* * *

When she'd gone, Allegra brought up the security camera feed from the salon on her laptop. She'd had hidden cameras installed so she could always see who was coming and going. None of her staff knew about these cameras. She found the table Maria always used for her manicures and studied the beautiful, willowy woman with long light brown hair sitting there. The way she constantly looked around the room, studying everyone who walked by, made Allegra very nervous. She watched the woman converse with Maria, smiling and laughing before paying and walking out. Allegra switched to the camera on the front of the building, and noticed the woman glance back over her shoulder at the salon as she went.

'Did my father send you?' she murmured as the figure turned the corner and vanished from view.

Allegra sat back in her chair to think, stamping down the rising tide of panic. Either everything had been in Maria's imagination and the woman was a genuine customer, or she knew Allegra was still alive and was looking for her. Maria was a clever, practical woman, not prone to letting her imagination run away with her. Maria's instinct had told her something was wrong and she'd felt strongly enough to mention it.

Making a snap decision, Allegra shot to her feet, snatched up her handbag and hurried downstairs, sneaking out of the back of the salon. She headed down the back street and turned right onto the same street she'd last seen the mysterious Claudia. She walked through a grand archway that led her into a busy piazza lined with pavement cafes, bustling with tourists, Allegra almost falling over two of them when they suddenly stopped to take a selfie, arms around each other. Pigeons pecked at the ground and a band of three elderly men played some traditional music on a cello, violin and guitar, a crowd gathered around clapping along and tossing money into the open guitar case on the ground. Just then ahead of her she saw Claudia. Allegra had thought it would be impossible to spot Claudia in the crowd but she was a tall woman, taller than Allegra herself, and her long hair meant she stood out too.

Keeping her head down, Allegra followed the woman across the square; Claudia paused to watch a large golden carousel slowly turning, children clinging onto the pink-plumed horses, before carrying on her way. Allegra watched as she took a seat at a table outside one of the cafés, a large beige parasol providing shelter from the sun, giving her a good view of the immediate area. Only once she was seated and distracted by the waiter taking her order did Allegra skirt around the edge of the square, passing an elderly woman selling flowers, the sweet scent bursting into life as she passed by, fading as she left her behind. Allegra wondered if getting any closer to the mysterious woman would be a stupid thing to do but she had to know if Claudia Gallo was a danger to her and she wouldn't find that out by watching her from a distance. The advantage she had was that if Claudia was looking for her, she would have no idea what she looked like now.

Allegra took a seat at a table outside the café next to the one Claudia was in. She chose a spot where she was sitting behind her and partially hidden by a potted tree. A waiter came to take Allegra's order and she asked for a cappuccino before turning her attention back to Claudia, who had taken out her phone. Allegra got to her feet, using the tree as cover to listen in.

'Hi, Gavin, it's me,' said Claudia in a strong Glaswegian accent. 'No, I've not been able to confirm. One of her employees told me she's gone away for a few days, but I couldn't be sure she wasn't suspicious of my questions. I'm hanging around to see if she goes back to the salon. No, no photos anywhere online under the name Helen Wilkinson. No social-media profiles either. If it wasn't for the salon and passport she wouldn't exist.'

Allegra was starting to question how smart she'd been setting up that salon, but she hadn't thought anyone would look for her, certainly not under that name. The man who had made the passport must have grassed to someone. Had her father sent this woman here or was she connected to the police?

'I'll confirm, don't worry,' added Claudia. 'I might try getting access to something of hers that only she's touched for a fingerprint or DNA sample.'

Allegra's stomach lurched. She hadn't even considered that and there was nothing she could do to alter her DNA. She did recall watching a film where the main protagonist had his fingerprints burnt off, but she didn't know if that was a real thing.

'I'll keep you informed,' said Claudia, before she hung up as the waiter fetched her coffee and a pastry.

Allegra ducked back out of sight behind the tree, wondering what she should do now. It was imperative she find out exactly who this woman was. A police officer? Interpol? Private investigator? Or someone else she hadn't even considered. How she would love to get hold of the woman's phone, but even if she did she probably wouldn't be able to access it because it would be fingerprint or password protected.

Briefly she considered calling Jamie, but there was nothing he could do and he would only worry. The only way to get rid of this woman was to give her Helen Wilkinson.

* * *

Jamie had agreed to take the evening shift to check on Donald. He'd received a phone call from Digger that afternoon informing him that Donald was fine and had cooked himself eggs and beans on the small camping stove, leading to an enormous amount of flatulence. He'd said the inside of the workshop smelled like rotting cabbage. So Jamie wasn't exactly looking forward to this errand.

He unlocked the door to the workshop, hurried inside, closed the door behind him and locked it before turning to Donald, who was watching television.

Donald failed to realise Jamie was there because he had his back to the door and was wearing headphones, so the noise of the television wouldn't be heard from outside.

'Bloody hell,' exclaimed Donald, all his limbs jumping when Jamie appeared in front of him. He yanked off the headphones. 'Are you trying to give me a heart attack? Is that your game?'

'Didn't you hear me come in?' said Jamie innocently.

'Don't try and pull that one on me, boy. Have you brought my vodka?'

'No. I didn't know I had to.'

'But I need more vodka,' Donald said petulantly.

'You've already got a full bottle,' Jamie replied, pointing to the one on the floor by Donald's chair.

'That won't see me through to tomorrow.'

'If you're no' careful you'll die of alcohol poisoning or liver failure.'

'Good. That would be better than being trapped in here like a rat. There's no natural light in this place. It'll send me peculiar. I saw it on a documentary once. If you don't get regular access to natural light then you go insane and your skin falls off, or something. I wasn't paying much attention, to be honest.'

'I'm sure you'll be okay. It's only for a few days.'

'Very well, but if you walk in one day to find me a skinless sack of meat then on your head be it.'

'I'll take full responsibility,' said Jamie flatly.

He was tempted to ask Donald who he was and why the McVays were hiding him, and he had the feeling Donald would tell him, but he wanted his eyes to stay in his head, so he refrained. 'Is there anything you need?'

'Oh, I don't know,' Donald said wistfully. 'A purpose in life, a meaningful connection with someone, to feel like a fully functioning member of society again, a pretty pert brunette.'

'Is there anything you need that I can get you?' retorted Jamie.

'No, I suppose not,' the man sighed. 'Unless you can get me the last one? I'm sure there are some pretty girls on this estate somewhere who haven't grown old before their time, around the mid-twenty mark. Any older than that and they get too bolshy. I like the eager-to-please type.'

'No,' said a stony-faced Jamie. 'No one else is allowed in here.'

'Fine.' Donald sighed again. 'I suppose there'll be plenty of young nubiles on the exotic beach Toni promised to send me to.'

Jamie wondered if Donald would end up on a tropical beach being serviced by beautiful women or in a shallow grave minus his eyes. 'So, apart from the vodka, do you need anything?'

'I'll manage,' Donald said with a martyred sigh.

'Good. Gary will be round first thing in the morning.'

'Is Gary the fat one?'

'Aye, but don't call him that.' Jamie glowered. 'It won't be good for your health.'

As Jamie turned for the door Donald said, 'I knew Allegra.'

His words turned Jamie's body to stone. Once the initial shock of the statement had worn off, he slowly turned to face him. 'You did?'

'Oh, yes. I was a friend of her godfather, Tarquin. We did a lot of business together. Lovely girl. Owned every room she walked into.'

Jamie just nodded, afraid that if he started talking Donald would stop.

'I met her at several charity events. I knew her mother too, Rebecca. Such a divine creature – her daughter was very much a chip off the old block. I couldn't believe Rebecca married a monster like Cameron. Everyone said she was a gold-digger, but I believed she genuinely loved him. Like her daughter, she had the ability to see the best in people, but whatever was best in Cameron Abernethy died when he murdered his wife.'

'You know for certain that he killed her?'

'Of course I do. I heard him discussing it with that thug of his, Neil.'

Jamie stared at him with his mouth hanging open before he recovered himself. 'Why did you never tell the police? You could have saved her life.'

'Simple, boy. Because I didn't want to be murdered too. That man has killed more people than anyone realises. His wife was just the tip of the iceberg. It's such a shame he added his daughter to that list.'

Jamie loomed over him, hands bunched into fists. 'If you hadn't been such a fucking coward Rebecca Abernethy would be alive now and Allegra—' he broke off when he realised he was on the verge of saying *wouldn't have gone away*, catching himself '—would be here too,' he ended instead.

'I understand how annoyed you must be...'

'Annoyed?' Jamie exclaimed. 'Try fucking furious.'

'I was terrified for my life and I wouldn't have seen the inside of a courtroom. Cameron would have had me killed before I'd got anywhere near.'

'Then why hasn't he tried to have me killed again?'

'Because everyone would know who was responsible if anything happened to you, but he will try again, mark my words. While the trial is ongoing you're safe, but the moment it's over he will come for you again, regardless of whether he's found guilty or innocent.'

'Is that why you've been stashed here, to keep you hidden until you can give evidence in court? The police are reopening the investigation into Rebecca's death.'

'Sorry to disappoint, but no. I'm here for a very different reason.'

'Do you have any proof Cameron had Rebecca killed?'

'Just what I heard and saw. I don't have anything concrete, unless...'

'Unless?'

'Get me a bottle of vodka and I'll consider telling you.'

Jamie's lip curled. 'You never met any of the Abernethy family, did you? You're just trying to get more booze out of me. You haven't said anything that hasn't been in the newspapers or on the telly.'

'How about I describe the interior of the Abernethy home? That hasn't been on the news.'

'Go on, then,' said Jamie, folding his arms across his chest.

Donald did indeed describe the interior perfectly, including the huge swimming pool.

'It doesn't mean you know the family,' said Jamie when he'd finished. 'You could have done some work there.'

'What work?'

'I don't know, like fixing the plumbing or doing some decorating.'

'I am not a plumber or a decorator.' Donald sniffed. 'I'm a stockbroker. Oh, but I've said too much. Scratch that last part from your mind. Toni will have our guts for garters if she found out I'd said that.'

'You have to tell the police what you overheard Cameron saying about his wife,' said Jamie almost desperately.

'I'm sorry but I couldn't do that. At the moment I'm trying to avoid the police.'

'Shit,' sighed Jamie, raking his hands through his hair. 'There must be some other way, like a signed statement you can send them...'

'Toni really wouldn't like that and Cameron's smart lawyer would ensure it wasn't admitted as evidence, not without me to back it up. No, I'm sorry, Jamie. I couldn't possibly.'

'If it can be proved that he had his wife murdered the jury would be more likely to believe he killed his daughter too.'

'You won't need my evidence. From what the media's saying he's very likely to be found guilty anyway.'

'But there's always a chance he won't be and her mother's death tortured Allegra. She knew her da had arranged it and she wanted to see him punished for it. You could make that happen.'

'No, I couldn't. I really shouldn't have said anything. It's the gin's fault, it makes me talkative.'

'Is there anything I can say or do that would convince you to do this?'

'No. You seem an intelligent, together lad, so if you want to remain hale and hearty you'll forget I ever mentioned it.'

'Please, Donald...'

'No. I'm sorry, Jamie, that's the end of the conversation.'

His tone was such that Jamie knew further pleading would just be a waste of breath. It was still possible that he was making it all up for his own amusement. Fortunately there was someone he could ask.

Jamie stormed out, slamming the door shut and locking it. He took out the phone he used to call Allegra and dialled the only number on it.

'Dangerous,' she breathed when she answered.

'Princess,' he said, as usual aching inside at the sound of her voice.

'Are you okay? You sound angry.'

'How can you tell? I only said one word.'

'Because I know you. What's wrong?'

'Did you ever meet a stockbroker in a bad blond wig, likes to wear colourful clothes and is a total tosspot?'

'Do you mean Derek Baker?'

'I don't know his real name.'

'Is he a raging alcoholic who loves gin and vodka?'

'Yes, that's him.'

'I do. He was a good friend of my godfather's, although he did more business with my father. Tarquin was straight down the line. He liked Derek as a person, but he was too crooked for him to work with.'

'Which is why your da liked him?'

'Yes. They went in on a lot of nefarious schemes together. Why, have you met him?'

'Aye. He's the secret Toni wants us to look after.'

'Oh, hell. If that's the case, then he's probably done some dodgy work for her too. Maybe the police have cottoned on and she's hiding him so they won't be able to get him to talk?'

'Then why not just kill him?'

'He might be too valuable to her. The man's a mathematical genius and he has a sixth sense for investment. He made my father a lot of money.'

'He said he overheard Cameron and Neil discussing having your mother killed.'

There was silence on the other end.

'Are you okay?' he asked her.

'Yes, sorry. That was a bit of a shock.'

'No, I'm sorry, I should have broken the news more gently. I told him to give a statement to the police, but he refused. I was so fucking angry because if he'd done that in the first place your maw would still be alive and you would probably be here, with me. But he was too fucking cowardly to do anything. He said he was scared of Cameron.'

'I understand why you're angry but don't be too hard on him. My father has that effect on people.'

'If he is telling the truth we cannae do anything about it because he can't go to the police and he has no evidence.'

'That's typical where my father's concerned. Everyone knows what he's done but everyone's too scared or has been bribed, so nothing happens.'

'Until you got the better of him,' he said fondly.

'Don't push the issue with him, babe. It will only get you into trouble with Toni. My mother's gone and there's no bringing her back. I don't want to lose you too.'

'Okay, if that's what you think is best.'

'I really do. You're everything to me, Jamie. Please look after yourself, for my sake.'

'I will,' he said gently.

'I'm glad you called, actually, because there's something I need to tell you. I wasn't going to mention it at first because I didn't want you to worry, but I think it's best you know.'

'Know what?' he said, concerned.

'Someone came to the salon asking questions about Helen Wilkinson. Maria, who works for me, got suspicious and told her I'd gone away for a few days. I followed this woman and overheard her on the phone talking to either her boss or someone she works with. She pretended she was Italian but she's Glaswegian and she said she wants to get Helen Wilkinson's fingerprints or DNA for testing.'

'Oh, bloody hell. Who put them onto you?'

'I'm guessing my father. It's possible she's a police officer but I don't think so.'

'Neither do I. They're convinced you're deid.'

'Then it's probably someone my father hired. I don't know who they are, although she did call the man Gavin.'

'You need to get out of there.'

'I can't. All my money is tied up in the salon and I like it here. I've made friends. I've come up with a plan – I'm going to give her Helen.'

'What?' he exclaimed. 'That doesnae sound a good idea.'

'Wait, just hear me out.'

As she explained her plan he fell in love with her all over again.

19

Jackie and Scott walked arm in arm along the banks of the River Kelvin that ran through Glasgow's Botanic Gardens.

'Why have I never been here before?' She sighed with happiness. 'It's so beautiful and peaceful.'

'Not in the summer months,' he replied. 'It's hoachin' then.'

'I can imagine. I don't often get to places like this. Thank you for bringing me.'

'Any time.' He smiled. 'Does Jamie not take you anywhere?'

'He does his best but he's a man now, he doesnae want to go everywhere with his maw. But now he's got a car we'll be able to get out and about more. He mentioned taking me and Charlie for a day out at Stirling soon. Charlie's always wanted to visit the castle. He's got a thing about castles.'

'Jamie seems a very together young man. He's a credit to you,' said Mullen, glad to be able to steer the conversation in that direction.

'He's a cracker. Since Jason walked out on us he took it upon himself to be the man of the house, even though he was so young. I don't know how I would have managed without him, and he's wonderful with his younger brother.'

'It must have been so difficult for him when Allegra died. I'm sorry, I shouldn't have said that,' he added when her smile fell.

'No, it's all right. Her death hit us all very hard and we're still feeling her loss. She just fitted right in with our family, even though we came from very different worlds. That girl didn't have an ounce of snobbery, which was a miracle given that she was raised by that stuck-up bastard of a father of hers. I wish you could have met her. She was so special. I know everyone says that about people who have died tragically but Allegra really was. I would have loved to have her as a daughter-in-law. Jamie's shown no interest in anyone else since, which isn't surprising because she's a tough act to follow, but I worry about him thinking being with another woman would be betraying Allegra. I know he's lonely, I can see it in his eyes, and the girls on the scheme throw themselves at him but he's no' interested. There's only one woman he wants and he can't have her. She was his first love.'

'I'm sure he'll meet someone else one day. He's probably still grieving.'

'I hope you're right.'

'Course I am,' Mullen said, wrapping an arm around her.

Jackie smiled and rested her head on his shoulder. 'I'm just so afraid for him. I know Cameron will try to hurt him again, and with his father coming back to the scheme he's distracted, not looking over his shoulder as much as he should.'

'He's a smart lad, he can handle it.'

'But he's still so young.' Jackie smiled sheepishly. 'Sorry, I expect you don't want to hear me bleat on about my problems.'

'On the contrary, I'm glad you feel you can confide in me. I like you very much, Jackie. You're different.'

'There are plenty of gobby cows like me about.'

'You're not gobby. You're strong and self-confident.' He stopped and turned her to face him, taking her face in his hands. 'And beautiful.'

'Is there something wrong with your eyes?' She blushed.

'No,' he breathed, leaning in to kiss her. 'My vision is perfect.'

Gently he brushed her lips with his own, pulling back slightly to regard her, enjoying the way her cheeks bloomed with colour and her pupils dilated. He kissed her again, harder, feeling her hands run up his neck and into his hair, the sensation sending tingles down his spine. He had to admit that Jackie Gray was a good kisser and he was rather enjoying this particular assignment.

The kiss ended and they smiled at each other, Mullen brushing a stray strand of hair out of her eyes.

'That was very nice,' he said.

'It was,' she replied, wondering if it was too early to move onto the next stage. She was a mature, sensible woman, not some daft teenager who leapt into bed with anyone, but it had been a very long time since she'd desired a man so much. She'd thought feelings like that were behind her, but they'd returned with a vengeance.

Mullen, for his part, was wondering about the best way to gain access to her home. He had hoped she'd invite him over for dinner but so far that invitation didn't seem to be forthcoming, probably because she was thinking of her children. To her credit she always put them first. He reasoned that if he invited her to his own home then she might be more inclined to extend the same invitation to him.

'Would you like to have dinner at my place tomorrow evening?' he said.

'Oh, wow, that's fast,' she replied.

'I didn't mean for... that,' he hastily added. 'I just thought it would be a quieter, more intimate setting where we could get to know each other better.'

'Yes, that sounds nice,' Jackie replied, hoping she didn't look as thrilled as she felt.

'Great.' He smiled, taking her arm as they continued their stroll along the riverbank.

Mullen was delighted. Inviting her into his home would create a deeper level of trust and intimacy between them, meaning she would be much more likely to allow him into her own home and finally he could search Jamie's room. At least, he hoped that was why he felt so excited. He'd never fallen for a woman in his life and now was not the time to start, but there was something about those green eyes of hers that melted the ice around his heart.

* * *

Jamie hung up after talking to Allegra, feeling troubled. He couldn't just sit back and do nothing after what Donald, or rather Derek, had told him, so he called his dad and asked to meet him.

'This is a bit of an odd place to meet,' said Jason when he found Jamie standing by the hanging tree on the expanse of untouched land in the very centre of the scheme, known locally as The Gallows, where criminals had been executed until eighteen sixty-eight, when public hangings in Scotland had ended. It was already dark, the tree casting an ominous shadow across the ground. A chill hung in the air and thick black clouds were amassing overhead. Jamie hoped the threatening rain held off until he'd got home – he had no wish to be soaked all over again.

'This is where Cameron and Craig tried to kill me,' replied Jamie, staring up at the tree. 'I could have ended up dangling from it like so many people have in the past.'

'That's a bit morbid, son.'

'But true.' Jamie snapped himself out of it and turned to face his father. 'Thanks for coming.'

'Any time for you, Jamie, and I mean that.'

Jamie just nodded. 'I want to ask you something, Da, and I need you to tell me the truth – is Donald really Derek Baker?'

Jason blinked at him in astonishment. 'How do you know that?'

'It doesn't matter. Why is he here?'

'You already know too much. It's not safe for you to know more.'

'He works for Toni, doesn't he? He probably knows all the secrets of her finances and investments, but the police have got too close, so she's hiding him so they don't find out the truth.'

'So you don't know it all, then. No, that's not why he's in hiding.'

'Are you going to tell me why?'

'No, for your own sake.'

'He told me he overheard Cameron and Neil discussing having Rebecca Abernethy killed.'

'Allegra's maw?'

Jamie nodded.

'Christ.'

'You have to convince him to tell the police.'

'Toni would never allow that.'

'You don't know what it would mean to me if you made this happen, Da.'

'I thought you were never going to call me that ever again. You've changed your tune now you want something from me.'

Jamie's eyes flashed. 'You owe me this, after how you've let me down my entire life.'

'Listen, son, I can only imagine how eager you must be to throw everything you can at Cameron and ensure he's sent down for life, but if you push this it won't hurt Cameron in the slightest, it will only hurt you and me, and in turn Charlie and Jackie.'

Jamie grunted and kicked at the ground.

'Are you sure he was even telling the truth?' said Jason. 'He's known for telling tall tales.'

'He described the inside of Cameron's house perfectly.'

'He might well have been in the house, he could even be friends with Cameron, but it doesn't mean he's telling the truth about over-hearing the plot to kill Allegra's mother. I mean, surely they would have been very careful to make sure they weren't overheard before discussing something like that?'

'That's true,' Jamie muttered.

'I know it's not easy, but you have to let this go. This is your first real job for Toni and if you bugger it up she'll just get rid of you. I don't mean to sound harsh, but you need a reality check, son. Allegra's dead and gone. You've got to think about those who are still living, like your maw and brother, as well as your friends. Play your cards right and you could improve all their lives, as well as your own. Let this go before it buries you. Allegra wouldn't want you putting yourself in danger for this.'

'You don't get it,' Jamie muttered to the ground.

'There's something you're keeping back, isn't there? I can see it in your eyes. You can confide in me, Jamie. I'll keep it to myself.'

'I'm not keeping anything back.' Jamie shoved his hands into his pockets. 'Thanks for nothing.'

'Wait,' said Jason, jogging after him as he strode away. 'I'm only trying to help you. I want you to start looking to the future. Why don't you get yourself another girlfriend? What have I said?' he added when Jamie rounded on him, hands bunched into fists.

'It doesn't matter,' Jamie said through gritted teeth before continuing on his way. He sighed and shook his head when the heavens finally opened, drenching him in icy rain. 'Oh, no' again,' he exclaimed.

Jason pulled up the hood of his coat against the pounding rain, watching Jamie recede into the distance. If he got his son what he wanted, then he might forgive him, but Toni would never allow Donald to give evidence.

There must be another way...

* * *

Allegra refused to touch the silk scarf she'd selected as part of her ploy to put off Claudia, or whatever her name really was. She pointed to it in the shop and got the assistant to take it off the rack and wrap it for her. As she didn't want the scarf traceable back to her, she'd made the hour-long drive to Siena to purchase it. No matter how good an investigator the mysterious Claudia was, no way would she be able to visit every shop in Italy that sold silk scarves.

Allegra paid for her purchase in cash, returned to her car carrying the paper bag containing the scarf in a gloved hand and drove back to Florence. Rather than risk going back to her apartment, she was staying in a hotel under the name Evelina Russo, which she thought was a beautiful name. Already she was working on changing hers to that permanently.

Once she was back in her elegant suite, she called Maria.

'I need to ask a favour,' she began.

* * *

Natalie returned to the salon for the massage she'd booked to try and discover more about Helen Wilkinson. To her relief, it wasn't Maria, who'd done her nails, it was a short, round woman called Aida who had a grip like iron. Natalie only realised how wound up she was when Aida's fingers dug efficiently into her muscles, releasing all the knots.

'You are very tense,' said Aida as she worked.

'Work has been hectic,' murmured Natalie, who was face-down on the massage table, feeling all the recent stress draining out of her. It felt so good she was disappointed when Aida announced the thirty minutes was up. No wonder this salon was so popular – all the staff were excellent at their jobs.

'I'll leave you to get dressed,' said Aida in her soft, soothing voice. 'Take your time getting up, there's no rush. You need to drink some water,' she added, pointing to the sparkling jug and glass on the table in the corner of the room.

'Thank you,' replied Natalie, too chilled out to move, hoping she didn't fall asleep.

* * *

Aida exited the room, quietly closing the door behind her. After washing her hands, she hurried back into the main salon where Maria was waiting at the till.

'She is finished,' Aida told her. 'Now we need to wait for her to get dressed.'

'Good,' replied Maria. 'You remember what to do?'

Aida smiled and nodded, enjoying the drama.

'Remember, act natural. She can't suspect a thing.'

'I know.'

Maria made herself scarce, heading to the small staff room at the back of the salon. Aida was waiting at the till for her client to finally emerge from the massage room.

'You look much more relaxed.' Aida smiled.

'I feel it,' replied Natalie, taking out her card to pay. 'I can safely say that was the best massage I've ever had.'

'That's because I am the best,' said Aida with another smile and a huge amount of immodesty.

'I won't argue with you there.' Natalie smiled back. 'Add on an extra 10 per cent as a tip.'

'That is most generous, thank you.' Aida beamed.

Once payment had been made, Aida stepped out from behind the small counter to the coat rack beside it.

'This was yours, wasn't it?' she said, producing a thin black jacket.

'Yes, thank you.'

Aida assisted her on with it. 'Is that your scarf too?' she asked her, indicating the elegant cream and pink flowery scarf that had been hanging underneath her coat.

'No, I've never seen it before.'

Aida peered at it closer and rolled her eyes. 'Oh, of course. It belongs to Helen, who owns the salon. It is her favourite and she has gone away on holiday without it.'

'Really? Has she gone anywhere special?'

'Yes, she is visiting friends in Venice.' Aida sighed wistfully. 'She is so lucky. Venice is one of my favourite cities.'

'It is a fascinating place.'

'Helen won't be happy. She adores this scarf.'

'Oh, that is a shame,' replied Natalie, forcing her expression to remain deadpan.

Another customer came through the door and Aida bid Natalie, or Claudia as she thought she was called, goodbye.

* * *

Natalie made a show of pulling on her gloves. Glancing around to make sure no one was looking, she snatched the scarf from the rack and rushed out. Once on the pavement she produced a clear plastic bag from inside her handbag and slipped the scarf inside before carefully sealing it.

Only once she'd turned the corner into the busy piazza did she call Mullen.

'You won't believe what I've got,' she told him.

'What's that?' was his cool reply.

'A scarf belonging to Helen Wilkinson. I'll send it to you for testing.'

'It's definitely hers?'

'According to one of her employees, yes. It's even pink and cream, the same colours the salon's decorated in. It's just Allegra's style and I've also found out where she's gone – Venice.'

'Head over there immediately.'

'I will, as soon as I've sent you the scarf. I'll send it priority postage.'

'Excellent work, Natalie.'

'Thank you.' She smiled before hanging up, very pleased with this day's work.

* * *

Allegra sat in the office, watching the mysterious woman steal the scarf she'd bought from Siena. Hopefully next she'd go to Venice and Allegra would never have to deal with her again. She'd chosen Maria and Aida to pull off this stunt because they were her most loyal employees and could be trusted to keep their mouths shut. Naturally they were curious about the reason for the subterfuge and Allegra had told them she wanted rid of this woman, who had stalked her in Scotland and who was a danger to her. This had satisfied them and they'd agreed to help.

Maria popped her head around the door holding a Jiffy bag.

'Come in.' Allegra smiled.

Maria stepped inside and held out the Jiffy bag to her. 'This just came for you.'

'Thank you,' said Allegra, taking it from her.

'The woman stole the scarf.'

'Excellent. You and Aida did very well. As promised, you will have double wages this week.'

'That's very kind.' Maria smiled. 'But not necessary. I was happy to do it.'

'It's a thank you for your help. That woman is an old girlfriend of an ex-boyfriend of mine and she stalked me for years. I really didn't think she'd find me all the way out here.'

'Let's hope she doesn't come back.'

'I think we've seen the last of her.'

'I don't understand why she wanted the scarf though.'

'She likes to steal things of mine. She's quite insane.'

Maria shuddered. 'I'm glad it's all over. I'd better get downstairs. I have a client waiting.'

When she'd gone, Allegra tore open the Jiffy bag and smiled. Inside was a false passport, driver's licence, identity card and Italian birth certificate in the name of Evelina Russo. She should have got her Italian forger to make her documents in an Italian name, not the name on the passport she'd got from Glasgow, but she really hadn't thought anyone would find out about Helen Wilkinson. She'd already set up a dummy corporation under the name of Evelina Russo, who would shortly buy the salon and Helen Wilkinson would never be heard from again. She couldn't wait to tell her Dangerous, he would be so proud.

* * *

'Will you be all right here on your own with Charlie?' Jackie anxiously asked Jamie.

'I'll be fine, Maw, don't worry.'

'But I do worry with everything going on.'

'The lads are coming round to watch a couple of films. Does that make you feel better?'

'It does. Can you get at least one of them to stay over?'

'Aye, I will. We'll be fine. Go and enjoy your date.'

'Well, okay, if you're sure, but I will be back late.'

'I don't mind if you don't come back until the morning.'

'Jamie,' she exclaimed.

'I'm an adult, Maw, I know what happens on third dates. Go and have some fun. I don't mind. You've been alone for so long.'

She kissed his cheek. 'I don't know what I did to deserve you and your brother, but every day I'm so grateful for you both.'

He beamed at her. 'Thanks, Maw. We feel the same about you.'

'That's him,' she breathed when the doorbell rang.

'I'll get it.' He grinned.

'Hello, Jamie.' Mullen smiled when the front door was pulled open.

'All right, Scott? Come on in.'

'Thank you,' he replied, stepping inside.

He smiled at Jackie, who looked lovely in a knee-length black skirt and a dark red blouse. Smart but casual, the perfect combination for the evening. 'Are you ready to go?' he asked her.

'I am, I just need to say goodbye to my boys,' she replied. 'Charlie's in his room. I'll be down in a minute.'

She rushed upstairs, leaving Jamie and Mullen alone.

'So,' began Mullen. 'How have things been lately? Any more trouble from that shower who attacked you?'

'Naw,' Jamie replied, trying not to think about battering John Lawson. 'All quiet.'

'That's good. I did worry they'd retaliate.'

'Not after we kicked the shite out of them.'

It just struck Mullen that Jamie seemed to admire him for his skills.

'You'll treat my maw nice, won't you?' said Jamie.

Mullen realised this wasn't really a question, it was a warning. 'Of course I will.'

'She's been through a lot and she doesn't deserve to be hurt. I like you, Scott, but, seriously, it would be better for you if you're nice to her.'

'I fully intend to be, Jamie, you've no worries on that score. I really do like her. She's a very unique woman.'

'Aye, she is,' Jamie said with a fond smile.

If Jamie thought he was serious about his mother, then he would be more likely to open up to him, trust him, allow him further into their lives. That was what Mullen told himself anyway when Jackie reappeared and his stomach flipped over. By Christ, those eyes of hers were amazing.

'Charlie's nearly done in the bath,' Jackie told Jamie. 'When he's finished make sure he comes down for his supper. Don't let him skulk about up there reading comics.'

'I won't'.

'See you later, Jamie, love,' Jackie said, kissing his cheek.

'Maw,' he muttered, embarrassed, although he was smiling.

'I've got my phone, so call me if you need me.'

'We'll be fine, now go and have a good time.'

Jackie gave him a little wave before leaving with Scott.

Charlie, as his mum had told him to, came down for his supper after his bath, wearing his pyjamas, his hair damp. Just as he was tucking into his crunchy pop pop crinklies in front of the television, the rest of the Blood Brothers turned up.

'We got a carry out from Mr Cavenie,' said Gary, a blue poly bag dangling from each hand. 'He said it was on the house. The Reids havenae bothered him since.'

'That's good news,' said Jamie. 'Did you check on Donald?' he asked Gary.

'I did and he's tucked up cosy for the night.' Gary seated himself on the couch and took out two six-packs of lager, along with numerous bags of crisps and nuts, and dumped them on the couch.

'Where are we supposed to sit?' said Logan, gesturing from himself to Digger. 'You've given our seats to the snacks.'

'Because they're more important than you.'

'Charming.'

'Why, did you want all four of us to cosy up together on the couch?'

Logan picked up the crisps, hurled them at Gary and plonked himself down on the now vacant spot at the opposite end of the couch to his friend.

Jamie watched all this from the comfort of the armchair with an amused smile.

'I'll take the floor.' Digger shrugged, seating himself beside Charlie and crossing his legs, looking like an overgrown child. 'I'm no' proud.'

'We already guessed that when we saw your art magazine,' said Logan.

Digger turned his head to glower at him.

'So, what do you fancy first?' said Gary, producing the DVDs he'd selected. '*High School Halloween Slasher from Hell, Chainsaw Chop Shop* or *The Revengeist*?'

'*The Revengeist*?' Logan frowned. 'That's no' even a word.'

'Aye, it is. It's on the cover. See,' Gary said, pointing to the word above an image of a muscular man, head bowed, vest artfully torn, a shotgun resting on one shoulder.

'Let me guess,' sighed Logan. 'A drug cartel kills some ex-military guy's wife, or possibly his entire family, and he goes after them all one by one.'

'You've already seen it, then?'

'Aye, I have, about a hundred times. There's loads of films with the same storyline. I don't know why we let you pick the DVDs. You always choose utter shite.'

'Oh, come on, the slasher one sounds great. A bunch of teenagers get trapped in their school in a blizzard at night and there's a mad slasher on the loose.'

'Why are they at school at night?'

'Err...'

'You cannae put them on yet,' said Jamie, gesturing to Charlie.

'Oh, sorry,' said Gary. 'What are we watching, wee man?'

The Dude and the Dog,' replied Charlie, eyes not leaving the screen. 'It's awesome. It's about this guy at high school who takes on the bullies with the help of his dog, a wee poodle. But the poodle can talk and only the dude can hear him.'

'Sounds better than what Gary picked,' commented Digger.

Jamie went rigid when he felt the phone he used to contact Allegra start to vibrate in his pocket. He pulled it out and rushed for the stairs. 'I'll be back in a sec,' he said before hurrying up them.

'Oh, God,' said Gary. 'I hope that's no' the McVays wantin' something. I've been looking forward to tonight.'

* * *

'All right, Princess?' said Jamie when he answered the phone.

'Oh, sorry,' she replied. 'Did I call at a bad time? You sound a bit breathless.'

'Because I ran up to my room to answer your call. The lads are downstairs.'

'What about Jackie and Charlie?'

'Charlie's been hypnotised by the telly and my maw's out on a date.'

'With the same man?'

'Aye. Third date and he's taken her to his place for dinner.'

'Wow, go Jackie. I've got some news.'

'Oh, aye?'

'I dealt with that woman who came looking for me. Helen Wilkinson is now no more. You are talking to Evelina Russo.'

She said the name in an Italian accent and lust swept through him. 'That is so sexy.'

'I know,' she said, a grin in her voice. 'I just wanted to let you know that it's been sorted and you don't need to worry. I'm safe.'

'That is good news, but it was a close call. Maybe you should move on somewhere else?'

'Maybe, but I'm happy here. I'll see how it goes. So, any news your end?'

'Naw. Me and the lads are having a film night. Gary's chosen some utter shite for us to watch but it's always more of a laugh when we watch crap films.'

'I like crap films. I watched one the other day about killer llamas. Tacky but, in a strange way, genius.'

'I'll look out for it.' He smiled.

'Any update on your father?'

'That walloper? I told him what Donald, I mean Derek, had told me. I wanted him to help me convince him to tell someone what he knows about your maw's death.'

'And what did he say?'

'That he couldn't. Toni would go mad.'

'I hate to say it, but he's right. No way would she allow that. You have to let it go, Jamie.'

He sighed. 'Okay, I will.'

'Thank you. We need to be so careful. This separation is just temporary and I'm terrified of something happening to make it permanent.'

'I won't let that happen, I promise you.'

'I know.'

They chatted for a few more minutes before he reluctantly said goodbye and headed back downstairs.

'Who was that?' Gary asked him when he walked into the living room.

'Oh, no one,' he mumbled, feeling awful for referring to Allegra as no one.

'It didn't look like no one,' said Digger. 'You ran out of here like you had a ferret down your trousers.'

'It was just personal, all right?' said Jamie, retaking his seat in the armchair.

'If you've met another bird, it's all right,' said Logan gently. 'No one will think bad of you. You've mourned long enough.'

'It wasn't another bird,' snapped Jamie. 'Just leave it.'

Logan held up his hands. 'Whatever you say, Jamie,' he replied, glancing at Gary and Digger, who appeared equally puzzled.

Jamie glared down at the floor, avoiding the searching gazes of his friends, wondering how long he could keep up this exhausting charade.

20

'This is a lovely flat,' said Jackie.

'Thanks,' replied Mullen. 'I like it.' In truth it wasn't his own place, it was one he only used for business, but it was impressive and he wanted to impress her. 'The best thing about it is the view.'

He strode across the living room to pull open the curtains covering the enormous window. Jackie gasped at the magnificent view looking out over the River Clyde, the Finnieston Crane lit up in the glow of the city lights.

'Wow,' she said, wide-eyed. 'That's amazing.'

'Isn't it?' He smiled, pleased with her enthusiasm. 'Would you like a glass of wine?'

'Yes, please.'

'I've got a lovely red,' he said, walking into the open-plan kitchen. 'It's like drinking velvet.'

'Perfect.'

He poured them a glass each and joined her back at the window. When he put his arm around her, she rested her head on his shoulder.

'Something smells good,' she said.

'I'm not sure whether you're referring to my aftershave or the food.'

'The aftershave is very nice, but the food smells amazing.'

'I've been busy in the kitchen all day. To start is a Roquefort cheese and caramelised onion tart. As you said you enjoy stews, I made ratatouille for the main course, and chocolate mousse for dessert.'

'Wow, you have been busy.'

'Well, I did buy the mousse because I never got the hang of making mousse, but the rest is all my own work.'

'You didn't need to go to so much trouble.'

He smiled down at her. 'Yes, I did.'

Gently he pressed his lips to hers and pulled back slightly to gaze at her, running his fingertips down her face, smiling when her cheeks bloomed with colour again. He took her glass from her hand and put both glasses down on the windowsill, before taking her face in his hands and kissing her hard.

Jackie's arms went around his neck, their bodies pressing against each other as the kiss grew more passionate. Her leg went around his waist and his hand slipped under her skirt and up her thigh.

'You're so beautiful,' he breathed, kissing her neck.

'Where's your bedroom?' she gasped.

'Really? You're ready?'

'Yes, but I want you to know that I'm not easy. In fact, it's a long time since I had sex but I'm a grown woman and I know what I want. We're not daft kids, so what's the point in fannying about?'

'I couldn't have put it better myself.' He smiled.

'Oh, but what about the food you cooked? You put so much effort into it, I don't want it to spoil.'

'It'll keep,' he said, scooping her up and carrying her down the hall to the bedroom.

Jackie laughed out loud and kissed him. He made her feel so young.

* * *

Jackie lay in Scott's arms after the most satisfying sex of her entire life. They were both hot and sweaty, the duvet shoved entirely onto the floor. She ran her hand up and down his stomach, which actually resembled a washboard. She'd never been with a man with such a great body and she loved the feel of his muscular arms wrapped around her.

'So that's another talent to add to your list,' she told him. 'Fighting skills, cooking and sex.'

'I think that skill lies with you,' he replied. 'You're a dynamo.'

'Really? I've never been called a dynamo before.'

He smiled and kissed her, running his fingers through her hair. Mullen hadn't expected things to move so quickly, in fact he hadn't intended to sleep with her at all. For the first time in his life, he'd overstepped the bounds of professionalism. If any of his employees had slept with a mark he would have sacked them, but it had felt so right. No longer could he kid himself that Jackie was merely a means to get closer to Jamie. He genuinely liked her, and it was all going to end in heartache, but he didn't want to give her up just yet.

Her fingers brushed the scar on his abdomen. 'Is that where you got shot?'

'Yeah,' he replied. 'It was a sniper in Afghanistan. It was touch and go. I lost a lot of blood and it ended my career, but at least I'm still alive.' A shadow passed across his face. 'I'm luckier than some who were deployed out there.' The shadow was dispelled when she hugged him tighter, filling him with warmth, and he clung onto her.

'Sorry for asking,' she said. 'I won't mention it again.'

'I don't mind you asking,' he said, running his fingers down her bare back. 'Well, I don't know about you, but I've certainly worked up an appetite.'

'Me too.'

'How about I bring the food through here? That way we can stay in bed.'

'All right.' She smiled. 'Shall I give you a hand?'

'No, I can manage. You stay here and relax.' He picked up the duvet and placed it on the end of the bed. 'I'll put that there in case you get cold, but I do hope you don't use it,' he added with a playful wink that drew from her that deep, dirty laugh he was growing so fond of.

Mullen pulled on his grey robe and wandered barefoot into the kitchen, smiling to himself. His smile fell when he saw he had a missed call from Steven, one of his employees. Fortunately he'd put his phone on silent before Jackie had arrived.

'It's me,' he told Steven when he answered.

'Oh, hi, boss. Just to let you know that the scarf Natalie sent has arrived. I've handed it over to our man for DNA comparison. He's rushing it through, so we should have the results in a couple of days. Hello, are you still there?'

'Yes, I'm here,' he replied. He'd got lost in the thought that the results of the comparison could well end his relationship with Jackie. He found himself hoping Helen Wilkinson wasn't Allegra Abernethy. 'Let me know the moment you find out.'

'Will do. Oh, and Natalie's in Venice but so far nothing.'

'All right, thanks,' Mullen said before hanging up.

He sighed and tossed the phone onto the worktop. One day soon he would lose Jackie. She wouldn't discover the truth of who he was, he would see to that, but when the case was over he would have to break it off with her.

Shoving aside all thoughts of breaking up with her, he took the food out of the oven, artfully arranged it onto plates and carried it through to the bedroom on a large tray, along with the bottle of red wine. He had big plans for the chocolate mousse.

* * *

It was Jamie's turn to check on Donald the next morning and he was looking forward to it. He'd made a mental note to always think of him as Donald, not Derek, to avoid any slip-ups.

He stopped by the workshop after dropping Charlie off at school.

Once again Donald was watching television, but this time he realised Jamie was there before he could surprise him. He'd switched the chair and television around so he could see the door. Jamie wrinkled his nose. The room was starting to smell of body odour.

'Hello, Jamie,' said Donald when he walked in. 'I expected to see you sooner.'

'Why?'

'You seemed rather keen on me telling the police what I know. I thought you'd be back to plead your case more.'

'You mean you wanted me on my knees begging you?'

'Sorry, you're not my type. I like them a little less masculine.'

'So, you haven't changed your mind about telling the police, then?'

'No, sorry,' said Donald, staring at the television. 'That's just how it is.'

'Well, I've made a decision of my own. I've decided that me and my pals aren't going to bring you any more booze.'

Now he had his attention. 'What?'

'Either you give me a statement detailing what you saw or you go cold turkey.'

'But... you can't do that. You're supposed to take care of me.'

'And we are. We're bringing you food and water. You know, the essentials. Booze isn't an essential.'

'It is to me. In fact, it's more essential than the sodding food.'

'Here's the water,' Jamie said, taking two large bottles out of the carrier bag he held and placing them on the floor, along with the food. 'Much healthier than the booze. Enjoy.'

'You can't go, I've only half a bottle of vodka left.'

'That's no' my problem.'

'Wait,' Donald cried when he made for the door.

Jamie stopped and turned to face him.

'Don't you see what an impossible situation this is? Toni will have us both killed.'

'I'm no' asking you to go to the station. I just want you to record a statement about what you saw and heard, that's all.'

'And what will you do with it?'

'Nothing. It'll just make me feel better having it.'

'Okay, you win,' the man sighed. 'But it must stay between the two of us.'

Jamie took out his phone and filmed a miserable Donald detailing hearing Cameron plotting to kill his wife. Apparently Donald had been at the Abernethy home for a meeting with Cameron. He'd left after the meeting and realised he'd left his gloves when he got to his car, so he went back into the house, entering without knocking. Cameron was already talking with Neil. Neither of them had realised he'd come back, so he'd overheard everything.

'Cheers,' said Jamie, saving the footage and slipping the phone back into his pocket. 'Gary will bring you more booze at dinnertime. You can have whatever you want.'

'Great.' Donald's smile returned. 'One bottle of gin, one vodka and I want a nice single malt. None of your blended shite. Make it a

Glenlivet or a Glenfiddich – you can't go wrong with one of the glens. Or perhaps a Lagavulin.'

'How about all three?'

'That would be bloody superb.' He beamed.

Jamie assumed he was forgiven. 'See you later, Donald.'

'Remember, Jamie,' he called after him. 'Tell no one about this.'

* * *

Mullen parked his car outside the Gray home and switched off the engine.

'Thank you for a wonderful time,' said Jackie.

'No, thank you.' He smiled, taking her hand.

'I've never done that with chocolate mousse before.' She giggled.

'Yes, that was a lot of fun. I do have a very interesting idea about what we could do with French vanilla custard.'

'Intriguing,' she said as he kissed her.

'I could always call in sick to work,' he breathed.

'Tempting, but I'd better go home. Jamie will worry if I don't go back and I'm meeting up with my friend Tricia for a coffee.'

'Shame. Can I see you tonight?'

'It wouldn't be fair if I asked Jamie to babysit again. How about you come to mine for dinner?'

'Are you sure? I know it's a big thing for you to ask me with your children there.'

Her expression turned serious. 'I'm not a woman who likes wasting my time. If you're not in this for the long haul, then say now. I have weans I need to think about, so I don't get involved with men I don't think there's any future with. There'll be no hard feelings if you don't want to get involved, I'll completely understand...'

'I'm in for the long haul.'

'Really?' she said, a little startled by how quickly he'd answered.

'I'm a serious man and I don't like to waste my time either. I really want to see where this goes.' He ran his fingers down her face. 'No way am I giving you up yet.'

'That's all right, then.' She beamed. 'I can't do any fancy French cooking but I do good simple, plain food.'

'I'm sure it'll be lovely. In fact, I bet you can teach me a thing or two. You certainly did last night.'

Mullen kissed her again, Jackie moaning into his mouth. She spied one of her elderly neighbours slowly progressing down the street on her Zimmer frame and tore her mouth from his. 'Mrs Kelly's there.'

'So? She's probably as blind as a bat.'

'She isn't. She's got eyes like a hawk and she's a gossiping old biddy.'

'Okay,' he said, releasing her.

'I wondered if I could ask you a favour.'

'Of course.'

'Would you be able to teach Jamie some of your moves? Not those moves.' She laughed when he grinned and slid his hand up her skirt. 'I mean your fighting moves.'

'My fighting moves?' he replied, amused.

'Aye. He's a very handy lad but he's had no formal training and I constantly worry about him getting attacked again. It would make me feel so much better if he could do what you can do.'

'I'm happy to show him a few moves, if Jamie agrees, of course. Anything for you.'

She smiled back and pecked him on the lips. 'Is half five too early tonight? My boys won't be able to wait until seven to eat.'

'It's fine.'

'See you then,' she said before climbing out of the car.

Mullen watched her go into the house, looking forward to the evening ahead. He should have been pleased. Finally he'd been given access to the family home. But he knew that wasn't the real reason he was happy, no matter how much he tried to tell himself it was.

* * *

Jamie returned home to find his mother doing the dusting, happily humming to herself.

'Well, if it isn't the dirty stop-out.' He grinned.

'You cheeky wee sod.' She smiled, throwing the duster at him.

'You had a good night, then?'

'Aye, I did. It was lovely actually.'

'So, he treated you well?'

'He did,' she said dreamily. 'He made me feel so special.'

'I suppose he must have done, seeing how you spent the whole night with him.'

'Yes,' she replied, trying not to smile at the mischief in his eyes. 'And that's all I'm saying. Actually, I've invited him for tea tonight.'

'Really?'

'You sound surprised. Oh, I knew it was too soon, but I had such a wonderful night and I got a bit carried away...'

'No, it's fine, Maw. He must be special.'

'He is. I'm really falling hard for this one.'

'Wow.'

'What do you mean, wow?'

'I've never heard you talk about a man like this before.'

'Because I've never felt it before. Well, not since the early days with Jason and we both know how that ended.'

'Scott is not Jason.'

'Aye, you're right. I've got to stop worrying. Well, he's coming for tea, so you can get a better read of him. By the way, I asked him to give you some lessons, in fighting. I think with everything going on you need to learn some new techniques.'

'Actually, that's a good idea. His moves are pretty awesome.'

'You're telling me,' she murmured, the dreamy look returning to her eyes.

'Oh, aye?'

She blushed and cleared her throat. 'You can do the vacuuming. I want everything spotless.'

'Maw, it's already spotless. It's always spotless.'

'I can see crumbs on the couch.' Her eyes narrowed. 'Gary brought snacks last night, didn't he?'

'He was eating tortilla chips while we were watching some stupid slasher film and he jumped when the bad guy leapt out at the dumb blonde and dropped them everywhere.'

She smiled and shook her head. 'Oh, Gary, the poor love. Right, you, get the vacuum.'

'I can call him and tell him to clean up his own mess.'

'Like that'll work.'

'I need to get that,' he said when his phone rang. 'All right, Logan, what is it? You're kidding?' he exclaimed. 'For fuck's sake.'

Jackie watched him questioningly but didn't interrupt.

'Aye, thanks for letting me know. We need to get together to discuss how we're going to handle it. I'm on my way.'

'What's happened now?' said Jackie when he'd hung up.

'Sasha Reid's been stirring things with the Lawsons.'

'What do you mean, stirring things?'

'She's gathered all the Lawsons together at the snooker hall and is riling them up to attack us. She's saying they should hit back after what we did to John.'

'Oh, Christ. Isn't there enough going on without that lot adding to it?'

'I'm meeting the lads at Digger's,' said Jamie, before hurrying into the kitchen and grabbing his bike chains.

'At least you've got the car,' said Jackie. 'So I don't need to worry about you walking the streets.'

'Sorry, Maw, the vacuuming will have to wait.'

'Don't worry about that, I'll do it. You go and get it sorted.'

'Cheers,' he said, kissing her cheek before dashing out.

Jackie pondered the problem of Sasha Reid. The boys wouldn't be able to deal with her. It was to their credit that they wouldn't hit a female. There were too many men on the scheme who didn't have a problem with it, but it meant they wouldn't be able to negate the threat she posed.

Jackie fetched her frying pan from the kitchen, slipped it into a carrier bag, pulled on her jacket and shoes and left the house. She made the short walk to the McVitie house and banged on the door.

Dave pulled it open and rolled his eyes. 'Oh, what is it now? I haven't done anything, for God's sake.'

'Aye, I'm well aware of that, Davey boy. You've done nothing your entire life but here's your chance. I need your help.'

'Sod off,' he retorted. 'Why should I help you?'

'Because our boys are in trouble.'

'They're more than capable of sorting it out themselves.'

'Not this time. They need help and we're going to give it.'

'What have you got in mind?' he said curiously.

'Just come with me to the snooker hall, will you? Not for my sake,' she pressed when he still looked reluctant. 'For the boys.'

'Fine,' he sighed. 'Let me grab my coat.'

She impatiently waited on the doorstep while Dave dithered, searching for his trainers. Eventually he located them under the armchair. He pulled on his anorak and they started the walk together to the snooker hall.

They had to go by Jackie's house to reach the snooker hall and she groaned when she saw the pink ice-cream van parked outside.

'Oh, great,' she muttered.

'Ephraim will go pure mental if he sees me with you,' said Dave. 'He'll think we're dating and lop my head off with a machete.'

'Me date you?' she retorted. 'Urgh. Even Ephraim's not mad enough to believe that.'

'If you want my help then I suggest you start being a wee bit nicer to me.' He sniffed.

'Let's cross the street. If we go behind the van he might not notice us.'

'Good idea.'

They crossed the road and thought they'd got away with it, until they heard Ephraim's voice call, 'Hey, Jackie.'

She stopped, sighed and turned to see him jogging across the road towards them.

'Are you off out somewhere, Jackie, hen?' Ephraim said.

'Aye, just a bit of business to take care of.'

'With him?' said Ephraim, nodding aggressively at Dave, who retreated a couple of steps.

'Yes,' Jackie replied, spotting a much better ally than Dave McVitie. 'The boys are in trouble, so we're going to help.'

'What, the Blood Brothers?'

'Sasha Reid's stirring up the Lawsons at the snooker hall. The boys won't hurt a woman, so I'm gonnae deal with the wee cow.'

'You cannae go in there, they'll tear you apart.'

'They can try,' she said, tilting back her head.

'You're some woman, hen,' Ephraim said, eyes sparkling with admiration. 'I'll come with you. Just let me grab a couple of my pals first.'

'Does he mean actual people or weapons?' Dave asked Jackie as they watched Ephraim hurry back to his van.

'I'm hoping he means weapons. I'm not sure he has any friends. Yep, I was right,' she added when Ephraim jogged back over to them with a machete in each hand.

'Jesus Christ,' Dave murmured under his breath.

'Don't let him hear you say that,' said Jackie. 'I've heard he's killed people for taking the Lord's name in vain.'

Ephraim had donned a long black leather coat and he slid the machetes into the deep inner pockets he'd specifically created for his weapons. 'Are we ready?' he said, gaze on Jackie, ignoring Dave.

'Aye,' she replied. 'Let's go.'

He placed a hand on her arm. 'I just want you to know, Jackie, hen, that I've got your back in there. If any of them lays a finger on you, I'll chop off their hands.' Ephraim ended this statement with a bizarre facial twitch.

Jackie forced a smile. 'I appreciate that.'

He beamed like a child who had been told they were good. 'Get in the van. I'll gi'e you a lift. It's a bit of a trek from here to the snooker hall.'

'Dave too?' said Jackie, not wanting to be alone with Ephraim in his van.

Dave swallowed hard when Ephraim's hawk-like stare was turned on him.

'Why does he want to tag along?' demanded Ephraim.

'Because this is about all the Blood Brothers,' replied Jackie. 'No' just Jamie. He wants to help his son.'

'Oh, aye, all right, then,' Ephraim said, looking a bit happier with this explanation. 'Let's get going, then.'

As they walked back to the van, Jackie noticed the line of customers waiting.

'What about them?' she asked Ephraim.

He waved a dismissive hand. 'I'll sort them out.' He jabbed a finger at the queue. 'None of you fannies had better go anywhere. I won't be long.'

The waiting customers watched the three of them hop into the van and drive off.

'But I've got a pan on the boil,' said one of the customers.

'Then call someone to switch it off for you,' replied another customer. 'If you leave he will know and he'll come after you.'

The customer paled, took out his phone and frantically dialled his wife. 'Hi, Francesca, hen. I'm gonnae be longer than I thought.'

21

Jackie tried not to grimace during the drive to the snooker hall. Ephraim had insisted she take the seat beside him, which meant she had him on one side and sweaty Dave McVitie pressed against her other side.

'Can't you move up a bit?' she told Dave.

'No, I cannae,' he retorted. 'I'm jammed up against the door as it is.' He gasped and grabbed onto the handle above his head when Ephraim took a corner at speed.

'You'd better gi'e Jackie more space,' Ephraim barked at him. 'Or I can always slim you down with the help of my machetes.'

Dave's sweating went into overdrive and he crossed his legs and tilted his body to the left, attempting to create a sliver of space between him and Jackie, wishing the daft cow had left him out of this.

'That's better, Dave,' said Jackie, not wanting to get him into trouble with Ephraim. 'Thank you.'

He gave her a grateful smile.

Ephraim slammed on the brakes outside the snooker hall, jolting them all in their seats. He threw off his seat belt and flashed them a disturbing grin. 'Let's go and handle these wallopers.'

They got out of the van, Dave a little unsteady on his feet after the wild drive, and walked into the snooker hall. Jackie led the way, slapping the door open with her palm, holding the carrier bag containing the frying pan in one hand.

There were about fifteen members of the Lawson family gathered in the centre of the room, listening to Sasha, who was standing on one of the snooker tables, ranting and raving about the menace that was the Blood Brothers and how they must be stopped, her face bruised from Jackie's fist.

The manager of the snooker hall was standing off to one side, sweating and wringing his hands. He lacked the courage to tell them to move their little powwow somewhere else, but he didn't want the Blood Brothers finding out he'd allowed it to happen.

'Jackie,' he breathed with relief when he saw her walk in.

He rushed towards her, hoping she was the answer to his dilemma, coming to an abrupt halt when Ephraim entered behind her.

'All right, Duncan,' she said.

The Lawsons were so busy listening to Sasha, who was rather an impressive public speaker, that they didn't notice the new arrivals.

'I'm s-so sorry about this,' stammered Duncan. 'I've told them to leave but they just ignore me. I want you to know that this is nothing to do with me.'

'Calm yer jets,' she said. 'I know. It's that mad wee pixie's fault. She's aff her heid. Leave it to us, we'll sort it.'

'Oh, thank you,' he gasped, standing aside to allow them to pass, Ephraim giving him a hard look as he passed by, while Dave reluctantly shuffled behind them.

'Oy, you,' yelled Jackie, striding towards the assembled group.

Sasha finally went silent as they all turned to look at Jackie.

'What the fuck's this, then?' demanded Jackie. 'You got a problem with my boy and his pals?'

'Aye, we have,' retorted Sasha, feeling brave because she was standing above everyone else. 'Not only did they batter my brothers and Nick Lawson and his pals, but they attacked me and John.'

'Oh, aye? And have you told this lot why they attacked you and John?' Jackie smiled when Sasha pursed her lips. 'That's a no, then.' Jackie regarded the Lawsons, who all appeared hostile but were making no move. In fact they were nervously eyeing Ephraim, who stood by Jackie's shoulder on bodyguard duty. Dave stood on her other side, the fear Ephraim was clearly instilling in them boosting his own courage.

'Her and John were robbing the auld yins who live near the church,' said Jackie. 'They broke in, tied them up in their beds and ransacked their places. They left three old women shaking and traumatised.'

'You're a lying old cow,' screeched Sasha.

'Oh, am I? We caught you in the act. I gave you that bruise to the face myself.'

'Hey, you,' said Ephraim, pointing at Sasha. 'Jackie Gray doesnae lie. You'd dae well to remember that.' His deep, gravelly voice was full of threat and not even Sasha would dare contradict him.

'Actually, I heard something about that,' said a young Lawson cousin. 'My pal's gran got done over and it was just like Jackie said – they tied her up when she was in bed and robbed her blind, and she didnae have much to begin with. They badly bruised her and she became really jumpy and afraid.'

Murmurs and whispers were exchanged before all the Lawsons looked back at Sasha with scowls on their faces.

'It wasn't me,' she screeched. 'I'm innocent. The Blood Brothers have a vendetta against me and my brothers.'

'You and your brothers were smashing up Mr Cavenie's shop and stealing from him,' countered Jackie.

'Only because your husband paid us to,' she replied with a triumphant look.

The Lawsons' scowls were turned back on Jackie.

'He is not my husband,' she snapped. 'He's my ex-husband, and what Jason Gray gets up to is nothing to do with me or the Blood Brothers.'

'Mr Cavenie's all right,' piped up another Lawson. 'He gave my maw tick when we were totally broke and couldnae afford any food.'

'He did the same for my granddad,' said another Lawson.

'Well, she and her brothers cost him a small fortune in damages,' said Jackie, pointing at Sasha.

'Everything's been peaceful on the scheme lately,' she continued. 'Everyone can go for a pint in peace, play snooker, go to the shop. Do you really want to ruin that because it's what she wants?' she asked the Lawsons, gesturing to Sasha as she spoke. 'She's using you to attack my son and his friends because she and her brothers aren't up to the task themselves. Are you going to let yourselves be used like that?'

There were more murmurs and whispers.

'The Blood Brothers came in here and twatted Nick and his friends,' announced one Lawson. 'They hadn't done anything wrong, but they battered them anyway.'

Jackie inwardly cursed. She'd known that assault would come back to haunt them. 'That is nothing to do with this.'

'Aye, it is. They attacked them for no reason.'

'And my son was attacked when he was walking alone by some

of your lot.' Her grin was broad. 'But he still managed to beat them all.'

'Only because a passer-by helped.'

Jackie noted his bruised face. 'Oh, aye. Were you there?'

He blushed and glanced nervously at Ephraim when he grunted. 'No.'

'Then what do you know about it?'

'Nothing,' he mumbled to the floor.

'The last thing anyone wants is a repeat of the Battle of Gallowburn,' said Jackie in a reasonable tone. 'Let's keep the peace.'

'I don't want to keep the peace,' announced Sasha, stamping her foot on the table, the dent she made in the green baize making the manager wince. 'I want revenge.'

'I'll tell you what – rather than drag all these people into your personal vendetta, how about me and you go one on one right here right now?'

'What?' Sasha laughed. 'Seriously?'

'Aye. Why, are you scared?'

'Me, scared of an old woman like you?'

'I think you are. I've already decked you once.'

'Only because you took me by surprise in the dark.'

'You mean in Mary McAlpine's bedroom when you tried to rob her?'

Sasha's eyes widened when she realised what she'd said. 'No, I meant—'

'Don't give us more of your lies, we're no' stupid. So, do you accept or not?'

Sasha looked around the Lawsons and realised she was losing them. Some of them looked positively angry by what she and John had done. It was a code of honour on the Gallowburn that the old folk were left alone. 'Aye, I do. I'll hammer you into the ground, you old witch.'

'What the fuck did you call Jackie?' roared Ephraim, drawing one of the machetes from inside his coat and pointing it at her.

'It's all right,' said Jackie gently, patting his shoulder. 'I can handle her.'

He gave her a wink. 'I know you can, hen.'

'Oh, God,' breathed the manager, standing off to one side, biting his nails as he watched Sasha jump down off the snooker table and march over to meet Jackie, who put down the carrier bag she was holding and removed her jacket.

'Is this a good idea?' Dave whispered in Jackie's ear. 'That girl's mad mental.'

'Don't worry, Davey boy,' she replied. 'I've dealt with nuttier than her in my time.'

The Lawsons started cheering and chanting as the two women circled each other.

Sasha lunged for Jackie, swinging her fist. Jackie dodged and slammed her own fist into the girl's face. Sasha tottered backwards, eyes wide and stunned. Jackie followed this up with a second punch that put her on her backside.

'Experience over beauty,' Jackie sneered down at her.

The Lawsons appeared disappointed that it was over so quickly. They'd hoped for blood and had got a five-second fight.

Jackie turned to smile at her friends.

'Nice one, Jackie, hen.' Ephraim winked at her.

Dave's eyes widened when he saw Sasha pull a knife from inside her jacket and drag herself to her feet.

'Look out,' he cried.

Jackie snatched the frying pan out of the carrier and swung it in an arc as she turned, slamming the pan into Sasha's hand. Sasha screamed and dropped the knife. Jackie snatched up the weapon and dragged it along the floor, snapping the blade, leaving a gouge in the manky carpet.

Jackie pointed the frying pan at Sasha, who had dropped to her knees, cradling her injured hand. 'John will be able to sympathise,' she said. 'I did the same to him when he brought a knife to my house. Now you listen to me, lady, and listen good – you will let this stupid vendetta go. It only exists in that mad heid of yours. And you shower,' she added, addressing the Lawsons, 'will break this up and bugger off home.'

When they all stared at her stupidly, Ephraim drew the second machete from inside his jacket and stood beside Jackie. 'Are you all fucking deaf?' he roared. 'If you're no' out of here in five seconds flat I'll start chopping off heids.'

They all scrambled for the exit, Dave having to leap aside to avoid being knocked down in the rush. Sasha hauled herself to her feet and left with them, glaring back over her shoulder at Jackie.

'That little girl won't learn her lesson,' she murmured sadly to herself.

The snooker hall manager breathed a sigh of relief that the only damage to his premises was a dent in one of the tables and a tear in the already-crappy carpet.

Jackie replaced the frying pan in the carrier bag and left the snooker hall with Ephraim and Dave, expecting some people to be milling about outside, but the street was deserted. They got back in the van and drove back to Jackie's house, Ephraim pulling up at the kerb to find his customers still waiting. He made a show of performing a head count through the window.

'Are they all still there?' Jackie asked him.

'Nae idea. I didn't count, but they don't need to know that.'

Jackie chuckled. 'Thank you so much for your help, Ephraim.'

'It looked like you had it under control yourself, hen.'

'Things could have turned a lot nastier if you hadn't been there.' She planted a kiss on his cheek. 'Thank you.'

He stared at her in astonishment, pressing his fingertips to his cheek, watching in numb shock as she got out of the van with Dave. Jackie closed the door behind them and gave him a wave, before walking towards her front gate, carrier bag in hand.

'That Sasha's no' gonnae gi'e up so easily,' Dave told Jackie.

'I know, but I think she's been stopped for a while. Mad as a box of frogs, that one.'

'You're no' wrong there.'

'Well, thanks for your... help,' said Jackie. Although he hadn't done anything, she was grateful for him coming along.

He stopped and stared at her. 'Did you just say thanks, to me?' he said, pointing at himself.

Jackie smiled at his astonished look. It seemed today was her day for shocking men. 'Aye, I did, but don't get used to it. See you around, Davey boy,' she said, before heading up her garden path.

Jamie returned to the house with his friends in tow half an hour after she'd got back.

'All right, boys?' She smiled. 'Would you like a brew?'

'We've just been to the snooker hall,' said Jamie, ignoring the question.

'Oh, aye?' she casually replied. 'Did you have a nice game of snooker?'

'We went to confront Sasha and the Lawsons, but no one was there. Duncan said you'd already been along and sorted it for us.'

'I did,' she said, tilting back her head. 'What about it?'

'What's everyone gonnae think?'

'No one will dare say anything about it. Ephraim scared them shiteless. Dave came along too. And by the way, I'm fine. I sorted out that little madam good and proper.'

'I'm sorry, Maw, I should have asked that first,' Jamie said more gently. 'But I knew you could take her no problem. Everyone will think I need my maw to sort out any trouble for me.'

'No one's going to think that. I knew if you went in there Sasha would try something, and none of you would be willing to give her the hiding she deserved. I sorted her out and set a few things straight too for the Lawsons. She was trying to rile them all into attacking you.'

'But you could have been hurt.'

'Not with Ephraim there. He had his machetes. No one would have touched me, and he made sure they left nice and quietly. He also made it clear that he'll be very pissed off if anyone goes near me. That's better protection than having the SAS as personal body-guards. Just relax, will you? It's over and done with. You've enough to get stressed about without worrying about all that too.'

'Jackie's right,' Logan told Jamie. 'It's sorted. Let's forget about it and move on.'

Gary and Digger nodded in agreement.

'Okay,' said Jamie, dragging his hands down his face.

'By the way,' said Logan. 'Did you say my da was there?'

'I did,' replied Jackie. 'He didn't do anything but he was there, which was more than I expected from him.'

Logan got the feeling she hadn't given him much of a choice.

* * *

That evening Jackie opened the door to Scott, who looked so smart in his long grey woollen coat and matching grey scarf. In one hand, he held a bottle of red wine.

'Hi.' She smiled, annoyed when her voice took on an embar-rassing high-pitched tone.

'You look lovely, as always.' He smiled back, kissing her cheek and handing her the bottle. 'It's the same as the wine we had last night.'

'Great. I really enjoyed that. Come on in, then.'

He stepped inside. Jamie and Charlie were in the front room

and had got to their feet to greet him. It appeared Jackie had forced them to wear their best clothes, their hair neatly combed.

'Hello, Jamie,' Mullen said, stepping forward to shake his hand. He wasn't sure what the boys' reaction to his presence would be now he was dating their mother, but they both seemed friendly enough.

'All right, Scott.' Jamie smiled back.

'And you must be Charlie,' he said, turning his attention to the younger boy.

'Jamie said you're proper hard,' the boy eagerly replied.

'Charlie,' chided Jackie. 'That's no way to greet a guest.'

'Sorry, Maw.'

'That's okay, cutie.' She smiled and ruffled his hair.

'Don't, Maw, I've just combed it,' he said, self-consciously running his hand through it to flatten it down again.

'I think he's becoming a teenager early,' Jackie told Mullen, who smiled. He found the warmth between the three of them rather touching.

'I'll take your coat,' said Jackie.

Mullen removed his coat and scarf and handed them to her, and she hung them on the hook by the door.

'Dinner will just be a few minutes,' said Jackie. 'I won't be long.'

Mullen felt a little awkward when she vanished into the kitchen, leaving him alone with the boys. He'd never been comfortable around children. Even though Jamie was in his twenties, he still wasn't sure what to say.

'Maw said you're going to show me some of your moves,' said Jamie, who was trying not to sound eager and failing miserably.

'I will, if you want me to?' replied Mullen.

'Aye, I dae. Shall we try now while we wait for dinner?'

'Err, if you like.'

Jamie moved the armchair back against the wall, giving them just a little more space in the poky room.

'The important thing to remember,' began Mullen, 'is that defence is the best form of attack. Being able to retaliate is all well and good, but if someone can't get through your defences in the first place, then they'll never be able to get the better of you.'

'You mean blocks and that?' replied Jamie.

'Yes, blocking strikes. I'll show you one where you use your wrist to block the wrist of your attacker. Speed is the essence with blocking, and anticipating what move your opponent's going to make. You can judge this by their stance.'

He showed Jamie a few blocks while Charlie sat in the armchair to watch.

'If you can,' said Mullen when Jamie had performed a very few competent blocks, 'block and attack at the same time. While you're bringing up one arm to block, strike with your other hand.'

Jamie blocked the punch Mullen sent his way and mimicked driving his fist into his face.

'Excellent.' Mullen smiled. He enjoyed passing on his wisdom and Jamie was a very fast learner. 'You're a natural. Don't forget you can block with your legs too if someone tries to kick you, but the best move is to go for the knee. No matter how tough someone is, one boot to the kneecap and they'll go down.'

Jackie popped her head around the door and smiled at the scene. 'Tea's ready.'

'Can you show me more after tea?' Jamie asked Mullen.

'Jamie, let him have a rest,' said Jackie.

'I'm happy to show him more if he wants,' said Mullen.

'That's very good of you, Scott, but don't let him take advantage.'

They all piled into the kitchen and took their places at the table while Jackie fussed around them, piling their plates up with spaghetti bolognese, and ensuring they all had garlic bread and cheese.

'This smells delicious.' Mullen smiled.

'Well, it's not as fancy as your cooking, but it's one of the boys' favourites, along with pizza. They do like Italian food.'

Mullen caught Jamie's look at the mention of Italy. His eyes widened slightly and filled with sadness, and he swallowed hard and looked down at his food. Wanting to be certain he hadn't imagined it, Mullen asked, 'Have you been to Italy?'

'No,' sighed Jackie. 'We've never left the country, sadly.'

'Have you been to Italy, Scott?' Charlie asked him.

He glanced again at Jamie, whose head had dropped even lower onto his chest.

'Yes, I have, a few times. It's a beautiful country. I've been to Rome and Pisa and Florence.'

Jamie's head snapped up at the mention of Florence. 'What's it like?' he asked him.

'You mean Rome?'

'No, Florence.'

'Why are you asking about Florence?' Jackie asked him.

Jamie shrugged. 'Just curious.'

'It's a fabulous place,' enthused Mullen, who had genuinely visited Florence. 'I love renaissance art, so it's the place to go. Some of the greatest masterpieces are in museums in Florence.'

Jackie was thrilled that she'd finally found a cultured man who didn't talk constantly about football and lager.

'Da Vinci painted the Mona Lisa in Florence.' Mullen smiled. 'Sadly the painting is in the Louvre in Paris.'

'I meant what's the city like?' said Jamie. 'Is it a nice, safe place?'

'Why so curious?' Jackie asked him. 'Are you thinking of going?'

'I'd like to, one day, maybe,' he mumbled.

'It's a beautiful, romantic place,' said Mullen with a pointed look at Jackie that made her smile. 'And very safe. If you like art and architecture, it's fascinating.'

This seemed to cheer Jamie a little and he nodded. Mullen wondered if he wanted to know if it was safe so he'd know Allegra in turn would be safe.

'This is excellent, Jackie,' said Mullen as he ate. 'You've got the perfect balance of garlic with the tomato.'

'Wow, a compliment about my cooking.' She smiled. 'Did you hear that, boys?' She looked back at Mullen. 'Normally they just inhale their food, then go back to their rooms or sit in front of the telly.'

'I always like your cooking, Maw,' said Charlie.

'Thank you, sweetie.' She smiled.

'It's better than when Jamie cooks. He burns everything.'

'I do not,' his brother retorted.

'You burnt my pancakes the other day.'

'Oh, aye, I forgot about that,' Jamie replied with a sheepish but very charming grin.

Mullen smiled when the family all grinned at each other.

When they'd finished eating, the boys tore back into the living room.

'Making their escape before they have to help clear up.' Jackie smiled, shaking her head. 'I shouldn't complain because they help me in a lot of other ways. They are such good boys.'

'They're a credit to you,' said Mullen.

'Thanks,' she said, draining her wine and getting to her feet. 'Right, I'd better get to it.'

'I'll give you a hand,' he said, rising too and picking up two plates.

'No, you're a guest and guests don't lift a finger in my house.'

'But it means I get to be in here, with you.' Mullen smiled down at her, getting lost in those lovely green eyes.

Quietly he closed the kitchen door and pulled her to him.

'Finally,' he whispered, running his thumb down her cheek.

He pressed his lips to hers, sliding his hands up and down her waist, pressing her up against the kitchen unit as the kiss deepened. They jumped apart when the door burst open.

'Oh, sorry.' Jamie grinned. 'Am I interrupting?'

'Scott was just helping me clear up,' replied a pink-cheeked Jackie, running her hands through her hair.

'Aye, right. I just wanted to grab a can of lager,' he said, taking a can from the fridge before heading back into the living room, closing the door behind him.

The mood broken, Mullen helped Jackie clear the table and wipe it down.

'You've done your bit,' she told him as she started to wash up. 'You can go and relax. Do you want a coffee?'

'Yes, please. Milk, no sugar.'

'I'll bring it through.'

'Can I use your bathroom?'

'Course you can. Upstairs, second on the left.'

'Thanks,' he said, giving her a peck on the lips before exiting the kitchen and walking through the living room to the stairs. At the top he paused to get his bearings and peered into the first bedroom on the right. Judging by the double bed and dressing table holding make-up and perfume bottles, this was Jackie's room. It was small but pretty and neat, and he took a moment to drink it in before moving on to the room next door. The posters and toys said this was Charlie's.

Opposite Charlie's room he found Jamie's. There wasn't much in it, just a double bed, wardrobe and a shelf holding a couple of nick-nacks. A collage of photos was arranged on a corkboard that hung from the wall, most of them of Jamie and Allegra and a few of his friends and family. The only possible hiding places were the wardrobe or under the bed. Dropping to his knees, he peered under the bed and saw nothing.

Laughter from downstairs gave him a completely new sensation – guilt. It wasn't the first time he'd gained the trust of his marks and used it to access their home, but it was the first time he'd ever felt guilty about it. He got up and continued down the hall and went into the bathroom. He locked the door and leaned against the sink, gripping onto it.

'Get yourself together,' he told himself. 'You've got a job to do.'

He thought of bloated, angry Cameron Abernethy who was paying him to infiltrate these people's lives. A man who had tried to kill Jamie and had possibly murdered his own wife and daughter. Then there was the Gray family – decent, kind people who were just trying to get by.

He gazed at his reflection in the mirror, his usually steely, determined gaze softer and conflicted. Jackie Gray had got under his skin and made him doubt everything about himself. The smart move would be to leave right now and tackle this case from a completely different perspective. He involuntarily smiled at the sound of the three of them laughing together downstairs. But he didn't want to leave. This was the first time since childhood that he'd been in a close, warm family environment. After his mother had passed away when he was twenty, all his siblings had scattered to the wind and they rarely saw or even spoke to each other any more. Their mother had been the glue holding them all together and, without her, their family had fallen apart. Here he felt back in that comforting, familial warmth and he was reluctant to give it up. The Gray family had already given him so much and inwardly he rebelled against the thought of betraying them.

Mullen flushed the toilet and washed his hands, before heading back downstairs where Jamie was waiting to ask him if he could show him a few more moves.

'You're on.' Mullen smiled. 'What would you do if I snuck up on you from behind?'

'Drive my elbow into your face and then turn around, punch you to the ground and jump on your baws.'

Mullen burst out laughing. 'What can I say? Ten out of ten.'

Jackie walked into the room carrying two mugs of coffee, the sparkle in her green eyes warming his heart. Jesus, he was screwed.

22

The two employees who were already in the office by the time Mullen arrived at work the next morning both frowned when he walked in whistling a happy tune.

'You okay, boss?' asked Steven, who had modelled himself on his employer with his smart suits and long woollen coats.

'Fine,' he replied.

Steven was even more freaked out when Mullen actually smiled at him. 'Okay,' he said slowly, glancing at Adam, his colleague, who appeared equally puzzled.

They watched in confusion as Mullen dumped his briefcase on his desk and walked over to the coffee pot steaming in the corner, continuing to whistle to himself as he poured himself a cup. He was unaware he was whistling, too caught up in memories of the previous night. He'd ended up staying over at Jackie's and they'd made silent love up against her bedroom wall, stifling all sound so the boys wouldn't hear, which had only made it even more passionate and intense. He'd enjoyed Jamie and Charlie's company too. They seemed to have no problem with him dating their mother, and he'd had fun showing Jamie some more moves. The boy was a natural and Mullen had recommended he have professional lessons. Charlie, eager to be included, had joined in and he'd taught him how to punch, but he lacked his older brother's killer instinct. Charlie would always be too sweet and gentle to hurt anyone.

'We've had the results of the DNA test on the scarf Natalie sent,' added Steven.

'Already?' said Mullen, taking a swig of coffee.

'They pushed them through faster as a favour to you.'

'And?'

'It's not Allegra. It looks like you could be right. Someone else got hold of the passport and used it.'

'Probably,' Mullen said, turning his back so they wouldn't see his expression.

He couldn't decide if he was pleased with this news or not. On the one hand, it meant the investigation was still ongoing and he could legitimately keep on seeing Jackie. On the other, they still had no idea if Allegra was dead or alive. Natalie had been certain she was Helen Wilkinson.

'Or it's possible the scarf was touched by someone else,' commented Adam. 'Natalie said it was hanging on the rack in the middle of a busy salon.'

'Good point,' said Mullen, turning back round to face them. He considered Jamie's curious questions about Florence. 'Is Natalie still in Venice?'

'Yes,' replied Steven.

Mullen found himself standing at a crossroads, for the first time professional integrity losing out to personal feelings. If he pushed this and found Allegra, then it could lead to Jamie being arrested and thrown into prison. The thought of what that would do to Jackie was too terrible to contemplate.

'Tell her to come back,' Mullen told him. 'We have to follow the evidence, and so far everything's indicating Allegra never left the country.'

'But the passport—' began Steven.

'Is a dead end. We're chasing shadows. Let's focus the investigation on Glasgow.'

'If you say so, boss,' said Steven, glancing again at his colleague, who looked equally uncertain.

'Yes, I do,' retorted Mullen, not feeling the confidence of his words. 'I'd better go and break the bad news to Mr Abernethy.'

'Do you think he killed her?' Steven asked him.

'Yes, I do. Allegra Abernethy's dead and gone,' Mullen replied, before putting down his coffee cup and stalking out of the door.

* * *

Cameron was almost breathless with excitement as Mullen walked into his lounge. 'I take it you've had the DNA results back?'

'Yes, we have,' Mullen replied, trying not to look disdainful. Cameron was a mess. He was unshaven and he had huge bags under his bloodshot eyes. His clothes were rumpled and his hair uncombed. The man was unravelling.

'Well, don't keep it a fucking secret,' Cameron barked, taking a swig of whisky despite how early it was in the day.

'It wasn't a match to Allegra.'

Cameron blinked at him in astonishment. 'What?' he roared. 'But it must be.'

'I'm sorry, Mr Abernethy, but it's not.'

'You said your agent in Italy felt sure it was her.'

'She did, but she was wrong.'

'But... she can't be.'

'DNA evidence doesn't lie, Mr Abernethy. It's not Allegra.'

'But what about the name, Helen Wilkinson?'

'We think someone found her passport. Perhaps Allegra was carrying it when she staggered off injured and dropped it. A lost passport is gold to some people. The person who found it isn't necessarily the one who used it. They could have sold it on to someone who needed to leave the country.'

Cameron's jaw went slack and his eyes flicked around the room, as though seeking something stable he could cling onto in the storm of this fresh shock. His reddened eyes suddenly blazed with wrath, every muscle in his body snapping taut.

'Then what fucking use are you?' he roared.

'I wouldn't recommend it.' Mullen glowered when Cameron drew back his arm to hurl the heavy lead-crystal whisky glass at him.

Cameron decided to heed that warning and threw it at the wall instead, which it hit with a smash, splattering expensive single malt across the carpet and wall.

The door was opened by Fenston, who had been lurking behind it, attempting to listen in on the conversation. 'What's going on?' he asked.

'Get the fuck out, you useless little worm,' Cameron bellowed at him.

Fenston squeaked with fear and ducked back out, closing the door behind him.

'Mr Abernethy, please calm down,' said Mullen. It occurred to him that his actions might have condemned Cameron to life in prison, but it would have troubled his conscience a lot more if he'd contributed to tearing Jackie's family apart.

'Calm down? You do realise that DNA test was my last hope of not going to prison.'

'I think the most likely scenario is that Allegra staggered off somewhere and died from her injuries. It's possible she's not been found yet because she fell down somewhere that's difficult for the search teams to access.'

'What a load of bollocks,' the furious man retorted. 'The little bitch did this to me. She's out there somewhere, laughing up her sleeve at me, Cameron Abernethy,' he said, pointing grandly to himself.

'All is not lost. We've decided instead to concentrate our investigation in the city.'

'You think there still might be something to find?'

'I do.'

'I hope to Christ there is or I'm fucking done. I feel like I'm losing control. All the usual bribes aren't working and my enemies are determined to see me go down. I'm sure my business rivals have got together to ensure I'm thrown into prison.'

Mullen wouldn't be surprised if that was the case. Cameron's bullying tactics had got a lot of backs up over the years, and with him out of the way, they could tear his businesses apart and keep the pieces for themselves. If he'd spent the years forging real alliances rather than using blackmail and coercion, he might have more people wanting to help him out of this mess. Instead he found himself isolated and abandoned. Everyone had to face a reckoning one day. Mullen wondered what form his own reckoning would take.

He was dismissed by an aggressive nod from Cameron, who glared at his retreating back.

'He's supposed to be the best,' muttered Cameron. 'But he's fucking useless like all of them.'

Cameron took out his phone and stabbed at the screen before putting it to his ear.

'Yes, it's me,' he growled when his call was answered. 'Enough fucking about. Get it done.'

* * *

Jamie and the rest of the Blood Brothers were in Raymond's Rolls, enjoying a late breakfast together. Jamie had just told his friends about the previous evening with Scott.

'He sounds pretty awesome actually,' said Gary.

'Aye, he's no' bad,' replied Jamie. Coming from him that was high praise indeed.

'He could end up being your stepfather,' said Digger. 'Which would be bloody useful – he could help us sort people out.'

'He is a big handy bastard and my maw's proper smitten. I've no' seen her this happy in a long time.'

'Good,' said Logan. 'If anyone deserve happiness, she does.'

'Too right.'

'I just hope Jason does the right thing and gi'es her a divorce.'

They all looked to Jamie when the phone in his pocket started to ring.

'That's the McVay phone, isn't it?' whispered Gary.

'Aye, it is,' said Jamie, taking it out. 'Hello?' he said into the handset. He rolled his eyes. 'What is it, Jason? Now? Fine.'

'What did that prick want?' said Digger when he'd hung up.

'To meet up at the workshop. He wants to talk to me.'

'Just you?' said Logan.

'He said to come alone.'

'Bugger that. We're coming with you.'

Although he didn't say it, Jamie had hoped they would.

When they arrived outside the workshop, Jason was already waiting, carrying a holdall.

'I told you to come alone, son.'

'I don't gi'e a shit what you tell me,' he retorted.

'I wanted to talk to you about Donald.'

'On you go, then.'

'I mean, about what we discussed earlier, at The Gallows.'

'You can say it in front of my pals. I trust them with my life.'

'Fine. I want you to let me in so I can persuade Donald to make a statement about what he overheard.'

'What did he overhear?' Digger frowned, looking to his friends.

Logan and Gary shrugged, while Jamie and Jason ignored the question.

'You're too late,' replied Jamie. 'I've already got it.'

Jason planted his hands on his hips and shook his head. 'Jesus, Jamie.'

'What?'

'Do you know what Toni would do if she found out?'

Jamie studied his father carefully. 'You've already told her, haven't you? What fucking right did you have to do that?'

'Told her what?' said Digger.

'Shut up,' Logan hissed at him.

'She has to know,' continued Jason. 'If you want to stay alive you don't keep anything from Toni McVay.'

'And what did she say?'

'She hates Cameron Abernethy. In fact, she wants some of his businesses for herself, so it's in her interest to see him sent down. His fucktard of a son won't be able to fend her off.'

'So she wants to use this to make sure he gets sent down?'

'Yes.'

Jamie chewed his lip, mulling it over. Toni was his only way of getting Donald's statement into the public domain.

'All right,' he said, taking out his phone. 'I'll forward the file on to you.'

He jabbed at the screen and a few seconds later Jason's phone beeped. Jason took it out and nodded. 'Cheers, son.'

'What will she do with it?'

'She has a lot of police contacts. She'll probably forward it on to one of them. Can I see Donald?' He held up the bag. 'I've brought him some fresh clothes.'

Jamie nodded, took out the key and unlocked the door. Donald smiled when they all walked in, Gary closing the door behind them.

'What's this, then, a party?' said Donald.

'We brought you some more supplies,' said Logan, placing the two carrier bags he held on the floor.

Donald's smile fell. 'I don't hear the heavenly music of clinking bottles.'

'Because Gary's got those,' he replied.

Gary placed another two carrier bags beside the ones Logan had already put down.

'Gin, vodka and whisky, as requested,' said Jamie.

Jason grimaced at the smell. 'It's a bit ripe in here.'

'That's because there's no windows and no bath,' retorted Donald sniffily. 'You try keeping clean in a sink that's not big enough to drown two white mice.'

'Have you got everything you need?' Jason asked Donald.

'Apart from the nubile brunette I asked for and a hot tub, I suppose so. How much longer am I going to be here?'

'Not long now, just another day or two.'

'This really is intolerable.' Donald sighed.

They left a rather subdued Donald, who started tucking into the gin before they were even out of the door. Jamie locked up and slipped the key back into his jacket.

'I feel sorry for him,' said Logan. 'He looked pretty depressed.'

'He won't be there much longer,' replied Jason.

'Where will he go after here?' said Jamie.

'You don't need to know that.'

'But if he's gonnae gi'e evidence against Cameron...'

'Let Toni worry about that. Do you fancy coming for a drive, son?'

'No, thanks.' Jamie looked to his friends. 'Let's go.'

'It's about the... situation,' he called after him, making Jamie hesitate.

'What situation?' said Digger, rolling his eyes when Gary and Logan told him to shut up.

Jamie looked back over his shoulder at his father, obsidian eyes narrow and suspicious. 'Where will we go?'

'I dunno. Maybe a pub that I'm allowed to go in.'

'You don't drink.'

'I'll be on the orange juice.'

Jamie didn't want to spend a second longer in Jason's company but he was willing to if it would help Allegra. Although she'd told him not to pursue it, he wanted to hammer every nail he could find into Cameron's coffin. 'All right, then.'

'Cheers.' Jason smiled. 'I appreciate it.'

'Whatever.'

'Are you sure this is wise?' Logan whispered in Jamie's ear.

'How?'

'I don't know, I've just got a weird feeling.'

'Don't worry, I can handle him. Scott taught me some new moves.'

'But even so...'

Jamie patted his shoulder. 'I'll be fine, pal.'

Logan watched Jamie head out of the alley with Jason, feeling uneasy, although he couldn't have said why.

Jamie and Jason climbed into the BMW.

'So,' said Jamie as they set off. 'Where are we headed?'

'There's a nice pub I know not far from my flat.'

Jamie wondered if he was going to show him his flat, but thought Jason probably wouldn't want him knowing where he lived.

'I appreciate you spending time with me,' said Jason.

'Only so we can discuss Donald, or rather Derek. That's the only reason.'

'I hope I can win your trust again.'

'Doubtful,' Jamie replied, keeping his gaze on the window.

Jason decided further small talk would be futile and remained silent for the rest of the journey.

'Well, this is different to The Bonnie Brae,' said Jamie when they walked into the pub, which was fresh and modern, the two barmen wearing red lumberjack shirts and sporting beards. Jamie glowered. He hated hipsters. Rather than a snooker table, it had a ping-pong table.

'Take a seat and I'll get the drinks in,' Jason told him.

Jamie elected for a table in the corner by the window and Jason returned with a pint of lager for his son and an orange juice for himself.

'So,' said Jason, taking the seat opposite Jamie. 'Donald's evidence could really blow Cameron's defence out of the water.'

'Not really,' replied Jamie. 'He'd have to have a whole separate trial for Rebecca's murder. It would just have meant so much to Allegra if he got sent down for it.'

'I can imagine. Was the SIM card okay, by the way?'

'SIM card?' Jamie innocently replied.

'Aye, the one that got waterlogged. You seemed pretty desperate about it.'

'It was fine, fortunately, but my phone was knackered.'

'I'll get you a new one.'

'I already got a new one.'

'Tell me how much it was and I'll give you the money for it,' Jason replied, taking out his wallet.

'It doesn't matter,' snapped Jamie. 'Just forget about it.'

'I did notice that phone wasn't your main phone and it wasn't the one Caesar gave you.'

'It was a back-up phone.'

'You got pretty upset about a back-up phone. In fact, you were raging.'

'I was, because you pushed me into the sea, not because of the phone.'

'So, you didn't lose any data off that SIM card?'

Jamie realised his father was watching his reaction very carefully. 'No,' was all he was willing to reply.

'Good.' Jason nodded, sipping his orange juice. 'I heard Jackie's seeing someone.'

'How do you know that?'

'You know the Gallowburn, you cannae keep anything quiet.'

'Suppose.'

'Who is he?'

'It's none of your business.'

'I'm not trying to interfere. I just want to make sure she's safe and happy.'

'Aye, she is. Scott's all right.'

'So that's his name, is it?'

Jamie nodded.

'What does he do?'

'I'm no' discussing it with you. It's my maw's business, no one else's.'

'If he hurts her or you and Charlie, I'll fucking have him.'

'Good luck with that. He's one hard bastard.'

'So am I.'

'Nae offence but he could kick your teeth down your throat.'

'Told you that, did he?' his father retorted a little jealously.

'No, he showed me. He helped me batter some Lawsons.' He looked around the room. 'Where's the bathroom?'

'Past the bar on the left.'

Jamie got up and strolled across the room with his usual swagger, a table of three women watching him as he passed by. When he'd disappeared from view, Jason looked to Jamie's jacket, which hung over the back of his chair. The corner of Jason's mouth lifted into a smile.

23

'Only me,' called Jamie as he walked through the front door of his home.

He frowned when he saw his mother sitting on the couch, her arms around a pale, scared Charlie.

'What's going—?'

'Jamie, duck,' yelled Jackie.

Jamie reacted immediately, ducking and throwing himself forward, feeling something pass over the top of his head. Looking round, he saw an enormous figure in a black bomber jacket and jeans emerge from the bottom of the stairs, wielding a big, heavy cosh. Two more men emerged from the kitchen, similarly dressed.

'Did Toni send you?' he demanded.

Confusion filled their eyes. 'Who?' muttered one of them.

'Never mind,' he sighed. This told him they weren't connected to the McVays, and they certainly weren't from the Gallowburn. Besides, if Toni was angry at him she would have come to scoop out his eyeballs personally. That meant Cameron must have sent them.

Jamie pulled his bike chains from his pockets and smashed one of them into the face of the man who had snuck up on him from behind, knocking him back into the wall, clearing a path to the front door.

'Go, Maw,' he yelled.

Jackie shot up off the couch, dragging Charlie along with her. The two who had come from the kitchen attempted to chase after them. Jamie whacked the chains into the left leg of one of the men, recalling what Scott had told him about going for the knee. He missed the knee but got him in the thigh with such force the man's leg crumpled under him. Jackie successfully got Charlie out of the house and ran out onto the street, yelling for help, while Jamie hurled himself at the third man and the two tumbled violently around the room. Jamie was just gaining the upper hand when the man he'd hit in the face grabbed him and wrapped his arms around him, pinning Jamie's arms to his sides. The third man drew back his fist to hit him. Leaning all his weight back on the man holding him, Jamie kicked out with both feet, hitting the man in front of him right in the face. He slammed his foot down on the kneecap of the man holding him, who howled with pain and released him. Jamie turned and delivered a powerful right hook into the side of his face with such force the man was spun round, so he was facing the other way.

The third man in the room pulled a large knife, his eyes bulging, startled by this turn of events.

Jamie whipped up the bike chains, making them buzz as they cut through the air, looking cool and calm in comparison to his panicking opponent, who started to wildly lash out with the knife. Jamie brought the chains down diagonally on his opponent's hands rapidly one after the other. There was an audible crack of bone, a squeal and the knife fell to the floor. When the one whose knee he'd busted scrambled for it, Jamie kicked the weapon under the couch, out of reach, before kicking the man in the face, who dropped, hands going to his injured mouth.

With a war cry, the one he'd punched rushed him, grabbed him by the waist and slammed him up against the wall, making Jamie grimace. The man was too close to use the chains, so Jamie tried thumping his fists off his back, creating a dull thud, but the man refused to release him and Jamie felt the breath being squeezed from his body.

Jamie brought up his knee, once, twice, feeling it connect with his opponent's solar plexus, forcing him to release Jamie, who managed to drag in a breath. When his assailant brought back his leg to kick him, Jamie instinctively formed an x-shape with his forearms to block the kick, grimacing as he was struck, but he managed to hold the defensive posture. He chose his moment carefully, when his attacker drew back his leg again and he hurled himself at him, knocking him to the floor. Jamie landed on top and started pounding his fists into his face, snapping the man's head from side to side.

When he was satisfied he was subdued, Jamie dragged himself to his feet, breathing hard, staggering for the door before they could regather and attack him as one.

As he reached the door he groaned when a fourth man rushed in, holding a knife and a length of rope.

There was a loud clang and the man toppled to the floor unconscious to reveal Jackie standing behind him with a frying pan.

'Cheers, Maw,' breathed Jamie.

He glanced over his shoulder to see the other three attackers getting to their feet, including the one Jamie had knocked out. They were injured, bleeding and limping but still more than ready to continue the fight.

At that moment the rest of the Blood Brothers charged up the garden path towards the front door, eyes wild with fury. The injured men decided a tactical retreat was in order. Grabbing their unconscious friend, they rushed for the back door.

'Get 'em,' yelled Logan.

Jackie stood aside so he could enter, Digger and Gary following as he tore through the house after the intruders.

'Wait here, Maw,' said Jamie, before following his friends.

He rushed through the backyard and into the alley to find the rear door of a black Transit van standing open. One of the men was already in the driver's seat while Digger pounded at the window with a brick he'd found lying on the ground. The two men who'd jumped into the back of the van were locked in a game of tug of war, pulling at their unconscious friend's legs while Logan and Gary pulled back. When the driver slammed the van into reverse they were forced to release him and leapt aside to avoid being hit. The van continued speeding backwards out of the alley. Digger hurled the brick in an astonishing display of strength. It smashed into the windscreen before the van could reach the mouth of the alley. Unfortunately it didn't stop the driver, who steered onto the road, making the tyres scream and sped off down the street out of sight.

'You okay, pal?' Logan asked Jamie.

'Aye,' he said, wincing at the pain in his forearms, which were badly bruised from being kicked. 'You got here just in time.'

'Looks like you had it under control. You hammered the lot of them.'

'Thanks to Scott. His moves gave me the advantage.'

'Who the hell were they?' demanded Digger. 'Lawsons?'

Jamie shook his head, still catching his breath. 'Naw. They weren't off the scheme.'

'Something to do with Cameron Abernethy?'

'I think that's more like it. Let's check on my maw.'

They returned to the house where Jackie was surveying the damage done to her front room.

'Sorry about the mess,' said Jamie.

'Sod the mess,' she told him, taking his face between her hands. 'Are you okay?'

'Fine. What about you and Charlie?'

'We're fine too. I left him next door with Maureen.'

He pointed to the frying pan. 'Where did you get that from?'

'It's Maureen's. It's not as solid as mine, but it did the trick.'

'How did they get in?'

'There was a knock at the front door. When I answered it, the bastards barged their way in. When I demanded to know what the hell they thought they were doing they said we had to wait for you to come home.' She gestured to the rope the fourth man had dropped. 'I think they wanted to kidnap you. And probably me and Charlie too because we were witnesses.'

'But Cameron's had months to do something to you,' said Logan. 'Surely if he was going to make a move he would have done it before you could give evidence against him, so why now?'

'If it is him, then something must have happened to push him to this,' said Jackie. 'I mean, kidnapping. He must know if he was caught it would be the final nail in his coffin.' Anxiously she bit her lip. 'What if it's something to do with the McVays?'

'You know about that?' a startled Gary asked her.

'I do,' she replied. 'Jamie never lies to his maw.'

'Relax,' Jamie told his friends. 'She knows not to tell anyone else.'

'Does Dave know?' Jackie asked Logan.

'God, no. If I told him he'd be straight down the pub to tell the entire scheme, although he has an idea that something's going on.'

At the sound of a car engine, Jackie glanced over her shoulder through the front door, which was still standing open.

'Scott's here,' she said. 'Oh, God, I forgot. He said he'd pop round after work. Shall I stop him from coming in?'

'Looks like it's too late,' replied Jamie as they watched Scott climb out of the car and produce an enormous bouquet of roses from the passenger seat.

'What's going on?' Mullen said, looking at them all. 'Why are you holding a frying pan?' he asked Jackie.

'Some shower of shite burst in here and attacked us,' she replied.

'Jesus,' he breathed, dumping the flowers in Digger's arms and gently holding her by the shoulders. 'Are you all right?'

'I'm fine, we all are.'

'All? Was Charlie here when it happened?'

'Aye, he was. It was just me and him when they barged in and told us to sit and wait for Jamie to come home. When he did, he battered the shite out of three of them.' She lifted the pan. 'I sorted the fourth one out with this wee beauty.'

'You are so amazing.' He beamed. 'Where's Charlie now?'

'Next door with Maureen being distracted by ice cream and cartoons.'

'Are you okay, Jamie?' Mullen asked him.

'Aye, fine. They hardly touched me. I remembered everything you taught me.'

'I'm so glad it came in useful,' Mullen replied with a genuine smile.

'Can you show us some moves too?' said Gary, gesturing from himself to Digger and Logan.

'I suppose, one day,' he replied distractedly.

'Can someone take these off me?' Digger grimaced, holding out the roses.

'I will,' said Jackie, snatching them from him. She inhaled their scent and smiled. 'Beautiful.'

'Let's get this place straightened up,' said Mullen.

He didn't need to lift a finger as Jamie and his friends started picking up overturned furniture, so he followed Jackie through to the kitchen, watching as she bustled about putting the flowers in a vase.

'Are you sure you're all right?' he asked her. 'That must have given you a hell of a shock.'

'It did, but Jamie sorted it. You should have seen him,' she said with a proud smile.

'I can imagine. He has a lot of natural ability.' Mullen was frantically thinking, wondering if this latest assault was something to do with his client. 'Have you any idea who they were?'

'No,' she sighed. 'They definitely weren't off the Gallowburn. I think it was to do with Cameron Abernethy.'

Mullen forced himself not to react as she confirmed his worst fears. 'How do you know?'

'I don't. It's just a feeling. They weren't here to give us a kicking, they were here to take Jamie. Me and Charlie were just collateral damage. I shudder to think what would have happened if they'd managed to abduct us.'

'Christ,' he breathed.

Cameron had to be stopped.

* * *

Mullen spent an hour at the Gray house before excusing himself, saying he had to pop back to work as an emergency had cropped up. Mullen insisted all the Blood Brothers stay at the house until he got back, and he headed straight to the Abernethy home.

He hammered on the front door and it was opened by a frowning Fenston.

'Mullen,' he said. 'What are you doing here?'

'I need to speak to your father.'

'He doesn't want to be disturbed.'

When he tried to close the door, Mullen kicked it open and it whacked Fenston in the face.

'My nose,' he cried, dabbing at it with his fingertips. 'You made me bleed.'

'Get over it,' muttered Mullen as he stormed inside.

He burst into the lounge to find the man himself talking to four large men wearing black bomber jackets and black jeans. He took in their battered and bruised faces. One of them held an ice pack to the back of his head and another had one pressed to his knee while a third cradled a badly swollen hand. The sight of them caused him to go into an uncharacteristic rage.

'I knew it,' he spat. 'You sent this lot to the Gray's house, didn't you?'

'If I did it's none of your fucking business,' retorted Cameron.

'It's my business because you hired me to do a job.'

'And what a waste of money that was. You've achieved fuck all.'

'What do you want me to do, fake the results of a DNA test to suit you? Helen Wilkinson isn't Allegra and do you know why? Because you killed her.'

'I fucking didn't,' Cameron bellowed at him like an angry bear.

'I don't know who you're trying to kid with your lies. Yourself maybe?' Mullen snapped back.

'How dare you speak to me like that?'

'You might be able to intimidate other people but to me you're just a bloated, perverted wretch who wanted to have sex with his own daughter and got angry when she refused.'

Cameron turned a livid shade of purple, jowly mouth opening and closing as his thoughts spun so wildly through his head he was unable to grasp onto a single one. Never, in his entire life, had anyone spoken to him like that. Even when he was a child, being dragged up on a scheme in Possilpark, everyone had been too afraid of him to discipline him. He'd always been large and enjoyed using his fists. Even his tough-talking, hard-drinking father had been unable to control him.

'You fucking what?' he eventually managed to splutter. 'That's it, the job's cancelled. You are fired.'

'Fine by me, as long as you pay what you still owe me.'

'You barge your way into my home, verbally abuse me and you expect me to pay you? Well, you can piss right off.'

'I'm going nowhere,' said Mullen, thrusting his face into Cameron's. 'Until I get my money.'

Cameron stared into his eyes and smiled. 'Oh, I get it now.'

'Get what?' replied Mullen in a bored tone.

'You've fallen for Jackie, haven't you? That's why you got all arsy about that lot turning up at her house,' he said, waving in the general direction of the four injured men.

'I'm a professional, Mr Abernethy. I don't fall for marks.'

'Bollocks. I can see it in your eyes.'

Mullen's face turned to granite as Cameron's wild death stare bored into him.

'Pay me my money so I can be on my way,' said Mullen, reining in his anger. It was unusual for him to lose control as he had.

'You're not getting another penny out of me.'

Mullen's lips curled with amusement when Cameron nodded at the four heavies and they slowly got to their feet, one of them limping. He turned to face them.

'Do you really want to do this after you got your arses handed to you by a twenty-two-year-old?' He looked back at Cameron. 'This is why you hire professionals, not untrained thugs.'

'These thugs are going to shut your smart mouth,' Cameron smirked.

Mullen rolled his eyes and shook his head.

The first thug lunged at him clumsily with a cosh. Mullen coolly grabbed his wrist and twisted, snatched the cosh from his hand and slammed it into his extended elbow. There was a sickening crack and he screamed, his cries silenced by a blow to the face from the cosh. A headbutt put the second man on the floor.

'Really?' Mullen said as the man with the busted knee limped towards him.

The thug's response was a battle cry. A kick to the groin turned the cry into a whimper and he fell sideways onto the couch and curled up into a ball.

Mullen looked to the fourth man, who had slumped back into the armchair, the ice pack still pressed to his head. 'Wise man,' Mullen told him before looking back at Cameron, who was regarding him more warily. 'Jamie thought those men were there to kidnap him and you are his prime suspect, by the way.'

'I'm quaking in my boots.'

'What did you intend to do with him if your men had been successful?'

'I was going to make him tell me where Allegra's hiding, something you've failed to do. Then I was going to shut the little rat's mouth.'

'Permanently?'

Cameron didn't reply.

'And what about Jackie and Charlie?' Mullen's blood pressure spiked when Cameron failed to reply for a second time. His look said it all. 'Do you seriously think you would have got away with that? The police would have come straight to you.'

'Bad things happen to people on that scheme. They would have become just another sad statistic.'

'You wouldn't have got away with that.'

'Yes, I would.'

'No, you wouldn't.' Mullen glowered. 'I would have made sure you were done for it.'

'I knew it,' said Cameron with a humourless smile. 'You're in love with Jackie. I expected more from a man like you.'

'I suggest you transfer the rest of the money you owe me. Now.'

'Fine,' muttered Cameron, taking out his phone and stabbing at it. 'There. Happy now?'

Mullen took out his own phone when it pinged and smiled at the screen. 'Very. Thank you, Mr Abernethy. That concludes our business.'

'Too right it does. Fuck off and never come back.'

Mullen just gave him a sideways smile before leaving, the smugness hanging around him infuriating Cameron.

'I'll get you back, you fucking prick,' Cameron hissed after Mullen had gone.

24

It was Gary's turn to check on Donald, so he left his friends still standing guard at the Gray house to head to the workshop, stopping at the corner shop on the way to pick up more supplies for their charge.

'Only me,' he called as he stepped inside and closed and locked the door behind him.

As always, Donald was sitting in front of the television. Gary could only see the back of his head as his chair faced away from the door. The usual strong smell of alcohol and body odour was overwhelmed by something else that made him feel sick.

'Have you shat yourself?' Gary frowned. 'Aww, man, that's manky,' he added, wafting his hand before his face. 'No way am I changing you. You'll have to sort yourself out, you hear me?'

Fear froze Gary's blood in his veins. He'd never known Donald not come back with a sarcastic comment. It also just occurred to him that the chair was again facing away from the door and the TV facing towards it . Why had they been moved? Was it to hide something?

Heart thumping, Gary dumped the carrier bag on the floor and slowly walked around the armchair. Donald didn't move or make a sound.

'Oh, Jesus,' Gary cried.

Donald's face was colourless, mouth slightly open and eyes wide in baffled surprise. A knife stuck out of his chest. The stench was because Donald's body had evacuated itself when he'd died.

Shock turned Gary numb and he just stood there, staring at the body for almost a full minute. Then panic shattered the shock and he started running around in a circle, flapping his arms.

'Oh, God, oh, God,' he said over and over.

He'd never seen a dead body before and this was doubly worse because Donald had been murdered. Who had done it? Jamie had the only key which he'd given to Gary and no way would he do something like this. What the hell had happened?

He turned his back on Donald, unable to look at his face any longer, switched off the television and took out his phone with shaking hands.

'Jamie,' he gasped. 'You need to come to the workshop right now. No, it can't wait,' he snapped. 'Get your arse here pronto. It's Donald. He... he...'

Jamie told him not to say anything else over the phone, and added that he was on his way, before hanging up.

Gary shoved the phone into his pocket and hastily exited the workshop, locking the door and rushing to the mouth of the alley to wait for his friends. No way was he waiting with the body.

It felt like hours before he saw the familiar and comforting sight of Jamie and Logan appear at the top of the street and approach him with their long-legged strides. It seemed to take them forever to reach him. He forced himself to wait, hopping from one foot to the other with agitation.

'Finally,' he breathed when they reached him.

'What's up?' Jamie frowned, taking in the fine sheen of sweat on

Gary's face, his pale skin and wild eyes. The most disturbing thing was the way he couldn't keep still. Gary only moved when he had to.

'I'll show you,' he replied. 'It's not something I want to say out loud.'

'Oh, God, what's Donald done?' said Logan as they followed Gary to the workshop door. 'Has he gone mental and smashed the place up?'

'Or thrown up everywhere and you're wanting us to clean it up?' said Jamie.

Gary just shook his head, his friends frowning when his hands trembled as he unlocked the workshop door. He pushed the door open and made no attempt to go inside. Jamie and Logan glanced at each other before walking in. Only once they were inside did Gary follow and pull the door shut.

'Fucking hell,' cried Logan. 'He's deid.'

'Aye, I know, Sherlock,' replied Gary, feeling a little better now someone else knew.

'How did this happen?'

'I'm no forensic expert, but I'm guessing it's something to do with the knife sticking out of his chest,' said Gary sarcastically.

'But... but... how?'

'Don't you mean who?' said Jamie, the knot of muscle at the base of his jaw throbbing with anger. 'Who the fuck would do this?'

'The door was locked when I turned up,' said Gary. 'It hadn't been broken into, meaning someone had a key.'

'The only person with a key is me.'

'And no way was it you, meaning someone else has a key.'

'Maybe someone in Digger's family has a key he doesn't know about?' said Gary.

'You're saying his maw or da found the key, got in, found

Donald, stabbed him in the chest for no reason and left?' said Logan.

'No, course not, but I cannae think of another way anyone could do this,' he snapped back. 'I mean, it's just fucking horrible.'

Logan looked back at Donald and sighed. 'Poor bastard. He might have been a drunken mess but he didn't deserve this.' He glanced at Jamie and was rather taken aback to see he was practically quivering with fury. 'Jamie, you all right?'

'This is a set-up.'

'Set-up?'

'The only people who knew Donald was here were us and the McVays.'

'Why would the McVays do this? They wanted us to look after him.' Logan's sad gaze settled on Donald's body. 'Which we fucked up big style.'

'We didn't fuck up. I had the key in my jacket when I went for a drink with my da. I left the jacket on the back of my chair when I went for a pish.'

'Was it still there when you came back?'

'Aye, I checked.'

'So, he didn't steal it.'

'No, but he could have taken an impression of it and had his own cut.'

'Does that work or does it only happen in films?' said Gary.

'It's a real thing,' replied Jamie. 'That's what must have happened. It's the only thing that makes sense.'

'But why?' said Logan. 'This wouldn't benefit him.'

'He was pissed off when Toni said the Gallowburn would be used for hiding secrets. If we fuck up she might change her mind and use it for dealing instead.'

'Surely not even Jason Gray would do that? It would put you in danger.'

'We're all gonnae lose our eyes for this, aren't we?' said Gary, starting to sweat even more.

'No, we're not,' said Jamie. 'Because we're gonnae get the person who really did this.'

'And you're sure it's Jason?' said Logan.

Jamie nodded.

'But would he kill someone just so he can deal drugs?'

'That bastard would do anything to get what he wants and he's killed before, in prison. Plus, it makes sense that it's him. He knows about our security system. Someone using the key wouldn't set off the alarms, meaning it wouldn't send an alert about an intruder to our phones.'

'Actually that does make sense, but he's our contact for Toni. We can't tell her what he's done directly. We have to go through him.'

'I'll call him and get him to come down here. You're not to let on we suspect him. We'll pretend to be clueless.'

'And what about when Toni wants to take our eyes?' said Gary.

'She won't if we play this right. Trust me.'

Gary took a deep breath and nodded. 'I do. Oh, Christ, is that your da?' he asked when Jamie's phone rang.

'No, it's Digger,' Jamie said, glancing at the screen before putting the phone to his ear. 'Aye, all right. Come to the workshop.' He hung up and looked to his friends. 'He said he's coming here because Scott's turned up at the house, so he can watch over Charlie and my maw.'

'Don't you think you should have warned him first?'

'We'll meet him at the top of the alley. I didn't want to break it to him over the phone and have him go mental in front of my maw.'

'Aye, good call.'

'Let's get out of here,' muttered Jamie. 'The smell's giving me the boak.'

Gratefully they stepped outside into the fresh air and waited for

Digger to arrive. His enormous form soon hove into view and he grinned when he saw them.

'What's up with your faces? Has Donald given you another slagging?'

'He'll never give anyone a slagging ever again,' replied Logan.

Digger's forehead creased with a frown. 'What are you on about?'

'We'll show you,' said Jamie, unlocking the door.

'I cannae believe I'm going in there for a third time,' said Gary, following them inside.

They all thought Digger was going to throw up when he went white and ran for the door. After a few gulps of air, he started kicking the wall.

'I'll kill them,' he spat. 'I'll fucking kill them.'

'Kill who?' said Logan.

'Whoever did it. I will rip their head off with my bare hands and bounce it about like a... a...'

'Bouncy ball?' offered Gary.

'Aye, one of them.'

'You liked Donald, didn't you?' said Logan.

Digger nodded. 'He was rude and insulting but he made me laugh. He didnae deserve that.'

'No, he didn't,' said Logan sadly.

'We should go back in there and say something.'

'Like what?'

'I don't know, the Lord's Prayer or something.'

'I could ask Valerie for advice on what to say,' said an eager Gary.

'I think it's best we don't involve her,' said Logan.

Jamie explained to Digger his theory about what had happened to Donald and immediately wished he'd kept his mouth shut when

Digger went into a fresh rage. After managing to calm him down Jamie explained the plan.

'You've got to keep it together,' Jamie told him. 'Jason can't know that we know or everything is fucked, including us.'

The hard look in Jamie's eyes and the way he spat his words at him encouraged Digger to get his temper under control. 'I understand. I'm calm.'

'You'd better be, because Jason's our contact and I'm gonnae have to call him and get him to come down here.'

'I won't let you down, Jamie.'

Jamie nodded and stared down at the phone in the hands, wrestling with his own anger. If he and his friends didn't manage to put on a good front, they were all dead too.

* * *

'Are you sure you're okay?' Mullen asked Jackie, wrapping an arm around her.

'Fine,' she replied, leaning into him and sliding her arms around his waist. 'I don't let wallopers like that get me down.'

'What a woman.' Mullen smiled down at her before kissing her.

They were ensconced in the kitchen together while Charlie happily watched television in the front room, recovered from the trauma.

'Would you like me to stay over tonight?' Mullen asked her.

'Well, I do feel a little vulnerable,' she purred. 'I need a big strong man to make me feel safe.'

'I'm very happy to oblige,' he replied, running his fingertips down her face.

Already he was working out how he could tell her who he really was without arousing her suspicions. The case was over, so by rights he should cut ties with her and ensure they never saw each other again, but he didn't want to give her up. The job had always come first with him, at the expense of his private life, and now, for the first time, he was putting himself before the job. He wanted to make Jackie a permanent fixture in his life.

They kissed, jumping apart when the kitchen door opened and Charlie wandered in.

'Maw, can I have some ice cream?'

'You already had a bowl at Maureen's,' she replied.

'Oh, right,' he mumbled, sticking out his bottom lip.

'How about some toast with jam?'

'Yeah, all right, then.'

'I'll bring it through, sweetie. You go back to watching your programme.'

Charlie smiled up at Scott. 'Do you like jam?'

'I do, especially cherry.'

'Urgh, cherries are horrible. Strawberry's my favourite.'

'I like strawberry too.'

'Do you want to eat your toast on the couch with me?'

Mullen, as ever the fish out of water with children, glanced at Jackie, who was positively beaming at her son. Obviously this was good. 'That would be nice. Thank you, Charlie.'

The boy gave him a sweet smile, before returning to the living room.

'He likes you,' said Jackie. 'He doesn't ask everyone to eat toast with him on the couch.'

'He's a good boy.'

'He's nothing like his loser father, thank God. I dread to think what my boys would be like now if Jason had hung around. Running out on them was the best thing he could have done, otherwise they might have ended up terminal losers like him.'

'Has he bothered you again lately?'

'No, he's left us alone. Jamie's the only one he's interested in because he can use him.'

'Use him, how?'

Jackie realised how close she'd come to revealing the truth, but this man made her drop the barriers, which told her how special he was. 'He's tried to get the Blood Brothers involved in something heavy.'

'And have they got involved?'

'They're not stupid enough to fall for any idea of his. They've kept him at arm's length.'

Mullen knew she was hiding something but decided not to press the issue. She would tell him when she was ready. It was a relief that he didn't have to get any information out of her any more. He could just enjoy the relationship.

* * *

'Remember, keep it together,' Jamie whispered to his friends when Jason pulled up outside the workshop in his BMW. 'We know nothing.'

The rest of the Blood Brothers nodded.

'All right, son?' said Jason. 'Why are you all standing out here?'

'I'll show you,' said Jamie. 'You lot wait out here,' he told his friends before leading his dad inside.

He watched Jason's reaction to the gruesome sight carefully.

'Jesus Christ,' breathed Jason when he saw Donald's body. 'What happened?'

'No idea. Gary found him like this.'

'Did someone break in?'

'All the doors and windows were intact.'

'What about the cameras? Did they capture anything?'

'Aye, a figure in black. It showed them fumbling at the door but their back's to the camera, so we can't see what they were doing. We've nae idea how they got in. The door was locked and Gary had the only key, which had been with me until I gave it to him this morning to bring Donald his supplies.'

'Can you see the intruder's face on the camera?'

'No. They were wearing a mask.'

'So, no alert was sent to your phone that someone had got in?'

'Nope, meaning a key must have been used, which is why we can't work out how they got in.'

'I hate to say this, son, but how much can you trust your friends?'

'They've been my best friends since school and we're blood brothers – we made a blood pact.'

'Pacts can be broken and all three of them had access to the key. They could have had a copy made before giving it back to you.'

'This isnae them. What would they have to gain?'

'Maybe one of them blabbed to someone and they paid them to sabotage your arrangement with Toni.'

'Like who?'

'I don't know, the Lawsons. Or maybe Cameron Abernethy.'

Jamie made a point of looking thoughtful. 'You've got a point there. That bastard would do anything to hurt me.' He sighed heavily. 'What do we do now? Toni's gonnae kill us all.'

'No, she won't. She can be reasonable. We need to get her down here, but let me do all the talking. You never know, this could lead to her getting rid of Cameron for you.'

Jamie's eyes turned to flint. 'I told you, I want to do that.'

'Take it from someone who knows what it's like to kill – you really don't, son. Anyway, we'll talk about that later. Now I need to call Caesar.'

* * *

The Blood Brothers and Jason all watched Caesar climb out of the large Audi four-by-four, walk around the car and open the passenger door. A long, elegant leg appeared, followed by the rest of Toni, wearing her traditional fur coat over a revealing short black dress. Caesar took her hand and assisted her over the cobbles, ensuring she dodged all the dog turds. Out of the back of the car climbed two large heavies. Jamie's hands went into his coat pockets, the feel of his bike chains reassuring. Behind the Audi was a large white Transit van. Two men were sitting in the cab but they made no move to get out. The presence of so many heavies made him extremely nervous.

Everyone stood aside to allow her entry, but her only reaction to Donald's corpse was a curl of the upper lip.

'Well, this is an almighty fuck-up, isn't it, boys?' she said, shark-like black eyes darting between them all.

They all nodded like naughty children and hung their heads.

'Anyone care to explain? How is it that my men got the shite kicked out of them when they tried to get in, but you let someone swan in and stab poor old Donald?'

'Because they had a key,' replied Jason.

Her eyes flashed. 'A key? Just how the fuck did they get that?'

'We're not sure,' he said while the Blood Brothers remained silent.

'I was under the impression there was only one key, which your son was in charge of.'

'That's right.'

'And there are no more keys?'

'None.'

'Well, obviously there's a second one that no one knows about. What did the cameras show?'

'Just someone wearing a mask unlocking the door with a key,' said Jamie, bringing up the footage to show her.

'Hmm,' she said, eyes narrowing at the image. 'That could be anyone. I'm disappointed, boys. I thought you were up to this, I trusted you and look,' she said, gesturing to the body. 'I'm left with a corpse sitting in its own shite.' She nodded at Caesar, who waved to the men sitting in the van.

'Relax,' she told the Blood Brothers when they all looked at each other nervously. 'They're not here for you. They're here to clean up this mess. Go home. It's not wise to get in their way.'

'What happens now?' said Jamie.

'I've yet to decide that,' she replied, voice low and dangerous.

Jamie glanced at Jason, who urged him to remain silent with a shake of the head. When he looked to Logan, his friend nodded his encouragement. 'I've also got this...'

He was forced to move out of the way by Toni's men entering the workshop carrying cleaning products and a long sheet of plastic. Jamie found it sad that Donald was going to end up wrapped up like a parcel and buried in a shallow grave.

'I've got this other—' Jamie continued.

'Not now,' snapped Toni. 'We need to get this mess moved.'

'But I've—'

'I said not now,' she positively snarled at him. 'I will speak to you later, unless you'd like to press the issue?' she added, producing a glasses case from her pocket. 'It's black, to match your eyes.'

Deciding now wasn't the time, Jamie nodded at his friends and they all filed out in silence, looking back over their shoulders as they made their way down the alley, but someone had closed the door of the workshop and they could no longer see inside. Jason had remained behind to help clean up.

'She didn't even give me a chance to show her what else we have.' Jamie sighed.

'You had no choice,' said Logan. 'Don't worry, I'm sure you'll get another chance to explain.'

'I don't know,' said Gary. 'She might just decide to slaughter us all and use the Gallowburn for dealing.'

'That would be stupid and she's no' a stupid woman,' said Jamie. 'She wouldn't dare do that with so much media attention on me.'

'But there hasn't been any for a while,' said Gary. 'You gave your evidence, we scared off the journos waiting for you when you got home and they haven't come back.'

'Gary's right,' said Logan. 'Maybe you're overestimating the protection that gives you and, even if it still makes her wary, that protection will only last for so long.'

'I guess we'll find out.'

While Jamie strode on ahead, his friends all regarded each other uneasily.

25

Jackie saw Scott off to work the next morning before taking Charlie to school. Jamie had stayed over at Logan's to give them some time together. She worried what he'd say about Scott staying over again, but he seemed too preoccupied to really notice. She hoped to God nothing bad had happened with the McVays, but Scott left her with a big smile and a promise to stop by on his lunchbreak to make sure everything was okay. Jackie found his concern for her safety and that of her children very touching.

She was doing some dusting when there was a knock at the door. After what had happened the previous day, Jackie was a little nervous about answering it.

After shoving her mobile phone into the back pocket of her jeans, she picked up her trusty frying pan and approached the door, making a mental note to have a spyhole installed. After putting on the chain, she opened the door a crack and peered out, sighing with relief when she saw it was a delivery man in a high-vis vest.

'Jackie Gray?' he said.

'Aye, what of it?'

'I've got a package for you,' he replied, holding out a large Jiffy bag.

Deciding she'd done enough cowering, she removed the chain and flung the door open, the man arching an eyebrow at the pan in her hand.

'I was... about to clean it when you knocked,' she said, snatching the bag from his hand and closing and locking the door.

She replaced the pan in the cupboard then sat at the kitchen table to open her package, wondering what it could be. She frowned when she tipped a stack of documents and photographs onto the tabletop.

'Oh, Christ,' she breathed when she saw the photos were of Scott, only the attached documents said his name was Gavin Mullen and he owned a private investigation business in the city.

Also in the package was a handwritten letter, the signature at the bottom of which turned her blood to ice. *Cameron Abernethy.*

The letter informed her that he'd hired Mullen to investigate her family to discover the whereabouts of his daughter, who he was convinced was still alive. The letter oozed smugness and superiority and Jackie's temper rose with each word. Apparently Mullen felt nothing for her, she was just a mark, a way for him to gain their trust and in turn gain access to their home. Jackie wasn't one for crying but hot tears rolled down her face as all the joy Scott – or rather Gavin – had brought into her life froze and fell away, leaving her cold and heartbroken. She had only just realised that she had been falling in love.

Molten anger flowed through her veins, melting the ice, and she scrunched up the papers as her hands curled into fists.

'The bastard,' she spat. 'The lying, manipulative bastard.'

She buried her face in her hands and sobbed. The only males who had never let her down were her boys. All the others were fucking useless. Why should Scott be any different? Inwardly she sighed. Gavin. She hated that name. She'd gone to school with a Gavin and he'd been a total twat.

The fact that he'd used her was the worst. He'd put on a front to get to her son. They'd trusted him, given him free rein of their home. He could snoop all day and there would be nothing to find, she knew that for a fact, but it was the betrayal that cut her deep.

Jackie lifted her head, dried her eyes and took out her phone.

'Jamie,' she said. 'Can you come home? I need you to help me with something. No, just you,' she added when he asked if she needed him to bring his friends.

* * *

Mullen knocked on the door of the Gray home that afternoon, running a hand through his hair, the other holding a box of Jackie's favourite chocolates. He'd arranged a surprise for her. She deserved a treat after those bastards had burst into her home.

'Hi.' He beamed, as always his heart lifting at the sight of her. 'Are you okay? Has something else happened?' he anxiously asked. 'You look so pale.'

'I've got a headache,' she replied flatly. 'I've taken something for it, but it doesn't seem to be shifting.'

'Oh, I'm sorry to hear that,' he said, stepping inside and closing the door behind him. 'Do you get them often?'

'Only when I'm stressed. I think it's what happened yesterday that did it.' She forced a smile. 'Are those for me?' she said, indicating the chocolates.

'They are,' he replied, handing them to her.

'My favourites.'

'I know, I remembered you saying.'

'That's very sweet.'

'Are you sure it's just a headache?' he said. 'You look so sad.'

'Well, it's not just that. Cameron's trial is coming to an end soon and we're really feeling the pressure. If he doesn't get sent down I don't know what we'll do.'

'He will. The prosecution's case is watertight.'

'Let's hope so,' she sighed. 'Brew?'

'I'll make it, you're not feeling well.'

'I can manage a brew. Take a seat, it won't be long.'

Mullen watched her shuffle into the kitchen, looking the essence of misery. He was glad that he'd arranged his surprise for her – it would take her mind off her worries for a while.

She returned to the living room with a cup of tea for each of them and the box of chocolates and sat beside him on the couch.

'I came to tell you that I've arranged a surprise for you,' he said.

'Oh, yes?' she replied with a small smile before taking a sip of tea.

'I've booked a night for us at a hotel in the city tomorrow. It's a five-star hotel with a fantastic spa. You could have a few treatments, get a massage. It'll help you relax.'

He drank his tea as he watched her digest this news, expecting her to be overjoyed, but she barely reacted.

'Tomorrow night?' she said. 'But it's short notice. What about Charlie?'

'Well, I thought Jamie could look after him or he could stay with a friend.'

'I don't know, I've left them on their own a lot lately.'

'They'll be fine.' He nervously drank his tea as she appeared to drift into her own world. When she didn't reply he added, 'Is it too soon for a night away together? I'm sorry if I've jumped the gun.'

'No, it's a lovely idea but some warning would have been nice.'

'Oh,' he said, looking down at his hands. Was she losing interest already? She sounded so cold and aloof. Had he just broken all his own rules of professionalism for nothing? As this was the first time he'd ever had serious feelings for a woman, he had no idea what to do or say and he frantically hunted around for an answer. 'I suppose I could change the booking to next week, so you've more time to prepare.' His head suddenly swam and he put a hand to his forehead.

'Are you okay?' she asked him.

'Just feeling a little dizzy,' he murmured.

When he reached out to take her hand she got up off the couch and put her mug down on the coffee table.

'Jackie?' he said, confused.

His grip on his own mug weakened and she caught it before it fell to the floor. She folded her arms across her chest and watched him swaying on the couch, ice in her eyes.

'Night night, Gavin,' he heard her say before he fell unconscious.

* * *

It wasn't a gentle return to consciousness for Mullen. He jumped awake, as though something had startled him, but he couldn't have said what that was. It took his muddled brain a few seconds to process what was going on. He was still in the living room of the Gray home, only now he was tied to one of the kitchen chairs, unable to move. Jackie loomed over him, looking very pissed off, frying pan in one hand. Beside her was Jamie.

'What... what's going on?' he mumbled, tongue feeling thick in his mouth.

'I slipped a few tranquillisers into your tea,' said Jackie. 'They won't do you any harm. My GP prescribed me them for stress after Allegra died.' Her gaze hardened. 'We know who you are, Gavin Mullen.'

His heart sank. His cover had been blown and he thought he knew who was responsible.

'Don't even try to deny it,' Jackie said, producing a sheaf of documents and throwing them at him.

As he couldn't move his arms, they hit him in the chest and landed on his lap, some of the papers fluttering to the floor. He noticed one of the items on the floor was a photograph of himself in his marine uniform. Cameron had got hold of his military records to prove his true identity.

'Christ,' he sighed, closing his eyes and shaking his head.

'Cameron sent me this lot. It told me everything – how you used me to get close to Jamie, that I was just some mark to you.'

'I'm so sorry,' he breathed.

'I thought I'd finally found a decent man when in fact you're just another lying scumbag, like all the rest,' she said, lip curling with disgust. 'No wonder you were on hand to help Jamie with the Lawsons that night. You were following him, spying on him, you dirty bastard,' she yelled.

'It's true, Jackie, Cameron did hire me. He's convinced Allegra's still alive, but I told him where to stick his job. I knew he was the one who sent those four men here and, before you ask, no, I didn't know he was going to do that. I went to his house to have it out with him. He didn't like what I had to say and he ordered the same four men to attack me but they failed miserably and received a second beating.'

Hope surged through him when he saw the corner of Jamie's mouth lift into a smile at that. If he could convince Jamie of the truth, he might be able to convince his mother.

'I told him what he could do with his job,' continued Mullen. 'And do you know why?'

'Why?' she said, green eyes bright with fury.

'Because I fell in love with you, Jackie.'

Tears filled her eyes before that iron will of hers took over and she blinked them away. 'What a load of shite. You're only trying to talk your way out of trouble.'

'I'm not, I really mean it. I've never felt like this about anyone before. For the first time in my life, I put my personal feelings before business. I told Cameron to stick his job up his arse for you, Jackie, because I love you.'

'Stop saying that,' she snapped. 'You don't love me.'

'Yes, I do. If you only knew what I'd done to protect you. I could have got Cameron the evidence he needed to prove Allegra's alive.'

'That proves you're lying, because that lassie's dead,' she yelled. 'How dare you use her too?'

'She's not though, is she, Jamie?' Mullen said, eyes flicking to the strong, silent figure standing in the corner of the room. 'She's alive and well in Florence, isn't she?'

Jackie gave her son a sideways glance, but Jamie was giving nothing away, eyes dark and inscrutable.

'I called off the investigation into Allegra's disappearance,' said Mullen, 'because I knew it would hurt you, Jackie, if your son went to prison, which he would if Allegra was ever found alive, and the case against Cameron would collapse. I damaged my reputation and possibly my business for you.'

'Why are you banging on about Allegra being alive?' she said. 'I don't understand.'

'Ask your son. He knows all about it, don't you, Jamie?'

When they both stared at him, Jamie shrugged. 'He's bullshitting you, Maw. He's been caught out and he's trying to worm his way out of it.'

'No, I'm not. Allegra set up her father for her murder and fled the country. But she came back to see you the day of the memorial, didn't she, Jamie?'

'I've nae idea what he's talking about,' Jamie told his mother again.

But Jackie was recalling the day of the memorial and how she'd frantically searched the hotel grounds for her son when he'd said he was going for a walk. He'd been devastated and depressed and she'd feared he'd do something silly. After she'd found him, he'd seemed a little lighter, as though the weight bearing down on him had become easier to bear. Jamie was avoiding her gaze, keeping his attention on Mullen.

'Your secret's safe with me,' he told Jamie. 'I don't want your mother to get hurt, or you and Charlie. Believe it or not, I've become very fond of you two as well.'

'I don't believe you,' Jamie replied stonily.

'I wish you did because it's true. I had the opportunity to search your room when I came for dinner, but I didn't take it. You've no idea how much I surprised myself, but you'd welcomed me into your home and I was enjoying your company. I didn't want to break your trust.'

'That flat you took me to with the view of the Finnieston Crane,' said Jackie. 'That wasn't your flat, was it?'

He shook his head. 'No. It's one I use for undercover work.'

Jackie turned her back on him when more hot tears threatened. That flat had been the place where she'd given all of herself to him, shown him the most trust she could ever show a man, and it had all been a lie.

Jamie produced his bike chains from his pockets. 'Want me to batter him, Maw?'

'No,' she replied, wiping away her tears and turning back round. 'You betrayed me in every way possible,' she told Mullen.

'I know it seems that way, but I didn't—'

'Just stop lying,' she yelled at him. 'You can't help yourself, can you? I loved you and you threw it back in my face.'

'You love me?' he breathed.

'Not any more.'

'Yes, you do. You can't turn emotion like that off like a tap. I know because I tried so many times to deny what I felt for you, but couldn't. So that's how I know that you love me, like I love you.'

Jackie bit her lip as fresh tears spilled down her face. Sensing he was getting through to her, Mullen decided to keep pressing his point. 'We can start again, Jackie, this time with no lies. I'll tell you everything about myself, I'll keep nothing back. We can be a proper couple.'

'I already thought we were a proper couple,' she exclaimed. 'Was all that you told me at the restaurant true or more lies?'

'It was true, every word. I was so surprised that I opened up to you like that, but I felt so comfortable with you, which is why I'm sure we have a future together.'

'You don't get it, do you? You've already broken my trust, made me think you were someone you're not. You've destroyed any chance we had of a future together.'

He shook his head as an unfamiliar pain swelled inside his chest. 'No, we can get over this. I know it.'

'It's already over,' she said in a tired, flat voice. 'And it's all your fault.'

'But I love you, Jackie.'

'You can stick your love up your arse. I don't want it.'

Mullen looked down at the floor as her words tore his heart in two.

Despite what Mullen had done, Jamie felt a bit sorry for him. Mullen looked like he'd felt when he'd thought Allegra had died.

'Let him go, Jamie,' sighed Jackie.

'Seriously?'

She nodded. 'I want him out of my sight.'

Jamie produced a penknife and cut through Mullen's bonds,

before taking a few steps back, bike chains at the ready. Once he was free, Mullen slowly got to his feet, massaging his wrists.

'I'm sorry, Jackie,' he said.

'Piss off. I never want to see you again.'

Mullen nodded and pulled on his coat. He opened his mouth to say something, thought better of it and closed his mouth again. On his way to the door, he pulled her into his arms and kissed her. Jackie allowed herself a moment of indulgence to say goodbye, before shoving him away.

'Get lost, Gavin.'

He could see the pain he'd caused her shining out of her eyes and he felt terrible. Realising further pleading would be futile, that he'd ruined the best thing that had ever happened to him, he quietly left.

When the front door had closed behind him, Jackie let the frying pan drop and buried her face in her hands.

'Maw,' said Jamie, dropping his own weapons and rushing to her.

'I feel like such an idiot,' she sobbed on his shoulder.

'Don't. It's on him, not you.'

'I should have known something wasn't right, but I didn't have a clue. He fooled me so easily.'

'You didn't realise because he truly loved you, I really believe that. It wasn't all a lie.'

'Maybe you're right, son,' she said, wiping her eyes and taking a few, deep calming breaths. 'Anyway, I never want to talk about the prick again. There's something else we need to discuss.'

Jamie nodded, knowing what direction the conversation was headed.

'And I want the truth, Jamie. Don't lie to me like all the other men in my life have.'

'I won't.'

'Is Allegra still alive?'

He nodded.

'Jesus,' she breathed before collapsing onto the sofa. 'But... but... how...?'

'Calm down, Maw,' he said, taking her hand when she started to shake and cry.

'God, I'm blubbing a lot today,' she said. 'How long have you known?'

'Since the memorial. She came to see me after the service.'

'When you went out for a walk?'

'Aye. I didn't know she was there. She was in disguise. I got the shock of my life,' Jamie said with a fond smile at the memory.

He went on to explain everything, leaving nothing out. She deserved the full truth. Jackie just stared at him with her mouth hanging open.

'Scott... I mean, Gavin was telling the truth,' he added when he'd laid it all out. 'He could have kept the investigation going but he didn't, to protect us. If he had told Cameron the truth the police would have been round by now.'

'Don't start sticking up for him. He doesnae deserve it.'

'Probably not, but I just wanted you to know that not everything he said was lies.'

'I appreciate that, sweetheart,' she said, patting his hand. 'But you've been hiding this massive secret all this time, telling everyone she's dead, including the police and the media, giving evidence in court.' Her heart shattered all over again at what her son had endured.

'I had no choice. Allegra thought Cameron had killed me, so she was trying to get revenge, for me. If anyone found out the truth we'd both be arrested. It's been such a burden, Maw,' he breathed. 'I'm sorry for keeping it from you, but I didn't want you to get into trouble if anyone found out.'

'Don't worry about me,' she said, hugging him. 'It's you I'm concerned about and I'm over the bloody moon that Allegra's alive and well,' she said, voice cracking. 'But what about your future together?'

'When all this dies down, I'll go out there to be with her.'

'So you're still planning on leaving the country?' she said sadly.

'Aye, but no' for a few years. You don't mind, do you, Maw?'

'Do I mind you living in a beautiful country with the woman you love? No, course not. I'm happy for you. No wonder you've no' been interested in other lassies. Does anyone else know?'

'Naw, not even Logan. Do you want to talk to her?'

'Oh, that would be smashing, son. So that's what that phone's for,' she said when he produced the phone he contacted Allegra on. Jamie dialled her number and waited.

Jackie smiled at the way his face lit up when Allegra answered.

'There's someone here who's desperate to talk to you,' he said into the phone. 'Naw, it's okay. Trust me.'

Jackie's heart was thumping as he handed her the phone. 'Hello, Allegra.'

'Jackie,' she squealed.

'Oh, sweetheart, it's incredible to hear your voice. Jamie's told me and I'm just so happy... oh, God, I'm greetin again. I've been doing it all day. Just some bastard man, nothing for you to worry about.'

Jamie smiled as he listened to them talk, catching up after all this time. Every so often a tear would slide down his mother's cheek and she'd hastily wipe it away, but this time they were tears of joy. That bastard Gavin had taken something from her, but he'd given her something back.

26

Jamie prowled the house restlessly for the remainder of the day, wondering when he was going to hear from the McVays or Jason. His friends kept calling him for updates but he had nothing to tell them. The only time he left the house was to pick up Charlie from school in his car.

He watched his mother carefully, worried about her after the double shock she'd received, but she was the type to keep soldiering on. Her mood was bitter-sweet. On the one hand she was down about what Gavin had done to her, but on the other she was delighted about Allegra still being alive. He decided not to tell her about Donald's murder. She'd been through enough for one day.

After tea there was a knock at the door and Jamie steeled himself to answer it.

'What are you doing here?' He sighed.

'We're going demented waiting at home,' said Logan, flanked by Digger and Gary.

'So you decided to go demented here instead?'

'Aye.'

'You can come in, but don't say anything to my maw. She doesn't know about what happened to Donald.'

They received a warm welcome from Jackie, who was glad of their company. Their presence always cheered her up; she loved listening to their banter, which would be just the tonic after the day she'd had.

'Gary.' Charlie beamed when they walked in. 'Maw got me a new cereal – flumpy crunchy lumpies. Do you want to try some? It's got marshmallows.'

'Oh, aye, wee man. I pure love marshmallows.'

'I'll get you a bowl.' Jackie smiled. 'Does anybody want anything else?'

'I'll have a lager, if there's one going,' said Digger, his friends murmuring their agreement.

Happily she set about serving them all, glad of the distraction.

'We have to do something,' Logan whispered when Jackie had gone into the kitchen along with Charlie, who was eating his cereal at the table. 'We cannae just sit around waiting for Toni to come along and scoop out our eyes and cut off our baws. We have to play this the right way and think carefully about any move before making it.'

'Right now, Jason thinks he's safe,' said Jamie. 'That no one knows what he's done, and I want to smash that confidence with a fucking sledgehammer.'

They all looked at each other when there was a knock at the door.

'We'll answer it together,' said Logan.

They nodded at each other before making their way to the door.

'Jesus, Da,' breathed Logan when Jamie pulled open the door to reveal Dave. 'What are you doing here?'

'I cannae find the remote. Where is it?'

'You mean the remote for the telly?'

'Aye.'

'Why didn't you just call me?'

'Because I've lost my phone too. Have you seen it?'

'Jeezo,' Logan sighed. 'No, I haven't. Are you sure you didn't flog it down the pub when you were pissed again?'

'No, I...' He hesitated as a vague memory returned. 'Actually, I might have sold it to Neville last night.'

'For what?'

'A pork pie.'

''Oh no' again.'

At the sound of chimes, Dave turned. 'Here comes Ephraim.'

The big pink van couldn't pull up outside the house any more because of Jamie's car, so it parked behind it outside the house next door.

'My maw will be pleased I've got that car now,' commented Jamie.

Ephraim got out of the van, ignoring the customers who were already congregating on the pavement, and stomped down the garden path of the Gray home, Dave hastily jumping out of his way.

'I heard your maw's got a new fella,' snarled Ephraim, left eye twitching.

'She did,' replied Jamie. 'But she kicked him into touch.'

The twitching stopped. 'Really?'

'Aye, really.'

'Why?'

'Because he's a walloper.'

'Oh, right, then.' The big man smiled, tense body unfurling, to all their relief. 'Is she okay?'

'She'll be fine. You know my maw.'

'Aye, I dae.' He beamed. 'Do you think she'd like an icey?'

''No' at the moment, she's doing some housework, but it's good of you to ask.'

Ephraim peered over their shoulders, hoping for a glimpse of Jackie, but she'd heard his voice and was hiding in the kitchen. 'Right, well, I'd better get tae work, then. Gi'e her my best.'

'I will, Ephraim.'

They all breathed a sigh of relief as he returned to his van, but before he could get in, a gleaming black Mercedes S-Class rolled down the street.

Dave whistled. 'Nice motor. It can't have been on the scheme for long, it's still got all its wheels.'

A sense of impending doom settled over Jamie as the Mercedes slowed, before pulling up at the kerb on the other side of Jamie's car, so his motor was penned in between a pink ice-cream van and a seventy-six-thousand-pound car. The sight was so surreal he wanted to laugh, but any sense of amusement was eradicated when Caesar got out of the back.

'Oh, good,' Caesar called to them. 'All the wee fannies are here.'

'Is he calling me a fanny?' said Dave, pointing at himself.

'Naw, Da,' said Logan. 'You're best going home. You don't want to get involved with this.'

'Why, what's going on? Bloody hell,' he added when Caesar held the back door open and out climbed Toni, clad in her fur coat, diamonds glittering in the fading light.

'Oh, shite,' said Digger and Gary in unison.

Caesar took her hand and escorted her to the kerb. The driver, who, judging by his enormous size and threatening demeanour, was a heavy, hauled his bulk out of the car too. Jason got out of the front passenger seat and the four of them progressed up the garden path of the Gray home.

Excited whispers emanated from the queue at the ice-cream van as they all recognised Toni, who gave them a regal nod, revelling in her notoriety. Ephraim stared at her with a puzzled frown. Toni gave him a nod too and he nodded back, looking confused.

'Toni,' said Jamie nervously. 'We didn't know you were coming.'

'I do like to surprise people.' Movement caught her eye when she spotted a figure exiting a house two doors down and her eyes widened.

The figure seemed equally shocked to see her and came to a halt on the pavement, the two women staring at each other.

'What the hell are you doing here?' demanded Toni, striding towards the woman.

Valerie's smile was grim. 'Long time no see, Antoinette.'

'She knows Toni?' Digger whispered to an equally astonished Logan, who shrugged.

They both glanced at Gary, who was staring in amazement at his angel coolly conversing with the most dangerous woman in the country.

'Surely you're not surprised?' Valerie told Toni. 'You must already know that I'm reverend on this scheme?'

'I do, but I expected you to be holed up in your stone temple,' sneered Toni. 'Babbling to your god.'

'I see you're still the heathen, Antoinette.'

'And you're still the God-botherer, Valerie,' Toni retorted.

Jamie noted that Valerie's profession seemed to intimidate Toni, as though it brought all her sins home to her.

'Why are you here?' said Valerie, glancing at the Blood Brothers before her eyes swept back to Toni. She knew better than to keep her eyes off her for too long.

'If you were still part of the family I might have told you, but you lost all rights to any information when you left to marry your Christ.'

'She's a McVay,' murmured an astonished Logan.

'I'm not a nun,' Valerie told Toni.

'Why are you hanging around here?' Toni replied.

'I've just been to visit a parishioner. Why, what are you doing?'

'I'm telling you nothing,' Toni hissed. 'Aunt Janet nearly died when you put on your dog collar.'

'My mother always was overly dramatic. I do hope you're not dragging Jamie into your world. He's a good boy.'

'Good boy.' Toni snorted. 'Still living in a dream world, Valerie.' A cruel smile curled her lips. 'If you're here to save his soul, you're going to lose.'

'I've never lost once in my life. I thought you of all people would remember that.'

Toni's eyes turned black and shark-like and she leaned in to whisper in her ear, 'There's a first time for everything.'

Valerie's only reply was a tightening of the jaw and a tilt of the head.

Toni smiled triumphantly, pleased she'd got in the last word, before stalking back up the path to the Gray home, ignoring the way everyone looked from her to Valerie with their mouths hanging open. She frowned up at the house. 'Well, this looks... small.'

'It's homely,' said Jamie, eyes narrowing.

'Aren't you going to invite me in, then?'

Jamie's eyes flicked to Jason, who nodded almost imperceptibly.

'Aye, all right,' he said, realising he had no choice, although he didn't know how his maw was going to take this fresh shock.

'Thank you.' Toni looked to Dave, who swallowed nervously. 'Who are you?'

He just gaped at her, unable to believe he was face to face with Toni McVay.

'This is Dave, my da,' replied Logan.

'Doesn't he speak? Is he deaf and dumb?'

'Naw, he's just... shocked.'

'That is the effect I tend to have on people. Piss off, Dave.'

'Oh, right. Thank you,' Dave replied with a small bow that

seemed to please her, before scurrying down the garden path and out of the gate.

They all piled into the house, the tiny front room practically taken up by all the bodies inside.

Jackie emerged from the kitchen, dropping the four cans of lager on the floor that she'd been holding when she saw Toni McVay in her living room.

'Sweet Jesus,' she breathed.

'Not quite.' Toni smiled, tossing back her head. 'You must be Jackie Gray.'

'I am,' Jackie murmured, eyes wide with shock.

'I'm glad you're here, actually, because there's a lot to sort out.'

'There is?' Jackie said, glancing at Jamie.

'I understand this must have come as a shock,' replied Toni with such understanding she surprised everyone. 'Please, sit down.'

'Oh, thanks,' said Jackie a little sarcastically before taking a seat on her own sofa. 'Charlie, sweetheart,' she added, trying not to panic when her younger son emerged from the kitchen. 'Go back and finish your supper.'

'I've finished it,' he replied.

'Well, do your homework.'

'I've already done it.'

'Then why don't you go to Kieran's?'

'Can I?' He grinned.

'Course you can,' she replied.

Charlie frowned at the room, surprised to see so many people standing there. 'Who's she?' he asked, gesturing to Toni.

'She's a... friend,' replied Jackie, glancing uncertainly at Toni.

'She's really pretty,' said Charlie, who was already developing an eye for the ladies.

Toni was always ready to accept a compliment, even if it was from an eleven-year-old. 'What's your name, wee man?'

'Charlie.'

'Charlie. Do as your maw says and go to your pal's. Just some grown-up business. Nothing for you to worry about.'

He looked to his older brother for confirmation, and Jamie nodded. 'It was nice to meet you,' Charlie told Toni in his most respectful voice.

'And you too,' Toni replied with a smile.

'Gary, can you take him to Kieran's, please?' Jackie asked him, continually glancing at Toni, wondering if she was going to object, but she seemed content with this plan.

'Aye, nae bother,' he replied.

'Come straight back, Gary,' said Toni.

'I will.'

Gary waited for Charlie to pull on his coat and shoes before leaving with him.

'I don't like weans,' said Toni. 'But he's a wee cracker.'

'Aye, he is,' replied Jackie in a tone that said she didn't give a shit who Toni was, she would rip her head off if she laid a finger on her child. 'And I don't mind you and your pals being here, but I want that pig's arse out,' she said, jabbing a finger at Jason. 'His own son didn't even have a clue who he is. Charlie didn't look at him twice.'

'That's true,' said Toni, narrowing her eyes at him.

'I want to make that right, but you won't let me near him,' Jason told Jackie.

'Because you're a toxic rattlesnake.'

'No domestics, please,' announced Toni. 'I'm so glad I never got married. We're here to discuss something else, and Jason needs to be here for it,' she told Jackie.

'Fine, as long as he stays well away from me or I won't be responsible for my actions,' Jackie replied, folding her arms across her chest.

Jamie feared his mother's attitude would enrage Toni, but, on the contrary, her smile said she respected her.

'You messed up royally, boys,' Toni told the Blood Brothers. 'I trusted you to look after something valuable and now Donald's dead.'

'What?' said Jackie, turning pale.

'I can't tell you how disappointed I am,' continued Toni in a tone that made her sound more like a teacher than a gangland boss. 'I really thought you had potential but obviously, for the first time in my life, I was wrong.'

'You weren't wrong, Toni,' said Jamie. 'We do have potential and we're good at what we do.'

'Tell that to Donald,' Toni said, eyes turning even blacker.

'If it helps, we know who did it.'

'It's obvious who did it – one of you four.'

'It wasnae us. It was him,' Jamie said, pointing at Jason.

'You lying wee shite,' exploded Caesar, who was standing right beside Jason. 'I didnae do it.'

'No, I mean him, my da.'

'Wow,' said Toni. 'You really do hate him, don't you?'

'You mean he really hates me. He stole the key out of my jacket when we went for a pint together after our last visit to Donald, and had a copy made.'

'So, the key is missing?' said Toni.

'Naw, I still have it. He made an impression of it and had his own cut.'

Toni looked to Jason. 'What have you got to say about this?'

'I'm not angry, son,' Jason replied, addressing Jamie directly. 'You're in trouble and you're panicking, but blaming me isn't the solution.'

'I can prove it.' Jamie smiled at the fear that flickered through his father's eyes. He looked to Toni. 'After Caesar's men tried to break in, I installed another camera at the entrance to the alley. It covers the street that runs across the top of it, to capture anyone approaching the alley. It shows Jason heading to the workshop just after Digger did the last check.'

He turned his phone round for them to see, and their eyes widened at the sight of Jason strolling down the street and into the alley. Jamie swiped at the screen when the footage stopped. 'He walked through the blind spot between the camera at the top of the alley and the ones on the workshop. When he appears again he's wearing a mask.'

'You nasty, sneaky sod,' Jackie yelled at Jason, leaping to her feet. 'That's just the sort of vicious thing you'd do. All you've ever cared about is yourself. The boys never meant anything to you.'

'Don't you fucking dare,' Toni told her driver when he drew back his hand to slap Jackie across the face. 'If you so much as touch her, not only will I take your eyes, but I'll take your hands too.'

The driver paled, lowered his hand and hung his head in shame.

'This is why I wanted to do this in front of your ex-wife,' continued Toni. 'To get the truth about you, Jason. The ex-wife always knows.'

'I'm happy to tell you everything,' said Jackie, spitting with rage. 'He used to batter me and Jamie senseless, he put us both in hospital. Until I fell pregnant with Charlie. Then I held a knife to the useless bastard's throat and told him if he laid a finger on any of us again, I'd cut him open. He was so scared he pissed himself.'

'You bitch,' snarled Jason, lunging for her.

The Blood Brothers all rushed as one to put themselves between him and Jackie.

'You,' said Toni, jabbing her finger at Jason. 'Calm down.'

He nodded and raked his hands through his hair, shaking with fury.

'Now,' said Toni. 'Would you care to explain what you were doing in this footage?'

'I was just keeping an eye on things, that's all. I was trying to help out my son.'

'I'm asking the questions,' yelled Toni when the Blood Brothers and Jackie all started shouting at him as one. 'That's better,' she said when they went silent. 'Now, Jason, why are you wearing a mask?'

'That's not me. That's the killer and Jamie's joined that footage together to make it look like it was me.'

'We don't know how to do that,' exclaimed Jamie.

'But I bet you know someone who does. Logan has a friend who's a tech genius. What's his name, eh, lads? Mark, isn't it?'

Logan and Jamie glanced at each other. Jason was frighteningly well informed about their lives.

'We haven't seen Mark in months,' said Logan.

'But he's capable of doing this, isn't he?'

'Nae idea,' said Jamie coldly. 'We've never asked him to doctor any footage.' He looked to Toni. 'Give it to an expert to analyse. They'll tell you it's no' been tampered with.'

'I can't be arsed pissing about like that. I want this settled now. One of you killed Donald and I want to know who it was.'

'It wasn't me,' said Jason and Jamie in unison.

'If you don't tell me in the next few seconds,' she said, 'I'll have to use more persuasive techniques.'

Caesar grinned and produced a small blowtorch from inside his jacket.

'You carry that around with you?' Digger frowned.

'Aye. Your maw likes me to cook her a sandwich every time I shag her.'

'Don't you talk about my maw,' he bellowed, Jamie and Logan having to hold him back when he charged at Caesar.

They all recoiled when Toni produced a gun from the depths of her fur coat and waved it around.

'The next person who speaks without my permission will have their eyes scooped out of their fucking head,' she yelled.

This made the room go silent again.

'It's like herding fucking cats,' spat Toni. She took a deep breath and replaced the gun in her pocket.

'Now, there's only one way to sort this out – we're going to go old school and use a method my brother Frankie used to resolve similar issues. In fact, he found it very entertaining, God rest his psychotic soul. Mortal combat.'

'What do you mean by mortal combat, Ms McVay?' said Logan politely.

'Gray Senior against Gray Junior.'

'You mean a fight?' said Jamie.

'Oh, yes,' she replied in a breathy purr. 'The first one who begs for mercy is the loser and I will take that person to be Donald's killer, which won't end very well for them.'

'No,' cried Jackie, leaping to her feet.

'It's either that or my men take them both away right now and you'll never see either of them again.'

'But Jamie hasn't done anything wrong. It's all on that prick,' Jackie said, gesturing to Jason. 'As usual.'

'But your son did do something wrong, didn't you, Jamie?' she said, turning to face him.

Jamie sighed and nodded. 'I fucked up.'

'Too right you did, gorgeous. You should never have taken that key with you to a pub and then left it unattended, and for that you need punishing. If you survive it'll teach you a valuable lesson.'

'But...' began Jackie, eyes filling with tears. She looked to Jason. 'Surely you're not going to do this? He's your son.'

'If that's what Toni wants, then I have no choice,' he replied.

Her lip curled with disgust. 'You're going to go all out to win this, aren't you?'

His black look told her everything she needed to know.

Jackie grabbed her son's face between her hands and pulled his head down to her so she could whisper in his ear.

'He won't hold back.'

'I know, Maw,' Jamie said, hugging her before releasing her. He looked to Jason. 'You were never here for me, were you? It was always about what you could get.'

'Course it was,' his father replied. 'You were a means to get control of the scheme for Toni, that's all.'

The coldness with which he made this pronouncement didn't surprise Jamie, but it still hurt.

'I thought I was the only one in the room with a block of ice for a heart,' said Toni. 'But it looks like there's two of us.'

'Let me fight him instead,' said Jackie, glaring at Jason. 'I'll rip his fucking head right off and stick it up his arse.'

'I don't doubt you could,' said Toni. 'But this is your son's responsibility.' She looked from Jamie to Jason. 'The rules, gentlemen – no weapons, only your fists and feet. The fight isn't over until one of you concedes defeat.'

'Oh, God,' breathed Jackie, burying her face in her hands. She knew that neither her ex-husband nor her son were the type to concede defeat, so she was terrified that they wouldn't stop until one of them lay dead on the ground.

'Let's take this outside,' said Toni. 'There's not enough room in here for the brutal delights we're about to see,' she added with a disturbing smile. 'It'll be safe enough. As Jamie has so often mentioned, no one grasses to the police on the Gallowburn. Jackie, you can sit with me to watch.'

Toni linked her arm through Jackie's as though they'd been friends for years. Jackie had to force herself not to shudder, feeling very unnerved about being so close to this lunatic.

Logan shook Jamie's hand. 'Rip the bastard apart,' he told him while glaring at Jason.

Jamie just nodded, feeling a bit sick about fighting his own father.

'Me and Jackie require seats,' announced Toni.

Her driver took a couple of chairs from the kitchen table, carrying one in each huge hand.

The party filed outside. Dark clouds were gathering overhead, matching the mood of the two combatants.

Dave had been hanging around chatting to Ephraim, who had dealt with all his customers, both of them hoping to find out what was occurring in the Gray home.

'What's going on?' Dave asked his son as he filed by.

'Jamie's gonnae fight Jason,' he whispered to him.

'Bloody hell. Why?'

'I'll tell you after.'

Ephraim got out of his van and joined Dave in standing on the pavement to watch.

Toni directed her driver to place the chairs in the middle of the road.

'What if a car comes along?' said Jackie.

'Then they'll have to fucking wait,' said Toni. She spotted Valerie, who was hanging around on the pavement, wanting to know what her notorious cousin was up to now. 'I see you stayed to watch the action,' she called to her. 'I do remember how much you used to enjoy a good fight. There are a lot of people in this city minus their original teeth thanks to you and your antics. Still, you did a lot of good for the dental industry.'

'Shame I can't say the same for you and the local opticians,' she retorted, causing Toni to narrow her eyes at her. 'Do you still carry glasses cases about, just in case?'

'Oh, yes.' She smiled. 'I've got a blue one in my coat pocket right now.'

Most people would have trembled at such a threat, but Valerie's blue eyes were absent of any fear.

'As fun as this reunion is,' said Toni, 'there's business to attend to.' Her eyes filled with slyness. 'We'll have to have a proper catch-up, one day soon.'

'Just name the day. I'll be ready.'

'I always had a feeling the reverend was hard,' Digger whispered to Logan, who nodded in agreement.

Toni, pleased she'd tarnished her sainted cousin's reputation in the eyes of her parishioners, took a seat on one of the chairs, crossing her legs, dress riding up to reveal a lot of thigh. Caesar stood at her shoulder on guard duty while the driver took up position by Jackie's side, although he felt more like a jailor than a bodyguard.

27

Jamie and Jason stalked into the middle of the road, glaring at each other with identical brooding eyes.

'All right, boys,' began Toni. 'You can—'

'I'm back,' called a voice, cutting her off.

They all turned to see Gary half running, half staggering up the street, face bright red and damp with sweat.

'I came as fast as I could,' he panted.

'How wonderful,' said Toni flatly before turning her attention back to Jamie and Jason. 'Now—'

'What's... going... on?' said Gary as he stood by Digger and Logan while attempting to catch his breath.

'Shut up,' Toni snapped at him.

'Sorry,' he replied, wiping the sweat from his brow.

'Finally,' muttered Toni when he didn't speak again. 'You can begin,' she told the two Gray men. 'And make it a good show. I don't want any pansy punching.'

'You really want to do this, do you, Da?' Jamie asked him.

'We've no choice,' replied Jason.

'You brought us to this. You should have left Donald alone.'

Jamie just managed to dodge the jab to the face from Jason's fist. 'You total cunt,' exploded Jamie before hitting back.

Jason dodged but he wasn't as quick and Jamie's fist just grazed the left side of his face. He responded with a blow to the stomach, which Jamie managed to deflect with the block Mullen had taught him, and he enjoyed the surprise in his father's eyes, eyes that were just like his own. That single moment of sentiment was to prove to be Jamie's undoing because Jason took full advantage of it, swinging a punch into his face, quickly following it up with a right hook that spun Jamie round into his own car.

'How can you do this to your own son, you piece of shit?' yelled Jackie, leaping up, stricken as she watched Jason grab Jamie by the shoulder, turn him around and drive his fist into his stomach, doubling him up.

Toni took hold of her arm and encouraged her to sit back down.

Jamie dropped to all fours, coughing, attempting to catch his breath, Digger, Gary and Logan yelling at him to get up.

Jamie formed his arms into a cross, blocking the kick Jason aimed at his head. He grabbed his foot, keeping hold of it as he rose to his feet, tipping Jason onto his back. Jason hit the tarmac hard and rolled.

By now all the neighbours, curious as to what was going on, had come out of their homes and were watching the fight from their gardens. Some of them recognised Toni and were frantically whispering and pointing.

Jamie made a half-hearted attempt at stamping on his father's face as he rolled but found himself unable to do it. Even after everything Jason had done, he still felt something for him.

Tears stood out in Jackie's eyes as she watched her boy being torn apart by internal conflict. He knew his father wouldn't stop until the job was done but he was unable to bring himself to really hurt him. She knew Jamie was capable of winning this fight, but his good heart wouldn't let him. Whereas Jason's eyes were full of coldness and determination, Jamie's were wide with pain, and she was helpless to do anything for him.

Jason grabbed Jamie's left leg, the one that had been broken by Cameron Abernethy's thug, and punched him in the back of the knee. Jamie howled with pain and staggered backwards. Jason was up in an instant and all Jamie could do was dodge the punches he rapidly threw at him until the pain eased off in his leg.

'Fuck this,' said Digger, storming into the middle of the road with Gary and Logan, all three men intent on intervening.

Before they could help their friend, Toni had given her men the nod and Caesar and the driver rushed to stop them.

'Be sensible and get back, lads,' Caesar growled at them.

'But this isn't fucking right,' exclaimed Digger.

'I don't gi'e a shite what you think. Get back before I cut off your tiny wee boabies and throw them down the gutter.'

Logan and Gary grabbed hold of Digger's arms and encouraged him backwards while glowering at Caesar.

Jamie chose his moment well and when Jason drew back his fist again, he left himself exposed and Jamie punched him in the solar plexus. Jason's eyes widened and he tottered backwards a few paces, gasping for breath. Taking advantage of this, Jamie punched him twice rapidly in the face, snapping his head from side to side, blood erupting from Jason's burst lower lip.

'Yes,' cried Jackie, punching her fist in the air.

'Oh, great,' said Logan when cold drops of rain started to fall, swiftly turning into an icy downpour. 'What's next, a zombie apocalypse?'

The driver retrieved an umbrella from the boot of the car to hold over Toni, who slapped him in the stomach and told him to hold it over Jackie too.

Jamie and Jason continued to beat on each other but Jason was rapidly gaining the upper hand, not because of his skill but because Jamie was holding back, unable to bring himself to hurt his own father, no matter how shitty he was.

'Da,' breathed Jamie as he blocked more of his punches. 'This is fucking mad.'

'I thought you were cut out for this life,' panted Jason. 'I thought you were like me, but I was wrong. You haven't got what it takes, you lack that killer instinct.'

'And what about family and loyalty? Don't they mean anything to you?'

'Family and loyalty don't get you the good things in life.'

'They are the good things, you prick,' Jamie retorted before lashing out at Jason, who grabbed his arm, twisted and threw him against the ice-cream van.

'Hey, watch the paintwork, you walloper,' yelled Ephraim.

Jason didn't even hear him as he stalked up to his son. He was in a frenzy, bloodlust lighting up his eyes. To him the flailing, bleeding figure on the ground wasn't his son, it was merely an obstacle to everything he wanted and he was determined to get rid of it.

The rain was by now lashing down, soaking them all, and everyone except the two fighters was shivering.

Jamie rolled onto all fours, resting his weight on his forearms and attempting to push himself upright, but being thrown into Ephraim's van had left him stunned and disorientated, and everything was swimming in and out of focus. He could hear his mother and friends yelling at him to get up, but he lacked the strength.

Jason, gaze pitiless, kicked him in the face, causing him to collapse onto his front, and it took Jamie everything he had to cling onto consciousness.

'I'll kill you myself, you bastard,' yelled Jackie, leaping up and running at him.

But Toni's driver was quicker and he wrapped his arms around her and hauled her backwards, still kicking and screaming.

'Get angry, Jamie,' Logan frantically yelled. 'Get angry.'

'Who do you think he is?' retorted Digger. 'The fucking hulk? Do you think he's gonnae turn green and tear off his clothes?'

'Aye, I dae,' Logan roared back at his friend, so furious his hair looked to be standing on end.

'Oh, yeah,' replied Digger as realisation dawned.

'Think of everything he's done to you,' Logan continued to yell. 'Use all that pain and rage.'

Images flicked through Jamie's mind from when he was a kid – of his father lunging at him with his fists, the pain, the snap as his arm broke, hearing his mother's cries as he battered her in the kitchen. Of Jason producing packets of drugs in the pub, taking him to see Toni McVay and pushing him into the icy water. Taking him to the pub just so he could copy the key and kill Donald. It was like watching a horror movie on fast forward, the anger inside him rising with each frame, the emotion he'd kept locked up for years fighting against the prison he'd put it in. He felt something inside him snap as it finally broke free.

Then everything turned to darkness.

The assembled crowd watched in astonishment as Jamie shot to his feet, suddenly free of the pain of his injuries, and unleashed a roar that echoed down the street. His eyes seemed even blacker, all the muscles and tendons popping out in his arms and neck. Jason's eyes widened and he stumbled backwards, startled by this terrifying display. Jamie's predatory gaze settled on him, lips drawing back over his teeth as he sprang, launching himself at his father.

'Yes,' exclaimed Digger. 'He's gone green.'

Jackie stopped struggling in her captor's arms, astonished as she watched her son batter his father. Jason was helpless against the savage onslaught as Jamie knocked him to the ground, straddled him and repeatedly smashed his fists into his face and torso. When he got bored of that, he leapt up, grabbed Jason by the back of his jacket and dragged him towards his Vauxhall Vectra. He hauled him onto the bonnet as though he weighed nothing and began repeatedly slamming his head off it, that same animal cry flying from his lips. Jackie had seen the footage of him going berserker on Cameron Abernethy, but seeing it in the flesh was much more disturbing. Jason hadn't managed to get in a single hit and he was growing limper by the second, blood spattering the bonnet of Jamie's car.

'Jason's done,' Jackie told Toni. 'End this now.'

'Why? The fun's just beginning,' Toni replied, eyes alight with pleasure as she watched the show.

The crowd had swelled even more, but everyone was ignoring the now furious rain that washed away the blood spatter as soon as it landed, hypnotised by the gruesome spectacle of Jamie obliterating his own father.

The helplessness overwhelmed Jackie. The way Jamie was going on, he was going to kill him. She didn't give a shit about Jason, but she knew killing him would destroy her son.

'Jamie,' she yelled, struggling against her captor, but he was just too strong. 'Jamie, snap out of it.'

But he couldn't hear her. Growing bored of bashing Jason off the car, he threw him to the ground and circled him, enjoying his weak struggles to get up, figuring out the best way to finish him.

An explosion down the street knocked them all off their feet. Jackie found herself released and fell into Dave, knocking him to the ground, his flab providing her with a soft landing.

'Aww, Jesus,' he groaned.

She sat up to see a large fireball shooting into the sky further down the road. 'What the hell is that?' she cried.

Everyone slowly dragged themselves to their feet. Even Toni

had been knocked off her chair and was very unimpressed about her hair getting wet. Caesar scrambled to retrieve the dropped umbrella and held it over her, but the damage had been done and her dark curls were wet and limp.

'It's a car,' gasped Logan. 'It fucking exploded.'

'Jamie,' cried Digger.

They all looked round to see him unconscious on the ground.

'No,' cried Jackie, racing to his side. 'Jamie, son,' she said, gently shaking him.

He jumped awake, eyes swivelling about in his head. 'What happened?'

'Don't you remember?'

'I was on the ground and Jason was standing over me, then everything went black.'

'You went green,' cried Digger excitedly, having rushed to him, along with Logan and Gary.

'Eh?'

'He means you went berserker again,' said Logan.

'It was fucking awesome, man,' said Digger. 'You hammered the ever-living shite out of the walloper.'

'Where's he gone?' said Gary.

They all looked round, but Jason was nowhere to be seen.

'The coward must have done one when we were all distracted by the explosion,' said Logan.

'Are you okay, sweetheart?' said Jackie, relieved to see the Jamie she knew shining out of his eyes.

'Aye, just really sore and tired. And I'm freezing.'

'Take my jacket,' said Digger, pulling it off.

Jackie wrapped Digger's jacket around Jamie, leaning over him to shield him from the worst of the rain.

'Everyone clear the street,' yelled Caesar. 'Before the fire brigade turn up to put out that fire.'

The crowd dispersed, everyone returning to their homes. Logan noticed Sasha Reid was there, flanked by a few Lawsons. Clearly her pact with them hadn't been broken, despite Jackie's best efforts. They all gave him a hard look before turning a corner and disappearing.

Jamie had been left so weak Digger had to help him up, holding him on one arm and escorting him into the house.

Jackie closely followed, hesitating when she saw a figure hovering outside a house a few doors down. Her heart soared when she realised it was Scott, or rather Gavin. It was then she knew he'd blown up that car to stop Jamie from killing his own father. She gave him a small nod, which he returned before walking away, vanishing into the darkness.

Pushing aside the emotion threatening to overwhelm her, she rushed into the house and switched on the heating, before retrieving a thick towel and a blanket from upstairs. Digger helped Jamie lie back on the couch, propping up his painful left leg, and Jackie wrapped the blanket and towel around him. Jamie was a mess. Both eyes were swollen, his lips were cut and bleeding and his face was a mass of swelling and bruising.

This time only Toni and Caesar came into the house, followed by Logan, Gary and Digger; the bodyguard relegated back to the car.

Just before she entered the Gray home, Toni paused to look back at Valerie, the two women staring at each other hard before Valerie turned and walked away, seemingly undisturbed by the rain.

'Not you,' Toni told Dave when he tried to follow them inside, slamming the door shut in his face.

For once Toni was not her immaculate self. As well as her hair being sodden and limp, her clothes were streaked with dirt from when she'd been flung into the road and there was a tear on one side of her dress. She regarded Jamie's prone form on the couch, where he was being fussed over by his mother.

'Well done, Jamie,' she said. 'All you had to do was tap into that rage. It took you a while, but you got there in the end.'

'You knew he would win, didn't you?' said Jackie.

Toni smiled approvingly. 'You're a very intelligent woman, I like that, and, yes, I did. After seeing the footage of him hammering Cameron Abernethy I knew Jason wouldn't stand a chance against him.'

'You wanted Jamie to win?' pressed Jackie.

'Aye. Why would I want a man working for me who betrayed me? This was a way for Jamie to prove he'll be a suitable replacement.'

'Replacement?' said Jackie, heart sinking.

'Yes. I've decided that I will continue to use the Gallowburn to hide my secrets and Jamie and the rest of the Blood Brothers will be in charge of that. Don't worry, they won't get involved in my main business. This scheme will remain free of that.' Toni's eyes settled on something over Jackie's shoulder. Jackie turned to see Ephraim standing right behind her. She physically jumped, having had no idea he was even there.

'We need to have a discussion,' Toni told him.

'Aye, we dae,' he retorted, folding his arms across his chest.

Toni stalked up to him, eyes roaming up and down him appreciatively. 'You look like a big, strong, capable man.'

'I am that,' Ephraim said, unfolding his arms, seemingly entranced by her, especially the way her wet clothes clung to her curvy body.

'The Blood Brothers have told me so much about your many talents. I'm sure we can come to a mutually pleasurable... agreement,' Toni breathed, leaning into him, so close their lips almost touched.

His eyes took on a dreamy, sensuous look. 'I've nae doubt about that, hen.'

Logan had to hand it to Toni, she was very smart. She'd already realised that Ephraim had an eye for the ladies and knew that she could use her feminine wiles to charm him. If she managed to cast her spell over him he would work with her. That would be preferable to fighting him. Even she was wary about taking him on as, not only did he pay off the police, but he wouldn't care who she was. Neither was he afraid of her. He would happily chop off her head if she got in his way.

'Later.' Toni winked at Ephraim, who eagerly nodded. She turned back to face the room. 'But Jason got away, thanks to that explosion. How the fuck did that happen, by the way?'

They all shrugged, clueless. Only Jackie knew the real reason and she certainly wasn't going to say anything.

'Maybe it was an accident?' said Digger.

'Cars don't just randomly explode,' said Toni.

'They can,' said Gary in the eager voice that always preceded one of his stories. 'I heard from Katie Pearson that she was driving through Easterhouse and a dog ran out in front of her and she slammed on the brakes, and the brakes started to smoke, so she leapt out and there were like flames coming out of the bonnet and the flames formed a big demon face that grinned down at her, and the face swallowed her car and it blew up and knocked her onto the pavement.'

The entire room gaped at Gary.

'Can I shoot him, boss lady?' said Caesar, breaking the silence.

'No,' she replied. 'We're going to need all four Blood Brothers, even the doolally one.'

Gary frowned and folded his arms across his chest, but didn't dare call them out about the insult.

'Maybe Jason had someone on standby to cause a distraction as a backup plan,' said Logan. 'In case Jamie was able to convince Toni that Jason had killed Donald.'

'I think that's a much more likely explanation than demon faces,' said Toni.

Jackie was relieved when this explanation seemed to satisfy her.

'I've already dispatched men to track him down,' said Caesar.

'Good. Right, Jamie,' said Toni, turning to him. 'Christ, you look like shite.'

'Cheers,' he replied before wincing.

'That was an extremely impressive display, one of the most impressive in fact and you wouldnae believe the things I've seen. You are the new king of Gallowburn and you will continue working for me doing what you were doing, with the help of your pals. I'll have the word put about the scheme that no one is to mess with you. That should keep those wee fannies off your back who live on the south side, what's their name again?'

'The Lawsons,' replied Logan.

'Aye, that's them. They won't dare bother you again.'

Jackie thought that not even Toni McVay could stop a mental case like Sasha Reid. That girl had a lot more trouble to throw their way, she could feel it in her bones.

'Jason told me he lost the plot in prison and battered someone and he didn't remember it,' said Jamie. 'That I got it from him. That was a lie too, wasn't it?'

'Aye, it was, sweetheart,' said Jackie. 'Like everyone else he'd probably seen the footage of you battering Cameron and Craig and decided to use it to try and bond with you.'

'Bastard,' Jamie muttered, looking down at his hands. 'He said he killed someone when he was in prison. Was that a lie too?'

'It was,' said Toni. 'He did batter a few people, but he never killed anyone.'

'Did he tell you about what Donald overheard?'

'What did Donald overhear?' said Digger. He scowled at Logan when he told him to shut up.

Toni nodded. 'He played me the footage, which is useless now Donald's gone.'

'Jesus,' sighed Jamie, hanging his head. 'You're no' pissed off at me for taking that video, are you?'

'No, in fact I expected it. Why do you think I sent Donald here in the first place?'

He blinked up at her. 'What?'

'I knew he had something on Cameron Abernethy, but he was too afraid to tell me. Knowing how loose his tongue was and that he wouldn't be able to resist bragging to someone, I thought he might open up to you. I want Cameron to get sent down because I want some of his businesses. I'll let that idiot son of his keep the shite.'

'You are scarily smart, boss lady.' Caesar smiled adoringly.

'I know.' Toni preened. 'But Gray Senior fucked it all up by killing Donald. I mean, did he really think I'd believe Jamie was responsible for that when Donald had such sensitive information about Cameron? That would only make him even more determined to keep him alive. I suppose you deserve to know why you were looking after him, boys. Donald was a genius financial advisor and investor but he got himself into some hot water with the exotic dancer daughter of a vicious Triad leader.'

'You were hiding him from another gang, no' the police?' said Logan.

'Precisely. After all he'd done for me, I thought the least I could do was protect him. Sadly, I didn't know I had a traitor in my midst.'

'I could have told you that,' said Jackie.

'Which is why I came here. The wife always knows.'

'Ex-wife. We never got divorced but I don't need a piece of paper to say he's no longer my husband.'

'Good for you,' said Toni with admiration. 'When I get hold of him he will be your ex-husband. In fact he'll be an ex everything. What do you have to say about that?' she added, watching Jackie's reaction carefully.

'I say Christmas has come early.'

Toni gave her a genuine and very rare smile. 'Right, you lads need to get on with finding a new safe place. The workshop is compromised. I'm sure your friends can do that while you rest up, Jamie. Hopefully in a few days your face won't resemble a pulverised pumpkin.'

Jamie was too exhausted and sore to respond.

'I'm glad that's finally sorted. Caesar, let's go.' Toni looked over her shoulder at Ephraim and winked. 'Ready for that wee chat?'

'You bet I am, sweetheart,' Ephraim replied, following her and Caesar out of the door.

Jackie breathed a sigh of relief when he didn't even look her way. Hopefully his unwanted attentions had been transferred onto someone else.

'Thank God for that,' said Jackie when they'd gone. She rushed to Jamie's side. 'How are you feeling? Do you need the hospital?'

'Naw, I'll be fine. I don't think anything's broken.'

'But you could have internal bleeding.'

'I'll be fine. It's no' the first time I've taken a beating,' he said a little sadly, thinking of what Jason had done to him when he was a kid. The memories that had returned to him when he'd gone berserker still felt fresh and raw.

'We need to get you out of those wet clothes. I'll bring some fresh ones down,' she said before bustling for the stairs.

'Aww, man, you were awesome out there,' said Digger. 'You were like a force of nature.'

'I cannae remember any of it,' said Jamie miserably, his speech a little muffled because of his swollen lips. 'I remember being on the ground, Jason standing over me and then everything he'd done to me came flooding back and I got so angry – then nothing.' He closed his eyes and shook his head. 'I hope me fighting my own da isn't put all over the Internet like the last time.'

'No one would dare with Toni there,' said Logan. 'Everyone knows she'd hunt them down if they did.'

'I hope so.'

Logan felt sorry for Jamie, he looked so miserable. 'You okay, pal?' he asked him.

'Jason was gonnae kill me,' he replied. 'He had absolutely no problem with it. I always knew he didnae gi'e a shite about me, but I didn't think even he would go that far.'

'He doesn't deserve you.'

'What if I turn out like him one day?' he said, eyes wide and earnest. 'What if I turn on those I'm supposed to love and protect?'

'You won't and you know why? Because you're your maw's son. You're nothing like him.'

'That's very sweet of you to say,' said Jackie, who they hadn't realised was standing at the bottom of the stairs holding Jamie's dry clothes. 'And very true. I lived with that bastard for years and you're nothing like him, Jamie. You never have been and you never will be, so don't you go worrying about that, okay?'

Jamie managed to lift the least injured side of his mouth into a smile. 'Cheers, Maw.'

'You're welcome. Now let's get you out of those clothes.'

'We should go if you're going to be stripping off,' said Digger.

'I thought you'd like to hang about and have a wee perv.' Gary grinned. 'Jamie has muscles and we all know how much you like those.'

Digger turned puce with anger. 'If he wore a dog collar, you'd probably fancy him.'

'What did you say?' snarled back Gary. 'Come on, then, you donkey, square go.'

'Not again,' sighed Logan, shaking his head.

'That's enough, the pair of you,' Jackie told them. 'We've had enough fighting for one night.'

'Sorry, Mrs Gray,' they said, hanging their heads.

'Your precious Valerie's a McVay,' Logan told Gary.

'What?' he exclaimed. 'Seriously?'

'Aye. It came out before you got there. We heard her talking outside with Toni. Her maw is Toni's aunt.'

'Jeezo,' Gary breathed. 'But her last name's Brown.'

'Either she changed it, which would be understandable, or maybe her da's last name is Brown?'

'Maybe. Wow. I always knew she was special,' he said adoringly.

'Right, you lot,' said Jackie. 'You can come and check on Jamie in the morning. Now get yourselves home.'

'Come on, you pair of fuds,' said Logan.

'Do you want your jacket Digger?' said Jackie. 'It's damp but it'll protect you from the rain.'

'Naw thanks Mrs G,' he replied. 'The rain doesnae bother me and I don't feel the cold.'

'You really need to stop the steroids,' said Gary.

The three of them said their goodbyes and left.

Jackie helped Jamie out of his wet clothes and into dry jogging bottoms and a thick jumper. She covered him with a fresh blanket as the other one she'd given him was damp.

'Do you want to talk about what happened?' she asked him.

'Naw. I feel better for what you said about me no' being like Jason,' Jamie said sadly, knowing he'd never see his father again. Toni's men would find him and kill him.

'You need to put this behind you and look to the future. And Allegra.'

Just the mention of her name brought the colour back to Jamie's cheeks and the sparkle to his eyes. 'Aye, I will.'

'Good. Oh, gosh, Charlie's still at Kieran's and it's after ten o'clock. He'll never get up for school in the morning. I'll go and pick him up.' She kissed his cheek. 'Won't be long.'

Jamie smiled as he watched her hurry out of the door. He nestled into the couch, eyes growing heavy as exhaustion took over. He was nothing like his father, but tonight had shown Jamie that he was born for this life and he was going to make a success of it.

28

Jamie and Jackie were back in court, sitting with DI Ross in the gallery, awaiting the jury's verdict. Despite the legal tricks Cameron's defence had tried to pull, finally he was about to face his fate. Thankfully a few weeks had passed since Jamie had fought his own father, so his injuries had had time to heal.

The jury had deliberated for three tense, hellish days during which the Gray household had been bombarded by journalists desperate to get their opinion on what the outcome would be; consequently they'd spent the last few days hiding in the house with the curtains drawn. It was the lack of a body that had given the jury such pause and the prosecution was worried because successful murder convictions without a body – although not unheard of – were rare.

Finally the jury were ready to give their verdict and they filed back into the courtroom. Jamie studied them carefully but it was impossible to judge their decision from their expressions. Fenston had finally shown his face and Jamie had been watching him carefully too. He appeared to be the only relaxed person in the room.

Cameron was sitting in the dock. He'd sacked the frosty twig shortly after Jamie had given evidence and his new lawyer was a grossly overweight man with very hairy hands. Intermittently Cameron would throw Jamie a glare, the confidence in his eyes that he would get away with it infuriating.

But he was wrong. The jury found him guilty of conspiring to incite the murder of Jamie, and then Jamie's entire body went numb as it was announced that Cameron had been found guilty of Allegra's murder too. Even though Jackie knew she was still alive, the emotion was too much for her and she started to gasp and cry. Jamie felt tears fill his own eyes. Finally Allegra was truly safe. Ross had already told them that in Scotland a life sentence had to be given for murder. The detective sighed with relief too, body sagging in his chair as the weight of getting this monster put away was finally lifted off him.

Cameron, who had been instructed to get to his feet, just stared at the jury in astonishment. He'd felt sure his own power and wealth would have got him out of this mess. His expression was almost comical.

Jamie listened with delight as the judge passed sentence, giving him life with a minimum term of fifteen years.

'This is justice,' yelled Jackie, jumping to her feet. She pointed at Cameron. 'You got what you deserve, you animal.'

A wildness filled Cameron's eyes and he leapt out of the dock before the court security officer could stop him. 'I know she's alive and you know where she is, you vicious little scheme rat,' he yelled at Jamie. 'I'll find her, and when I do I'll slit her fucking throat, and then yours.'

Members of the jury as well as those assembled in the gallery gasped, and shocked murmurs raced around the room.

Jamie got to his feet and stood defensively in front of his mum when Cameron attempted to dive into the gallery, but Ross and the other police officers in attendance as well as court security tackled him to the floor before he got near them, snapping on the hand-cuffs as he struggled against them.

'She's not dead, she's not dead,' yelled Cameron over and over. 'I've been set up.'

He was still proclaiming his innocence as he was dragged down the stairs leading into the cells below.

'It's over,' breathed Jackie. 'Finally.'

Jamie took her hand. 'Let's go home, Maw.'

They watched Fenston leave with a smile on his face. No doubt he was looking forward to taking over all of his father's businesses and having free rein of the house and bank accounts. He was in for a shock. Toni had already put plans into motion to take the majority of it from him.

Ross had told Jamie that it would be best if he gave a statement outside the court to the hoard of waiting journalists. It was the quickest way to get them off his back. So, for the first time, he addressed the press, who were eagerly gathered on the pavement outside the High Court.

'Jeezo, I'm shaking, Maw,' he whispered.

She took his hand. 'You can do this, sweetheart. It's the last leg of a very long journey.'

'Aye,' he said, gently squeezing her hand before looking back at the crowd. Allegra's case had attracted so much attention the horde wasn't just made up of journalists, but members of the public too.

He took out the piece of paper on which he'd composed his speech, with his mum's help. He was so relieved to be reading out this one and not the one he'd written if Cameron had been found not guilty.

'I'd like to say how happy me and my maw are that justice has finally been done for Allegra,' he began.

A memory of her rolled through his head, her beautiful blue

eyes staring up at him from his pillow, bright and happy, and a lump formed in his throat. He cleared his throat to shift it.

'The last year has been a nightmare and it's a huge relief that it's finally over. I'd like to thank the police, especially DI Ross, for the great job they did on Allegra's case, as well as the procurator fiscal and his team, the judge and the jury for seeing through Cameron's lies.' He'd thought he'd feel more of a hypocrite reading this out, but he didn't. This was justice. 'Allegra's still out there somewhere, so the search for her will continue. The police have assured me they'll never give up looking for her, but we're still grieving for the loss of this beautiful, bright, loving woman who brought nothing but joy to everyone she met. I ask that you respect our privacy and allow us to continue grieving in peace. Thank you.'

With that, he stuffed the piece of paper into his pocket and, taking his mother's hand, walked towards the taxi Ross had made sure was waiting for them at the kerb, refusing to answer all the questions the journalists shouted at them.

The beast had been slayed. Now all Jamie had to do was wait until he could join Allegra in Italy and they would never be parted again.

EPILOGUE

SIX MONTHS LATER

Jamie walked up the steps and inside a huge, gothic four-storey hotel on the bustling North Bridge in Edinburgh, an overnight bag clutched in one hand. He walked through the grand reception and took the lift up to the fourth floor.

Heart hammering with excitement, he knocked on the door of one of the rooms. The door was immediately opened by a woman with short black hair and wide green eyes. They stared at each other, both hardly able to believe what they were seeing before he stepped inside, kicking the door shut behind him.

'Dangerous,' she breathed, gazing up at him.

He cupped her face in his hands, her skin as soft as he remembered. He half expected her to evaporate like a phantom dreamed up by his tortured mind but she remained solid and real. 'Princess.'

They kissed, arms locking around one another. He was afraid that during their time apart their passion for each other might have waned, but it was stronger than ever. They just held onto each other for a while, revelling in being back together.

'I can't believe you're here,' she breathed, running her hands up his chest and along his shoulders. 'You look different – stronger, harder.' Her lips curved into a wicked smile. 'Even sexier.'

'And you're as gorgeous as ever.'

'You like the hair?'

'I do.' He stroked her face with his thumbs. 'Beautiful.'

'I still wear your ring,' she said, raising her left hand to show him. 'I never take it off, not even in the shower. What?' She smiled when his eyes flared.

'I was just thinking of you in the shower.' He looked around the room, which was in fact a large, sumptuous suite. 'I take it this place has one?'

'It does.' She grinned. 'As well as a huge roll-top bath.'

They kissed again, Allegra already pushing his jacket off his shoulders.

'Can you do me a favour?' he said.

'Anything,' she breathed as he kissed her neck.

'Can you take out the contact lenses? I need to see your eyes.'

They managed to tear themselves away from each other, Jamie frowning as he watched her remove the lenses.

When she looked at him with her large blue eyes, he smiled. 'There she is.'

With a giggle, she hurled herself at him and they fell onto the bed together, frantically kissing.

Allegra unbuttoned his shirt to reveal the ring she'd given him on a chain around his neck. He pulled the chain off, discarded it and slid the ring onto his finger.

'That's better,' she said before kissing him.

Jamie had imagined their physical reunion being fast and frantic but, on the contrary, it was slow and tender as they reconnected after being apart for so long. It felt strange not being able to slide his fingers through her long soft hair, but she was still his princess in every single way. He gazed up at her as she moved on top of him, constantly running his hands up and down her body, knowing it would be a long time before they were able to be together again, wanting to memorise every sweet inch of her.

He flipped her onto her back, making her laugh, their sweat-soaked bodies moving together, her thighs locking around his waist, pressing his forehead to hers and gazing into her eyes.

'Jamie,' she cried, arching her spine as she came.

They clung onto each other as their bodies shuddered together, months of longing and frustration leaving them in a rush.

Jamie's body eventually went limp and he could breathe again.

'God, that's better,' she breathed as he rolled onto his back and pulled her into his arms.

'You're telling me.' He grinned, hugging her.

Allegra nestled into his chest, running her fingers up and down his damp skin. 'I loved the growl you made when you came. I've never heard you do that before.'

'It's being celibate for so long that did it.'

After they made love again, Allegra announced she was hungry, so they ordered room service. They donned the complimentary fluffy robes and sat on the bed to eat, talking and catching up.

'Did the McVays ever find your father?' she asked him.

'Naw. He dropped off the face of the planet.'

'He's a piece of shit for what he did to you. And he wasn't even reluctant about the fight?' Naturally Jamie had called her to tell her all about the fight, so she was up to speed.

'Not at all. He saw a chance and he took it.'

'Until you went berserker and beat him,' she said, running an asparagus tip down his skin.

'That's an unusual sensation,' he said, looking at the butter smear that had been left on his chest. 'And that's even better.' He moaned as she licked it off.

'So, you're in charge of the Gallowburn now?' she said as she kissed his chest.

'Mmmm,' he murmured, enjoying her attentions.

'I always knew big things would happen to you, right from the moment I saw you.'

'You did?'

'Oh, yes.'

She pushed him back onto the bed and opened his robe, moving her attentions lower down his body.

'You're so special, Dangerous,' she breathed into his skin, scattering goosebumps across his body.

'I'm no' the only one, Princess. Your father's no' gonnae gi'e up. He's sure you're still alive.'

Allegra rested her head on his stomach, looking up at him along the length of his body. 'And you're sure this Mullen won't give away my secret?'

'Sure. He really does love my maw. In fact, I think he even likes me and Charlie.'

'Then we're free and clear. To the rest of the world, I'm dead. No one will be looking for me now. It's a shame Jackie couldn't get over what Mullen did. He might have been good for her.'

'Even after he lied to her?'

'He did the right thing in the end. So many men wouldn't have.'

'He might have acted like a twat, but I think deep down he's a decent man.'

'She's adamant it's over?'

'She seems to be.'

'Shame. I sold the salon in Florence.'

'What? But you loved that place.'

'I know,' she said sadly. 'I'd made some great friends there too, but it had been compromised. I didn't feel safe there any longer. On the bright side, I sold it for forty grand more than I paid because it was doing so well. I'm enjoying Seville, though.'

'Isn't Spain a bit risky? It gets a lot of British tourists. What if you're recognised?'

'With how I look now? I doubt it.'

'True, you do look very different, especially with the contact lenses. Can you speak Spanish?'

'Not as fluently as I can speak Italian, but I get by. Seville is the birthplace of Flamenco dancing. I'm having lessons.'

'So you're okay out there? I worry about you all the time.'

'Don't worry about me, I'm fine. I've rented a lovely villa and I'm looking to open another salon, I so enjoyed it the last time.'

'You don't let anything slow you down, do you?' He smiled as she kissed her way back up his body.

'No, I do not. Actually, I had an idea I wanted to run past you.'

'What's that?' he said as she delved into her handbag. His eyes widened when she produced a small knife. 'Jeezo.'

'You know how you made a blood pact with your friends?'

'Aye,' he slowly replied.

'I thought we could make one of our own, seeing how we can't marry yet.'

'You're still keeping me on my toes, Princess,' he said, the corner of his mouth lifting into a smile. 'All right, then.'

'Great. I brought bandages and antiseptic cream and I've sterilised the blade.'

'Go on, then,' he said, holding out his right hand. 'I want you to do it on the opposite hand.'

She nodded, Jamie inhaling sharply as she scratched the knife across his palm, creating a shallow cut. She handed him the knife and held out her left hand. He held the blade over her palm.

'What's the matter?' she said when he hesitated.

'I cannae do it. I cannae hurt you.'

'I'll help you,' she said softly, putting her hand over his and pushing it downwards and along, the blade slicing through her skin.

They pressed their palms together, threading their fingers through each other's.

'Bonded for life,' she said.

'For life.' He smiled, kissing her.

Allegra cleaned and dressed their wounds, then straddled him.

'Feeling up to more now you've had something to eat?' she said.

'Too right I am,' he replied, pulling her down to him.

* * *

Jamie and Allegra barely slept that night. They enjoyed both the bath and the shower together, briefly dozing off in between bouts of lovemaking before waking again to talk, revealing things they hadn't had the chance to tell each other before.

When it came time for Allegra to leave the next morning to catch her flight back to Spain, they found themselves unable to let each other go.

'I got into the country no problem,' she said as they clung onto each other. 'So at least we know we can meet up more often.'

'Do you think you'll get back okay?'

'No problem.'

'I don't want you to go,' he said, burying his face in her hair.

'I don't want to go. These last few hours with you have been the best of my life.'

Tears filled her eyes and he held her tighter.

'We'll see each other again soon,' he said, pressing his cheek to the top of her head. 'Promise.'

'Please be careful working for the McVays.'

'I will. Working for them will mean I'll be able to save some serious money to come out to you with.'

'Hopefully in a couple of years.'

'It'll happen before we know it.'

They both forced a smile but separating again was tearing them apart.

She glanced at her watch. 'I really have to go or I'll miss my flight,' she said, a tear sliding down her cheek. 'The room bill's paid, so you just have to hand the key back to reception.'

'And you've got the towels you stole?' He smiled.

'Of course.' She smiled back, more tears slipping down her face. 'Give it an hour before leaving.'

'I will.'

They grasped onto each other's hands.

'I don't think I can let go,' he rasped.

'I was so excited to see you I didn't think about how hard it would be to say goodbye.' She kissed him. 'Goodbye, Dangerous. I love you so much.'

'I love you too, Princess.'

With one last kiss she was gone, pausing to glance back at him over her shoulder before leaving.

Jamie sank onto the bed and dragged his hands down his face. It felt as if he was grieving for her all over again. He picked up her pillow and inhaled her scent. Coconut. He replaced the ring she'd given him on the chain and fastened it around his neck, ensuring it was hidden beneath his clothes.

It took him the full hour to get himself back under control and he left the hotel and drove back to Glasgow. He'd replaced Jason, driving clients between the airport and casinos, so Toni had given him a flash black Audi four-by-four.

Jackie was anxiously waiting for him at home.

'How did it go?' she asked him. 'Oh, come here, sweetheart,' she said, hugging him when tears welled in his eyes.

A knock at the door made him force all his emotion deep down inside while Jackie went to answer it. The rest of the Blood Brothers walked in.

'All right, boys?' Jackie smiled.

'No' bad, Mrs G,' replied Logan. He looked to Jamie. 'We've got a job on.'

Jamie nodded, his expression once again hard and controlled. 'See you later, Maw.'

'Bye, sweetheart,' she replied, watching him go, confident he'd be all right. Her son had the inner strength of ten men.

The four of them stalked down the street together, everyone nodding at them respectfully as they passed by. Now they worked for Toni they no longer ruled just the north side of the scheme. They owned the lot of it.

The Blood Brothers had come of age.

ACKNOWLEDGMENTS

Many thanks to everyone who reads and supports my work, it is so appreciated. Also, many thanks to Sarah, my fabulous editor, as well as Nia, Amanda and all the wonderful people at Boldwood Books for helping me bring the Blood Brothers to life.

MORE FROM HEATHER ATKINSON

We hope you enjoyed reading *Bad Blood*. If you did, please leave a review.

If you'd like to gift a copy, this book is also available as an ebook, digital audio download and audiobook CD.

Sign up to Heather Atkinson's mailing list for news, competitions and updates on future books.

http://bit.ly/HeatherAtkinsonNewsletter

The first book in the Gallowburn Series, *Blood Brothers,* is available now.

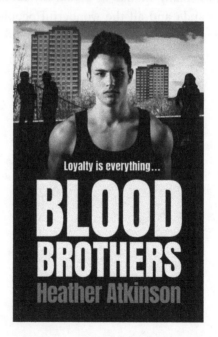

ABOUT THE AUTHOR

Heather Atkinson is the author of over fifty books - predominantly in the crime fiction genre. Although Lancashire born and bred she now lives with her family, including twin teenage daughters, on the beautiful west coast of Scotland. Her new gangland series for Boldwood, set on the fictional Gallowburn estate in Glasgow began with *Blood Brothers* which was published in December 2020.

Visit Heather's website: https://www.heatheratkinsonbooks.com/

Follow Heather on social media:

twitter.com/HeatherAtkinso1

instagram.com/heathercrimeauthor

bookbub.com/authors/heather-atkinson

facebook.com/booksofheatheratkinson

ABOUT BOLDWOOD BOOKS

Boldwood Books is a fiction publishing company seeking out the best stories from around the world.

Find out more at www.boldwoodbooks.com

Sign up to the Book and Tonic newsletter for news, offers and competitions from Boldwood Books!

http://www.bit.ly/bookandtonic

We'd love to hear from you, follow us on social media:

facebook.com/BookandTonic
twitter.com/BoldwoodBooks
instagram.com/BookandTonic